The Block Island Charade

Bekah Overbey

First edition May 2022

For Eli, because you always believed I could

Chapter 1

Harper had two, possibly three minutes before her composure dissolved.

Bubbles of laughter were surging *up, up, up,* threatening to catapult straight through her veneer of polite interest.

The impending hilarity was problematic for two reasons: one, she was pathologically polite, and it was rude to laugh at someone's name; and two, one of her current train car companions was named Mr. Womblesrump.

Wom.

Bles.

Rump.

Yes, that was his real name, and *yes,* he had introduced himself with the natural pride of a man who possessed a far less provocative surname.

While Harper sat wedged beside him (his considerable girth seemed only apt for a man by the name of Womblesrump,) a governess named Ms. Nelly and her two young charges sat across from them.

The boys, obviously brothers, were covered in swaths of freckles and impressive mops of curling ginger hair, and they shared Harper's own predilection for hilarity regarding their train companion.

When the five of them had first settled into the train car together at Kingston Station, Mr. Womblesromp had greeted them promptly and majestically, repeating each of their names and bowing over each set of hands with great pomp and affection. When he had shared his own name, the two boys had howled with laughter for an entire half a second before their governess had administered a painful-looking pinch to each of their chubby legs. The howling stopped immediately, but their eyes still danced with mirth.

Harper couldn't blame them.

She was only grateful that she had stifled her own laughter in time. She was convinced that Ms. Nelly might have pinched her as well.

Fortunately, Mr. Womblesrump seemed happily oblivious to the reaction his surname incited and proved early on in their journey to be a garrulous companion.

Their train car was currently being treated to a retelling of his recent safe—*dare he say heroic*—delivery of a breech calf. Being a veterinarian by trade but an orator at heart, his narrative was rife with sentient detail, much to the delight of the two young boys and the mingled disgust and umbrage of their guardian.

"And that is when I reached into the birth canal—which, if you've never delivered a calf before"—Mr. Womblesrump chuckled happily here—"can be *quite* warm. And the squidging—goodness, what a sound! So memorable! So poignant of birth and new life, as the blood and viscera of the mother are rearranged to accommodate offspring! And I righted that calf and delivered it out into the world. Within moments—moments!—it stood on its own legs, the near-disaster of the past hour forgotten!"

He finished with a triumphant clap.

Harper wrestled masterfully to keep her expression placid.

"Mr. Womblesrump, please! I'm sure we've heard enough!" Poor Ms. Nelly. Her face had become an unnatural shade of red.

The two boys in her care clapped in gleeful appreciation until they each received another pinch.

While Harper had endured the story with mild but silent revulsion, Ms. Nelly had interjected vehemently and regularly to say, "Mr. Womblesrump, really!"

Unfortunately for Harper's composure, each time she said it she emphasized the last syllable of his name by raising her voice.

Mr. Wombles*RUMP*!

Mr. Wombles*RUMP*!

Mr. Wombles*RUMP*!

Because Harper was only human, there were only so many times she could hear *rump* in polite company before she laughed uproariously.

One more exclamation from Ms. Nelly would set her over the edge.

In Harper's defense, the last few weeks had been especially harrowing.

One month ago, her estranged maternal grandmother had shown up unexpectedly at the farm, and after an hour closeted in the study with Harper's father—her grandmother's historic enemy!—the two had announced that Harper would be leaving the farm and her father to move to New York to have her debut under the stern chaperonage of her grandmother.

To which Harper could only sputter—

New York! A debut! Grandmother!

The whole proposition was unfathomable.

The first issue was New York itself. Harper had been born and raised in Rhode Island, and truth be told, had never had the desire to live anywhere else, least of all among the affluent Knickerbocker society that her mother had abandoned in order to marry her father.

Second, at twenty-one, she was a bit too old to be having a debut. It wasn't common for a girl in rural Rhode Island to have one anyway—that was a rite of passage mostly relegated to the upper echelon of society—and she had no desire to simper and charm her way into a marriage whose primary function was financial and social advancement. Marriages among affluent New York families were not based on anything so gauche as affection or love.

Finally, they hadn't seen Harper's grandmother since the day of her mother's funeral—over a decade ago—at which time her grandmother and her father had had a fight so spectacular that a comparison with Vesuvius was not at all out of the question.

But when her father had looked her in the eye and said with unusual solemnity that he thought it was the best thing for her, Harper could only agree to the scheme in wide-eyed shock, keeping her thousand and one questions locked tightly behind her lips.

She and her father had always been close, and the sense that he was sending her away made something very deep inside her crack. But it was what he wanted, and so in her last month at home with him she had not wept, wallowed, or moped about the unexpected and unwelcome turn her life was taking.

The forbearance had taken its toll.

As had the breech calf story. So many graphic adjectives in such a short span of time.

"And where is it you are bound for, Miss Whitley?" Mr. Womblesrump's question jolted her from her reflections, and she turned to face him.

"New York. Grand Central Station." She managed a small smile for him. Silly name or not, he was not unkind. Merely… regrettably named. And an extremely gross storyteller.

"How marvelous! And what takes you there, my dear?"

"Mr. Wombles*RUMP*! That's quite a probing question. Please, let's all sit quietly now, shall we?" Ms. Nelly looked invitingly at the two boys in her care, who in turn looked rather put-out. They had quite enjoyed the calf birth gore.

Before they could object, however, the train rolled to a stop in front of a sparkling expanse of sapphire ocean, and a porter announced the station.

"Now stopping at Point Judith, Block Island Ferry!"

Later, Harper would not be able to identify the exact impetus for what she did next.

It may have been that last utterance of *RUMP!*, or Ms. Nelly's unfortunate use of the word *probing*. Maybe it was the mental exhaustion of the last month or the sudden view of the vast cerulean water. Perhaps it was the temptation to have one last day of freedom before she was trussed up as a marriageable, well-dowered debutante.

But before she could check her impulses, Harper jumped up with a start.

All eyes turned to her in surprise, and when Harper reached under the seat for her valise and parasol, the eyes widened. "I believe this is my stop."

Obviously, it was not.

But when the porter had called out the station, a completely outrageous thought had occurred to her: she was expected at her grandmother's today, but it was still early in the morning, and surely she could take the ferry and spend a few hours on the island, then return in time to catch another train to New York to arrive that night, couldn't she? She would need a send a telegram to inform her grandmother of her delayed arrival, but the station had a telegraph clerk on-site, and that could be accomplished easily enough.

Harper had been to Block Island once before, the summer before her mother died. The island was only a few miles off the coast of Rhode Island, and while it had all of the sunshine and sandy beaches of the mainland, it also had a tucked-away charm and quaintness all its own. Suddenly that connection to her mother and the halcyon days of her childhood held a nearly irresistible appeal for her. It was rash and inadvisable and perhaps even a bit dangerous, but again, her composure had been set to expire in two, possibly three minutes.

She was now pushing four.

And could she truly endure another three hours of listening to the word *rump!* shouted with varying degrees of indignation without laughing uncontrollably and offending her loquacious but otherwise very genial carriage companion?

No. No, she could not.

"But Miss Whitley, we're still a ways away from Grand Central Station. We've not even left Rhode Island yet."

"Mr. Wombles*RUMP*! I'm sure Miss Whitley knows her own mind," Ms. Nelly cried in outrage.

Harper suspected that Ms. Nelly said this mostly because she wanted another excuse to reprimand him, as Harper herself had only just declared her intention of disembarking elsewhere. But she appreciated the show of concern from both of her erstwhile companions and told them so as she made a very awkward curtsy and fled the train, much to the shock and dismay of the rest of the train car.

As she stepped down onto the platform, she finally released a gurgle of laughter. She was off to her day of freedom.

***

"I'm sorry miss. The Block Island Ferry is closed."

"Closed!" Harper blinked rapidly at the clerk, wondering if it would change his words. "But I don't understand. The schedule says it departs at nine, and it's only," she slipped her watch from the pocket of her dress and looked down, "eight-thirty."

The clerk at the counter shifted uncomfortably. "Yes, well. I've been told not to allow any more passengers aboard the ferry. If you want to visit Block Island, you'll be able to take the ferry when it opens again on the first of July."

"July!" Harper didn't have until July—today was only the first of June. She barely had until the end of the *day*. In her hasty flight from the train, it hadn't even occurred to her that the ferry would have run out of tickets. The prospect of one last day of freedom had flashed through her mind with such dazzling allure that she hadn't considered the inherent flaws in her plan.

She felt mildly nauseous as she considered them now.

The clerk tugged at his collar. "Yes. Unfortunately, the ferry won't run as scheduled until then."

Harper gave the clerk a tepid smile, then took a rallying breath. "I understand. Thank you, sir."

Understand was a bit of an exaggeration. She did *not* understand why the ferry was not running as scheduled. She did *not* understand why she had fled a safe, semi-comfortable train car and scrambled into the long, serpentine ferry line at Point Judith. She did *not* understand how desperately she began to long for Mr. Wombles*rump*.

Dire times indeed.

Things were not going to plan. Not at all.

Although she hadn't actually made a plan at all, had she?

Harper turned to step out of the line, but her boot slid awkwardly in the gravel. She lurched forward and collided with a formidable chest, staggering backward and only regaining her balance because the owner of that chest steadied her by the arms and muttered a gruff *"mind your step."* She smiled her thanks without bothering to look up, then wandered into the growing crowd that had formed behind her.

June was the official beginning of tourist season on Block Island, which was why it was so odd that the ferry was closed, not only for today but for the remainder of the month. As she walked away, she heard another would-be passenger's sharp reaction to the ferry closure.

In fact, the further she got into the crowd, the more outrage she heard. A particularly put-out man with a bowler hat and bristly mustache was cracking his knuckles, threatening to storm the ferry by force. Several of the men around him (and a few of the women) agreed with his scheme, and the menace in their voices made Harper genuinely nostalgic for Ms. Nelly and Mr. Womblesrump.

Though now that she considered it, perhaps Mr. Womblesrump's narrative about the calf birth might be a factor in her nascent nausea.

The thought did nothing to assuage her unease.

As she struggled to make her way through the throng of people at the docks and ticket counter and back toward the train platform, the shifting crowd and growing unrest made her realize what an unwise thing she had done in leaving the train in the first place. It was one thing to be a woman traveling alone for the duration of a train ride—her father had wanted to accompany her, but she assured him she would be just fine, and the farm would not run itself—but it was quite another to be a woman alone while being jostled amidst an overly warm mass of angry bodies.

Furthermore, it was quite, *quite* another thing to be a petite woman in such a situation. Harper was only five feet tall on the best of days, and she freely admitted that today was not one of those days. It is a fact acknowledged by small women everywhere that the world holds innumerable indignities for them—*high shelves! Tall people! Too long skirts!*—but the disadvantages of their plight are never so acute as in a crowd of people (especially of the tall variety.)

Very quickly did indignity yield to outrage as bowler-hat-bristly-mustache-ferry-stormer knocked into her, followed by his ill-tempered compatriots, knocking several pins out of her hair and almost wrenching her valise from her hand. She held onto the bag with a white-knuckle grip and clutched her parasol to her chest.

Losing *that* was the real danger.

Before she had left home her father had given her an impromptu and enlightening lesson in self-defense, which made use of naught but a parasol and a man's inherent vulnerabilities. *"Swing like you mean it, Hopsy,"* he had told her, and as she was jostled amidst the Point Judith mob, she understood the wisdom of her father's lesson.

At the time she had been confident in her ability to defend herself in any situation, but when the crowd made a sudden surge towards the ticket counter and her feet slipped out from under her, that confidence deserted her entirely.

***

Thomas ran his hand through his hair, frustration radiating off of him in waves.

"Yes, I know you've been instructed not to sell any more tickets for the ferry, but it's imperative that I'm on that boat. I'm willing to pay double—no, *triple*—the usual price for a ticket."

The nervous clerk eyed Thomas's outstretched hand, overflowing with crisp bills, but only shook his head.

"I'm sorry, sir, but orders is orders. Can't sell another one, no matter what you're offering. Now if you'll excuse me." The clerk moved to step back.

"Wait!" Thomas set his hands on the counter, leaning towards him. He *had* to get on that ferry. He unclasped his watch from his wrist, holding it out to the clerk. "Here, I'll throw my watch into the deal."

"Sir, I—"

"I will give you my firstborn son." Safe to offer, as he had no intention of having a firstborn son (or daughter, for that matter.)

"That's not nece—"

"Acclaim. Do you want acclaim? Fame? Prestige? I'm a journalist. I'll write you an article. I'll say whatever you want."

Thomas recognized the note of desperation in his voice and decided to change tactics, straightening to his full height and presenting his fiercest scowl.

Thomas *excelled* at scowling and was gratified to see the clerk's eyes widen in dismay.

"Now see here. Either you're going to let me on that boat, or I'm going to take that unused wad of tickets and wedge it straight up your —"

Thomas never did get to say where he would wedge the tickets, as the clerk hastily reached behind him and pulled out a wooden board with CLOSED painted across it, then dropped it on the counter before scampering further into the ticket office. He turned around only long enough to shout over his shoulder, "Sorry folks, ferry's closed until July. We'll see you then!"

Thomas could only growl at the man's back as he disappeared. He adjusted the satchel on his shoulder, then hefted the hard case of his Remington typewriter off the now abandoned ticket counter.

He *needed* to be on that ferry.

His fingers drummed impatiently on the counter as he turned around, eyeing the restless crowd behind him.

Everything hinged on him getting on that boat.

For the last month, his primary task at the *Manhattan Herald* had been to track down the location of the O'Malley wedding. His agreement with Luther, his editor, was simple: if Thomas found out where Charles O'Malley's daughter was getting married this summer and covered the story, then Luther would publish his exposé on the mills, the articles Thomas had spent years and countless hours researching.

Except there was nothing simple about discovering the location of the wedding of the century.

That was what the press had taken to calling the wedding of Adeline O'Malley, only daughter of the shipbuilding titan Charles O'Malley, to the Gray Star Line's wunderkind, Wesley James. Wedding of the century was a bit of a stretch, as the new century was only a few months old, but the moniker had taken.

Even before the engagement, the press and public alike had been fixated on O'Malley's daughter. Though the New York four hundred refused to allow Charles O'Malley into their ranks because his money was too new (even if he was richer than the lot of them combined), the same could not be said about his daughter Adeline.

She was relatively unknown until she appeared at a charity ball hosted by her father, but the press had taken one look (and dozens of photos) of her wide violet eyes and cascading blonde hair, and the public had been enamored. Tall enough to be considered statuesque but still lithe and graceful, the press dubbed her a modern Helen of Troy, a nod to her beauty and status as the shipbuilder's daughter. Even the highest sticklers of old Knickerbocker society acknowledged that Adeline's looks were unparalleled.

And so began the press's infatuation with her and the end of her private life. When she had become engaged to her father's right-hand man at a New Year's Ball at the exact moment that 1899 became 1900, the masses had been enraptured.

Or at least they *were* until O'Malley announced that his daughter's wedding would be a private affair and refused to disclose the date or location of the upcoming nuptials.

With that, the gauntlet had been thrown. Newspapers up and down the east coast were in a frenzied race to discover where and when the wedding would take place; Luther had made himself and his staff half-mad in trying to parse together any details about the wedding.

Thomas himself hadn't taken much interest in the whole affair. The gossip columns were neither his concern nor his responsibility, which is what he told Luther when the editor asked why his best reporter wasn't trying to nail down the date and location of the wedding of the century.

The writers in that branch of the newspaper were by and large a fickle, mercurial lot, jumping from one tidbit of gossip to another. Before the O'Malley engagement had been announced, they had been agog at the prospect of a long-lost Knickerbocker granddaughter returning to the city to make her belated debut. Unfortunately, Luther was well aware of Thomas's personal interest in and time spent on his exposé on the mills and saw an opportunity to force Thomas's hand.

Which is why when Thomas inadvertently overheard an inebriated group of Block Island Ferry workers toasting their good fortune in a *full month's paid leave* while the ferry was closed for the *whole of June*, he knew he had struck gold. Why would the Block Island Ferry close for the first month of tourist season unless someone had asked them to do so? And who else was rich enough to essentially buy out the ferry and its employees for all of June, not to mention had such connections in the shipping industry?

None other than Charles O'Malley, and for no other reason than to throw the wedding of the century on a perfectly idyllic, conveniently secluded island.

As personally distasteful as Thomas found it to invade someone's privacy and either coerce or force his way onto that ferry, that was exactly what he needed to do to publish the exposé and atone for all that he and his father had done.

To his everlasting shame, Thomas had done so very, very much.

The angry shouts in the crowd at the docks began to crescendo, and Thomas realized that he was not the only person considering taking the ferry by force. Just as a brawny man in a bowler hat led a charge towards the ticket counter, Thomas saw the woman who had run into him earlier. He hadn't gotten a proper look at her then, noting only the gray of her dress and diminutive stature—but it was with a thread of alarm that he saw that small gray figure begin to sway and fall into the chaos of the mob.

Without consulting his brain, his body began to move towards her, using his sturdy typewriter case to clear a path against the crowd. Just as her feet slipped out from under her, his free arm came around her waist and pulled her clear of the stampede and onto the docks.

Thomas avoided people as a general rule, but specifically young, marriageable women, as he had no intentions of marrying. But suddenly, standing on the Point Judith docks with his arm wrapped around a tiny hazel-eyed woman who, he noticed absently, smelled like strawberries and spring rain, he momentarily forgot why. Her closeness was so disorienting that he also forgot to release his hold on her.

He would pay dearly for the lapse.

With a ferocious jerk of her arm, she took her parasol and slammed it down against his foot with enough force that he bent forward in surprise and pain.

"Let—" she shrieked, "Me—" she changed directions, and the parasol collided with his nose—"Go!"

The pain of the blows was stunning, but it was nothing in comparison to her coup de grace. He was about to take a step back from her when the tiny, beautiful, terrifying woman before him took her lacy white parasol and swung it directly between his legs.

Stars flitted across his vision and he forgot how to breathe.

He was only vaguely aware of his knees hitting the damp wood of the docks, of crumpling onto his side and making a noise that sounded very much like the cry of a felled woodland creature.

Chapter 2

Dying, Thomas thought blankly.

Surely he was dying.

Never again would he underestimate a woman's upper body strength *or* her accessories.

He had rolled away from the woman when he first curled into fetal position, but when he turned the other way in hopes of recovering both his breath and his dignity, he saw the woman scurrying towards him, her eyes wide.

"No, no, no," he mumbled, turning away from her and giving up his dignity as lost irrevocably.

"Oh, sir! Oh sir oh sir oh sir!" She moved around to meet him face-to-face, kneeling on the ground in front of him and removing her gloves to set her bare hands against his cheeks. "Oh, sir, I'm very sorry! You were helping me, weren't you?"

She looked out at the water with a frown. "The toes, the nose, the family jewels," she said in a sing-song voice before turning back towards him. "It was all so different when I practiced on the hay bales! I hardly realized how.... Oh, dear. I should never have..." She mumbled something that sounded oddly like *rump,* then moved a hand to his forehead, as if she thought that a man deprived of his manhood might develop a sudden fever.

Which, based on his current pain level, seemed plausible.

Because he wasn't sure if he had regained the power of speech yet, and because he had no idea what she was talking about, and because it was oddly soothing to have her hands on his face, Thomas simply laid there and stared at her while he recovered.

She was younger than he was, likely no more than twenty. Rough handling from the mob at the ticket counter had knocked her hat askew, and a mass of wild auburn curls tumbled down flushed pink cheeks.

Though his eyes were open, she spoke to him as if he was unconscious.

"Sir, can you hear me? Do you think you can stand?"

Something about her question reminded him of his long-lost dignity and the urgent need to get onto the ferry. With what he hoped was a convincing show of strength, he sat up, then pushed himself to a standing position.

When his voice came out at the normal octave, he was inordinately relieved. "Yes, yes of course. I'm quite fine." Which was not entirely accurate. That jittery frustration to get on the ferry had returned, and he was angry with himself for being distracted by a pretty face and rogue impulse to gallantry.

Having already risked life and limb to pull her from the mob, he felt compelled to escort her somewhere safe before he found a way onto that ferry.

But before he could come up with a plan to do just that, she stood and eyed him warily, her gaze straying to his beltline before flying back up to his eyes.

"Are you certain? What about your... erm... how are your... your jewels?"

He stared blankly at her. "I beg your pardon?"

"You know... your... *ahem*..." she leaned forward and whispered, "your *family* jewels?"

***

Sweet merciful heavens above.

Why, why, why did she ask him about his jewels!?

That was the term her father had used in their little self-defense lesson, so it was the first one that came to mind, but of course—of course!—no respectable woman would ask a man with whom she was not acquainted about the welfare of his family jewels. She probably wouldn't even ask a man with whom she *was* acquainted. In fact, a respectable woman probably would never even use the term *family jewels* with a gentleman *ever,* let alone after she had whacked said jewels with a parasol.

And then the look. Why did she look down?

But she had been so panicked!

When the crowd closed in and Harper felt the ground beneath her shift, such wild terror gripped her that even when she saw that she was free of the crowd, that *he* had pulled her free, some sort of muscle memory had kicked in. *"Swing like you mean it, Hopsy,"* came her father's voice, but she was now very certain that he had not meant her to swing at formidable-looking good samaritans.

And goodness, he was tall. Her head only came up to his chest—the very chest, she realized, that had belonged to the man in line who had kept her from falling earlier. His height had been apparent from the moment he pulled her from the crowd, but she hadn't gotten a proper look at his face until she knelt down beside his colossal form.

He had wide, puppy-dog brown eyes framed by sweeping lashes, which were at complete odds with the rest of his face. His cheeks and brow were lined with austerity and firmness, and the set of his mouth was straight, almost grim, as if unaccustomed to smiling. His hair was dark, and though it looked like he had begun the day with it neatly styled, it was haphazard now, likely from their encounter with the mob.

He was glaring down at her now, and she couldn't blame him. Even *she* was surprised that her swing had felled him. There was no doubt about it: she had gotten herself into a proper mess, and she would just have to brazen it out.

"Yes sir," she said uncomfortably. "I swung rather hard, I'm afraid, and I'm terribly sorry about the misunderstanding. So I only ask about your..." oh goodness, she would never in her life say these words aloud again, "*family jewels* to ascertain if I've done any lasting harm. Again, I'm quite sorry." Her cheeks flamed in embarrassment.

That formidable expression didn't waver. He may have puppy-dog eyes, but his scowl was strong enough to conjure an actual raincloud over a parade of happy children.

"I'm fine." His voice was cold and unyielding—he sounded like he might actually *want* to rain on a children's parade.

"Are you certain?" She willed her eyes not to glance south again.

"Yes, quite."

She blew out a breath. "Well, good. Based on your reaction, I was afraid your jewels—er rather, *they* were rather more delicate than I had previously thought."

A muscle ticked in his jaw. "They're not delicate."

"Oh. I see." That was *not* the impression she had gotten. "It's just that when you fell over I assumed—"

"I didn't fall over."

"You were on the ground," she pointed out reasonably.

He clenched his teeth. "The dock is slippery when wet. I lost my footing."

"You were also wheezing."

"I am unused to the briny sea air!"

Harper's eyes widened in surprise, and he straightened, apparently in an effort to regain his composure. "I assure you, I'm quite fine now." He dragged a hand down his face, and it occurred to her that he looked exhausted, like he was in desperate need of a proper night's rest. "Hm. Police."

Harper bristled. "I hardly think we need to involve the police. I *did* apologize, sir!"

His eyes flicked down to her, and he shook his head. "No, the police have been called to break up the mob." He gestured with his chin.

Harper turned behind her, and sure enough, the screech of police whistles heralded several policemen mounted on horseback, and for all the trouble the hopeful ferry passengers had caused, they dispersed quickly enough, most moping off in the direction of the main road towards waiting carriages or hansom cabs ready to be hailed.

For a moment they both stood in silence, watching as order was restored to Point Judith. But when Harper turned back towards the open ocean and saw the Block Island Ferry bobbing happily off the dock, and remembered that in a few hours' time she would begin her new life in New York with her grandmother, she couldn't help the sigh that slipped out. "So much for a day of freedom."

"What's that?" Her rescuer was frowning down at her again, which, if she hadn't recently swung her parasol between his legs while he was saving her, might have hurt her feelings. Since she had, in fact, done exactly that, it seemed ungracious of her to take offense.

"Nothing, nothing at all." She rallied a smile. "Thank you again for your assistance, sir. Good day." Harper bent to retrieve her parasol and valise, then slipped her gloves back onto her hands. Her shoulders sagged in disappointment as she turned her back on the ocean and headed in the opposite direction towards the train platform.

"Wait."

Harper looked over, startled to see that her rescuer was following her. "Yes?"

"I'll accompany you." He said it with such obvious reluctance that he might as well have offered to have his teeth pulled.

"Excuse me?" her eyebrows flew up.

He closed his eyes, then began again. "What I mean to say is, may I accompany you back to your carriage? Or perhaps to whomever you planned to ride the ferry with?"

His tone was curt and begrudging, his expression dour. She had no idea what had possessed him to make such an offer at all.

"That's very kind of you, but that won't be necessary."

"I assure you that it is." His voice was like a stone wall, and she had to bite back a sharp retort.

Until their encounter this morning, she had always been unfailingly civil—she had even resisted the urge to laugh at Mr. Wombles*RUMP*! —so although she was disappointed about her foiled escape to Block Island and prickly about the man's gruff manners, she would be polite. She was *always* polite.

"In that case, you may escort me to the train platform. Thank you."

They walked together in uncomfortable silence. Now that the police had cleared out the mob, the ticket counter and the train platform beyond were quiet except for the shouts of dockworkers around the ferry. Harper took a seat on the bench on the train platform, feeling suddenly exhausted. In the last month she felt like she had lost control of the trajectory of her life, and the person who had always made her life so steady, her father, was the person who had set the unexpected path in motion. She pushed the unsettling thought to the back of her mind, focusing instead on the man before her.

Harper tucked her loose curls back into her hair and righted her hat, mustering the energy to rid herself of her erstwhile rescuer.

"Thank you again for your assistance, sir," she said, offering a perfunctory smile.

But he didn't smile back. Or leave. He just stood there, hovering over her, that same thundercloud expression in place.

"You're here alone?" It was more accusation than question, and the *V* in his forehead deepened.

Ms. Nelly's words on the train floated back to her. *"That's quite a probing question!"* Harper resented the implication that she had done something foolish in being at Point Judith alone—mostly because she knew that she absolutely *had*—but it really was none of his business. So she would do her best governess impression and send him off—although without the word *probing*, for obvious reasons.

"That's hardly your concern, sir. Again, I thank you for your help.

Good day."

But he didn't accept her clear dismissal. He just stood there, holding a satchel and what she assumed was a typewriter case, and glowering down at her. Why wasn't he accepting her dismissal? This was the second time she had told him *good day*, which was her most polite way of saying *Our interaction is at an end! Leave me alone! Take your frown elsewhere!*

"You shouldn't be here alone. It isn't safe."

He managed to sound both pompous and irritated, and Harper felt her own irritation mounting. Surely he wouldn't say such a thing if she were taller! Realizing her inherent disadvantage in remaining seated before him, she stood to her full height. Because five feet was still considerably lower than six feet, it was less impressive than it might have been.

"As I have said, that is none of your concern, sir. And I am perfectly capable of taking care of myself. I have my parasol, after all!"

He winced slightly before assuming the thundercloud expression again. "That parasol did little to help you when you were trapped in the middle of an unruly crowd."

His words stung because they were inarguably accurate, but now Harper was getting well and truly angry. Who did this man think he was?

"Thanks to your timely intervention, I came to no harm. But please do not feel that your earlier intervention makes you responsible for me now."

Something flashed in his eyes, gone before she could name it. "Unfortunately, that is exactly what that means."

Unfortunately? Unfortunately!? This man was an affront to good manners and knights-errant everywhere.

"Has anyone ever told you that you have the bedside manner of a wet blanket?"

"No."

Harper scoffed. "Perhaps not to your face." Apparently, her good manners had their limits.

He did not dignify this remark with a response and instead walked to the adjacent wall of train schedules. Feeling doubly offended at being referred to as his responsibility—*unfortunately!*—and then being ignored, Harper sat back down on the bench, ready to stew and mope in peace.

She was not so fortunate.

"What train are you taking?"

Maybe if she ignored him, he would go away.

"What train?" Now he was standing in front of her, practically shouting down at her from his lofty position of six feet above the ground.

"If I tell you, will you leave?"

"Possibly."

Hm. Worth a chance. "New York. Grand Central Station."

"Grand Central?" He looked over his shoulder at the train schedule, then back towards her, his forehead scrunching in dismay. "The next train won't arrive for nearly three hours."

She sighed. It would be a long penance for her impulsive decision to leave the train in the first place. "Indeed. *Now* will you leave me alone?"

In lieu of an answer, he sat down beside her. Harper practically gaped at him. "What are you doing?"

His jaw ticked. "I am sitting beside you." His lips curled in apparent distaste.

His demeanor was so utterly provoking that Harper had to curl her toes in her shoes to keep from stomping on his foot.

He turned to her again, "Miss, I—"

"Oh don't *Miss* me. If you're going to insist on speaking to me, just call me Harper."

His frown grew impossibly deeper. "Do you normally give strange men leave to call you by your Christian name?"

"Only the ones I hit with my parasol."

He muttered several words that one should *not* use in polite company, then turned back to her. "I'm not going to call you by your given name."

"Harper. My given name is Harper."

He ignored her interruption. "But if you will forgive the impropriety, I will address you by your surname, Miss…?"

Harper sighed, feeling resigned to his unsolicited company. "I believe most of our interaction thus far has fallen into the realm of impropriety." She looked over at him. "My name is Harper Whitley."

He nodded, apparently satisfied. "Miss Whitley."

"And how would you like me to refer to you, as it seems that you are determined to be responsible for me, in spite of any real need?"

He held out his hand. "Thomas Montgomery."

She wasn't immediately inclined to take his hand—he *had* referred to his concern for her as *unfortunate*—but it would be churlish not to, so she reluctantly extended her gloved fingers.

Thomas took her hand into his own large one, his fingers engulfing hers in a grip that was surprisingly gentle. His eyes lingered on hers for a moment, then he released her hand abruptly.

"As I was saying, Miss Whitley, it's hardly proper for an unchaperoned woman to be waiting at Point Judith for the next three hours."

"Thank you for that enlightening piece of information," Harper snapped, then cringed at her own rudeness. She never spoke like that—his poor bedside manner must be rubbing off on her. "What I mean is, I will be just fine, and there is no need for you to wait with me."

"I certainly cannot wait with you for three hours."

Did he think she *wanted* that? She was actively trying to dismiss him! "Then it is fortunate that I have not asked it of you," she ground out.

He studied her, his brow scrunching improbably further. "How did you come to be here, Miss Whitley?"

"Excuse me?"

"At Point Judith. Did someone drop you off here?"

Harper set her chin, sensing the direction of his question. "I arrived here on the train."

"To take the ferry?"

"*Yes,* to take the ferry." Every question made her feel more waspish.

"I *see.*"

He looked like he saw quite a bit about her, none of it flattering to her judgment or capability. She was tempted to reach for her parasol again.

"So, if I understand correctly, you departed from your home this morning—wherever that may be—to board a train, with an ultimate destination of Grand Central Station, but disembarked here instead. Had your train broken down, Miss Whitley?"

Harper narrowed her eyes. "It had not."

"I see. Did you have some sort of medical emergency that required your immediate exit of the train?" His voice was laced with irritation, and she wanted to take her parasol to his windpipe.

"I did not."

"Then was there some imminent threat to your person that forced you to leave the relative safety of a fully functioning train while in perfectly adequate health, in order to board a ferry for which you had not previously obtained a ticket?"

Harper thought of Ms. Nelly and Mr. Womblesrump. Compared to Mr. Montgomery, another three hours of farmyard birth narratives and exclamations of *Rump! Rump! Rump!* sounded heavenly. "There was not."

His jaw ticked. "That was an extremely unwise decision."

Oh, *this man.* Of all the nosy, condescending tones! "I don't recall asking your opinion, sir, nor do I recall asking for your help."

He was the one who implied he would wait with her, hadn't he? And why did he insist on being here with her against his will, when she had actively discouraged him? He felt responsible for her without actually wanting to spend time with her.

With the force of a wave, a thought struck her: was that how her father had felt about her? They had always been close, but maybe now that she was of age and unmarried, she was becoming a burden? He had never given any indication that he felt anything but pleasure in her company, but if that was the case, why was he sending her away to her grandmother, a woman whom he could hardly even mention without exasperation?

Harper felt a telltale warmth behind her eyes and realized with dawning mortification that she was about to cry. Exhaustion always made her weepy, but surely her tear ducts could read the situation well enough to know that it was not the time for a spontaneous bout of ugly crying!

Apparently, they could not, because the heat behind her eyes only increased, and her nose began to prickle, and she knew it was coming. Here, in the middle of a train station, sitting next to the world's grumpiest example of chivalry, she was going to cry.

The first tear fell and she swiped it away before Thomas noticed, but then another fell, and another, and then her nose started to run and before she could stop herself she sniffled, and of course, *of course*, he noticed.

"What's that?" His voice was curt, borderline abrasive.

She swiped beneath her eyes and resisted another sniffle. "Nothing."

"No, I heard something."

Her head was angled away from his, but he leaned forward on the bench to look at her.

"Are you... are you *crying*?" He sounded equal parts confounded and irritated, and her mortification swelled.

"Of course not," she said, but it came out weak and watery and completely unconvincing.

"Then why are you doing that—that *sniffling*?"

Harper closed her eyes, willing herself to disappear. If a person could die from embarrassment, she was, without a doubt, about to pass on to glory.

Chapter 3

She was crying.

Why was she crying? Had *he* done that?

And what in the world was he supposed to do about it now?

It wasn't that Thomas had never seen women cry before—he had grown up with a younger sister and had covered all manner of stories that had put him in close proximity with grieving widows or mothers. But this time was different.

After pulling her from the crowd at the ticket line and realizing she was alone, Thomas could not possibly abandon her. However improbable, he now felt responsible for the well-being of this tiny woman.

And if she was crying, then she certainly was not *well*.

Her hazel eyes were glossy with tears, and she let out a sob, so small and tragic and obviously inadvertent that he found himself balling his fists. Because sitting next to her, hearing her sniffles and watching her quietly wipe away tear after tear after tear—it was unacceptable. Women cried all the time, he reminded himself, and they generally survived the ordeal. But he was not sitting next to *women* in the abstract—he was sitting next to an actual woman, Miss Harper Whitley, and for the first time in such a very long time, he *felt*.

He felt concern and dismay and something else that was oddly soft and a little warm and very compelling—something that felt dangerously like.... tenderness. Such an unexpected thing, to feel anything at all, let alone *tenderness*, and especially for this tiny, headstrong woman who had brought him to his knees with a parasol and had exasperated him every moment since.

Perhaps, he conceded, he had been a *bit* brusque with her—but he *was* helping her now—or at least trying to—wasn't he? What did it matter if he had the bedside manner of a wet blanket?

And why should it offend him that she thought so?

In general, he didn't need to have a bedside manner at all. He interacted just fine with his coworkers and sources and by and large kept the world at arm's length, but there was nothing wrong with that. He had his career for company, and once he covered the O'Malley wedding, his expiation for what he and his father had done would be complete.

And as soon as he saw her safely off somewhere, he would push the world back to arm's length and restore the status quo. Being responsible for Miss Whitley was a one-time aberration.

Except the more time he spent with her, the more he realized how complicated seeing her safely off *anywhere* would be.

The first step, at least, was to make her stop crying.

How did he do that? What did men do when women cried?

A handkerchief. Thomas would hand her a handkerchief.

Yes, excellent. He would hand her a handkerchief, and then she would stop. Thomas patted the pockets of his jacket, then his pants, but came up with nothing more than a few broken pen nubs. He always carried handkerchiefs, didn't he? He went through his pockets again, then his satchel, finding nothing, then ran his hand through his hair in irritation. For goodness sake, was there not a single scrap of linen to be found on his person?

Harper hiccuped again, and Thomas realized with mounting alarm that her shoulders were trembling.

Unacceptable. That was all he could think as he watched her cry; her grief and whatever prompted it, whatever made that pink lower lip tremble—unacceptable. And this tug in his chest that she evoked, this feeling—this *tenderness*—also unacceptable.

Maybe he ought to talk to her. Women like talking, didn't they? It had been an embarrassingly long time since he had interacted with a woman socially; his experience with them in the last few years had been confined to one who was related to him and those who he interacted with as a reporter, but the principle seemed sound.

Thomas cleared his throat gruffly. "Why don't you talk about it?"

She was facing away from him, but her back stiffened when he addressed her.

He set his jaw, trying to soften his tone. "The sniffling, I mean. Why are you doing it?"

There. That was soft.

"I would rather not talk about it."

Well. So much for that. The trembling in her shoulders seemed to be subsiding, though, so that was a something. But the sniffling—that unacceptable sniffling that provoked that unacceptable tenderness in him—that was still present, and the longer it went on the more agitated he became.

Thomas was *not* tender. She *had* to stop.

"Miss Whitley, I… I apologize for my tone just now."

He wouldn't apologize for his words because he meant every one of them. Getting off a perfectly good train was both rash and irresponsible. He just hadn't meant to make her cry. Never in his life had he made a woman cry. He felt—there it was again, he *felt*—like the worst sort of cad. She hadn't responded to him, but he had to say something, say *anything*, to make her stop crying.

"You wanted to go to Block Island." His robust conversational overture was met with silence, but Thomas was a persistent man, if a wet blanket, so he continued. "I've never seen it. Today would have been my first time." He cleared his throat. "Have you been before?"

To his relief, she turned and faced him, but his relief was short-lived. Her face was streaked with tears, dripping over the perfect cupid's bow of her top lip and down her chin. Thomas had the sudden and unlikely urge to run his thumb across her lip to dry her tears.

Which was preposterous.

"I have, yes," she answered as she patted her face with her gloved hands, then stared out over the empty train tracks. "I went with my parents, the summer before my… When I was a child. It's one of my favorite memories. It's why I came to Point Judith today. I know it was reckless, leaving the train"—she sent him a wry look—"but I… I just wanted one day. One last day of freedom on Block Island, to feel the sun and wind and hear the ocean and let the real world slip away, to just be myself for a little bit longer."

He studied her, intrigued in spite of himself. "Will you not be yourself in New York?"

"Not really, no."

Well. That was… troubling. Not that he cared. He did *not* care about this woman.

"You said you'd never been before? To Block Island, I mean?"

"I have not."

She perked up at this, then gave him her first sincere smile. "Oh, it's wonderful. You would absolutely love it. The beaches are spectacular, and the whole island feels like the most charming seaside town, a world all unto itself. I'm sorry you won't get to go today." She glanced down at his typewriter case. "You're a writer?"

Thomas felt his jaw clench. He wasn't ashamed of his profession, but his current assignment to ferret out the wedding and write covertly—that was a much more complicated matter. He only inclined his head.

Unaware of the tension that he felt, Harper looked down at his typewriter, then behind them towards the water. "Then I'm doubly sorry you won't get to Block Island today. It would have been such an idyllic setting for writing a novel."

Thomas let out a breath he didn't realize he had been holding. No need to correct her assumption—it was better all around that she assumed he was a novelist.

Before he could respond, a commotion at the docks grabbed their attention. A well-dressed couple was storming off the ferry and onto the docks, their voices raised loud enough that they could hear them even from the train platform.

"Vivi, enough! Just get back on the boat and we can talk about this." The man yelling was following closely behind the woman, but he struggled to keep up with her furious clip.

"You are the most difficult, selfish man I have ever encountered!"

"For pity's sake, you're making mountains out of molehills!"

"Mountains out of molehills?" Vivi shrieked. "Neville Jones, you are the most insensitive, unsupportive husband. All I'm asking for is a bit of moral support!"

"Moral support? Moral support?" Neville threw his head back and laughed, and Thomas was relieved that they were off the docks and walking past the ticket office. Otherwise, Thomas suspected that she might have tried to throw him bodily into the Atlantic. "Vivienne, you don't need moral support. I have seen you take on the most formidable matrons of the New York four hundred. I've seen you reduce grown men to tears. And need I remind you of just what you did to poor Mr. Rockefeller at the charity gala last year?"

The couple barreled past Harper and Thomas on the bench, accidentally dropping their ferry tickets onto the dusty train platform, and though they heard the woman let out a gasp worthy of Vaudeville, they never did get to hear what she did to poor Mr. Rockefeller, as the couple had moved on past Point Judith and disappeared down the road of lingering carriages. As they walked by, however, Thomas saw the woman's face, and he nearly let out a gasp of his own.

The woman looked uncannily similar to Harper Whitley. The same wide hazel eyes, gently sloping nose, and pink-tinged cheeks—even the same perfect cupid's bow lip.

As Thomas glanced again at Harper, it struck him that the women were more than similar—they could easily pass for twins, and as his gaze slid from her to the forgotten ferry tickets near the bench, a ludicrous, borderline mad idea struck him.

Thomas had to be on that ferry—it was the last one departing for Block Island before the O'Malley wedding, and everything hinged on him covering that wedding—and Harper had already told him that she wanted to go to Block Island, hadn't she? Discarded on the ground were two tickets that would otherwise go to waste. If the two of them were to use the tickets, impersonate the couple…

There would be complications, of course. If he brought her to Block Island, his sense of honor demanded that he find a way to covertly keep watch over her for the day, then see her off on the return ferry. He wouldn't be able to accompany her then or see her onto the train safely, but if he could align the schedules properly, surely he could ensure that she had a minimal wait between disembarking from the ferry and boarding another train to Grand Central Station?

His conscience balked at the idea of her doing even that by herself, but there was no way that he could return with her to Point Judith, nor could he sit on this bench for three hours to see her safely off. And wouldn't she be better off in his care than by herself?

The thought had nothing at all to do with that niggling inclination to tenderness—it would simply be a practical business arrangement. Nothing more.

Thomas rose and walked towards the tickets, brushing them off as he picked them up off the ground. In simple block print were the words BLOCK ISLAND FERRY, and handwritten were the names Neville and Vivienne Jones. He and Neville had been of similar height, if not features, but Harper was a dead ringer for Vivienne. What was the likelihood of anyone on the boat looking closely enough to know that the couple who had just stormed off the boat was not the one who got back onto it before the ferry departed?

It was madness, he knew, but he was desperate. Publishing the exposé meant everything now, and he wouldn't stop until he had accomplished it.

Harper had watched him in silence while he stood and now studied him as he returned to the bench. She was no longer crying, but her lashes were still wet, sparkling in the sunlight when she looked up at him.

"The happy couple has forgotten their tickets?"

"They have." He tapped them idly against his hands, weighing the risks of this outrageous idea.

He couldn't. He couldn't ask her to pretend to be someone else, and he certainly couldn't make himself responsible for her for the duration of the day on Block Island.

But then she looked behind them at the water, at the boat sitting in the early summer sunlight, and she sighed.

Such a small thing, a sigh. But in that moment it wasn't so small. It was longing and sadness and soft wistful hope, and that tremulous little sigh pricked that tender spot in his chest.

His words came out before he could stop them.

"I have a proposal."

She jerked her gaze from the water and back to him, startled. "A proposal?"

No. He did *not* have a proposal, and he was *not* going to ask her to impersonate Vivienne Jones.

"In regards to the ferry."

In regards to nothing! There would be no proposal!

His mouth paid his brain no heed.

"Miss Whitley, I'm not sure if you noticed, but you bear a striking resemblance to the woman who just passed us, Mrs. Jones, according to their tickets. As the couple is unlikely to return for them, let alone board the ferry, it occurs to me that the tickets are about to be wasted. I understand how disappointed you are that the ticket office was already sold-out when we arrived, but I wonder if we might be able to help one another out?"

Her eyebrows lifted, an unspoken encouragement, and he continued. "I also hoped to get to the island today, and like you, arrived too late. Normally, I would not condone any sort of deceit"—the O'Malley wedding exempted—"but perhaps, for the duration of the ferry ride, you and I might," he cleared his throat, wondering when exactly his brain had lost control of his mouth, "temporarily assume the identities of Mr. and Mrs. Jones."

This was madness. Utter madness. His rogue mouth plowed forward.

"Though they were on the boat earlier, the bottom of their tickets has yet to be stamped. The ferry seems crowded enough that no one is likely to realize that you and I are not the same Mr. and Mrs. Jones who just left."

Thomas held his breath, wondering if she would hit him again with her parasol. Sweet mercy, *please*, don't let her swing again. But she didn't reach for her parasol—she only stared at him, biting her lip.

The sound of the ferry's fog horn blared out in the distance, rattling the silence that stretched between them.

They were out of time. Thomas was out of time.

He shut his eyes. How in the world would he get Luther to publish the exposé now?

"I'll do it."

His eyes flew open.

"You will?"

She gave a single nod. "But I have terms."

"All right." He forced his voice to remain even, resisting the urge to sprint to the dock.

"I will only impersonate Mrs. Jones for the length of the ferry ride. After that, I am plain Harper Whitley."

"Of course."

She nodded, then dropped her gaze to the ground, bringing it back up only to settle on a point just above his shoulder. "And although we will be masquerading as husband and wife, I will not allow any..." she cleared her throat. "There is to be no... *ahem*..."

"No...?" Thomas tried to be patient, but he could see the ferry workers behind her start to unwind the rope from the dock.

"Canoodling." A crimson flush flooded up her neck, into her cheeks.

"Canoodling?" What on earth was canoodling? Apparently, it had been a *very* long time since he interacted with a woman.

"Canoodling," she repeated, more decisively this time. He must have looked as adrift as he felt because she continued on, circling her wrist in the air and gesturing vaguely. "Monkey business, I mean."

"Monkey business?" His eyebrows jumped to his hairline. Did he look like the sort of man who participated in monkey business? He made a mental note to stop mussing his hair.

"Exactly. *No* canoodling, *no* monkey business, *no* tomfoolery." She was warming to her subject now, ticking the items off on her fingers.

"Tomfoolery?" His brain truly had stopped working because he had no idea what she was talking about and could do nothing more than parrot her words.

He didn't have time for this. They needed to get on that boat. *Now*.

She narrowed her eyes and pursed her lips, apparently misreading his confusion and impatience as something more sinister.

"Mr. Montgomery! Allow me to speak plainly. If we are to embark on this charade together, then allow me to be clear that there will not, without a shadow of a doubt, be any *liberties*!"

Liberties? *That* was what she was getting at?! Did she think he would… why hadn't she just said *that*?

"Yes yes, of course not. I would never—" he broke off, realizing for the first time in several years that he was blushing. He shoved his unexpected embarrassment aside and extended his hand to her. "Very well, Miss Whitley. I accept your proposal."

Chapter 4

What had Harper just agreed to?

And why had she used the word *canoodling*?! Not that tomfoolery or monkey business were much better. But honestly, what sort of gentleman needed a concept spelled out so clearly?

When she settled on liberties, she had seen the light of understanding in his eyes, followed by indignation and… a blush?

Who knew grumpy men blushed? It was the first time she had ever seen a grown man blush, and she found it oddly disarming.

Which was not at all the thing. The last thing she should feel in front of Thomas Montgomery was disarmed. He was peevish and rude and very nearly a stranger, and what did she really know about him? He could be a thief! A rogue! A deflowerer of innocents!

All of which, admittedly, seemed highly unlikely. He had, after all, helped her when the crowd rushed the ticket counter, which was a chivalrous thing to do, even if he had been rude and surly since then. But he had been… almost kind when she cried? Well, *almost kind* might be a stretch—his chronically-furrowed brow never did smooth out, and he had actually been rather insensitive and abrasive about the whole matter of the sniffling—but Harper had gotten the impression that he was *trying* to be *almost* kind, in his own prickly way. And she had stopped crying, so that counted for something, didn't it?

Also, a thief or rogue or deflowerer of innocents would probably have a nicer bedside manner. More flies with honey and what-have-you.

Nevertheless, he was a near stranger, and she had just agreed to act as his wife, which, even after her string of spectacularly poor decisions today, might actually be the poorest. But the charade would only last for the duration of the ferry ride. Nothing would happen to her while surrounded by people on deck, and once they stepped off that ferry, they would part ways; she would have her day of freedom before life with her grandmother, and he would be free to write in the perfect oasis that was Block Island.

Easy.

Harper realized that while she had been contemplating the various scenarios in which he was a villain or charlatan, he had been efficiently gathering up her things alongside his, and she hopped off the bench to help.

"Mr. Montgomery, you don't need to do that." She held out her hand expectantly, but he only frowned down at it.

How shocking.

"I can carry them for you."

"I'm sure you can, but there is no need."

"I disagree."

Patience. She willed herself to have patience. "Be that as it may—"

"Miss Whitley, do you want to get on that ferry or not?"

"Of course I do," she huffed.

"Then let's take the sixty seconds of our walk to the dock to acclimate ourselves to not fighting and mimicking a happily wedded couple."

"Much like the real Mr. and Mrs. Jones?"

His brow darkened. He was *not* amused. "Miss Whitley," he began, his voice pained.

"All right, all right, you may carry my things for me. But *only* so that we can get into character."

"Agreed."

"Agreed." She nodded firmly. "Oh! Just one moment though!" Without a backward glance, she hurried to the clerk at the train platform and filled out a telegraph sheet to her grandmother, explaining her late arrival. When she shuffled back to his side, his impatience was fairly palpable.

Thankfully, there were no other delays—the porter on the ferry stamped their tickets without comment—and within moments they were settled on the deck of the boat. While Thomas pulled out a notebook and scribbled hastily into it during the ferry ride, Harper drank in the panorama of sprawling azure skies and turquoise water, basking in the warmth of early summer sun. The salt air was fresh and crisp, and excited passengers chattered happily around them. Even

Thomas's aura of long-suffering grumpiness could not dampen her spirits.

Because she was actually doing it. She was going to have her day of freedom.

She did, however, find herself sneaking glances at Thomas, trying to make sense of the man who was helping her in spite of the fact that he clearly disapproved of and almost certainly disliked her.

He was well-intentioned but roughly-spoken, concerned but irritated about feeling concerned, on a boat to the best-kept secret in the North Atlantic waters yet unapologetically grumpy. She could make neither heads nor tails of him, but thankfully, she didn't need to understand him. In a short while, their acquaintance would be at an end.

When Block Island finally came into sight, Harper nearly squealed in delight.

Enormous rocks flanked the docks, and an immense whitewashed lighthouse lifted its head above it all, standing sentinel over the island. The blue of the ocean was a sharp contrast to the vivid green of the grass set further inland, dotted with cedar shake cottages and a system of turquoise ponds and waterways. Sailboats and schooners dotted the coastline ahead of them, a quintessentially New England welcome. The air smelled like fish and salt and sunshine, and Harper breathed her fill.

"We've made it," she sighed happily, smiling up at him even though she knew he wouldn't return the gesture. "While I will admit that our plan for getting here was a bit harebrained, I'm grateful it worked." A foghorn bellowed as the ship lurched into the harbor. "And I suppose we'll part ways now, Mr. Montgomery. Thank you for everything," she said sincerely. He hadn't been an ideal traveling companion, but after the scene at Point Judith, the fact that Harper had gotten here at all was a feat.

It was a moment before he looked down at her, and when he did, his eyes were inscrutable. He gave a decisive nod. "Right. Well, then. I'll escort you off the boat."

She wanted to protest but knew what his reaction would be, so she only nodded, resigned to his company for a little longer.

As the boat settled into the dock, the passengers on deck had begun to collect their belongings, and a queue had formed to descend the narrow steps.

Thomas leaned down to gather their own bags and was about to say something to her when a shriek erupted from behind them. When Harper turned, she was nearly bowled over for the second time that day.

A plump, gray-haired woman was barreling towards her with outstretched arms. Harper looked around her desperately, hoping she was not the intended recipient of the incoming embrace, but then the woman was in front of her, and the outstretched arms were around her, and Harper was crushed between the deck railing at her back and the ample, unfamiliar, rose-scented bosom everywhere else.

"Vivi!" came the muffled voice from somewhere above the bosom. "Oh my darling girl, you came!"

Shock and understanding assailed her, and Harper's eyes, which were the only part of her body that retained freedom of motion, flew to Thomas's, whose own brown eyes reflected her consternation.

No, no, no. No, this could not be happening. They had not made it all the way to Block Island on the ferry, only to be recognized—or misrecognized, in this case—when they were about to disembark. This woman was obviously acquainted with Vivienne, which meant that Harper was in deep, deep trouble.

"You see, Hugh, I told you it was our Vivi!" came the voice again, and a moment later Harper was released from the onslaught, only to be immediately gathered up by another set of arms and crushed into another unfamiliar chest, this one smelling like pipe smoke and cinnamon.

"Why, Bess, you're right! Vivienne O'Malley, as I live and breathe! Wait until Claire and Claudia see you, love! They took the early ferry yesterday morning with your Uncle Charles. Oh, you are a sight for sore eyes, my girl!"

"She's Vivienne *Jones* now, love!"

The arms released her as the man—Hugh, apparently—smacked himself in the forehead. "Of course! Of course, you're a married woman now, love! And you still look every inch the blushing bride!"

Harper was quite certain she was blushing, but not for the reasons that the man suspected. Suddenly she felt too hot—the breeze as the boat moved had kept her cool, but now that the boat was still, the sun felt scorching rather than welcoming, adding heat to cheeks that were already red with surprise and embarrassment.

Harper took advantage of the reprieve from spontaneous embraces and slid over to Thomas, shooting a look at him that she very much hoped conveyed *do-something-right-this-minute!*

To his credit, he seemed to understand the look but did not act quickly enough. Harper's shift to Thomas's side had drawn the couple's attention to him, and as they took in his tall, broad physique, the chiseled jaw set below wide, puppy-dog eyes, they looked as if someone had just told them it was Christmas morning.

"Neville!" they shouted in unison, then rushed him like he was wrapped in a bright red bow. The look on his face—shock, discomfort, horror—when they simultaneously wrapped their arms around him would have been amusing in any other circumstance, but right now, nothing was amusing.

Because right now, their charade was about to unravel.

"Look at him, Hugh, so handsome!"

"I had no idea he would be so tall!"

"Such strong bone structure. Look at his bone structure, Hugh!"

"Yes yes, mark my words, their children will be exquisite."

"Exquisite," Bess cooed.

The last comment about their unborn children seemed to snap Thomas out of his stupor. While Hugh and Bess had been crooning over Thomas, the crowds had started to move down the stairs, leaving ample space for them to make their way to the dock.

"Perhaps we should move our reunion off the boat?" He said it in his usual terse tone, but he might as well have performed a flawless opera, so enraptured were they with his suggestion.

"Of course, Neville!"

"Too right, dear!"

Before they turned to head down the stairs, though, Bess turned back at Harper, her eyes watery.

"Oh my sweet girl, I'm so happy you'll be at Adeline's wedding! You and Neville will share our carriage to the hotel, of course, so we can catch up!"

Thankfully, she had turned back to the stairs and did not see Harper's reaction. Her jaw dropped even as she turned to Thomas, digging her nails into his arm.

He winced as he looked down at her.

"Mr. Montgomery," she hissed. "Surely she cannot mean Adeline O'Malley's wedding?"

There was really no need to ask the question, as she already knew the answer. Because Bess and Hugh had already mentioned the name O'Malley, and with the mention of Adeline's wedding... there were only so many possible Adeline O'Malleys in the world who could be getting married this summer. Which meant that Vivienne Jones, the person who Harper had so casually chosen to impersonate, was going to the wedding of the century. Harper lived on a fairly tucked away farm, but even *she* had heard about Helen of Troy's upcoming nuptials.

She suddenly wished she had been more slack with her corset this morning. Her lungs felt too tight, too constricted. But in light of her grandmother's current opinions of Harper's manner of dress, she had donned her best traveling dress and wrapped her corset tightly enough to turn coal into diamonds, so that if nothing else, her décolletage would quite literally be above reproach.

At the moment, she would have preferred the ability to breathe.

Thomas somehow managed to collect all their luggage with one arm while Harper kept a vise-like grip on his other. Strange as it was, he felt like the only thing keeping her from flying apart at the moment, the only steady variable in the chaos of the morning. They had begun this charade together, and while he was not exactly a friend, he was her accomplice, and currently the only person she knew for several miles in any given direction.

Troubling as it was, at the moment, Thomas Montgomery was all she had.

"I'm afraid," he whispered down to her, "that is *exactly* the wedding Vivienne and Neville Jones were on their way to."

His words were not a surprise, but they took her breath anyway.

Or it may have been the corset.

Either way, Harper very much missed the feeling of oxygen in her lungs.

"What are we going to do? I cannot ride in a carriage with them to some hotel!"

The couple was descending the stairs now, and Thomas paused at the top. " I believe you're feeling seasick."

"I am?" She certainly had begun to feel ill in the last few moments.

"Yes," he said, his eyes boring into hers. "So seasick, in fact, that you cannot possibly endure a jarring carriage ride right now. So, unfortunately, we'll have to separate from your long-lost relations until you're feeling more the thing. Once you *are* feeling more the thing, hopefully they'll be halfway across the island and you will be tucked safely away on the opposite side of the island," he said meaningfully.

She nodded, understanding, then followed him down the steps, only to jerk his arm again.

His jaw ticked, and he looked at her. "What is it?"

"What if they insist on waiting with me until I recover?"

"Then we move onto Plan B."

"What's Plan B?"

He sighed, then shifted their bags in his arm. "We act like the real Mr. and Mrs. Jones."

"Meaning?"

"Meaning we have a very public, very noisy argument that ends when we angrily storm away from everyone."

Harper bit her lip. "That would probably work. It would seem awfully rude to Hugh and Bess, though. They seem lovely." Aside from their obvious infatuation for Thomas, who was… *not* lovely.

"Yes, it would, which is why it's Plan B."

"Oh. Right. Well, let's hope Plan A works, yes?"

"Let's hope," he agreed grimly.

When they reached the bottom of the stairs, the crowds had yet to disperse, and Harper couldn't see which way Hugh and Bess had gone.

Sensing her dilemma, he used his considerable height and weight to create a path for them through the crowds.

Even so, there were too many bodies, too many smells. Perfumes and colognes mixed with the smell of fish, and she felt her grip on Thomas's arm slacken.

Air. She needed *fresh* air. And shade, and quiet, and space. Wide-open space.

Her arm dropped from Thomas's entirely, and when he looked back at her, the *V* in his brow deepened. The bodies jostled her away from him, but he was bigger than anyone around them, and he reached back for her, taking her hand and interlocking their fingers as he plowed his way off the boat, using his typewriter as a battering ram.

When they made it through the worst of the crowds, Harper saw Hugh and Bess on shore, waving maniacally at them. She tried to smile, but she didn't know if her face was cooperating. As they stepped out onto the dock, her legs swayed beneath her. Surely there was a polite way to loosen her corset in a public place, wasn't there? A trickle of sweat dripped down her back, and she looked up at Thomas, but the bright sunshine behind him was darkening.

"Miss Whitley?" His voice was coming from so far away. "Miss Whitley, are you all right?"

The edges of her vision were turning black, but she saw Thomas's concerned face in the center of it, those puppy-dog eyes rounding in concern.

But then those disappeared too, and Harper swooned into oblivion.

Chapter 5

Thomas blinked.

He was having a nightmare. That was the only plausible explanation for what was happening right now.

Harper had looked pale coming off the boat, too pale for this heat, and when her hand slipped off his arm in the middle of the crowd, he had felt little bells of alarm going off in his chest—his *chest,* of all places. And then her eyes fluttered closed and her legs buckled, and before his brain could understand what was happening, his arms were throwing their bags to the ground and scooping her up, one arm behind her knees and the other at her back.

The crowds, heedless of the strange happenings in his chest, kept moving, kept shuffling and pushing and jarring so that the only way to keep Harper from harm was to lift her so high that she was flush against him, close enough that he could smell strawberries and spring rain again.

It was intolerable that she should smell like spring and new life. Equally intolerable was the fact that he had become responsible for her, and that she was currently lying unconscious in his arms.

And he had forgotten—how could he have forgotten?—how terrifying it was to see someone he was responsible for in distress. The miserable crack of tenderness in his chest was the reason for his terror. He should never have allowed it, never should have proposed this ridiculous charade. Surely there had been another way to get onto that ferry and write the article for Luther.

But there was no time for regret now. Right now, he needed to get Harper away from the docks and heat and people. And so he shamelessly shoved his way through the crowd, careful to keep Harper lifted above the fray. He was head and shoulders taller than anyone else in the crowd, and his terror and desperation likely made his scowl downright murderous. In the wake of his signature glower, considerable height, and determined strides, the crowd parted for him like the Red Sea.

By the time he made it to the gravel drive beyond the docks, Bess and Hugh had realized what had happened and had the carriage ready to depart. Thomas had been able to track down where the wedding guests were staying, the iconic River House Hotel, and knew from his research that it was a mercifully short ride from the docks. The couple regarded him with wide-eyed concern as he carried Harper wordlessly into the carriage, and though the couple fussed worriedly over Harper, Thomas endured the ride to the hotel in stiff-lipped silence.

Over and again, the same question flashed through his mind. *What had he done?*

The question was a steady crescendo of guilt and terror, drowning out all other thoughts. The woman lying unconscious against his chest —he didn't even know her, other than that her name was Harper Whitley. He didn't know where she was from or where she was going, her family or her friends, or why she wanted to escape to Block Island in the first place. And what had he been thinking, taking this strange woman with him on the ferry, asking him to impersonate his wife?

He hadn't been thinking, of course. He had been *feeling*. She puffed out that sad wistful sigh and Thomas had *felt* it—not heard or seen it—*felt it*, right against his ribs.

It needed to stop.

But when he remembered how enthusiastically Bess and Hugh had greeted Harper, it happened again. He felt… worried. Anxious. Afraid.

Vivienne O'Malley. Now that he was sitting, now that the urgency of the moment had died down, he allowed himself to process the revelation of that moment, and his stomach sank with the enormity of their deception. Because Vivienne and Neville Jones were not just two vacationers who happened to be taking a trip to Block Island.

They were guests at the wedding of the century.

Asking Harper to impersonate Vivienne Jones had been risky enough, but had he known that he was asking her to impersonate Vivienne Jones née Vivienne *O'Malley*, he never would have asked her to get on that boat with him.

In the time since he had made his agreement with Luther, Thomas had spent hours poring over the O'Malley family tree, reading about their various properties and habits, all in the interest of trying to figure out where they might have the wedding.

Charles O'Malley, the son of Irish immigrants, had two brothers, Michael and Hugh, both of whom worked at the Gray Star Line with him. Vivienne was the only child of Michael, the eldest brother, but had become the black sheep of the family four years ago when she broke off an engagement to a man of her parents' choosing to elope with the son of an affluent horse breeder—incidentally, the man Thomas was currently impersonating. Her parents had cut all contact with her after her marriage, and based on recent events, her extended family hadn't seen her since, either.

If Thomas remembered correctly, Michael and his wife were currently overseas, negotiating a shipbuilding contract with the British government. Adeline's wedding would have been the first time any of the extended family had seen Vivienne in years and the first time they met her husband. The youngest O'Malley brother, Thomas surmised, was currently sitting across from him in the carriage beside his wife.

Charles O'Malley, the middle brother, had founded the Gray Star Line and had quickly become the world's most prolific manufacturer of ocean vessels. He had accrued the largest fortune in American history in the span of a single lifetime, and the speculation about where his only daughter would get married varied from a castle in Ireland to one of his mammoth ships in the middle of the Atlantic. Their townhouse on the Upper East Side and the mansion in Newport were widely believed to be far too obvious for a secret wedding.

As Thomas took in the Block Island landscape out the window, he could appreciate what a perfect choice it was. The island, only five by seven miles, had the feeling of remoteness without being far from the mainland, set between Point Judith, Rhode Island, and Montauk, New York.

Block Island itself was convenient but private, close but secluded. No wonder O'Malley had chosen it for the wedding. He had enough contacts in the ports to halt the tourism ferry service for the month, no doubt for an exorbitant price. That done, he had effectively severed the island from press and public alike.

The plan was brilliant.

Thomas just hadn't expected to fall right in the middle of it. He had meant to be at the wedding, of course, but not as a guest—certainly not as a guest by way of abducting a woman from Point Judith and asking her to masquerade as his wife.

That train of thought inevitably led him back to, *what had he done?* And, more importantly, *What was he going to do to fix it?*

A particularly large rut in the road jarred the carriage, and Harper stirred in his arms, burrowing against him with a whimper.

Unacceptable.

That tiny fissure of tenderness towards this strong-willed, impulsive woman was spreading, and he needed it to stop.

Mercifully, the River House Hotel came into view, and Thomas, in spite of his newfound and entirely irrational onset of feeling, was able to appreciate the aesthetic perfection of the place as a wedding venue. An expanse of perfectly mowed green grass led up to row upon row of hydrangeas, shades of lilac and indigo and pink, perfectly framing the hotel. Painted white and topped with a red roof, a porch wrapped around the entirety of the building with inviting rocking chairs spread across it. There were dormer windows spaced perfectly across the exterior, a cupola and weathervane topping the structure's center. It was charming without being rustic, elegant without being overbearing, a study in relaxed New England luxury. The ocean beckoned from the hotel's east side, a brilliant expanse of cerulean, navy, and sapphire.

As the carriage rolled to a gentle stop in front of the wide front porch, Bess took charge again, marching out of the carriage before her husband could step out and help her, shouting instructions to the flustered staff of the River House.

"We have a situation! Ready the front parlor! Smelling Salts! Cold Water! Fetch Dr. Grayson! At once!"

Before Thomas could help or object or formulate any sort of solution to the problem that was currently lying unconscious in his arms, he was bustled into a bright front-facing parlor as a harried butler gently closed the door, muting Bess and Hugh's battle cries demanding *"assistance and aid!"* for their overwrought niece.

Other than the soft ticking of a grandfather clock in the corner, the room was completely silent, and the sudden quiet after the chaos of the morning was unsettling.

A whiff of strawberries and spring rain assaulted him, and he realized with a start that he was still holding Harper. He hurried to a settee opposite the window, then laid her down gently.

Thomas ran his hands through his hair, willing himself to calm, and was about to start pacing the room when Harper's eyes fluttered open. Their hazel color was muted now that they were inside, more brown than green. They opened slowly, timidly, but once they had lifted all the way, Harper sat up with a gasp.

Her hand flew to her chest as her eyes swung madly across the room, taking in her surroundings like a soldier who had taken a blow to the head and awakened in an enemy camp. She stood abruptly, but she was still weak, and she tottered back down as quickly as she had come up. She was breathing too rapidly, her hands shaking, and without thinking, Thomas came and knelt in front of her, taking her trembling hands in his.

"It's all right, Miss Whitley. You're all right."

But she made no response other than to widen her eyes at him and shake her head.

"Breathe. Just breathe, Miss Whitley. You're all right. *You're all right.*"

She held his gaze with a small nod, then slowly matched her breathing with his.

"Good, that's it now. Just breathe."

After a moment, she looked down at her hands, where his still rested over top of hers.

Had he done that?! When had he done that?

He was losing his mind.

He jerked his hands away from hers and rose to his feet to pace the room. He cleared his throat. "All right now?"

She nodded slowly, still staring at him.

Her gaze made him uncomfortable, and he strode over to the sideboard, pouring a glass of water for her and shoving it into her hands.

Startled, she took the glass, downing it quickly, and Thomas repeated the process, preferring a task to conversation at the moment. But when she drank the second glass and didn't hold it out to be refilled, he returned to his original task of pacing the room, keeping his eyes on the walls rather than on the woman in the settee. They were painted a soft blue, adorned with watercolor landscapes, likely views from here on Block Island. It was well past lunchtime now, and the sun from the wide windows bathed the room in light, making it almost too warm.

Or that might have been the company.

"Mr. Montgomery?" she asked, and he grunted in response, continuing to pace the room. She repeated his name, and he repeated his grunt, not slowing his pace. When she said his name the third time, she nearly yelled it, which startled him enough to stop and look at her.

"What?" he barked.

She raised her eyebrows. "While I hate to interrupt what is obviously an important pacing session for you, would you mind telling me exactly where I am?"

Ah. That. Why hadn't she just asked?

"I believe that's what I just did, Mr. Montgomery."

Hm. He hadn't meant to say that out loud. His unfortunate re-introduction of feelings must be to blame for his newfound madness.

"Block Island."

She really must be feeling better, because she gave him an extravagant eye roll. "Yes, I gathered that. But more specifically, I am…?"

"At the River House Hotel."

"What!?" She sprang off the couch, but this time her legs held. "You mean the jewel of Block Island? Beautiful white building on a hill? Cupolas? Red roof? Fancy? Wildly expensive? *That* River House Hotel?"

"I don't imagine there's more than one."

Her hands fisted at her sides. "Mr. Montgomery! I cannot be in the River House Hotel right now! I shouldn't even be on Block Island right now!" Her eyes grew impossibly wider. "Oh my goodness. The boat. And Bess and Hugh. Am I here right now as Harper Whitley or Vivienne Jones?"

"The latter, I'm afraid," he said tersely.

"Thomas!"

"I prefer you call me Mr. Montgomery."

She ignored him. "I cannot be here at all, let alone as Mrs. Vivienne Jones!" She shot a furtive look at the door. "I need to go before they come back." She ran to the window, wriggling her fingers under the frame to open it. "Quick, Thomas, my valise and parasol, if you please."

"I believe those were brought up to your room."

"I don't have a room here!" she shouted at the window. The frame gave no sign of budging, so she pressed her shoulder against it as she lifted. "It's fine. I don't need the bag anyway. And perhaps I can steal a parasol on the return ferry."

Thomas frowned. "Are you in the habit of stealing, Miss Whitley?"

"I've never stolen a thing in my life." She hit the top of the windowsill with the heel of her hands, then banged against it with her shoulder. "Except for my recent theft of Vivienne Jones's ferry ticket and identity." Her forehead fell roughly against the window. "Thomas.

You're right. I *am* a thief! They're going to put me in jail! Does Block Island have a jail? No—don't answer that. Quick—help me with the window!"

"Are you planning to jump out of it?" he asked reasonably.

She blew out an exasperated sigh. "Why else would someone open a window?"

"A breeze. Cooler temperatures. Fresh air. There are actually a number of reasons for opening a window other than throwing oneself out of it."

She turned fully at him now. "Thomas Montgomery, was that supposed to be a joke?"

"I don't tell jokes."

She scoffed. "Of course you don't. Now, will you please put those broad shoulders to good use and come open this window!?"

Harper tugged at the window again, and because Thomas had a genuine fear that she would try to break it open with her bare hands, he walked across the room and placed himself between her and her intended exit.

"Finally," she huffed. She stepped away from the window expectantly, then scowled when he made no move to open it.

"I'm not going to open the window."

"Then I'm going to break it open with my bare hands! Oh, this never would have happened with Mr. Womblesrump!"

Thomas ignored the bizarre statement, opting instead to reason with her. "Miss Whitley, what do you plan on doing after launching yourself out this two-story window? Are you still planning on having a day on the beach? Roaming the shops without escort or any of your personal belongings?"

Her eyes narrowed. "I suppose you have a point to make with these rude questions?"

"They aren't rude questions. They're perfectly valid."

"Just because a question is valid doesn't mean it isn't also rude to ask it."

That was... accurate. But he didn't have time to debate with her. "Miss Whitley. We have"— Thomas glanced at the clock—"roughly five minutes left before Vivienne's aunt returns to check on you and escort you to your room. I understand the difficulty of our current situation, but—"

"Difficulty? *Difficulty*? Mr. Montgomery, everyone in this hotel believes I am a former O'Malley heiress, here to celebrate Helen of

Troy's wedding. In the last few hours I've become an escapee and a con-woman, not to mention some wilting flower who faints in broad daylight. So, sir, I beg of you, if you insist on using a euphemism for our current predicament, choose something with a bit more accuracy than *difficulty*." Her eyes, bright green now that she stood in the light of the window, flashed at him.

He sighed, accepting the truth of her statements. "You're right."

His admission caught her off guard, and her mouth dropped open into a surprised *O*.

"I got you into this trouble, Miss Whitley, but I intend to get you out of it. You have my word, and for as long as you need it, you also have my protection." Seeing her unease, he tried to gentle his tone. "And for what it's worth, I'm sorry you won't have your day of freedom."

To his surprise, she gave him rueful smile, then shrugged. "You didn't get me into any trouble that I hadn't agreed to of my own volition. And I trust you."

Now it was his turn to be caught off guard, and before he could think better of it, he asked, "Why?"

A laugh bubbled out of her. "I don't know, actually. I suppose I have little reason to. Nevertheless, I find that I do." She tilted her head thoughtfully at him.

Thomas didn't know what to make of the admission, given so freely, so simply. There was no time to make sense of it now, though. They needed a plan to extract Harper that did not involve launching her out the window.

"Right. Well, then. In our remaining three minutes, shall we cobble together a Plan C?"

Chapter 6

As it happened, they had only *two* minutes before Aunt Bess returned to the room, flanked by her daughters Claire and Claudia. Even so, it was enough time for Thomas to explain to Harper everything he knew about Vivienne and Neville Jones and to arrange their getaway.

As planned, Thomas excused himself when the O'Malley women arrived and was off to find the nearest telegraph office to send the two messages Harper had hastily scrawled; one to her father, letting him know she had arrived safely (though she omitted any clear mention of *where* she had arrived safely), and the other to her grandmother, explaining another unexpected delay in her visit. Thankfully, Thomas accepted the messages without questioning their contents and told her to expect him at her room at six to escort her down to aperitifs and dinner.

Since the only ferry departing for Point Judith today was at eight o'clock, they agreed it would be better to make a brief appearance during drinks, then reprise Harper's illness and insist that nothing but the comfort of her own home and bed would restore her, at which time Thomas would whisk her away to the ferry.

After he left the parlor, Harper allowed her supposed relations to fuss over her, happy to prolong the appearance of exhaustion from her ordeal on the docks. Since she had no idea how Vivienne would normally interact with her aunt and cousins, it was far simpler to allow them to think her subdued nature was due to the lingering effects of her fainting episode. Even if she resembled the real Vivienne well enough to fool her family, Harper had no confidence in her ability to prolong the charade, and so was all meekness and frailty as they led her to her prepared room upstairs.

Harper would have preferred to avoid any further interaction with the O'Malleys this evening, but Aunt Bess had been so adamant that Harper needed a proper examination by the family physician that Harper found herself insisting she was perfectly well, if only a bit tired. She realized now that her fainting on the docks was caused by dehydration and exhaustion, but Aunt Bess argued that nothing short of a *full* examination from the family physician would satisfy her.

But there was absolutely no way that Harper was going to let an unknown doctor conduct a full examination on her. It took a bit of persuading on her part, but Harper managed to convince her not-aunt that an afternoon's rest was sufficient medicine, and *of course* she would be well enough to see the family at dinner.

In truth, Harper wished she had just jumped out the window.

Her sense of guilt over her deception was like a boulder resting on her chest. Because Aunt Bess and Claire and Claudia were lovely. They were doting and warm and perhaps a smidge overwhelming, but since her mother died, Harper had known so little in the way of affection and love from other women. Truth be told, she all but basked in their attention.

Which was absolutely terrible, because she was *not* their beloved niece and cousin, but an imposter who had stolen the real Vivienne's identity, not to mention her ferry ticket. Harper tried to remind herself of the fact as the three women, along with Adeline's maid, Rose, helped her into a silky soft nightgown to rest in, then tucked her into bed like a coddled child.

After they left, Harper had only meant to close her eyes for a moment, but when she woke it was nearly dinner, and Rose was already back in the room laying out her clothes for the evening—or rather, *Vivienne's* clothes. The idea of wearing any of her doppelgänger's clothes made Harper squirm, but when she asked Rose if she wouldn't mind just helping her back into her same gray traveling dress from earlier in the day, the maid had snorted a laugh, then hastily apologized for her impertinence while simultaneously forcing Harper into a gorgeous emerald evening gown that likely cost more than what the farm made in a year. The fabric was light and silky, and while the design was simple, the fit was perfect, falling and hugging in all sorts of places that Harper had never had a dress fall or hug before.

By the time Rose had arranged her hair and pinched her cheeks to bring back the color she had lost earlier, Harper looked in the mirror and hardly recognized herself. Which, all things considered, was probably a good thing, since she wasn't *supposed* to look like Harper Whitley at all. For the next hour, she needed to look like Vivienne Jones.

When Rose smiled approvingly at her, she felt a welcome wisp of confidence.

A knock on the door signaled Thomas, and when Rose opened it for him, Harper felt that wisp of confidence shrivel up and die. Because Thomas took one critical look at her and blurted out, "*What* are you wearing?"

Harper felt her cheeks flame but forced a smile. "It's an evening gown."

Rose, who looked as surprised and offended by Thomas's question as Harper felt, intervened. "We chose the emerald gown to bring out her eyes. Doesn't she look beautiful, Mr. Jones?"

Thomas looked at the maid, then tugged at his necktie uncomfortably. He had the grace to look sheepish.

"Yes, yes, of course. You look lovely, Mrs. Jones," he said, briskly taking her arm and leading her out of the room.

Once they were in the solitude of the corridor, she looked up at him. "Eventful afternoon?" she asked.

"You could say that," he answered, keeping his gaze straight ahead.

"The telegrams..?"

"Sent."

"Thank you." She glanced over at him, but his stare was still set on the hallway before him, his jaw clenched. "Did you find a way to entertain yourself for the rest of the afternoon?"

"I did. I ran into Bess and Hugh on my way back from the telegraph office, and they spent the afternoon introducing me to the rest of the family."

He looked so put out when he said it that Harper had to stifle a laugh. She could well imagine gruff, stern Thomas Montgomery spending the afternoon with Bess and Hugh.

"Well," she said lightly, "for the real Neville's sake, I hope you were your usual sunshiney self." He shot her a warning look so severe that she couldn't repress her laugh this time. "I'm only teasing."

"Teasing." He repeated it like it was a foreign word, his eyes fixed straight ahead.

She looked over at him. At some point, he had changed into evening dress, though judging by the too-tight fit of the jacket, he was wearing

Neville's clothes, rather than his own. The crisp lines of the vest and jacket accentuated the tight line of his jaw, and she realized that if one could get past that perpetual scowl, he was actually strikingly handsome.

Though the scowl was admittedly difficult to get past.

"Yes, *teasing*," she said, using the same tone he had. "Surely your friends tease you?"

"I don't have friends," he huffed, and if he hadn't already told her that he didn't tell jokes, she would have suspected him of telling one now.

"Not even one?"

In lieu of an answer, he clenched his jaw.

"You know, since I'm supposed to be your fake wife, it might help if I knew a bit about you."

"You already know a bit about me."

"I know your name."

"That's one."

"You're a writer."

"Two."

"You're curmudgeony well beyond your years."

Finally, he looked at her, and was he… offended?

Fascinating.

She would have thought someone with the emotional range of a half-dead cactus might be immune to taking offense, and she felt a sort of childish delight in having roused him.

"I wouldn't say I'm curmudgeony," he ground out.

"I wouldn't say you're sunshiney either."

He heaved a sigh so great that Harper was surprised the wallpaper didn't blow down, then let go of her arm and turned to face her, which again, brought her childish delight. She had never irked anyone for the fun of it, and though their circumstances should have made her feel a bit more serious, she found the urge to tease and nettle him irresistible. He was just so… *nettleable*.

"Since we need only endure one another's company for the next hour, perhaps we could spend it in silence."

Now it was Harper's turn to feel nettled. He had to *endure* her company, did he? She lifted her chin.

"Since Mr. and Mrs. Jones were so wildly in love that she broke a previous engagement to elope with Neville, I would think they might actually deign to speak with one another. I doubt most couples spend their time together in *silence*."

"Only the happy ones," he murmured, which she returned with a dark look. "Miss Whitley, let's just get on with this, shall we?"

"Fine," she said, reluctantly taking his arm again. "But that should probably be the last time you call me Miss Whitley."

"Probably so. I will refer to you as Mrs. Jones."

"Or just use an endearment," she said flippantly, then clamped her lips together. She regretted the words the moment they left her mouth. She had said them without thinking and realized that they probably sounded like an invitation. And she was not inviting him to use endearments with her. He was so cold and stern that he probably didn't even *know* any.

Thankfully, he chose to ignore her statement, opting for his own preferred method of silence.

Without the distraction of nettling Thomas, though, Harper found her nerves catching up with her. She had never enjoyed crowds to begin with, but right now, she was about to walk into a room full of strangers who would greet her as a niece and cousin, who would likely allude to a shared history that Harper knew next to nothing about. She felt her palms begin to sweat in her evening gloves, and once they were downstairs, she could hear the excited chatter of wedding guests coming from the front drawing-room.

She dug in her heels, forcing Thomas to stop beside her.

"Yes?" His tone was impatient, making her even more nervous.

"I don't think I can do this."

"Do what?"

She bit her lip, unwilling to look at him. He had already been present for her impromptu bout of weeping and a fainting episode, but for some reason, she was unwilling for him to see her afraid.

"I don't think I can go in there. I'm a terrible liar, a worse improvisor. They're going to know. They're going to know I'm not Vivienne and then they're going to hate me and then they're going to lock me up in the attic."

"I believe you've been reading too many gothic novels."

His dry tone was enough to provoke her, but she saw something flicker in his eyes. He didn't smile or unfurl his brow or even unclench his jaw, but something in him seemed to soften.

"You're going to be fine." He sounded so sure, so confident.

"Am I? You can't know that."

"Of course, I can. You're Vivienne Jones." He paused, considering her. "I have seen you take on the most formidable matrons of the New York four hundred."

Even in Thomas's flat, serious voice, she recognized the real Neville Jones's words from the docks.

"I've seen you reduce grown men to tears."

The corners of her lips began to tug.

"And," he continued, raising a brow, "need I remind you of just what you did to poor Mr. Rockefeller at the charity gala last year?"

Harper's lips jumped into a full smile. "No, that won't be necessary, Mr. Jones." She gusted a sigh. "Thank you."

He inclined his head, and as she followed him into the drawing-room, she wondered if maybe he might have the emotional range of a fully living cactus after all.

Chapter 7

Bess and Hugh saw them when they came through the door, and their beeline towards them caught the attention of everyone in the room. As Harper expected, the room was fit to burst with well-dressed men and women, and the golden haze of evening summer sun cascaded over them from the windows, coloring the lot of them in soft, gilded hues. In light of their wealth, it seemed fitting.

Not to mention intimidating.

She pasted a smile on her face and held tight to Thomas's arm, willing herself to believe his words. *You're going to be fine.*

Or sick. It was possible she was going to be sick.

But there was no time even for that because Bess and Hugh had already reached them, kissing both her and Thomas on each cheek. Harper felt a rush of her earlier delight when Thomas submitted to the pecks with obvious discomfort, though it was short-lived because Bess and Hugh were already dragging them to the middle of the room so that the rest of Vivienne's long-lost relations could fuss over her.

Since Thomas had met most of the family earlier in the day, he was able to whisper their names in her ear as they approached, for which she was grateful. The various O'Malley relations all came to offer belated congratulations on their marriage, kissing *Vivi dear* on the cheek and shaking Thomas's hand.

All of the O'Malleys were spendthrift in their endearments, and Harper warmed under their affection even as she reminded herself that it wasn't meant for her at all.

Because no one had ever met Neville, his role was fairly easy to play, and even with his stiff demeanor, everyone seemed determined to like him. As much as the newspapers heralded the O'Malleys as wildly rich and portrayed Charles O'Malley as a cutthroat businessman, they were all as warm and affectionate as Bess and Hugh, and Harper wondered what it would be like to be part of a such a family, of a group of people determined to love one's spouse simply because he married in, regardless of their personal taste.

Not that it mattered, because they were *not* her family, and in less than an hour she was going to feign illness and say goodbye and never see them again.

The thought was oddly disheartening.

For a time Harper was happy just to let the conversation swirl around her, but when a hand tapped her on the shoulder, she turned around and immediately lost her composure. Because she was face-to-face with Helen of Troy.

Adeline O'Malley was literally the most beautiful woman Harper had ever seen. She was over a head taller than Harper (which was admittedly the norm for the men of Harper's acquaintance, though less so for the women), with perfectly curled blonde hair and wide violet eyes, along with a flawless, radiant complexion and perfectly straight, white teeth.

She was, without question, the kind of woman who men would willingly go to war for, beautiful enough to launch a thousand ships and more.

Harper was so intimidated that she wasn't sure she could manage a smile, but it didn't matter, because before she knew it Adeline was bending towards her and embracing her, laughing as she did so.

"Vivi dear, I can't tell you how happy I am that you're here! We've all missed you so—gatherings just aren't the same without you, and I cannot imagine getting married without you by my side!" She pulled back, taking the arm of the man beside her. "Wesley, meet Mrs. Vivienne Jones, my dearest cousin."

Wesley took Harper's hand in his own and kissed her knuckles. "So happy to meet you, Mrs. Jones. Adeline has told me so much about you."

Wesley was taller even than Thomas, and as he stood beside his fiancée, they easily looked like they could have fallen out of the pages of Greek mythology, so aesthetically perfect were they. He had curling, sand-colored hair and bright, almost reptilian green eyes set above perfect cheekbones and a thin mustache across his upper lip. He languidly held a tumbler of amber liquid in his hand, his posture communicating both confidence and ease, strength and restraint, like a lion in repose.

His lips curled into a smile that was intimate and charming, and though she returned it out of habit, his regard unsettled her.

"So nice to finally meet you," she murmured, feeling flustered. Most of her companionship at home came from four-legged ungulates and her father, so she was feeling decidedly out of place amongst present company.

Thomas shifted beside her and stepped forward, extending his own hand to Adeline's fiancé. "Neville Jones."

Wesley took the proffered hand, and for the first time Adeline's gaze swung to Thomas, and she blushed. "Oh, please forgive my rudeness! I'm Adeline, Vivi's cousin."

She said it so simply, so unassumingly, as if there was anyone in the country who would not recognize the shipbuilder's gorgeous daughter at first sight. It endeared Harper to her instantly.

"No no, forgive me, Adeline," Harper interrupted. "My husband, Neville Jones."

"It's a pleasure, Miss O'Malley," Thomas said, dutifully taking her hand.

Adeline waved a hand, smiling at him. "Please, we're family now! You married my dearest cousin. You must call me Adeline."

Thomas looked like he wanted to object, but they were interrupted by another voice behind Adeline.

"What's this I hear about my favorite cousin gracing us with her presence?"

Adeline stepped aside and turned, revealing a man who so resembled her that he could only be her brother.

"The rumors are true, Rhys," Adeline said with a grin.

Rhys playfully set his sister aside as he came towards Harper, wrapping his arms around her and lifting her clear off the ground.

Harper let out a surprised laugh as he spun her around, then swayed on her feet when he set her back down. Rhys steadied her by the shoulders, then looked her up and down. He was a few years older than Harper, but his smile was boyish and infectious, and she couldn't help but return it.

"My my, Vivi dear, marriage must suit you. You're prettier than ever."

Harper blushed under the praise even as she recognized it as a patent falsehood. With a sister who looked like Adeline O'Malley, Rhys would probably think the *actual* Helen of Troy looked like a soiled dishrag.

"It's lovely to see you, Rhys," she said, and she meant it. Granted, she had never actually seen him *before*, but he was so obviously kind that it really was lovely to see him.

A throat cleared loudly, and Harper swung her head to its source, the glowering man beside her. Since Rhys hadn't greeted Thomas already, Harper assumed the men hadn't met earlier in the day, and quickly introduced them. Though Thomas said all that was proper to Rhys, his expression was especially austere, and when Rhys reclaimed his hand after their handshake, he had to shake out his wrist several times and waggle his fingers.

Harper wanted to send Thomas a warning glance, but their height difference was simply too vast to accomplish it with subtlety.

The plight of the short woman.

Harper held her smile rigidly in place as they were introduced to a friend of Wesley's, Lyle Jennings; Father Jessup, who would be marrying the bride and groom; Max Stevens, O'Malley's personal secretary; and finally to Wesley's parents, Marcus and Gwen. His father was as tall as Wesley, but while Wesley was lean and charming, Marcus was prone to roundness in the middle and had a brusque, booming demeanor. Wesley's mother, by contrast, was so pale and slight that she all but disappeared beside her husband. When they left to mingle with other guests, Harper felt inexplicably relieved.

"Wait until Daddy comes down, Viv," said Adeline. "I'm sure he'll be happy to see you, and to meet you, Neville," she added with a grin.

"I'm afraid that reunion will have to wait, darling. We're meeting with Max in the library again this evening to finalize some details for the Navy contract."

A shadow flashed across Adeline's face, but she covered it well, and when she spoke, her voice was even. "You and Father are working tonight?"

"Don't worry, love," he said, snaking his arm around her waist. "I'm sure we'll be able to stop back in at some point. Just a few details to go over."

In spite of her obvious disappointment, the smile Adeline managed for her fiancé was radiant. "Yes, yes of course. I understand."

Rhys intervened. "I notice you said *we*, Wesley. Is he expecting us in the library now, then?"

"No need for you to miss the evening's festivities as well, Rhys," he said smoothly. "We've got it well in hand. Besides, I'm sure you're eager to catch up with everyone's favorite cousin." Wesley directed his smile at Harper again, and she had the inexplicable urge to step back from him.

She forced a smile.

An uneasy silence hovered over their group as Wesley excused himself, and when Aunt Bess appeared beside her, Harper felt a surge of relief. The woman's effervescence seemed to buoy any interaction.

"Vivi dear! I see you had a chance to meet Wesley just now. Allow me to present to you our new family physician, Dr. Grayson. I know how fond you were of Dr. Atkin, but he retired just after your wedding, dear, and you're in good hands with Dr. Grayson."

As the doctor stepped beside Aunt Bess, inclining his head towards Harper, she was hard-pressed not to drop her jaw in shock. Because the man standing before her was not the snowy-haired, wrinkly-handed septuagenarian she had been imagining when Bess first mentioned being checked over by the family doctor.

This was the man whom Bess wanted to give Harper a *full examination?* Harper felt a fleeting rush of relief that she had demurred earlier. Dr. Grayson was young, near Thomas's age, with raven hair and steely gray eyes, though the most prominent feature on his face was the deep dimple in his chin. He was good-looking by any standards, and enduring *any* sort of examination from him would have been beyond mortifying.

Unfortunately, Harper was not to be exempt from mortification even now.

"Vivi dear, I've been updating Dr. Grayson about your little episode on the docks earlier, and he agrees with me that you ought to be checked out."

Panic bloomed in her chest. "Oh, well, that's terribly kind of him, but truly, I'm feeling much better." She tried to smile at him to soften the refusal, but she worried it might have come across as more maniacal than apologetic.

"But darling," Bess protested, "Rose told me you slept for the rest of the afternoon. Surely such fatigue warrants at least a cursory exam, don't you agree, Dr. Grayson?"

The good doctor managed what actually *was* an apologetic smile. "Since you were unconscious for a time, Mrs. Jones, I would think it best to at least check your vitals. Ideally, I would have done it immediately after you regained consciousness, but I was away from the River House at the time, and when I returned your Aunt informed me that you were already resting."

His voice, like his demeanor, was calm and soothing. He was by all appearances a perfectly respectable doctor, but there was absolutely no need for any sort of check-up. That ferry was going to leave at eight o'clock with or without her—the very idea that it would leave without her made her wish, yet again, that she had taken her chances jumping out the window. She had to put a stop to Bess's well-intentioned sabotage of her escape plan.

"Yes. Yes, I was. And my rest this afternoon was glorious. Marvelous, really. Restorative in every possible way. Quite the best I've ever had—I slept like a veritable Rip Van Winkle." She smiled brightly as proof of her words, but based on the stunned and bewildered faces around her, she had veered more into the realm of maniacal again.

Rhys joined in the sabotage. "Don't worry, Viv, his hands are much warmer than old Dr. Atkin's were. Remember how cold his hands always were?" He shuddered dramatically.

"Glacial," Bess confirmed with feeling. "A man with cold hands has no business going into medicine, that's what I've always said. Haven't I always said that, Ada?"

Adeline shot Harper an amused grin. "Always, Aunt," she said dutifully.

"You see?" Bess said to Harper, as if the former doctor's glacial hands were irrefutable proof that Harper ought to let Dr. Grayson examine her. "And you know, my dear, there can be all kinds of causes for such an *episode*. I would really be more at ease if Dr. Grayson checked you out."

Even Adeline chimed in. "I'm sure we'd all feel better knowing you were well, dearest."

With all eyes fixed on her, she took a steadying breath, wishing everyone would stop referring to her *episode*. It made her sound infirm and erratic.

Although at the moment, those descriptors seemed accurate. She needed to project competence. Soundness of mind. Capability. More smooth-sailing schooner and less wind-battered shipwreck.

But before she could attempt a smooth-sailing countenance, her reprieve came from an unlikely quarter.

"I'm so pleased to know you're feeling better, Mrs. Jones," said the good doctor. "Your family cares so greatly about you, and anytime you feel the least bit unwell again, I hope you won't hesitate to come to me." With a warm nod, he stepped aside to chat with Uncle Hugh across the room.

Though Aunt Bess still looked skeptical, she deferred to Grayson's assessment and joined him and her husband across the room, while Adeline and Rhys picked up the conversation by telling them all that they had seen so far on the island.

After a moment, Adeline's gaze moved to the entrance of the room, and though her posture remained impeccable, her shoulders seemed to droop. Her brother noticed the subtle shift in her, then followed her gaze.

In the doorway stood a middle-aged woman, rail-thin and beautiful but in the cold, impersonal way of a marble statue. The woman's eyes, the same ethereal violet as Adeline's, scanned the room.

"Ah. Mother has arrived. How fashionably late," Rhys drawled.

"Rhys," Adeline chided, elbowing him.

"Tell me you're honestly happy to see her, Ada."

"She's our mother, Rhys!" came her exasperated response.

"Not by choice."

"Rhys!"

"Ada!" he mocked, amusement in his brow. He turned to Harper. "Why don't we ask Vivi, hm? Isla isn't *her* mother."

"You shouldn't call her that."

"Vivi? It's her name."

"You know what I meant."

"Isla is much nicer than several other things I might call our mother."

His sister's eyes flashed in warning, and he laughed, returning his attention to Harper.

"Vivi dear, settle this for us, Have you *ever* been happy to see our mother walk into a room?"

Harper opened her mouth, at a loss as to how to respond, but Adeline spared her the trouble, tugging her brother away even as she smiled apologetically at Harper and Thomas."We'd better go and greet her before she gets worked up."

Rhys allowed his sister to pull him, but not before he rolled his eyes and began humming a funeral dirge.

***

Harper waited until they were out of earshot before she rounded on Thomas.

"What was that?" she hissed.

"Excuse me?" He had his stoic mask on, and Harper had the absurd temptation to poke him in the cheek, just to provoke a reaction.

"Why didn't you intervene when Bess asked Grayson to examine me? You cannot tell me that I'm going to be *fine*, then just stand by while I deteriorate from fine to addlebrained!"

"You weren't addlebrained," he said evenly. "Though the Rip Van Winkle reference was a bit obscure."

She narrowed her eyes. He *would* comment on that. "Well, perhaps if you had supported me while I told everyone that I was fine, I wouldn't have needed to resort to obscure Washington Irving references."

"Reference. There was only one. Multiple would have veered into addlebrained." He said it so stoically, as if they weren't discussing her recent behavior as a wackadoodle.

Her finger itched to bop him in the cheek.

"I believe, Mr. Jones, that is beside the point. I don't have time to let some strange man examine me—I need to be on that ferry."

The deep *V* appeared in his brow. "I was never going to allow some man, strange or otherwise, to *examine* you." He shot her a look that was as piercing as it was opaque. "I did, however, choose not to corroborate your marvelous well-restedness, because in about forty minutes' time, we need to convince everyone in this room that you are, in fact, so unwell that you need to flee the island immediately."

Harper's stomach dropped. "*Oh, no. Oh no oh no oh no*. I hadn't meant to.... I had forgotten the plan.... I wasn't thinking..."

"Quite," was what he said, and Harper decided she was going to push both of her index fingers into both of his cheeks. She would *not* do it gently.

"What are we going to do?" It was difficult to keep her voice low with the panic humming in her stomach.

Thomas looked out across the room, then down at her. "We're going to improvise."

"Improvise. Right. Of course." She bit her lip. "Are you... any good at improvising?" It felt like asking a statue if he knew how to do the can-can.

He lifted an eyebrow. "Actually, I've never asked a woman to act as my wife to catch a boat before, nor have I then risked stranding her on an island and been forced to improvise a way to extract her from a doting family that is not, in fact, her own."

She was going to shove her pinkies up his nose. "Thank you, *dear*, for that staggering vote of confidence."

Chapter 8

Harper was staring daggers at him, but he didn't have time to care.

Even if he *had* the time, he would not have permitted himself even a single ounce of care for her beyond what he had already given.

He had already given far too much.

It was also difficult to care about the nuances of someone's feelings when that someone had essentially blown apart their proposed getaway plan.

Thomas actually had little confidence in his ability to improvise a way out of dinner and drinks and get Harper onto that ferry on time, but he would find a way.

He *had* to find a way.

But to do that, he needed time to think, and since any sort of close proximity to Harper affected his ability to do so (as evidenced from that fateful moment when he first pulled her from the crowd), he decided some distance from her was just the thing. When he moved to step away, she gave a frantic tug on his arm.

"Where are you going?" she whispered.

Thomas tried not to notice the worry in her eyes. "To practice my improvisation."

"What about me? Don't you think I ought to practice too?"

"No," he said firmly.

Her eyes turned mutinous.

Good, he thought. Better she be mutinous than afraid. If she was angry enough with him, she wouldn't worry about how to get off the island.

He was worried enough for both of them.

"But what am I going to do while you're gone?"

"Mingle, I'd think."

"I can't mingle with these people! I don't *know* these people, and they all think they know me!"

"Then let them mingle, and you just smile along."

She opened her mouth to protest, and Thomas swiped a glass of champagne off the tray of a passing footman. "Here," he said, thrusting it into her hand. "Just hold this and smile along. I'll be back in a moment."

He turned on his heel before he could hear her complaint and only felt a slight pang of guilt about it. Her panic was understandable and justified—he felt it too—but if he was going to help her, he had to get away from her, even if it was only to the other side of the room.

At least there he wouldn't have the smell of strawberries and spring rain to distract him.

Thomas took a turn around the room, nodding politely and lifting his hand in greeting to all he passed, but not pausing to engage in any conversation. In the far corner was an oxblood leather chair, and he quietly sat down in it, willing himself to think.

They could still stage some sort of fight like the real Mr. and Mrs. Jones, but he doubted that either he or Harper could muster a convincing enough performance. He could feign some kind of work emergency, but since Neville was a horse breeder, Thomas wasn't sure there was any potential situation that would warrant an emergency dire enough to justify missing Adeline's wedding. The family all clearly adored Vivienne and was eager to meet Neville, which only added to Thomas's own mounting guilt regarding their deception.

If worse came to worst they would simply sneak out of the room and disappear, though such a stunt would inevitably reflect badly on the real Mr. and Mrs. Jones, not to mention crush the family that believed they had just been reunited with their long-lost niece.

What further complicated matters was that he needed to simultaneously send Harper home on that ferry and then disappear somewhere on the island until the wedding; he had already introduced himself to too many people as Neville Jones, and he couldn't risk any of the wedding guests seeing him again after tonight.

While he sat stewing over their situation, he kept an eye on Harper, who seemed to be mingling without difficulty. Claire and Claudia stood talking with her for a time, which boded well; Thomas had met the two girls earlier, and they chattered as much as a whole room filled with people.

But when they left and Adeline's mother approached her, he saw Harper stiffen. The room was too noisy to make out whatever Isla O'Malley had said to her supposed niece, but Thomas watched as unease and embarrassment flitted across Harper's face, and was on his feet in a heartbeat, his exit plan momentarily abandoned.

Unfortunately, he had stood up so quickly that he ran almost directly into Uncle Hugh, who accepted Thomas's hasty apologies with cheerful bonhomie, but to Thomas's dismay, proceeded to ask him a nearly endless series of questions about a pair of mares he was about to purchase for his daughters.

Before he could extract himself almost twenty minutes had passed, and he had only ten minutes to spare before a carriage would be waiting outside the River House to take him and Harper to the ferry. He had lost track of Harper during his conversation with Hugh and began to scan the room for her with a tightly-leashed impatience.

When he found her, she was tucked behind a potted fern so large that it had nearly hidden her entirely. She still held her glass in one hand, but with the other she was tugging at the fern fronds, not noticing him until he cleared his throat directly beside her.

She looked up at him, and instead of glowering at him as she had before, she smiled brilliantly. "Hello, darling!"

The warmth and enthusiasm of the greeting were so unexpected that he could only stare at her. Her cheeks were red and flushed, her eyes bright.

Almost… too bright. And it had taken a moment before they had been able to focus on him.

Thomas felt a sinking feeling in his stomach.

"Mrs. Jones?" he asked, keeping his voice low.

She either didn't hear him or was ignoring him. All of her attention was back on the leaf before her. She tugged on the end of it, humming happily to herself.

His stomach turned to lead.

"You know, love," she began conversationally, as if they had been in the middle of some intimate chat, "this fern is not at all fit for company." Her voice lilted strangely, playfully.

"Is that so?"

"Yes," she said, then turned to face him, maintaining her grip on the fern. "All of these leaves—they're enormous! Far-reaching! And, I might mention, terribly, *terribly*," she leaned towards him conspiratorially, "*handsy*."

The smell of champagne wafted towards him, and if he had felt worried before, he was downright terrified now. Still, he kept his voice gentle, quiet. "Handsy?"

"Handsy," she confirmed, widening her eyes and waggling her fingers. "You see, pookie, I was just walking by, minding my very own business, when this plant—this potted rogue!—came and sidled up to me." She curved her hip into the plant to demonstrate.

Pookie. Where was she getting these words? "The plant… sidled."

"Shamelessly, Thomas! And in broad daylight. The *temerity* of this plant."

Her voice was getting louder, and he tried to shush her, convinced she was about to give them away, but as he did, she took her index finger and pressed it against his lips, silencing him.

"Don't interrupt, dear. Now, the cheekiness displayed by this plant is beyond anything, and I just don't think I can stand for it." Her finger was still pressed against his lips, so he made no reply; he was also too nonplussed to respond. "And I insist you call him out."

Another whiff of champagne assaulted him, and he pulled her hand down.

"Harper," he whispered.

"Hm?"

"How many glasses of champagne have you had?"

"Oh, a few, sweet cheeks," she said airily.

He ground his teeth together, ignoring the endearment. "How. Many."

"Well, you told me to keep a glass in hand, so I just had a sip or two while I *mingled*," she gave a deranged wink, "and I found the more I sipped the more relaxed I felt, and then those charming men and their shiny trays kept coming by, handing me fresh glasses and taking the old ones for me, and I've just been having the loveliest evening." She set her hand on his chest, leaning against him. "I can't thank you enough for encouraging me to drink."

Thomas looked down at Harper, then over at the footman, appalled.

What had he *done*?

He hadn't actually *encouraged* her to drink, had he? He had only handed her the glass and told her to mingle while he came up with a Plan D. The question of whether or not she might sip the champagne didn't seem overly important then.

It seemed important now.

She was beginning to sag against him, and he set his hands on her shoulders, setting her upright and safely away from that tiny fissure of tenderness that resided right where she was trying to lay her head.

"Have you ever had champagne before?"

"Never! Daddy never keeps any alcohol in the house."

"You've never had alcohol.... Ever?"

"Not a once, love bug," she said brightly, then began to slump against him again.

He steadied her even as he struggled to improvise a plan. They only had a few minutes before they needed to meet the carriage that would take them to the ferry, and even if he could contrive a discreet exit, she was not fit to go anywhere in this state, let alone on a ferry and a train by herself. He knew all too well what could happen to a beautiful woman traveling alone.

For instance, she might get on a boat with a stranger and agree to act as his wife.

Thomas exhaled raggedly. What was he going to do? Even if he didn't have to stay on the island to cover the wedding, he couldn't escort her all the way to New York. Being alone with him for the better part of a night would destroy her reputation.

If he were honest, their day together already had the potential to destroy her reputation. Why hadn't he thought through the risks when he embarked on this charade? He had all but abducted her from the train station.

He had been so single-minded about getting on that boat, about writing about the wedding, about getting his mill articles published so that he could finally, *finally* absolve himself, but what sort of mess had he made in the meantime? If he didn't act quickly and wisely, the young woman slumped against him would be irrevocably ruined.

His usual tone was abrasive, he knew well, but he tried again to soften it now, for the sake of this woman who was leaning against him smelling like strawberries and spring rain and five or six glasses of very fine champagne.

"Sweetheart. Why were you traveling to New York today? Who was supposed to meet you at the train?"

A frown marred her flushed face. "I've been exiled to New York. To live with my *grandmother*." Then suddenly, she brightened. "You called me sweetheart! I'm so happy you decided to play the endearment game with me."

Thomas closed his eyes, ignoring the latter comment. "And your grandmother. Who is your grandmother?"

"She's *awful*, lovebug. A real harridan. Always proper, and so severe. Sort of like you. Her shoulders aren't nearly as impressive as yours, though." She gave his shoulders an appreciative squeeze. "And you know, I believe she's spent the last few decades with something very uncomfortable wedged up her—"

"Her name, sweetheart." Even when she was sober, he never knew what was going to come out of her mouth from one moment to the next. It was maddening and exhausting and untenably endearing.

"Oh, that. Heidi. Mrs. Heidi Amelia Verbeek," she said with a flourish.

Her words were like a blow to his solar plexus. Surely he had misheard. He had to have misheard.

"Verbeek. As in, the Astors, the Belmonts, and the Verbeeks?"

"Well, I've never met any Belmonts or Astors, although I suppose I will soon enough. But my grandmother certainly is a Verbeek. My mother was one too, I suppose, before she married my father. And my grandfather, obviously, though he died when I was a baby."

Thomas stared at her, willing his heartbeat to remain at a steady rate.

The situation was worse than he could have imagined. *She* was the long-lost Knickerbocker granddaughter that the gossip columnists had been writing about? He racked his brain, trying to remember all that he had overheard about her.

Her mother had been a reputed beauty in her own time but had disappeared abruptly from public life in the middle of the social season. The rumor mill had been rampant after that, but the Verbeeks never did make any official statement about where their daughter had gone. After a time, there was other more interesting gossip to discuss, and the Verbeeks were a good, respectable family after all, here since the earliest Dutch settlers, and little was ever said about the scandal after that season.

He understood now what she had meant about a day of freedom before her life in New York. Her grandmother, Heidi Verbeek, was regarded as one of the most formidable women in New York Society, second only to Caroline Astor herself. She was known to have an unyielding sense of propriety and little patience for those who went afoul of it. Rather ironic, given the behavior of her own daughter, but such was the nature of high society.

It took little imagining to see that Mrs. Verbeek meant for Harper's season to succeed where her own daughter's had failed. He didn't envy anyone who was tasked with pleasing the woman, and from what he knew already of Harper, she would have an especially difficult time of it. A debutante's greatest duty to her family was to marry well, and Thomas had no doubt that her grandmother meant to make a spectacular match for her granddaughter.

In spite of the widespread rumors about her impending arrival in New York, little was known about the Verbeek granddaughter's—*Harper's*—upbringing. Where she had lived or who had raised her, what had become of the mother who had so scandalously disappeared in the middle of the season. Her grandmother had brilliantly crafted a narrative in which her granddaughter had reappeared out of thin air, ready to dazzle and assume her place in society, without ever drawing attention to the parents who had sired her or why she had been absent from public life in the first place. Mrs. Verbeek had managed to build rampant intrigue about her granddaughter without prompting any questions about her background.

The anticipation of her arrival in New York was eclipsed only by the wedding of the century.

And now, that Verbeek debutante was slumping into Thomas, trying, it seemed, to poke him in the cheeks, three sheets to the wind and in real danger of missing the last ferry back to the mainland for the next month.

Thomas had kidnapped the long-lost Verbeek granddaughter.

He made up his mind, knowing what he had to do.

He would get her on that boat and escort her all the way to her family. They might want to run him through for derailing her trip in the first place, but if they could be discreet as they traveled, then her reputation could be salvaged. But he wouldn't sacrifice her well-being, her safety, just to cover the wedding and get the mill articles published.

Thomas could freely admit that he was not a good man—anyone acquainted with his past would readily agree—but he was better than this.

"All right. Here's what we're going to—"

"Do you know who else might like to play the endearment game with us?" she interrupted, straightening suddenly, her eyes glinting gold in the dimming light of the room.

"Who?" He sighed. He would humor her for the moment if only to keep her from doing anything untoward before he could get her away from company.

"Aunt Bess! She loves endearments! All the O'Malleys do. Let's ask her!"

"What?!" This was not humoring. This was madness.

Not the endearing sort.

"To play, silly." She scrunched her nose at him with a silent giggle.

"No, no, we need to g—"

"You hoo! Aunt Bess! Auntie!" Harper's voice was exuberant, loud enough to catch her not-aunt's attention from across the room.

"Enough," he ground out. "We don't have time for this. We need to leave. *Now.*"

But she wasn't looking at him. She was beaming at Bess, who was making her way toward them.

So help him, if he had to throw her over his shoulder and carry her out of this room and onto that boat, he would.

She shrugged his hands off her shoulders, and when he reached for her again she dodged him, skirting behind the potted fern and waving a leaf at him.

Handsy, she mouthed, her eyes wild.

Very well. Thomas was going to tear the outrageously large fern limb from limb and *then* throw her over his shoulder.

"Vivi dear! Look at the wonderful color in your cheeks! You truly are feeling better, aren't you?"

"The best," Harper cooed, coming away from the fern and taking Bess's hands in her own. "So well, in fact, that we've been playing a little game that I thought you would enjoy!"

Thomas coughed abruptly. He had to stop her. Her chatter was like a landmine. One wrong word and everything would explode.

"Are you? How lovely! Do tell, Vivi." She fluttered her fan excitedly.

Thomas coughed again, louder this time.

"Well, the premise is—"

Thomas coughed with greater intensity, and Aunt Bess thumped him on the back with her fan.

"Good heavens, Neville, are you quite well? Hugh," she called across the room. "Hugh! Neville is unwell." She thumped his back again, hard enough that his cough was no longer contrived.

"Got something in his throat, does he?" her husband shouted from across the room. "Give him a thump on the back!"

Aunty Bess's fan was about to lay down its life in the cause of thumping him on the back.

"I am, Hugh! I'm thumping!"

Thomas heard—and felt—her fan snap in half. He'd have a purple welt there by morning.

"Thump him harder!" Hugh called, striding towards them in the wake of the many eyes that were now on them.

"What's this, Aunt?" called Rhys from the opposite side of the room.

"He's choking, Rhys!" she said to her nephew, who began to make his own way toward them.

"I say, Aunt Bess, you're not thumping him hard enough." He reached them and stepped in front of his aunt, taking his own turn pounding on Thomas's back.

"She wasn't thumping hard enough, Uncle Hugh," he explained over his shoulder when Hugh reached the potted fern.

Rhys continued to pound Thomas with fervor while Hugh interjected with his own exhortations. "The heels of your hands, my boy! Use the heels of your hands!" He emphasized the point by pounding the heel of his left hand against the right with several vigorous staccatos.

Aunt Bess lifted her fan towards Thomas's face, presumably to cool him into relief, when she remembered that she had already broken it, and instead joined her husband in offering advice. "Right against the spine, Rhys! The vertebrae, the vertebrae!"

Meanwhile, Rhys took everyone's critique to heart and applied it with zeal. Conversation stopped altogether as all eyes turned towards the scene at the handsy fern.

Thomas very much wanted to feign relief in order to stop the assault on his person but found that the excessive pounding was having an adverse effect on that particular endeavor.

Out of the corner of his eye, Thomas saw Adeline lift her hand to her throat in obvious distress while Dr. Grayson strode towards him.

Hugh suggested that Rhys pound with both hands, and he quickly obliged.

A footman threw down a tray and leaped towards Thomas, apparently preparing to tackle him to the floor in order to dislodge the imaginary object caught in his throat.

To his left, Harper looked around the room, sighing audibly and rolling her eyes. Before he realized what she was about, she had turned around and swiped a glass off a nearby side table, throwing a full glass of exquisite Madeira into his face.

The thumping and shouted instructions stopped immediately, and Thomas was so shocked that his coughing did as well. He gaped at her as red wine dripped down his face, onto the delicate silk folds of his now ruined necktie—or rather, *Neville's* ruined necktie.

"There," she said, beaming up at him.

There was a general chorus of *"well dones"* and *"bravos"* and *"good girl, Vivis,"* but all other noise ceased as he heard the unmistakable sound of three foghorns.

The sound was another blow to his solar plexus, more jarring than any of the pounding on his back had been.

Because he was too late—they had missed the ferry.

The boat was leaving.

Which meant that Harper Whitley—the long-lost Verbeek granddaughter—was now stranded with him on Block Island.

Chapter 9

Harper turned restlessly in bed, her stomach churning. Even with her eyes closed, she knew it was morning.

Today was the day, the day she would take the train to New York to live with her grandmother, the sum of all fears lumped into one four-inch train ticket.

Gingerly, she opened one eye, then the other, noting with dismay that each lid seemed to hold the weight of a steel beam. Her head felt like it had been recently knocked about with a gong.

She braced herself against the barrage of sunlight.

Sunlight.

She must have overslept.

She would miss the train.

Harper catapulted herself upright, ready to throw off the covers and launch into her traveling dress when she took in the state of her room.

More specifically, the fact that it was *not* her room.

Where were her simple whitewashed walls? Why wasn't the top right corner of her bedframe creaking? What was this wonderful fabric that rested against her skin, and who had removed the worn, patched sheets?

And then, like the first strike of lightning in a darkening sky, she remembered.

Immediately, she wished she hadn't.

Leaving the train early. The ferry. Aunt Bess's arms around her. Elegant, long-stemmed champagne glasses. Big brown puppy-dog eyes boring into hers. A foghorn blaring out in the distance. Thomas grabbing her arm, excusing them from the evening meal. Harper jabbering like a loon until he deposited her in her room, *this* room, leaving her to the care of a bemused maid, muttering something about blasted strawberries and rain.

Although maybe she imagined the last bit. Seemed a bit off.

But the fact remained… *What had she done?!*

Of all the thoughtless, impulsive things to do, on all of the days to do them…

And what was she going to do *now*?

Trapped on an island in the Atlantic, hovering between Rhode Island and New York, where everyone believed that she was Vivienne O'Malley Jones.

Also, that she was married.

To a husband.

A *very* grumpy, *very* insensitive, *fake* husband.

Harper slipped out of bed, frantic to put on her own clothes and find a way to her grandmother in New York. Her telegram had been vague enough that her absence and delay were expected, but it was possible that her grandmother would interpret her absence as defiance, a refusal to comply with the cordial entente that her grandmother and father had reached without consulting her.

She forced down the bile that rose in her throat whenever she thought of the moment when her grandmother told her about their decision. The two of them had been closeted in his office for over an hour, and Harper hadn't heard even a peep of raised voices or broken furniture or walls cracking.

It had all been terribly disconcerting.

While her grandmother spoke, her father hadn't even looked at her. Instead, he had allowed her grandmother to explain her plan to provide Harper a generous dowry and belated debut into New York Society. He had stood by the window, his gaze on the floor and his hands tucked into his pockets.

He was never like that, so unsure.

Despite all the differences between his social standing and her mother's, her father had never been unsure of himself. He had the confidence of a man who had spent his life trusting that the sun would rise and set of its own accord, that seeds—and daughters—would grow and bloom in their own time.

Remembering the way he stood silent that day put an ache in some deep, tucked-away part of her, a part that she was too afraid to touch or examine or even admit that it existed.

Had he received her telegram? Did he miss her?

Harper couldn't bear to contemplate the thought.

Besides, thinking about her father and grandmother right now was useless.

In this moment, what would actually be useful was another set of arms to get her corset laced more quickly. Her fingers fumbled with the strings as she leaned against the bed for balance.

She silently cursed the footmen with silver trays who kept walking by last night, handing her glass after glass of fizzing, scrumptious poison.

She would never drink again.

Outside of her window—her enormous bay window, curtained with beautiful cream toile—warblers fluttered and chirped, oblivious to her plight. She frowned out at them, flying in the sunshine, wild and free. Life would have been much simpler as a bird. If birds were unhappy, they just flew somewhere new and let the ocean winds send them across land and sea and air.

They didn't need to escape from trains and make deals with strange gentlemen and impersonate their short-tempered upper-class doppelgängers in order to know a day of freedom.

Furthermore, birds did not wear corsets.

At long last Harper managed to lace herself in, and she was almost certainly about to cast up her accounts from the night before. She was leaning back against the bed frame still, setting her hands on the soft mattress behind her and preparing to brave the nausea to hoist herself upright and find her traveling dress, when the hinges of the door groaned and her bedroom door flew open.

Rose bustled in with a tray in hand, though when she saw Harper half-dressed and presumably looking like an animal that had recently been mowed down by a carriage, she paused.

The maid was about Harper's age and had strawberry blonde curls and an open, friendly face. Well, it *normally* looked friendly. At the moment, she was eying Harper dubiously.

"Forgive me for pointing this out, Mrs. Jones, but last night you seemed a bit… peaky."

They both accepted that *peaky* was a euphemism for grossly inebriated, but she appreciated Rose's diplomacy.

"And this morning you look a bit look you've been run down by a carriage."

Well. So much for diplomacy.

Harper couldn't argue, though, so she accepted the observation with a prim nod. "Indeed."

Rose flashed an impish grin, which Harper imagined got the maid out of all sorts of scrapes. "The cook here has just the drink to set you to rights—I took the liberty of bringing it up with your breakfast. I assumed you would prefer to eat in your room, rather than downstairs with the other guests?"

Harper nodded gratefully, taking a glass from the tray that Rose held out to her. Its contents were questionable at best. The drink was an unfortunate shade of puce, and it would be generous to call the concoction liquid at all. Chunks floated at the surface of the drink, bobbing up and down erratically. But Harper pinched her nose and drank it down, much to Rose's satisfaction. Though it threatened to come right back up, she found that after a moment it served to settle her stomach and mitigate the pounding in her head.

Though Harper was desperate to speak with Thomas and would have preferred to be alone, she allowed Rose to stay and help her dress. Much to her chagrin, Rose insisted on outfitting her in another one of Vivienne's dresses. The moment they were finished, Harper thanked the maid hastily and flitted from the room, bound and determined to undo the damage that her ill-advised foray into champagne had caused.

***

Thomas strode down the path to the beach, clenching and unclenching his fists with every step.

He needed time and fresh air and a physical task to clear his head, to formulate a solution. Because that's all the situation was: a problem that needed a solution. If he could frame it as such in his head, without the complication of the maddening, hazel-eyed woman who was the basis for said problem, then he could think rationally.

But who could possibly think rationally when it came to Harper Whitley?

The night before he had gone out for a walk on the beach after entrusting Harper to Rose's care, making sure not to return until she was asleep. Much to Thomas's horror, the O'Malleys had only reserved one room at the River House for Vivienne and Neville, and after the clerk at the front desk verified several times that there was not a single spare room in the hotel because of the number of wedding guests, he had reluctantly gone back to the room and settled on the bathroom floor with a pillow and blanket. Lavish as the bathroom was—the enormous clawfoot tub had cold and hot water on demand—it was *not* made for sleeping.

And so a scant few hours after he had laid down on the exquisitely tiled floor, he had pried himself back up, eager to be dressed and out of the room before Harper was awake and needed the bathroom. Based on her inexperience with alcohol and the volume she had imbibed the night before, she would have a monstrous headache, and he could well imagine her dismay if she realized they had shared a space for the night—it would have been equal to his own. But there had been nothing for it, and it was to be the *only* night that it happened. Before the end of the day, Thomas was determined to have Harper on a boat bound for her family.

It was feeling a bit like déjà vu.

After an early breakfast downstairs before the rest of the family was stirring, Thomas had explored the River House, making notes in his notebook for the wedding article. When he suggested taking the Jones's tickets, he was only looking for a way to get to the island and to help Harper, not to ingratiate himself into the family and spy on them from within the hotel.

He was enough of a journalist to realize what a boon he had been given in being mistaken for Neville Jones and enough of an honest man to be disgusted with himself for taking advantage of it.

And every time he remembered the way Harper had slumped into him the night before, tipsy and trusting and smiling up at him, he began clenching his fists all over again, trying to focus on simple problems with tidy solutions.

But there was nothing tidy about being responsible for Harper. He had spent so many years actively trying *not* to be responsible for anyone, not feeling care or concern for their vulnerability or well-being. Since he moved to New York and became a journalist, no one had penetrated the walls he built around himself, had even come close. He didn't socialize except for events that were necessary for the newspaper, and even then, he preferred to find a quiet corner and to speak only when spoken to. He had perfected his *do not disturb* face to use at such gatherings, and knew it to be wildly effective.

So how, *how,* could a pixie-sized woman with a parasol and a penchant for endangering herself in crowded places have breached the walls so profoundly that he was now in danger of being her protector —not to mention *husband,* to all interested parties—for the next month?

Inconceivable.

That's what he would have said twenty-four hours ago. Today, he wouldn't be surprised to see a whale sprout wings and fly out of the sea.

It was that kind of day.

The tide was going out, and when he reached the water he heard the scraping of hundreds of tiny crab legs on the rocks, making a mad dash back to the retreating water. In the water's wake were dozens of seashells and sand dollars, little clams tucking themselves back into the sand. His boots were a soft, worn leather and laced up nearly to his knees, so he waded out to the water's edge. He took a deep breath of briny sea air, willing himself to relax, to concentrate.

He touched the letter in the breast of his jacket, hearing the crinkle of his sister's letter. What would she think of him now, knowing what he had done to get to Block Island—who he had endangered?

She didn't approve of him writing about the wedding at all, and he didn't know how to make her understand. It wasn't about getting ahead in his career or becoming the next Nellie Bly.

It was about atonement.

And what could she know of that? His sister was lovely and gentle and innocent.

Which, of course, was why her disappointment in him had stung as deeply as it did. *"It's duplicitous, Thomas. Surely there must be another way to publish the stories."* But there wasn't. It had taken him years to establish his credibility as a journalist and earn the trust of his editor. If Luther wouldn't run his exposé, no other publication would.

And the articles needed to be published. The sooner the better. He wished he could crumble all of the guilt and shame and toss it into the ocean, let the water wash it out far enough that he would never see it again, feel it again. Never feel *anything* again.

He crushed his hands together, cracking his knuckles. This was not time for melancholy musing or self-pity. Not only did he need to find a boat to get the *problem* back to Point Judith, but he also needed to ensure that the *problem* got a train ticket and was safely delivered to her grandmother's.

Thomas bent down on his haunches, scanning the sand and pebbles. He picked out a handful of smooth, flat stones and began to skip them out over the water. The first one made it three skips, the second four. He continued on, grateful for the mundane task, the way it quieted his mind as he tried to set aside his sister's disappointment and his own guilt at stranding Harper and making her complicit in the ruse to write about the O'Malley wedding.

What would Harper's family do when they realized she was missing? She was not just any woman; she was *the* Verbeek granddaughter.

And he had just swept her out of a crowd. Handed her a ferry ticket and pretended to be her husband and stranded her on an island.

Why on earth had Harper been riding a train in the first place, let alone by herself? She should have been in the family carriage with the extravagant Verbeek family crest painted on the side, accompanied by a family member, or at the very least a maid.

There was something she hadn't told him, something important, and again he felt that frenetic impatience to speak with her, to find a solution.

Thomas rolled his shoulders, trying to work out the tension that a night on the floor and the stress of the situation had brought on. He wasn't sure how much time had passed when a voice called out to him.

Thomas turned around, using his hand to shade the sun from his eyes, and saw Wesley coming towards him.

"Got an early start on the morning, Neville?"

"I usually do, yes," he said carefully.

It required a deliberate effort not to use his *do not disturb* expression, but until he got Harper home and he disappeared somewhere on the island, he needed to act the part of Neville Jones. He would need to be sociable enough to avoid suspicion, without drawing so much attention to himself that anyone would think twice about the authenticity of his identity.

He really, *really* needed to get Harper on a boat.

Wesley gave him an easy smile, his gaze polite but assessing. "A man after my own heart, then."

Thomas sincerely hoped not. He had never met Wesley James in person but had read enough about him in the newspapers while he negotiated the Navy contract to know that it was not a comparison he wanted to cultivate. Wesley was shrewd and charismatic and had worked his way up in the Gray Star Line until he was Charles O'Malley's right-hand man. His innate knowledge of shipbuilding, coupled with a brilliance for numbers and rumored willingness to do whatever was necessary to win a contract had made him an invaluable part of O'Malley's company.

When he won the most lucrative government contract in modern history, he also won himself the hand of the shipbuilder's only daughter.

While most of New York's nouveau riche preferred to marry their daughters off to impoverished English aristocrats, O'Malley retained an Irishman's dislike of the English and preferred to marry his daughter to a man who would ensure the success of his company.

Wesley James continued to regard Thomas with a steady, practiced smile, and Thomas returned the smile even as he remained wary. If even half of the rumors about him were true, Wesley was dangerous as a snake.

"It promises to be a beautiful day," Wesley said, turning back towards the water. "A few of us have made plans to go sailing. Why don't you join us?"

Thomas tried for another social smile. "That's kind of you Wesley, but I was just about to find my wife. After a busy day of travel yesterday, I think we'll have a quieter one today." Thomas hadn't meant for his tone to be curt, but old habits were difficult to break.

Wesley gave him an enigmatic smile. "No need to find her. I just spoke with Vivi on the way here. She said she'd love to go sailing."

Thomas flexed his fist so hard that his knuckles cracked. "Did she now?"

Wesley's gaze flicked down to where Thomas's fist rested at his side, then raised a brow. "She did," he confirmed. "We're meeting down at the New Harbor in an hour."

An hour? To go sailing, likely for the rest of the morning? What had Harper been thinking, accepting Wesley's invitation?

Thomas met Wesley's eye, trying to mask his irritation. "Then I suppose we'll see you then."

Wesley's lips turned up in a half-smile. "Excellent. Until then, Neville," he said, and with a short nod, he turned back towards the River House.

Sailing. The thought filled him with slow-growing, *possibly* misplaced, fury.

Thomas was not going *sailing* unless that sailboat was taking Harper Whitley straight to the New York Verbeeks and far, *far* away from him.

"Sailing," he repeated under his breath. The word felt like a curse. "We are *not* going sailing."

Chapter 10

"I've never been sailing before." Harper stood beside Thomas, still too embarrassed to look at him. He was also radiating impatience, so she thought it best to give him a bit of space.

She hadn't *meant* to agree to go sailing, after all. He had all but chewed her head off when she ran into him on the way to the docks.

She had no idea where Thomas had been earlier this morning and had been frantic to find him.

She needed to apologize, of course. For the champagne incident, and for agreeing to go sailing, and for ruining his necktie—or was it Neville's necktie?

There was very little in their short history that she did *not* need to apologize for.

But when she ran into him on the path to the docks, he had been barreling along like a bull after a matador, and when she raised a tentative hand in greeting, he had only glared at her, then continued at his angry bull pace. She had broken a proper sweat trying to keep up with him—although perhaps that was a side effect of Rose's brew? Did raw eggs make one sweat?—and she was now out of breath as they stood at the New Harbor.

Fishermen were busy hauling in nets, and a crew of sailors was bustling around the promised sailboat, rigging masts and arranging ropes and fishing equipment. It was odd to see the docks devoid of tourists today, save the small group of wedding guests admiring the vessel before them. A steady breeze fluttered the sails, boding well for a day of sailing. But Harper was not supposed to be sailing at all—not unless she was sailing back to Point Judith.

It was not lost on her that the last time they were here was when she had swooned and gotten them into this debacle in the first place.

Had she apologized for swooning yet?

Perhaps she ought to make a list.

Thomas was still giving off a distinctly bull-like aura, though, and she was a bit afraid to disturb him. Not afraid *of* him, of course. For all his grumpy exterior, she knew she was perfectly safe with him. She didn't *like* him, per se, but she knew instinctively that he was trustworthy.

It was a strange word for the seething man beside her, but it was the right one, she was sure. He was prickly and insensitive, but there was a steadiness in him, something about him that invited others to depend on him. He probably didn't even realize it about himself, and she wasn't about to point it out to him, but she sensed it to be true all the same.

She wished that steadiness made him more approachable. He didn't seem to mind the silence stretching between them, but she was fair to drowning in it.

Harper bit her lip. "I feel I ought to—"

"Vivi, dear!"

Harper closed her eyes in dismay, then slowly turned.

"Aunt Bess, Good mo—oof!"

The novelty of seeing her long-lost niece had yet to wear off, for Bess's bosom engulfed her yet again. When her not-aunt released her, a fresh barrage came from Claire and Claudia, along with several rapid-fire exclamations.

"A lovely day for sailing!"

"Does my hat suit? Should I have worn the blue one?"

"Won't Neville look rugged holding a harpoon? Quick, grab him a harpoon!"

"Such rippling forearms!"

"Such promising shoulders!"

Harper managed to get a word in. "Harpoon?" she repeated. It truly was only the one word, as Claire and Claudia were quite dogged in their exclamations.

"The men will deep-sea fish while we're out there!"

"Wesley said you can spear them with a harpoon!"

"Such strapping arms, cousin Neville!"

"Captain Carraway once caught a six-hundred-pound tuna!"

"It was a marlin, Clairey—"

"No, I'm certain he said a yellowfin tuna."

"Just like you were certain that sailor was looking at you when we —"

"Girls!" Aunt Bess issued the word like a command, and it worked as such. They both fell silent.

Harper's shoulder's eased, grateful for the call to order.

"It was a swordfish," declared Bess grandly.

And with that, the debate continued anew, now with three raucous contributors.

While they argued, Harper turned to Thomas, still hoping for a moment to clear the air.

She leaned up and whispered. "Thom—*ahem*, Mr. Jones, I wonder if I might have a word—"

"Perhaps if you hadn't agreed to go sailing for the day, we would have had *more* time for words." His jaw was clenched so tightly that it was amazing he could whisper anything at all.

Harper barely resisted the urge to stamp her foot. "First of all," she whisper hissed, "it is *rude* to interrupt someone when they're speaking, and second, *excuse* me! I didn't *want* to agree to go sailing."

"Then why didn't you just say no?" He had yet to look at her. He might have been having the conversation with the ocean itself, with how little he regarded her.

She felt her temper flare, but *honestly*. If he would just listen, he would know that she was trying to apologize. "Because my cousin's fiancé invited me, and at the moment I was already flustered and failed to come up with a plausible excuse not to."

"You didn't need a plausible excuse—you simply needed to say no. Negative. My regrets. Apologies. No, thank you. Nein, if you think he understands German."

She glared up at him, thankful that her bonnet hid her expression from those around them. "The request was unexpected, and I'm sorry. I made a mistake. *Mistakes*. The drinks and the swooning and the sailing! Lots of mistakes." She shook her head roughly. "The first of which was sharing a train car with Mr. Wombles*rump*!"

In spite of her intentions to be conciliatory, her irritation was mounting. She wasn't some silly, irresponsible child in need of a scolding. She was a grown woman, for goodness sake! One who knew much better than he did what a mess she had made of their charade. She didn't need him to lecture her or clean up her messes.

She could handle herself.

* * *

***

Finally, Thomas allowed himself to look down at her. She was dressed in a simple cream-colored gown, lace dangling at her neck and her wrists, with a straw bonnet shading her face, only a few errant curls sweeping out the sides. The effect was strikingly lovely.

In the sunlight, her eyes were full green, all the glimmers of gold and brandy from the night before replaced with jade, bright and compelling.

And intolerable.

It was intolerable that she should look strikingly lovely and have beguiling hazel eyes, that she should look as beautiful in a gray traveling dress as she did in an evening gown because she was a problem.

Prob.

Lem.

How dare she be a pretty one.

And how out of character for him to notice.

All the tension he had managed to excise while skipping rocks returned with a vengeance when Wesley told him that Harper agreed to go sailing, and the walk from the beach to the New Harbor had not been nearly long enough to calm him.

"That's the second time I've heard you mention that man. Womblesrump. Do you have some sort of attachment to him?" The thought was accompanied by an unexpected flare of anger.

Harper laughed out loud at the question, which only fueled his anger. "Mr. Wombles*rump*?" Another laugh, as if he had told a joke—as if he *ever* told jokes—and he had to wait several seconds for her laughter to subside.

Very galling.

"That was not an answer." He gave her his darkest stare, the one he reserved for reporters who touched his Remington typewriter. *No one* touched his Remington.

"No, it wasn't," she said impudently, refusing to cower under his stare.

Also galling.

He clenched his jaw. "Is there a particular reason why you won't answer?"

"Because it's a ridiculous question!"

He took a deep breath to quell his anger. "I don't see why."

She gave him an incredulous stare. "His name is Mr. Womblesrump." Her voice was flat as if the words were self-explanatory.

They were not.

But no clarification was forthcoming, and when Bess and her daughters finally agreed that Captain Carraway had actually caught a small shark on his last deep-sea excursion, they turned back to Harper and Thomas expectantly, and the time for clarification and planning was lost.

With her natural effervescence, Bess linked her arm through his, oblivious to the tension between the happy couple. "Neville darling, you must grab a harpoon before we go. Try your hand at deep-sea fishing!"

Her daughters rapturously agreed.

"No, no, thank you. I'm sure Vivi would prefer that we just.... converse."

The tilt of Harper's eyebrow told him that she knew very well what kind of *conversing* they would do. Likely of the antagonistic variety, possibly in raised voices, if the natural sound of the sea allowed. But rather than agreeing with him so that they could discuss getting her back to the mainland, she gave a cheeky smile.

"No dear, you go ahead. I'm sure I'll manage without you."

And with that she flounced towards the sailboat, waving to Adeline as she approached from the beach path with her fiancé and brother, and easily falling into step with them.

He summoned a supreme willpower to stop himself from glaring at her retreating form. Honesty compelled him to admit that he hadn't handled the exchange well, that he had handled it, in fact, much like a dragon trying to sip from a porcelain teacup.

Thomas wasn't made for delicacy, for having polite conversations with pretty young women who drank too much and refused to answer his questions.

He allowed for the possibility that he had been heavy-handed, but only a *small* one.

But as the much-lauded Captain Carraway himself thrust a harpoon in his hand and Bess all but dragged him onto the boat, he resigned himself to another afternoon on a boat with Harper Whitley.

Hopefully, this one would be much less eventful.

***

* * *

Harper looked out over the water, letting the motion of the boat soothe her. Noxious as Rose's remedy had been, she was feeling much better, and if the circumstances had been different, she would have reveled in the moment.

Because here she was, on a luxury sailboat in the Atlantic, on a dazzling, cloudless day where the only sounds were the slap of water against the hull and the seagulls' calls and the delighted cries of a happy family celebrating the impending marriage of two beautiful people.

But her circumstances were rather more complex. She had let her wounded pride and temper get the better of her at the harbor, and in the face of Thomas's accusing, ridiculous line of questioning—an attachment to Mr. Womblesrump! Could the man even hear himself?—she had stormed off, thinking of nothing more than getting away from him.

A crucial miscalculation.

She had come straight upon Adeline, Rhys, and Wesley, and immediately regretted her impulsive behavior. Because fooling the O'Malleys into believing that she really was Vivienne Jones, beloved cousin, was far easier in a crowded room when she would only have to maintain the charade for an hour. Now, she had agreed to ride a boat with them for the better part of a day, with no reprieve but the beckoning cerulean water.

If she had a bit more confidence she might have jumped and tried to swim home.

She could well imagine Thomas's response to that.

Mrs. Jones, he would call her, that subtle note of irony in his tone. *Do you realize that water is wet? That your clothes are not buoyant? That the mainland is, in fact, sixteen miles from Block Island, and you hardly boast the physical prowess to accomplish such a feat?*

Even in her head, the man made her livid, and she blamed him for provoking her onto the boat and straight into Adeline.

Eager to be alone, she had taken advantage of Captain Carraway's explanation of boat safety and protocol to drift away from the family to the far side of the boat. She would let Thomas fend for himself with the O'Malleys and the promise of deep-sea fishing. A swift glance over her shoulder showed that he was still holding his harpoon, albeit grudgingly. Their eyes met briefly, and he must have seen the amusement in her face because his gaze grew impossibly darker. But then Dr. Grayson approached him, and Harper turned back to the water.

As gratifying as it would be to watch the O'Malleys bully him into spearing something, she preferred her solitude. For a while, her wish was granted, but after a time she felt a presence at her side and turned to see Adeline beside her.

"Do you mind if I join you, Vivi dear?"

"No, of course not." Harper shifted to give Adeline room to rest her arms against the railing, then looked up at her expectantly. The bride struck her as guileless and kind, not at all what one would expect from the daughter of the world's wealthiest shipbuilder and someone beautiful enough to be compared with Helen of Troy. Harper had expected to feel intimidated by the bride—and in truth, Adeline's mother was fairly terrifying—but Adeline herself was warm and endearing.

"I've been meaning to apologize to you, Viv," Adeline said ruefully.

"Apologize?" Whatever Harper had expected, it wasn't an apology.

Adeline's hands came up to her cheeks. "I know, you deserve so much more than that." Harper shook her head to disagree, but Adeline held out her hands. "Please Viv, let me get this out." Adeline's face was so sincere, and since Harper could see no feasible way to forestall her, she only nodded.

"It was horrible, the marriage your parents tried to force you into with Mr. Montague. That man is old enough to be your grandfather, and his reputation is appalling. I hoped your parents would relent, but whenever I broached the subject with my mother, she reacted just the way you would expect her to." Adeline grimaced.

"I had planned to ask my father to intervene, but before I had the chance, you and Neville had eloped, and then when your parents cut you off, the rest of us didn't know how to reach you. We all hated it, what they'd done, but I..." Adeline shook her head as if shaking off the unpleasant memories. "What I have been meaning to tell you is that I'm sorry I didn't stand up for you before, and it means the whole world to me that you and Neville are here now."

To Harper's horror, there were tears swimming in Adeline's violet eyes, and before she knew it, she was bundled up into a fierce hug. When Adeline pulled back, she gave a watery smile. "I can't imagine getting married without you with me, Vivi. I've always wanted to be as brave as you are."

Harper stared back at her, at a complete loss as to how to respond.

She felt like the worst sort of imposter, and even as half of her wanted to blurt out the whole truth and end the charade at that moment, the other half knew that the realization that her beloved cousin would not actually be present for her wedding would crush Adeline. She wished she had some of the bravery and spunk that the real Vivienne Jones possessed.

Instinctively, Harper glanced back at Thomas, craving his steadiness. He was still holding the harpoon and standing with Dr. Grayson, apparently engrossed in whatever the doctor was saying. As if sensing her regard, his eyes cut to hers. There was an odd glint to them—not anger, precisely, but something like suspicion—and after an almost imperceptible nod he turned back to Grayson, his posture tense.

But then, wasn't his posture always tense?

Harper looked back at Adeline, mustering a smile. "I suppose everyone's brave in their own way, aren't they?"

Adeline nodded and sighed wistfully. "I would like to think so." They stood in companionable silence, though after a moment, Adeline looked back at her. "You've changed, you know."

Harper's knuckles tightened their hold on the railing, but she forced a lightness into her voice.

"Have I?" Had she said something wrong, something the real Vivienne never would?

"Mm. You seem… more at ease. Content. Rhys was right. Marriage suits you." She tilted her head, as if she wished to say more, but only looked back out at the water with a satisfied grin.

Harper relaxed her grip. Perhaps it was a good thing that Adeline had noticed a change in her—hopefully any change in "Vivienne's" character could be attributed to her marriage.

Not that there would be many other opportunities for anyone to notice a change. The moment they were off the boat, Harper would put her pride and temper aside and work with Thomas to find a way home.

"Neville seems like a wonderful man," Adeline said warmly.

The comment startled her. "Oh. Yes. Yes, he is." Grumpy and high-handed were also apt descriptors, but that was neither here nor there. Because Adeline was talking about *Neville*, not Thomas. Except that the only "Neville Jones" Adeline had ever met was actually Thomas Montgomery. Harper could not with any real authority say *anything* about the real Neville, other than the fact that he made memorable exits from large steam vessels.

Recognizing that her response to Adeline's comment about her husband had been tepid at best, she wanted to elaborate, at least for the real Neville's sake but could think of nothing suitable. *Yes, the Neville you know is trustworthy at his core and disagreeable just about everywhere else. He has beautiful brown eyes, but they would be even lovelier if he ever smiled. He has a broad chest and impressively brawny arms, ideal for carrying tiny women out of crowded areas.*

Even as she listed these things in her head, she reluctantly admitted that their forced proximity and series of mishaps in the last twenty-four hours had born a sort of unlikely camaraderie between them. They couldn't hold a conversation for very long without irritating and offending one another, but from the moment he sat down on the bench with her—the moment he pulled her from the stampede, really—they had been bound to one another.

Which didn't make any sense at all. She didn't *want* to be bound to him. Truly, she didn't even know him. For all she knew he could be a pathological liar with a wife and seven children living in the backwoods of Kentucky.

Unlikely, but also unverifiable.

"How did you two manage to meet? Knowing your mother, I'd think she would have all but locked you in your room once the engagement to Mr. Montague was announced."

Adeline looked at her eagerly, and Harper let out a nervous laugh. The sound was borderline hysterical and had much in common with a braying donkey.

"How did we meet?" Harper's voice was unnaturally high. All of this deception was bound to trip her up, so best to stick as close to the truth as possible.

"Well, we were at a crowded... event, and I found it all a bit overwhelming. He came to my rescue." *And then I attacked his family jewels with my parasol and proceeded to discuss the state of his jewels with him.*

There *was* such a thing as too much honesty.

Hopefully, Adeline would take a *crowded event* to mean a Fifth Avenue ballroom, not a ticket line at Point Judith.

Adeline's expression turned wistful. "That sounds romantic. And you two didn't know one another very long before marrying. Was it love at first sight?"

Harper thought of her first proper look at Thomas. Those unnaturally long eyelashes sweeping over pools of molten chocolate.

The severe lines of his face, the brooding scowl. She shook her head, clearing the image. Obviously, it was not *love at first sight* when Harper met Thomas. It was more *charade after first conversation.*

Which would not be a helpful answer to Adeline's question.

"Our first meeting was truly unforgettable." There. That was true, wasn't it?

Adeline smiled again, looking back out at the water, twirling the small fortress of a diamond on her finger. The weight of such a thing would quickly grow uncomfortable.

"What about you and Wesley? Did you love him from the first?" Harper ventured.

Adeline dropped her hands from the railing.

"Perhaps not from the first, no. We had known each other a long time, you know, since he worked with daddy. We met on a number of occasions—he often dined with us, at home or out. We were put in one another's company, and…" She waved her hand in a circle. "It just seemed like the natural progression of things, when we began to court, and then it was New Year's Eve and…" Tucked in the folds of her dress, Harper saw Adeline's delicate fingers twirling the diamond again.

When Adeline didn't seem inclined to continue, Harper spoke again, very gently. "Sometimes love that grows softly can be the sweetest of all."

Adeline looked back at her, her smile beautiful but somehow dim.

"Yes, Viv. You're exactly right," Adeline said. She turned her gaze back to the water, bringing her hands up from the folds of her dress to the railing, smoothing over the contours of the weathered wood, the bands of her ring clacking gently against it. "Viv?

"Yes?"

"I'm so glad you're here," she whispered tightly.

When Harper went to reply, she found her voice oddly weak. "I'm happy to be here too."

The strange thing was, she was. She wasn't happy to be stranded on the island, or to be actively deceiving the O'Malleys, but for a girl who had grown up without a mother or sister, the sort of trust and friendship that Adeline's presence invited was a balm on a wound that she didn't know she had.

"Everything well, ladies?"

The sound of Wesley's voice startled them both, and they turned to him. He was holding a harpoon as well, and the effect was rather menacing, in spite of his solicitous words.

"Yes, yes, of course," Adeline said with a smile, smoothing down the lines of her dress. "Have you caught sight of anything yet?"

"A handful of swordfish but none worth chasing. I could use another set of eyes. Come with me, darling?" He held out his free arm to Adeline, and she took it with a nod.

"Vivi? Would you care to join us?" he added.

"Oh, you two go ahead. I'm just enjoying the view. I've never been sailing before."

Two minuscule lines appeared between Adeline's brows. "But your father used to take us out on *The Laurette* all the time when we were young."

Harper could have kicked herself. What a foolish thing to say. She let out an unconvincing laugh. "Yes, yes of course! I only meant I've never been sailing.... in such a very long time! It feels absolutely new, doesn't it? Such picturesque views." Her smile felt tight, but she formed it dutifully.

Thankfully, Adeline laughed with her. "Yes, I know exactly what you mean. The first sail of the summer always does feel like new. Enjoy the views, dearest." She looked up at her fiancé, but he wasn't looking down at her. He was looking at Harper, his eyes searching and unreadable. After a heartbeat of scrutiny, he brought his eyes back to Adeline.

"Shall we?" With that, he and Adeline walked to the opposite deck, leaving Harper alone to her picturesque views.

But she found that when she turned back, they had lost some of their luster.

Chapter 11

"How is your wife today, Neville?"

Thomas pulled his gaze from the water, meeting the doctor's eye. He felt fairly ridiculous still holding the harpoon, but every time he tried to lower it, both Captain Carraway and Aunt Bess looked at him in silent reproach, and after Harper sent an amused smile in his direction, he held onto it on matter of principle.

What principle, he couldn't say. But her amusement at his expense rankled, and he held fast to the harpoon, refusing to let her know that he felt as silly as she clearly thought he looked.

Made it rather difficult to hold a conversation, though, holding a six-foot deadly object. Thomas rested it gently on the railing, maintaining a loose hold.

"Quite well," he said to the doctor, not caring to elaborate.

Hopefully, the doctor would take the hint and leave him to his brooding. *Not* that he was brooding. He did not brood. He simply.... stood in solitude while thinking about problems. Not a brooder, Thomas Montgomery. His eyes had already returned to the water and his thoughts to the problem of Harper Whitley when the doctor spoke again.

"Do keep an eye on her symptoms, though. Fatigue and fainting like she experienced yesterday may have an underlying cause."

Thomas jerked his gaze back to Grayson, his attention unwillingly snagged. "An underlying cause?" He was pleased with the evenness of his voice.

"Possibly," the doctor replied, his tone noncommittal. An infuriating, tone, that. He was a doctor, not a fortune-teller. Surely he could do better than *possibly*.

"Not something serious, of course." Thomas meant for the statement to be declarative, but it came out more like a question, a need for reassurance. That infinitesimal fissure of tenderness pricked in his chest, and he knew a sudden urgency to rub his hand against it.

He held fast to the harpoon.

"I should think not, no. But some women do have a tendency to faint when they are in the early stages of pregnancy. Is Mrs. Jones…?"

Thomas's grip tightened. "Pregnant?" He said the word slowly, as if he was unsure of its pronunciation. No, impossible. His wife—his *pretend* wife—was certainly not pregnant. The notion was absurd.

At least he wanted to dismiss the notion as absurd. But what did he know of Harper, really? He had only met her yesterday, although the outrageous nature of their relationship and the events of the last twenty-four hours made it feel like much longer. But now that he replayed all that had happened, the notion that she was pregnant seemed… vaguely plausible.

She *had* fainted. She *had* been running away.

And hadn't he gotten the sense that she was withholding something of herself, something of why she had wanted to go to Block Island? Suddenly her desire for freedom took on all manner of new meanings, new possibilities.

I made a mistake. Lots of mistakes.

The prick in his chest flared into a fleeting but sharp pain, and he couldn't fathom why.

It would be shocking, but not unthinkable, for an unmarried young woman of her social status to be pregnant. But it would explain her behavior. Surely her grandmother did not know yet—she would not be so eager to thrust her into the limelight of New York Society if she did. Or perhaps she *did* know about the pregnancy, and that was the reason she was so eager to see her granddaughter married? A hasty marriage and a "premature" birth would easily conceal Harper's indiscretion.

Or perhaps Harper never meant for her grandmother to know about the pregnancy at all—perhaps she was planning on meeting the father of the child somewhere, intending to disappear entirely.

He glanced over his shoulder at her. She was on the opposite side of the boat with Adeline, and her bonnet obscured her face. From this side of the boat, with the bronze sun framing her tiny form, she was little more than a wisp of cream fabric, moving fluidly with the wind. She turned briefly in his direction, but her expression was hidden by her bonnet and the dancing shadows from the sail, and as quickly as she had looked towards him she looked away.

She looked lovely but ephemeral. The description felt poignantly apt.

But the entire train of thought summoned a shocking surge of rage, and suddenly Thomas was glad he was holding the harpoon, glad he had something heavy and dangerous in his grasp. He wanted to spear something, to hurl the sharpened steel far and fast out into the ocean. The impulse unnerved him, and he had to tighten his hold on the harpoon to keep from acting on it.

His reaction did not go unnoticed.

"You need not be alarmed. Such fatigue and light-headedness are common in your wife's condition."

Thomas was tempted to impale the harpoon on a much closer target. "She does not have a condition," Thomas ground out.

But the instinctive fear that she *could* be pregnant—that that was the reason she had been running away, the reason she had been ill—seized him, spreading through his thoughts like cancer. With alarming swiftness the possibility of pregnancy became *probability,* and then *certainty*. And that certainty, unfounded as it was, built until he was near to shaking with an anger he could not explain, even to himself.

Dr. Grayson wisely diverted his gaze to the water. "Of course," he said easily.

His tone was gentle, placating, as if years of ministering to the sick and anxious had smoothed out all the rough edges of the doctor's voice, like sandpaper brushed over and again on a rough piece of wood until the surface was soft enough to rest against. But the tone did nothing to soothe Thomas now. If anything, the gentleness and imperturbability of the doctor had the opposite effect on him, tugging at all the rough, splintering edges of Thomas's composure, so much so that he did not trust himself to speak.

No doubt the real Neville Jones would not rage against the doctor who was concerned with his wife's well-being and that of his unborn child. It was only his loose awareness of the need to maintain the charade that kept Thomas from acting rashly.

"They're not so bad, you know."

Thomas glanced sharply at the doctor.

"Children," Grayson clarified. "The first year is always difficult, but you would be amazed by how quickly you love them."

The doctor meant to be reassuring. He meant to be kind.

But Thomas felt another surge of anger.

"I don't doubt it," he said, controlling his temper with difficulty.

The doctor, sensing his mood, looked out at the water again.

"You need not be afraid."

"I'm not afraid," Thomas said instinctively.

Except he found that he *was* afraid, appallingly so. He was afraid that Harper was pregnant. He was afraid of the notion of babies and children in general.

No one knew better than he did how fragile children were, how easily they could come to harm.

But it wouldn't do to think about that now.

Right now, he had a more urgent problem to solve.

Specifically, a small, hazel-eyed problem. Who may or may not be with child.

The doctor turned towards him. "If, however, Mrs. Jones feels unwell again, or needs anything, know that I am here for her. My offer to examine her stands as long as we're here on the island."

The words, no doubt kindly meant, sent another shot of rage through him. Because Grayson didn't need to be *here* for Harper. *Thomas* was here for Harper. Whatever mess she had gotten herself into, he would take care of it. *He* would take care of her.

The doctor accepted Thomas's silence as an answer, nodded kindly, and stepped wordlessly from him to join Rhys, Wesley, and Lyle as they scoured the waters for their prey.

Though the spirits on the boat remained high, Thomas refused to engage with anyone for the remainder of the ride. Everyone was eager to catch sight of the elusive fish, and it was easy enough to stare out at the water under the pretense of looking for a fish worth spearing, but when he looked out at the water, he didn't see anything at all.

He thought only of a slight figure in a cream dress, swaying and rocking a bundle in her arms.

***

Their group never did find any fish worth spearing, and after another hour they all agreed to head back to the River House.

Maneuvering the schooner back into the harbor was a difficult endeavor. The island was surrounded by treacherous shoals filled with half-hidden rocks, even the smallest of which could damage or even sink the vessel, and any entrance into the dock needed to be done with time and precision.

The prolonged docking did nothing to improve Thomas's mood.

Mere seconds after Captain Carraway and his crew had the boat secured to the dock, he marched over and took Harper by the arm, escorting her off the boat before anyone had even moved towards the docks.

They were already halfway down the beach before she spoke. "Will you slow down?" she huffed.

"No."

"Thomas," she hissed, tugging on his arm.

"It's *Mr. Jones*." He tugged back, increasing his stride.

After a few more futile tugs, she changed tactics, twisting and stepping so that she stood directly in front of him. His speed and determination were such that he nearly mowed her down, but he recovered at the last moment. The movement was abrupt, though, and she faltered backward, nearly falling before he wrapped an arm around her waist.

Once righted, he released her quickly, having learned his lesson the last time. But her attention was on righting her tangled skirts, and by the time she looked back up at him, he had smoothed his expression back to bland stoicism.

"Would you like to tell me what that was about?" She was still catching her breath after his bruising pace, and he knew a flash of remorse. It was unkind of him to make her run in her condition.

"It was time to get off the boat."

"Indeed. But since the boat was neither ablaze nor under imminent attack, I'm wondering why you saw fit to disembark as if it were. People were looking at us!"

"Don't you think that's the least of your worries right now?"

He saw her square her shoulders for a sharp retort, but then her expression shifted as if something in her was deflating.

The sight of it made him feel like he was deflating as well.

Her voice was lower when she spoke. "Yes. I suppose I have a much bigger mistake to correct."

The words chafed; he saw in them the confirmation of her pregnancy.

"We need another way off the island. The telegrams I sent to my father and grandmother will afford me some time but without my appearance or further word from me..." She didn't need to finish the sentence, as they both knew full well what the repercussions of her disappearance would be. "I know that the regular ferry won't run again until July, but surely there are other boats that will need to venture out to the island in the meantime. Block Island must be dependent on all manner of things from the mainland."

She was right. "So what we need to do is find out which supply boats will still be running," he mused. "Things like food and medicine would need to be delivered regularly. The grocer or the apothecary would know. Or even some of the staff at the River House. Our questions would need to be asked carefully, but we could manage it."

Harper said his name, but he ignored her. His mind was churning now, running through the possibilities of which boats might pass through when. He would need to ensure that the captain of the boat was trustworthy enough to transport Harper, not to mention discreet. But discretion and silence could be bought. He had learned that from his father. *The ends justify the means,* his father would say. The inevitable pain that accompanied any reminder of his father hit Thomas like a punch.

But it was an actual punch to his chest—from a very small fist—that drew his attention.

"Ouch." He frowned down at Harper. "You hit surprisingly hard for such a small woman."

She looked inexplicably offended. "Why should it matter that I'm small if I can hit well?"

The sleep deprivation and hours in the sun had given him a headache, and her particular quirk of winding conversations in odd directions was making it throb. "Why should it offend you that I point it out?"

"Because petite women are chronically underestimated! As if what we lack in height we also lack in strength or cleverness or capability."

He rubbed his hand roughly down his face, striving for patience. "I'm sure that your cleverness and capability are quite average in spite of your deficiency of height. And I've already commented on your strength. *Now* can we discuss how to get you home?"

"*Deficiency* of height? You think I'm *deficient*? Oh, of all the insensitive, simple-minded—"

"*Mrs. Jones,*" he warned, cutting her a look. "Your way home."

Her look was mutinous, but she swallowed her retort, instead folding her arms against her chest. "I've already figured it out."

"You have? In the last two minutes?" He raised his eyebrows.

"Yes, you ogre."

He ignored the insult. "All right. Care to enlighten me?"

In response, she shoved against his shoulder until he was facing the water. And there in the distance was the unmistakable shape of a steamboat, making its way towards them at a sedate pace. With a flourish, Harper extended her hand. "May I present to you, the mailboat."

Of course. He ought to have thought of it himself—the mailboat carried the newspapers as well. Even all of Charles O'Malley's connections in the shipbuilding world would not have been able to halt federal mail from reaching the island during the month of the wedding.

He looked down at Harper. "Let's get you home."

***

The docking of the mailboat took an interminable amount of time, or so it seemed. While she and Thomas stood waiting, the rest of the sailing group had walked past them on the beach, smiling and making cheeky comments about their abrupt departure from the boat.

"Still in the honeymoon phase, are we? Awfully eager to get back to your room! Urgent matters to attend to?" There was a great deal of winking and nudging, primarily from Bess and Hugh and their enthusiastic offspring, and even Rhys gave them a knowing smile as he walked by, clapping Thomas on the back. The fact that Thomas's expression was fairly murderous didn't discourage them a bit. Apparently, their innate affection for *Vivi dear* extended to her husband, regardless of his faint aura of wet blanket. If she didn't have to stand with her arm linked with the wet blanket, Harper might have found their loyalty charming.

But since her close proximity to the man was still necessary, Harper endured the comments with a brittle smile, both embarrassed and bristling with impatience to speak with the captain of the mailboat. When the vessel finally eased into the harbor, she suspected her own expression resembled Thomas's.

The mailboat was a much smaller steam engine than the Block Island Ferry, built more for speed and efficiency than luxury or grandeur. Rust edged up from the bottom of the vessel, along with a smattering of mollusks that had embedded themselves near the stern of the boat. But the paint on the side of the boat, declaring it to be *The Nelesco II,* looked recent and neat, and while the boat was by no means new or embellished, it seemed serviceable and sturdy.

"Follow my lead," Thomas whispered as they neared the boat. "I'll talk to the captain, gauge if the mailboat might be a viable option for your return."

She had an instinctive urge to argue with him—it was *her* dilemma, after all, but she settled for a nod. The captain would probably respond to Thomas better anyway, and after her conversation with Adeline, she was more motivated than ever to end their charade. She kept her head down as they walked, then almost tripped when Thomas stopped abruptly. She looked up at him, and then in front of them, and immediately understood the reason.

They were standing ten feet away from Methuselah.

Or possibly Methuselah's grandfather.

Her memory for Old Testament genealogies being middling to poor, Harper could not recall the name of Methuselah's grandfather.

Maybe Adam himself?

Regardless of his forefathers, the man standing before them was old, appallingly so. Also, hunched. Possibly rickety, though she was not yet close enough to verify.

"*That* is the man who brings the mail to the island every day?" Harper whispered to Thomas. She realized too late that her incredulity was hardly gracious, especially since they were about to ask an enormous favor of the man. She changed her tone. "What a formidable chap he must be to still be rambling about the seas and delivering mail."

"That man," Thomas said, in none too gracious a tone himself, "has likely been rambling the seas since he was banished from the Garden of Eden."

She snorted an unexpected laugh and elbowed him.

"Be *nice*," she said. "If he is willing to return me to Point Judith, then he will be my rescuer, and I'll not hear anyone speak ill of him."

"Miss Whitley," he said, his voice stern. "Even if he is willing to take you with him, *I* am not willing to send you with him."

"What?" she said, her eyes snapping up to meet his. "Why ever not?"

"Look at him."

"I *am* looking at him. He's no spring chicken, to be sure, but what he lacks in youth he surely makes up for in experience. I'll be perfectly safe on his vessel. And I hardly need *your* permission to go anywhere."

The man in question had been slowly—so unbelievably slowly—unloading crates onto the dock and now straightened, pressing both his hands to his low back. They could hear the cracks from where they stood.

"I cannot entrust you to his care. One more large crate and he's liable to shatter. "

"I don't need you to *entrust* me into anyone's care. You are not my keeper."

He glowered at her. "In the time since we've met, I've pulled you from a stampede, caught you when you fainted, extracted you from a room while intoxicated—"

"You're the one who handed me the champagne! And I didn't ask you to do any of those things! I would have managed those situations just fine without your intervention."

Thomas ignored her blustering claims. They both knew she would have been trampled twice over if not for him, and who knew what sort of mischief she would have made if left by herself with the champagne? But he needn't be so ungallant about... well, his gallantry.

"I am not your responsibility," she said tersely.

"Miss Whitley, that is *exactly* what you are to me."

Harper reared back in shock, surprised by how much his words stung. It was hardly the first rude thing he had said to her, and truly, it wasn't even that rude. But for some reason, his curt and clinical assessment of their relationship—of Thomas as the competent adult and Harper as some inept child that he was obligated to assist—was like a paper cut. Small and swift, but disproportionately painful.

Jut then the postman stretched his ancient arms above his head and clasped him together, emitting another series of cracks. He bent his torso from side to side, and Harper could not decide if the resulting groaning came from his mouth or his age-old joints.

Neither aided her cause.

He had definitely had sprier days, but that hardly mattered. He was capable of bringing his boat from one port to another, and that was all that mattered. It wasn't as if she need him to defend her against a band of pirates. In the off chance that they did encounter any nautical miscreants, she had her parasol, though she thought it wise to keep the thought to herself.

"Thomas, if the United States government trusts him to deliver the post—and we must assume he delivers all matter of wildly important documents—then we can trust him to safely deliver me as well. Besides, it's not as if he needs to load me in a crate and lift me anywhere."

Thomas's expression was as severe as ever. "Be that as it may," he began, his tone dry, "delivering documents—*wildly important* though they may be—is very different from delivering an unchaperoned young woman to a train station."

"I don't see how." His comment about her being his responsibility—an *unwanted* and *begrudging* one at that—still stung, and she would have thought he would be eager to send her back to the mainland with anyone willing to take her. If he could have wrangled together enough seagulls, he probably would have strapped her to their backs and demanded that the birds drop her at Point Judith. "Would it make you feel better if he were a young strapping fellow? Brawny and virile?"

His jaw began to tick.

"It would not," he said through clenched teeth.

Well, now he was just being persnickety.

She sighed, then changed her tactic. "Maybe that isn't even the captain. Maybe he's just a dock worker."

Thomas gave her a skeptical glance.

"Let's at least talk to him."

After a small pause, he gave a minuscule nod and walked towards Methuselah. Or Adam.

Either one.

"Hello, sir. I'm looking for the postmaster of the *Nelesco*. Do you know him?"

Father Time squared his shoulders and tipped his hat.

"Silas McGarvy, at your service. What can I do for you?"

Thomas looked down and widened his eyes meaningfully at Harper, and she widened hers right back at him.

"You would not, by chance, be the captain for this fine vessel, would you?" Thomas asked.

"Yes, sir, I am! Been bringing the post to Block Island for the last sixty years, six days a week, excepting holidays, of course, and a week off every time the missus had a new babe. Seven in total," he said with pride.

"Of course," Thomas said, then lifted a brow at her. She pursed her lips at him, irritated, then turned to Silas with a winsome smile.

"How wonderful, Mr. McGarvy. You are a credit to both your profession and this fine island." Silas visibly puffed his chest. "My name is Vivienne Jones, and this is my husband Neville. I wonder if I might ask a small favor of you?"

Thomas tightened his hold on her arm.

"It would be my pleasure, dear," Silas said to her, offering her a smile that had lost about half its members.

Harper opened her mouth to respond, but Thomas did not give her the chance.

"A pleasure to meet you, sir, but my wife and I have an important appointment to get to."

"No we don't," she hissed at him.

"We really do."

"We do not. I haven't asked my favor yet."

"You don't need a favor." His eyes flashed a warning, which, naturally, she ignored.

"Yes, I do."

"Do. Not."

"Are you two newlyweds?" Harper and Thomas turned to stare at the sea captain, both of them aghast.

Silas didn't seem to notice their expressions. Instead, he regarded them with fondness, as if he was looking at a beautiful Rembrandt instead of a surly, bickering couple.

"Not exactly, no." Thomas's voice was taut as a bowstring.

"Ah, been together a while then."

"What makes you say that?" Harper blurted.

"The only couples who get on like you two are the mad ones. Madly in love. Makes you do all kinds of things, love like you two have."

Thomas looked horrified, which was *less* than flattering, even if she was sure her own face mirrored his.

"How kind of you to say so," Harper finally managed.

The reply pleased Silas immensely, and he winked at her. "Now, what was that favor, Mrs. Jones?"

Harper took a deep breath, then offered him another smile. "I was hoping you would—"

"Knots!" Thomas shouted, and both Harper and Silas turned bewildered stares toward him. He seemed almost as surprised as they were. "My wife has a passion for knots," he clarified, rallying quickly.

She could only gape at him, nonplussed.

"A passion," Thomas repeated. "And I imagine a seasoned sailor such as yourself would be able to show my wife a knot or two. If we could impose on just a moment of your time, it would make her day."

Knots? She had never considered knots beyond the ones she used to tie her shoes. He was treating her like a child, trying to redirect their conversation.

Harper was about to object, but at Thomas's request, Silas's face had lit up like a Roman candle, looking so elated that Harper had no choice but to nod with enthusiasm and add a reluctant *"please sir"* of her own.

As it turned out, it was Silas's pleasure not only to offer a *moment* of his time in which to teach her *a knot or two*; all said and done, he offered a full hour and taught her a bowline, figure 8, and a reef knot, finishing with a brief but trying exam of Harper's newfound expertise.

Apparently, Thomas's tactic of redirection was more than effective.

When they finally left the dock and a beaming Silas, the afternoon was nearing evening, and she was no closer to finding a way home. If Thomas hadn't intervened, she might be on the boat with Silas, bound for Point Juidth already. Anxiety over her situation and irritation at the man responsible for prolonging it had her seething.

The path from the docks down to the beach and back to the River House was not long, but it eventually became secluded enough that she could give vent to her ire without fear of being overheard.

"Thomas," she said, giving his arm a fierce tug.

He ignored her, becoming suddenly fascinated with a flock of seagulls squabbling over a scrap of biscuit.

"Thomas," she repeated, and this time she dug in her heels, forcing him to either drag her alongside him or stop fully. He stopped but was still engrossed in the plight of the biscuit.

Fine. She would talk to the back of his head.

"Why didn't you ask him? He would have said yes."

"I already told you why. He was too infirm to escort you safely."

"And *I* already told *you* that I would have been perfectly fine. I don't require a proper escort. Just a way to get from one place to another. And it isn't your place to decide how or with whom."

After a few more angry squawks the biscuit was devoured, and the seagulls flew off over the water.

Without the pretense of avid interest in coastal birds, Thomas was forced to turn to her.

"Of course you need a proper escort," he said. As he looked down at her, his gaze turned intense, inscrutable.

He paused, studying her as if she were a particularly complex equation that needed more theorems, more proofs. "Unless there was a particular reason you prefer to travel without one?"

There was an unsettling undertone to his question. It was too heavy, laden with some other question or implication she could not identify.

"A particular reason?"

His gaze flitted down her torso, then rapidly back to her face, as if the brief inspection was inadvertent.

"A particular reason?" she repeated.

Something flared in his eyes, and his brow furrowed impossibly deeper. "There's no need for the playacting. I already know."

She jerked her head back, now well and truly confused in addition to seething. She didn't have the time or inclination for a meandering or contentious discussion right now. "Just what do you *think* you know?"

He clenched his jaw, then seemed to steel himself for his next words. Inexplicably, he held out his hand, gesturing to her midsection.

"I know about the *baby*, Miss Whitley."

Chapter 12

Time was a strange thing.

A day was always twenty-four hours, an hour always sixty minutes, a minute always sixty seconds. But in spite of its apparent constancy, the nature of seconds and minutes and hours could shrink or expand, like wooden beams fluctuating in the elements.

If the last twenty-four hours felt as if they had been pulled and stretched to fit a much longer span—a week, perhaps a month—then the conversation that followed was a full day all its own.

A long, miserable, uncomfortable day.

On hearing Thomas's pronouncement—*I know about the baby*—she had run through a gamut of emotions—shock, incredulity, outrage—and then settled on just plain rage. Once that last one set in, she found her voice.

"How dare you. How *dare* you." Her voice had so perfectly captured the dangerous breadth of her anger that Thomas actually took a step back.

He did not, however, relent. "Running away from home. Fainting. How else can you explain your behavior?" He said it with such assurance, as if pregnancy were a foregone conclusion for any woman who had ever swooned. If that were the case, every woman who had ever felt light-headed would be thought to be with child. The world's population would be exploding.

Her next words were throttled into a hiss. "I don't need to justify my behavior to you."

Even as she said the words, though, she knew that she *would* justify herself. For what reason, she couldn't fathom. His good opinion hardly mattered to her.

"I didn't run away from home. Block Island was supposed to be a brief detour—I hardly planned on making a full-fledged escape! You know as well as I do that the events that transpired to strand us here were outside of our control! And I fainted because I neglected to eat and drink enough, then spent the majority of the morning in the sun!" *All while laced in a prison of whalebone and stiff fabric!* she added to herself.

If her outburst affected him at all, he didn't show it. "Really? Then explain to me how the long-lost Verbeek granddaughter came to be riding unescorted on a public train car."

She jerked her head back, stunned. "What did you call me?"

He scoffed. "As if you didn't know what your grandmother has been saying about you."

In spite of the heat, Harper had felt herself grow cold. Temperature was a strange thing as well.

The long-lost Verbeek granddaughter. Although she had known all along that her grandmother would be sponsoring her official debut into New York Society, it hadn't occurred to her that she would also be spreading word of Harper's arrival through the ranks or styled her as such. Why hadn't that occurred to her before? Of course her grandmother would want to stir intrigue about her—she meant for Harper to succeed in marrying well where her own mother had failed, at least by Knickerbocker standards. The thought that her arrival in New York had been announced and anticipated only added to her unease about the whole undertaking, and in light of her current predicament, that unease was easily rebranded as anger.

Thomas had watched her internal struggle with his usual stoicism. She lifted her chin, trying to maintain some dignity in the face of his outrageous claims. But then another question occurred to her. "How did you even know my grandmother was Heidi Verbeek?"

"You told me yourself. Last night."

Drat. She *had* told him. She was never ever ever *ever* drinking again.

"And you did not answer my question. What were you doing alone on that train? Surely your grandmother would have sent a carriage for you."

The impudence of his questions, and his expectation that she would answer them, sent her temper into a fever pitch. Was it only earlier today that she had thought him steady and trustworthy? He was rude, offensive, insufferable. In truth, her grandmother had offered her own personal carriage, but Harper had been adamant about riding the train.

She wanted that one last journey to be plain Harper Whitley, not a debutante or her grandmother's protegé. In this, at least, her father had taken her side and prevailed over her grandmother's protests.

But she didn't tell him that. It was unlikely that anything she said would change his opinion of her. "My goodness, is there no end to your presumption? My travel arrangements are none of your concern."

"*You* are my concern!" he shouted.

The words careened through the air between them with the force of a cannonball. A startled rabbit shot out from the woodland behind them, bolting down the path.

The ensuing silence roared between them.

Their gazes clashed and held, but his eyes—those wide, brown, puppy-dog eyes that seemed so out of place on his austere countenance—didn't hold the glint of reproach now. Something had shifted in him, and not just his eyes. His voice, when he had raised it to her, had been absent of the stiff pride that so often characterized it. In its place was something frustrated and untethered and, if she was not mistaken, aching.

His hand came up to his chest, as if of its own accord, and he tugged violently at the collar of his shirt before returning it to his side in a tight fist.

You are my concern.

His chest heaved in an apparent effort to restrain his unusual display of emotion. For a fleeting moment, she wanted to reach out to him, to rest her hand on his chest. To what end, she was unsure. To push against him? To steady him? To… comfort him?

The impulse was so jarring that she retreated from him, stopping only when her back came against the rough bark of a maple.

The gentle collision returned her to the moment, to his accusations.

"Let me be clear," she said to him, her voice cracking like a whip into the silence. "In spite of my impulsive decision to begin this charade with you, and almost every one made thereafter, I am not generally prone to rash decisions, certainly not rash decisions with gentlemen. Present company excluded," she added with an angry swat of her hand. "And although it is none of your concern, I am not currently, nor have I ever been, with child." She squared her shoulders. "I will find my own way off the island, sir. I'm sure you're eager to get on with your writing. And if I have not found a way home by evening, then I will see you at dinner." The last words she infused with as much scorn as possible.

And with that parting shot, she had fled back to the River House, not slowing until she had shut the door in her room and fallen back against the door.

Pregnant. He thought she was pregnant.

She tore the bonnet from her head, throwing it against the bed before remembering that it was not her own to manhandle. Moving to the luxurious bathroom connected to the room, she splashed her face with cold water, as if she could wash off their conversation, then flopped facedown on the bed.

She could try to go back to the docks, try to persuade Silas on her own to take her back to the mainland, but the task would be far more difficult now that she had introduced herself as Thomas's wife. Her request now would be conspicuous, arousing all sorts of unnecessary qualms and suspicion, which Thomas knew well.

Odious, judgmental, horrible man. She repeated the words in her mind like a mantra.

Except in between recitations, sometimes his face would intrude, that expression of almost ache, and she would see again the way his hand came up by his chest. Nothing about the man made sense, and it was far easier to think him horrible than to try to understand him.

Harper had no idea how long she had been lying on the bed when a knock came at the door, and before she could set herself to rights, Rose and Aunt Bess were already walking into the room.

"Vivi dear, are you feeling poorly again?"Aunt Bess was at her side in a flash.

"No, no, only tired from sailing," Harper reassured her, trying to put her hair and skirts in some semblance of order.

Rose, who had been carrying a tray of tea and a small mountain of sandwiches, set the repast on the table beside the bed and came to sit on her other side. "You should have rung for me! I would have come to help you get changed into something more comfortable."

The upper-class notion that a woman needed someone to help dress and undress her multiple times a day had always been a mystery to Harper; her grandmother would likely have conniptions if she knew her view. Vivienne's evening gowns and their intricate back fastenings required some assistance, she allowed, but there was no reason to bother Rose every time she needed to lie down.

"I'm fine, truly Rose," Harper said. "I'm sure you have more important things to do."

"I don't, actually." When Harper looked askance at her, she clarified.

"Normally I serve as Adeline's lady's maid, but for the wedding month Mrs. O'Malley *insisted* that Greta, her own lady's maid, look after her." Rose was well-trained enough not to roll her eyes, but the sour expression on her face told Harper exactly what she thought about Isla O'Malley's opinion. At the memory of her own brief interaction with the woman, Harper felt a certain kinship with the maid.

Aunt Bess was not similarly limited in what she could or could not say about her sister-in-law, and added stoutly, "Absolute rubbish, of course. So typical of Isla. As if anyone could do a better job than our Rosie!" She rolled her eyes magnificently, and Rose laughed.

"Why thank you."

"Oh, pish posh. It's no more than the truth. Now tell me Viv, are you truly just tired from the sailing?"

"I am." *Also, angry that her pretend husband was an odious, judgmental, horrible man.*

After a cursory look at her, Bess nodded. "Very good, then, dear. Now, I came because I have something for you."

"You do?"

To Harper's dismay, Bess proceeded to remove a ring from her pocket, a large emerald set in an intricately braided gold band, and slipped it onto the ring finger of Harper's left hand. The older woman let her hand linger over her supposed niece's.

Harper shook her head, guilt swamping her. The ring was exquisite; the craftsmanship was unparalleled, and it was likely worth a small fortune. All of them were being so kind to her, believing her to be their *Vivi dear,* and Harper couldn't bear it. "Aunt Bess, you don't have to give me your—"

"I want to, sweet." Seeing the question on Harper's face, she said gently, "I noticed, my dear, that you weren't wearing your ring. A married woman as beautiful as you should always keep one on. I'm sure Neville will thank me for it," she added with a wink.

Harper blushed, then struggled for a plausible explanation. "My wedding ring is… it's being resized. The jeweler didn't have it ready when we had to leave for the wedding."

Bess accepted the excuse with a sage nod. "I thought so, dear. Which is exactly why you ought to wear mine in the meantime."

"And that's so kind of you, Aunt Bess, but I cannot possibly take your ring. What would Uncle Hugh think?" She strived to make her voice light but was desperate for an excuse not to wear the ring.

Bess returned the smile easily, a warm glint in her eye. "He agrees with me, love." She waved away the protest gathering on Harper's lips. "Vivi dear, I insist that you keep this on while we're here on Block Island. It's bad enough that none of us could be at your wedding. Now, you know I would never speak ill of your parents, dear, but how any mother or father could be so heartless as to refuse to attend their only daughter's wedding, and then endeavor to keep our girl from us, is beyond me! We couldn't get a word out of them about where you and Neville had gone to after the wedding. I was in favor of beating it out of them, but your Uncle Hugh had objections." She said *objections* as if it were on a level with plague or parasite.

"Well, it was not to be born! So tragic that your dear mother and father are out of the country for Adeline's wedding." Based on her tone, it was no tragedy at all. "And so, my darling girl, wear it for me, will you? To make up for the fact that I couldn't be at your wedding, and that we're only now meeting your husband?"

Her tone left no room for arguing, and at her other side, Rose added, "Best not to argue with her, Mrs. Jones." Her tone was gentle and cajoling, and she sent her an impish grin and poured her a cup of tea.

In the face of such opposition, Harper could only nod, offering a small smile.

"Now, there's a dear," she said, patting Harper's cheek fondly.

The ease with which Bess touched her, the warmth and affection in her eyes, nearly undid her. How many times had she longed for her own mother's touch in the years since she had died? How many times had she longed for the reassurance of a mother's hand, the cradle of tenderness that came from being so fully loved?

Her father loved her deeply, Harper knew well, but he had never been a demonstrative man, and her grandmother would never do something so plebeian as to offer a hug. To her horror, she felt a gathering warmth behind her eyes, and just when she was afraid she might actually cry in front of the two women, another knock at the door heralded the arrival of Claire and Claudia.

"Knock knock, " Claudia sang as she and her sister bustled into the room.

"Are we interrupting?" Claire asked.

"No, no, of course not. Do come in," Harper managed, grateful for a distraction from her ill-timed tears.

"Are we having sandwiches?" Claudia's eyes widened at the sight of the tray and the pyramid of sandwiches.

"Those are for Vivienne, dear," said her mother.

"No, please, help yourself," said Harper.

"But Mrs. Jones, you ought to eat some." This from Rose, who looked faintly alarmed at the prospect of Harper sharing her food.

"I'm certain there's enough for all of us." Goodness, the women took their afternoon snacks seriously.

Claire and Claudia, taking Harper at her word, went eagerly to the tray, even as their mother furrowed her brow at them and pointedly handed several more sandwiches to Harper.

Bemused by Aunt Bess's interest in her appetite, Harper was happy enough to eat and let the girls chatter on their own, though when the subject turned to Neville, she was drawn into the discussion.

"He's so handsome, Viv," said Claire.

"All that brooding muscle."

"Tall, too. I've always liked tall men."

"Almost as handsome as Wesley."

"Is he taller than Wesley, do you think?" This from their mother.

"Does he have any brothers?" Claire asked hopefully.

In the silence that followed, Harper realized that the women did, in fact, expect a response from her. Which was a problem, as Harper had no idea if Neville Jones (or Thomas Montgomery, for that matter) had brothers. She floundered, unwilling to tell an outright lie.

"I'm sure you girls will both find handsome, tall husbands of your own one day."

Harper had no such views about her own impending husband-hunting in New York. She had nothing against the idea of marriage, of course—she wanted a family of her own one day. But until her grandmother showed up outside their little cedar shake cottage, Harper had been perfectly content thinking of marriage and children as a reality in the distant future, something that happened naturally and in its own time. She had never considered that she would be trussed up and sent out into the wilds of New York Society to capture that husband.

The younger girls sighed in unison, and Rose, who had been half tucked in the wardrobe while organizing dresses, laughed at them.

"I hope my husband looks at me the way Neville looks at you," said Claire.

Harper looked at her, startled. "What do you mean?" As far as she knew, Thomas generally looked at her with impatience and mild disgust, like a fly that had landed in his drink.

"Oh, you know," said Claudia dreamily, "like you're the only person in the room."

More like the most *irritating* person in the room, but it would be imprudent to say so.

"He has that… *intensity* to his gaze."

"It's the deep *V* in his brow," added their mother. "Very pronounced. *Very* attractive."

"It's different with Vivi though, the way he looks at her."

"It is."

"Like he thinks she's…"

"Almost like she's the most…"

The three O'Malley women tilted their heads, searching for a word or description that Harper could only guess at. She could only imagine that they were projecting on Thomas and Harper the things they wanted to see between their *actual* cousin and her *actual* husband. It didn't matter what they said or thought they saw; it was an illusion, a charade. Thomas didn't even like her, could hardly speak more than three civil words to her at a time.

"Precious."

Claudia and Bess's eyes widened, and they broke into rapturous grins.

"Claire, that's exactly it."

Precious? What a ridiculous notion. She wasn't any more precious to Thomas Montgomery than a thorn in his side. But then his words came floating back to her. *You are my concern.*

That expression.

That ache.

The hand that unwillingly came to his chest.

"Precious. Like he's found the only pearl in the ocean, and he means to keep it," Claire said.

"A pearl," repeated Claudia dreamily.

As the women moved on to discuss evening gowns and wedding details and upcoming plans to explore the island, Harper let the noise float around her, listlessly nibbling on the plate of sandwiches Bess had given her. In spite of her rash declaration that she would find her own way off the island, she hadn't the foggiest idea of how she might obtain information from the River House staff or locals about vessels that might still be coming from the mainland throughout the month.

Which meant that an hour later, she was allowing Rose to dress her in another elegant dress for another evening, alongside a man who didn't even like her, but who may or may not look at her as if she was precious.

Chapter 13

Thomas straightened his necktie in the mirror, grimacing again as he remembered his conversation with Harper. He had regretted his words the minute they left his mouth.

I know about the baby.

He *was* capable of tact. He *was* familiar with manners and social niceties and nuance. He was a journalist—he *knew* how to ask questions delicately, how to glean information with near surgical precision.

So he had no idea why he had confronted Harper with all the tact of a caveman with a club.

But once those first words were out, the rest of the questions—the interrogation, really—rushed out like a dam released. The shock of his conversation with Dr. Grayson and the disappointment of their encounter with the mailboat captain left him on edge, and the throbbing in his head was unrelenting, and suddenly he just… snapped.

Thomas Montgomery never snapped—his behavior was an affront even to himself. He was straight and unyielding, and until he embarked on this charade with Harper, he considered himself unsnappable.

The look on her face swam before his eyes, and his grip on the necktie tightened. Cheeks scarlet, lips pursed, eyes a blazing verdant, even in the shadow of her bonnet.

She had looked resplendent.

And somehow that made him feel like snapping as well.

Thomas frowned at his reflection in the mirror, pulling the necktie out altogether. It would be easier to start fresh than to continue adjusting the knot by fractions of inches.

He hadn't seen Harper since she stormed away from him on the path to the River House, though he had seen the maid, Rose, who assured him that she had already dressed for dinner and left the room. Harper had been angry enough that he didn't know what she was willing to do to get away from him, so when he casually asked Rose about his wife when he ran into her in the hallway, he was inordinately pleased that she hadn't left or done anything rash.

Because if she had, he knew it would have been his fault, that it was his tactless interrogation that had driven her to act impulsively.

He felt like the worst sort of blighter, knowing that she had never been pregnant, understanding the aspersions he had cast on her character by assuming that she was. Every bit of her anger had been justified. He was surprised—and more than a little relieved—that she hadn't rewarded his impudence with a slap across his face. Or a swipe with her parasol.

Thomas shuddered at the thought.

How could he have snapped? What had he been *thinking*?

He hadn't been thinking at all, just *feeling*. It was becoming a common affliction whenever he spent time with Harper. And feelings were, after all, an affliction. An affliction to reason, to good sense. Just look at what he had done when he felt tenderness towards her at Point Judith—that was how this whole ridiculous charade began in the first place.

His agitation flowed through to his hands, wreaking havoc on his necktie. Thomas abruptly let go of it, afraid to strangle it beyond recognition. He took a deep breath and smoothed the cloth down over his shirt. It wouldn't do to look as disheveled as he felt.

With a deep inhale, he gingerly set his hands at his tie again. If he didn't calm down—if he didn't stop *feeling*—he was liable to ruin the thin piece of fabric.

Then he would owe Neville *two* neckties.

A creak behind him caught his attention, and in the mirror, he saw the door swing slowly open. Harper took two steps into the room before she noticed him. Immediately she faltered, her eyes wide.

"Thomas." She was so surprised to see him that for a split second she forgot to be angry. The mistake was short-lived. "I… I forgot my gloves. What are you doing in my room?"

She had left the door ajar, and he rushed to close it, afraid of being overheard. He had to walk past her to do so, and she recoiled from his nearness as if he were a poisonous snake.

He couldn't blame her.

When the door was securely shut, he turned to face her. Rose had already told him that she was dressed for dinner, but he was unprepared for the sight of her. Her hair was up, with a few curls artfully falling over her shoulders, and her face bore the unmistakable pink glow and a fresh dusting of freckles that testified to hours spent in the sun. She was wearing another of Vivienne's dresses—this one a deep cranberry color, embroidered intricately with tiny sparkling beads that refracted the light from the window.

Inside, her eyes were no longer green but had changed to the softest shade of caramel.

All of this he took in at a glance, which unnerved him. Why was he noticing her freckles or eyes at all?

Useless things, freckles.

Eyes less so. But still. The color was irrelevant, and he was disappointed in himself for noticing.

Apparently, he had taken too long to respond because the pink in Harper's cheeks increased. "I said, what are you doing in my room?"

He cleared his throat. "Apologies. I hadn't meant to intrude. I only need to finish my necktie, and I will be out of your way."

"Can't you take care of your necktie in your *own* room?"

Ah. Another matter that required delicacy. If possible, he wanted to avoid letting her know that they had only the one room between them.

"I will be just a moment." He moved away from her and back to the mirror, willing his hands to cooperate. Unlikely, given his body's rogue instincts when Harper was present.

Unfortunately, Harper seemed disinclined to grant him his moment.

"Does your room not have a mirror, *Mr. Jones*?" She followed him to the mirror, crossing her arms over her chest.

"It does," he allowed carefully, trying to keep his eyes on the mirror and not Harper.

"Then would you care to—"

"This *is* the mirror, *Mrs. Jones*." He was mangling the tie again. And now his hands were sweating as well.

Simply grand.

Her expression turned wary. "What do you mean, *this is the mirror*? This is *my* mirror."

So much for delicacy and avoiding the truth of the room situation. He turned to face her squarely. "I mean, this is also *my* mirror. It is, in fact, *our* mirror."

Her eyes flared. "If this is our mirror, then do you mean to tell me that this is also *our room*?"

He faced the mirror again. "Yes," was his curt reply.

One would have thought he had developed a spontaneous case of leprosy, with how quickly she jumped away from him.

"But... but if this is our room... Then last night... what did you... where did you... " she was truly alarmed now and felt a flash of guilt.

"I slept in the bathroom, Miss Whitley," he said sternly. "I came in very late last night and was out very early this morning to ensure you as much privacy as our situation currently allows. I had hoped to have you home by now and spare you the awkward knowledge of our room situation."

Her mouth opened and shut several times before she could speak. "And since you thought I was pregnant, you just assumed that I would, that I... "

He held up his hands, a gesture of surrender. "I assumed nothing." At her skeptical gaze, he continued. "I would never have ventured in here now had I known you would be returning to the room. Rose assured me that you were already dressed and downstairs. Truly, I only kept the information from you because I didn't want you to be uncomfortable."

"Yes. You've made it so clear to me how much you value my *comfort*."

He sighed. Now was as good a time as any to apologize. "Miss Whitley, I—"

"For goodness sakes, just call me Harper."

Thomas cleared his throat. She already called him Thomas, didn't she? And since he had already abducted her and posed as her husband and slept on the floor of her bathroom, the impropriety of calling her by her first name hardly mattered. "Harper, then. What I said to you earlier, and the way I said it, was unconscionable." Thomas swallowed. He was no more accustomed to making apologies than he was to feeling tenderness, and it chafed. "You were right. Your personal matters are none of my business, and I spoke out of turn. For my assumptions and the offense they caused you, I am truly sorry."

Bravely he held her gaze, bracing himself for more recriminations.

At first, she made no reply. She just stood there, studying him. After what felt like an eternity, she shook her head, as if breaking a spell. "A pearl," she whispered to the floor.

He frowned at the non-sequitur. "I beg your pardon?"

She jerked her eyes up to him as if she had forgotten he was there. "I... well I..." she studied him a moment, and something in her seemed to relax. "I accept your apology. And I forgive you."

He nodded once, grateful for her unexpectedly gentle reaction. "Thank you."

After a beat of silence, he turned back to the mirror, hoping his hands could manage to do more than just crumple the necktie, and she went to the bedside table where long, elegant evening gloves lay draped across a book.

When she spoke again, she surprised him.

"We should probably get to know one another."

His fingers jerked against the fabric. "Excuse me?" He could see her in the mirror, but her back was towards him, and he couldn't read her tone.

"In case it takes a few more days to get me back to Point Judith. If we're going to maintain this charade, it seems safer to at least know a bit more about one another. Even if we don't know anything about Vivienne and Neville, it might serve us well to know one another."

She was nervous, he realized. Did *he* make her nervous? The thought caused him pain—actual pain—right in his chest again. Maybe he should have Grayson check his heart.

He answered carefully. No doubt she was a strong woman and a formidable one, but at the moment, she also seemed very young and very vulnerable.

And that caused him pain, too.

A part of him thrilled at the chance to know more about her. He still had dozens of questions about her circumstances, of course, but oddly enough, he also wanted to know more about her because...well, he wanted to know about her for her own sake, he supposed.

What an outlandish notion.

Before he could answer, she went on, her voice high and fast.

"For example, do you have any allergies? Or phobias? Or, I don't know," she said, walking back to the window, "a wife and several children somewhere in the midwest?"

His head snapped around to her.

A wife and several children? For goodness sake, did she think that he would be here with her, doing whatever it was they were doing if he had a wife and several children back home? In the midwest, of all places?

Perhaps they *should* have gotten to know each other sooner.

He cleared his throat, and she turned to look at him, her face wary. He didn't want her to be wary of him, or afraid of him, or uneasy around him. He wasn't sure *what* he wanted her to be around him, but all at once, he knew an urgent need to reassure her. To take away the wariness in those caramel eyes.

Only for the sake of the charade, he told himself. Because she was a *responsibility*. Responsibility was an excellent word. A non-emotive word. His favorite word, he decided.

"My full name is Thomas Morgan Montgomery. I was born and raised in Chicopee, Massachusetts. I have one younger sister, Kate. She lives in Chicopee still with her husband. Both of my parents are deceased, dying within a year of one another. I have neither a wife nor children, and the furthest west I have ever been is Philadelphia. No known allergies, though I admit to disliking snakes." He listed the information clinically, as if he were dictating a list for the market. He was *not* emoting.

She looked up at him for a time, her eyes surprisingly warm. "I'm so sorry about your parents, Thomas. It must have been unbearable, losing them both within such a short time."

"It was a mercy, actually," he said abruptly.

The curtness in his voice surprised her, but his reply had been instinctive. In the wake of all the devastation his father had caused, and with his mother's chronic indifference to life, it *had* felt like a mercy to lay them both to rest.

He wished he could have laid his and his father's sins to rest so easily.

But he regretted his words, for more reasons than one. He sensed they had upset her, and the notion that he had upset her was surprisingly distasteful to him. Then there was the fact that he *never* talked about his father. Ever. There were so many half-healed wounds and scars attached to the man that it was a matter of self-preservation.

"You're right, though," he added quietly. "Many things about the time were… unbearable."

He said it to spare her feelings, rather than to open a dialogue, and he was relieved when she nodded and understood.

"Have I omitted any pertinent information?" He desperately hoped not. He had no desire to invite her into any other parts of his life.

Thankfully, she shook her head. "No, I don't believe so. And I already know you're a writer." She shrugged guiltily. "I hope you still get the time you need to write your novel while you're here."

Thomas felt his jaw clench. The subject of his work hadn't come up since the ferry, and it hardly seemed relevant in light of all that had happened since. He had let her assume that he wrote fiction while they were on the ferry together—it seemed a harmless omission at the time. He should correct her now that he had the chance, now that they would be in close proximity to the very people who would be the subjects of his story.

But then he thought of his sister, the look on her face when he told her about the bargain he had made with his editor. He didn't think he could bear to see that look on Harper's face too, not now that she was smiling at him. It would be wrong to say something that would take the smile from her face.

"No need to concern yourself about that." He struggled to make his voice light. "Plenty of time to write while I'm here." Then, unable to hold her gaze, he turned back to the mirror. When he registered the limp, maimed state of his tie, he sagged. "Drat," he mumbled under his breath.

Harper watched the motion. "It is in rather a state." She came to stand beside him, regarding him through the mirror. "Here, let me help you." She turned and looked at him expectantly, and he frowned down at her.

"I don't need help."

"Yes, you do."

"I know how to tie a necktie," he insisted.

"I'm sure you do. But right now you're strangling it, not tying it."

A glance at the mirror confirmed her assessment. "And you would have me believe that you could do better?"

She quirked an eyebrow. "As a matter a fact, I would. Now, move your hands."

He white-knuckled the fabric. "You're not serious."

She rolled her eyes. "Thomas, you are well beyond your one minute, and if you take any longer we'll be late for dinner. Besides," she added, looking mournfully at the limp fabric around his neck, "soon we'll owe Neville *two* neckties."

Without waiting for a response, she stepped in front of him, hands hovering just over his chest, and he forgot how to breathe. When he remembered, he wished he hadn't, because now all he could smell was strawberries and spring rain.

"How do you know how to tie a necktie?" he asked, trying to

distract himself.

"My father," she answered simply. "I help him often enough. His hands are veritable bear paws, which helps in all kinds of things around the farm, but they can be an absolute nightmare when he needs to look sharp."

Her smile was rueful, and she craned her neck to look up at him, still waiting for his permission.

She stood close enough that he could see his own reflection in her eyes.

It would be churlish to refuse, especially so close to dinner, and the delicate silk of poor Neville's formerly pristine necktie could not withstand much more of his mangling.

"Fine," he said finally and was grateful that the operation required him to lift his chin and stare over her head.

She put her hands on his chest, smoothing out the wrinkled fabric. Her touch was gentle but confident, and, inexplicably, it felt like someone had set off a round of fireworks in his chest. A riot of color and energy and light exploded off of her fingertips as she smoothed the silk tie against his shirt. Every touch was a jolt of near combustible tension, radiating and pulsing from his chest outward, so frenetic and powerful that it took everything in him not to react, to stand completely still under her ministrations.

It wasn't as if he had never touched her before. Much of their interaction thus far had featured him physically extracting her from danger—but this was different. He couldn't say why, or even how. There was no reason for her hands to incite such a response. She was only helping with his necktie.

Maybe it was the way she looked in the early evening light, sun-kissed and freckled, an ethereal bronze glow silhouetting her in front of the window. Whatever it was had him holding his breath again.

Eons later, when she had finally restored the necktie to a respectably smooth shape, she began the knot, and he wasn't sure how much harder his heart could beat without flying straight out of his chest.

"It's your turn," he blurted, startling them both.

She froze, her hands under his collar.

"To tell me about yourself," he clarified, wondering how old he would be when this necktie was finally complete. How long had she been standing here with him? It felt like her hands had been on his chest forever.

He had the errant thought that they belonged there, should never move from there. He wasn't normally a proprietary man, so the sensation was new for him. He disliked it immensely. So as she stood before him, her still-ungloved hands working dutifully, he tried to dissociate himself from the moment.

It would be no trouble to put a bell jar over the errant thoughts, and if he could make his breathing more shallow, he might not even smell her.

Except that it wasn't working, the attempt at not smelling her, not sensing her, not being aware of every minute motion of every one of her fingers tugging the fabric at his neck. Every incidental graze of her hands against his chest was igniting tiny sparks, so volatile that the air around them fairly crackled.

For pity's sake, how long could it take to tie a single tie?

Which was an unfair question, as he had already spent a quarter of an hour attempting the feat.

The part of his brain that was still functioning rationally explained that it had been less than a minute and he howled inwardly. If she didn't start talking and distract him in the next nanosecond, he was going to lose his mind.

Her hands lifted from his chest, but his reprieve was only temporary, as fixing his necktie required her fingers to roam behind his neck, even into the hair on the back of his head.

He closed his eyes against the sensations, imagining the bell jar, willing it into existence over him.

"I grew up on a farm in Exeter. Rhode Island, that is. We have hens and a few cows, just for us, but most of what we grow are berries. The strawberries were starting to ripen just when I left—sweet little things, no bigger than a thimble. We have blueberries and blackberries that will be ripe in July, and by August we'll be picking peaches. My father and I do most of the work together, though Daddy hired a few local boys to help out for the summer. "

She smiled, her eyes focused on the knot but somehow distant.

"You and your father sound close," he said to the space above her head. He kept his tone neutral, noncommittal. He didn't want her to think he was truly interested, of course. He was being polite, rectifying his earlier rudeness. Just manners, he repeated, and imagined the words echoing around the bell jar.

"Yes, we were. We *are*. We've always been..." her voice trailed off, and he was suddenly frustrated that he couldn't see her eyes. She had the most expressive eyes; there were whole continents of emotions and thoughts splayed across them. Not seeing them was like navigating the ocean without a map, without stars.

No—that was another errant thought. He did *not* care about her eyes. Nor her feelings.

When she didn't continue, though, the silence was suffocating.

"He must be a good man," Thomas ventured. "And he must have excellent foresight to have taught you to tie his necktie for him."

"Mm," she said, looping her fingers through the silk fabric. "He never actually taught me. My mother used to do it for him, and I remember being a little girl watching her do it. Her movements always looked so simple, so fluid. The first time I tried to help my father, I closed my eyes and could still see her, the way her hands moved through the knot, and found that I could do it as well."

Her mother. She would have been Heidi Verbeek's daughter, the one who ended her season in a scandalous disappearance. So that's what happened to her—she married a berry farmer in Rhode Island. Suddenly the dearth of information about the long-lost Verbeek granddaughter made sense—Mrs. Verbeek would hardly want it bandied about town that her daughter had run away with a farmer and had chosen to raise her own child in rural Rhode Island.

"Your mother must be pleased that you're such a quick study."

"My mother is dead." Harper whispered the words so softly that if he hadn't been standing mere inches from her, and if the room hadn't been completely quiet, he wouldn't have heard her at all.

And once again, he felt like the worst sort of cad, speaking the way he had about the death of his own mother and father. She must think him heartless.

It bothered him that she was probably right.

"What happened?" he asked, keeping his tone as soft as hers.

She paused. "She died when I was ten. There was an accident—she slipped on the stairs and broke her collarbone, but when the bone didn't set properly, it became infected. Within a week it turned septic and.... the rest happened very quickly."

Her words ended on a hush, and he had an unprecedented urge to reach for her. To hold her.

He didn't.

Instead, he replayed her words in his head, listening for what she didn't say. Her relationship with her parents had been nothing like his own. When his parents died, it had been a relief, a merciful end to a legacy of constant, simmering vitriol. In the quiet anguish of Harper's tone, he heard the devastation that her mother's death had caused. It explained so many things about her—she was both strong and vulnerable, resilient and innocent.

He felt her fingers tense against his neck, the way her smooth movements become jerky, and with a swift tug against both ends of the neckcloth she stepped back from him. Strange that the loss of contact should make him feel so bereft.

"All set," she said, her voice louder now.

When she raised her eyes to his, he was surprised to find them dry, but surprise quickly yielded to dismay. They were *too dry*—barren, almost. Desolate.

"Thank you," he said, touching the knot absently. And then, because the look in her eyes was still there, he spoke again. He would distract her. Redirect her. Do anything to make her eyes lose that desolation.

"So your mother was a Verbeek, but you were raised in the country. And now you'll have a debut in New York. Was it always your parents' intention?"

She let the question hover in the air between them for a moment.

"No. The decision was… recently decided. Between my father and grandmother."

Ah. She hadn't any choice in the matter, then. Her last break for freedom on Block Island made more and more sense. The Knickerbocker society would make mincemeat of Harper and her warm, guileless nature. Perhaps it was fortunate that her grandmother was such a harridan.

"That must be… difficult." The word seemed insufficient for the expression on her face, the raw pain of it. It shocked him that it should also cause him pain. So much time had passed since he had let anything so messy as empathy affect him.

"Yes, it is." She gave him a hollow imitation of a smile, and he felt it right in his solar plexus. "And now you know me," she said with a shrug, eyes shifting to the ground.

But he didn't, not yet. And he was shocked again with the sudden desire to. That filthy, traitorous empathy had invited in all sorts of refuse. He *wanted* to know this woman. He wanted to know everything about her. Every moment that had ever given her pain and everything that had ever made her laugh. He wanted to memorize the constellation of freckles on her nose and categorize each shade of iridescent green in her eyes when she stood in full sun. He wanted to hear her talk for hours on end just to learn the rhythms and cadences of her voice. He wanted to walk the land she had been raised on and watch her hug her father.

But he had no right to know those things, to know her.

Because she was only a responsibility. He had a responsibility to keep her safe and bring her home, and he would. That's *all* he would do.

"I suppose I do," he agreed, because it was the right thing to say. The safe thing to say.

"And I imagine we'll find out more about one another as the charade goes on," she added.

"It will be over soon, though." His words were firm, decisive. For a hundred different reasons, not least of which was his own sanity, this charade *had* to end soon.

In the quiet that followed his statement, a creak from across the room yanked both of their gazes to the door, and what they saw there stopped him cold.

Because standing in the doorway, face as red and livid as an avenging harpy, was Rose.

Chapter 14

Rose slammed the door behind her in a manner more befitting a duchess than a maid, then crossed her arms over her chest. She might have been young and slight, but at that moment, she was every inch a lioness.

"I want to know exactly what's going on here. *Right. Now.*"

Harper looked up at him in panic, then quickly back to the maid.

"Rose, please, it's not what you think." Harper moved to step towards her but pulled up short at the darkening expression on the maid's face.

"It's not?" Rose lifted a brow. "Because what I think is that you're no more Adeline's cousin than I am, and for some reason that I cannot fathom, you're pretending to be."

Ah, well. It was exactly what she thought, then.

"Believe it or not, there is a perfectly reasonable"—or at least, semi-reasonable—"explanation for this," Thomas said.

"I'm dying to hear it." Rose's voice was bone dry.

Awfully cheeky for a maid, wasn't she?

Having no moral high ground to stand on, Thomas ignored the jibe.

Harper's gaze slid to Thomas, her eyes wide and guilty and questioning.

He understood that look well enough to know that Harper would be neither willing nor able to lie to Rose. She was too sweet, too innocent, and he knew well that the only reason she had agreed to lie and act as Vivienne Jones in the first place was because she thought it was a temporary ruse that wouldn't harm anyone. Somehow, even in their short acquaintance, he understood this about her: she would never willingly hurt or deceive anyone.

The knowledge that he had been the one to make her do so sat heavily with him. As did the fact that he was deceiving her as well by not telling her that he was a journalist sent to cover the wedding of the century.

Thomas tucked the thought aside, but he knew it was like burying something at the ocean's edge. Sooner or later, time and tide would reveal it.

But Harper's eyes were still locked with his, the question still there, and he ruthlessly returned himself to the moment, to the livid woman staring daggers at Thomas and Harper. With reluctance and trepidation, Thomas nodded to the petite woman at his side, giving her the permission she sought to tell Rose the truth.

Unfortunately, as Harper recounted the events of the last two days, her explanation sounded *less* than semi-reasonable. From start to finish, it sounded like an outrageous, ill-conceived farce. Downright embarrassing, to be honest. If she had been a more practiced liar, she might have twisted the facts to make them more believable, or at least glossed over some of the parts that were less than flattering for her.

But she wasn't a liar—she wasn't like *him*. He admired her honesty, even as it made him cringe.

Through it all, Rose stood there, an unyielding judge in a maid's uniform, her pretty face belying the iron in her eyes. Thomas half expected her to roll in a guillotine by the end of the explanation. Rose's silence following Harper's recollection of events was blistering, the moment rife with possible punishments and condemnations for the two of them for willfully deceiving the O'Malleys.

When she did speak, it wasn't at all what Thomas expected.

"Well, you'll have to finish out the charade now."

Shock, followed by incredulous fury, flooded through him. What utter nonsense—there was no scenario in which they could or would prolong their charade any longer than necessary.

Even if they could continue to fool everyone into believing they were the Joneses, there was no way that he could keep Harper—the long-lost Verbeek granddaughter, for goodness sake!—on Block Island for the next month. It would ruin her. *And* him. Her family would be beside themselves with worry, and when Thomas's involvement was discovered... he had no doubt her father would run him through with a pitchfork. And he would have every reason to do so.

Spending a month with Harper would be a punishment in and of itself. This improbable tenderness and empathy that she had awakened in him might very well be the death of him. He had spent years cultivating the unfeeling, distant composure that he had now, had spent years dissociating himself from the personal lives of others. To spend a month in Harper's company and pose as her husband would be nothing short of torture.

"I beg your pardon?" Harper's voice was little more than a squeak.

She gestured between Thomas and Harper. "This little ruse you've concocted. You've got to see it through until the wedding."

"Impossible." His voice was pure granite. "We never meant to deceive anyone other than the ferry workers. Surely you can understand that." The clear implication was that she *would* understand it, and she would let the matter rest. He was *going* to get Harper off the island. He was *going* to fix the problem.

"Oh, I understand plenty," Rose replied, her voice simmering with anger. "I understand that you two made an ill-advised decision to impersonate two people in order to obtain tickets to Block Island. I understand that a series of mishaps—admittedly, not all of your own making—has caused you to prolong your deceit. I understand that even if you never intended to harm Miss Adeline or any other member of this family, you are bound to do just that.

"Now I want *you* to understand something. Miss Adeline is one of the kindest women I have ever met in my life. For weeks, she has been talking about reuniting with her estranged cousin," Rose speared Harper with a glance, "and finally getting to meet her cousin's husband," the spear rounded on Thomas.

"This wedding has already put all sorts of undue stress on Miss Adeline, and I refuse to allow anything or anyone to harm, distress, or trouble her. *You* will not trouble her. Consider me a one-woman crusade with the single-minded pursuit of protecting Adeline O'Malley. If there is so much as a gnat that buzzes too close to her ear, I will annihilate it. I will make such an example of that gnat that every insect within a hundred-mile radius will live in sheer terror of me and the wrath I will bring down upon the head of any creature in Christendom who chooses to bother my mistress."

Rose was starting to breathe heavily with the exertions of her diatribe, and Thomas felt a grudging admiration for her loyalty to Adeline. He chose *not* to think about what Rose might do to him if she knew that he was actually a journalist sent here to cover the wedding.

"So," Rose said, straightening her shoulders. "You two will do whatever you have to do to make it through this wedding. I don't care what that entails, and honestly, I don't know how you've managed to deceive everyone thus far—but until Mr. and Mrs. Wesley James are announced lawfully wed, you two need to maintain the pretense that you are Neville and Vivienne Jones, and give no one reason to doubt it, least of all Adeline. *Am. I. clear*?"

As a man who could inspire terror with a single look, he recognized and conceded that Rose had the ability as well. But the trait was somehow more frightening in a woman.

The fierce look notwithstanding, there was no way that they could do what she was asking.

He was preparing to tell the maid exactly that when Harper stepped forward, laying a conciliatory hand on Rose's arm.

"Perfectly clear, Rose."

Good, thought Thomas. She would soften Rose up before telling her *no*—Thomas was incapable of softening, himself or anyone else, so it was better that Harper mediate now.

"You're absolutely right," she continued, which Thomas thought was a bit much. She was not *right*, certainly not *absolutely right*, but he would let Harper handle Rose. The two women seemed to have developed a rapport of sorts, so the let-down would be better coming from her.

"It was never my intention to hurt anyone." She lifted a hand to ward off Rose's inevitable objection. "But I realize that intentions are not the same as reality. I cannot bear to hurt anyone, *especially Adeline*, more than I already have—already *am*. So I give you my word, Rose, we'll carry this charade through until after the wedding. No one will be any wiser for it until after Adeline and Wesley leave for the honeymoon and the fallout can be mitigated."

If he hadn't already been clenching his jaw tightly enough to crack his molars, the whole thing would have unhinged in shock.

What was she *doing*? What was she *thinking*? Did she know the consequences of such an endeavor? Of disappearing from her family and her life for a month and keeping company with him? No doubt he would keep her safe for the duration, but the very fact that she would be *with him* for the duration was enough to make her a social pariah, especially among the cream of New York Society.

She couldn't possibly understand the consequences of maintaining this charade.

Rose looked at him expectantly, waiting for him to give his word as well, but it was madness.

Harper's reputation would never recover if their charade were discovered, and the recompense from both Harper and Adeline's families would be fierce. Everyone involved would want a pound of flesh.

"Miss Whitley, might I request a moment alone?" His voice came out strangled, but he was glad it came out at all. Because anger, fierce and dark and heavy, was throttling him. This charade *had* to end. *Now.* He would walk out the door this very minute and tear down trees with his bare hands and build a raft to take her back to Point Judith because there was no possible scenario in which he spent the next month pretending to be Harper Whitley's husband.

It would.

Not.

Happen.

But then.

Oh, but then.

Harper looked at him, and her caramel eyes widened in earnest entreaty, and she bit her lip in an unspoken plea. It was the sort of expression that Thomas had assumed existed only in stories and in the imagination of poets, the stuff of myth and legend. It was the sort of expression that would stop rivers or quench fires, that could soften despots and persuade generals and kings. It was the sort of expression that compelled a man to say *yes,* an expression that would eventually bring a man to his knees.

It was the only expression in the world from the only person in the world who could have convinced him to say *yes* when he wanted to say *no.*

Why that should be so he could not say. That blasted fissure in his chest, he supposed. That wretched tenderness, rearing its ugly head again.

But Harper had given her word to Rose, and for the life of him, he could conjure up no alternative but to give his word as well.

So he heaved a long-suffering sigh, running a hand down his face. And then he agreed.

***

The minute Rose left the room, Thomas turned to her, his voice dangerously low.

"Miss Whitley," he said tautly.

She recognized it as his way of demanding an explanation, but Harper didn't know what to say.

I'm sorry I forced you to continue this farce, but I would very much like to defer real life for a bit longer.

Aunt Bess gave me her ring to wear, and it made me want to weep.

Adeline told me she was glad I was here, and the feeling of being wanted was so intoxicating that it made me reckless.

No. That wouldn't do at all.

And he was entitled to an explanation. She knew full well that he had no intention of agreeing with Rose until she had looked at him, her eyes begging for him to agree.

In truth, she had as many qualms about continuing their ruse as he did, but the whole time Rose had been talking, Harper heard Adeline's voice in her head.

I'm so glad you're here, Viv.

She was not a complete fool. She knew that Adeline was not happy to see *her*. She knew that the affection and endearments lavished upon her were not meant for Harper Whitley at all. But all the same, the sense of belonging, of being wanted, was so utterly wonderful that a very selfish part of her wanted to continue this charade, wanted to pretend to be Vivienne Jones instead of the long-lost Verbeek granddaughter. Because she wasn't a debutante, or even a Verbeek, not really.

She was just a farmer's daughter, wondering why the father she had always adored was suddenly sending her away.

And the little battered place in her heart that was usually so full from her father's steadfast love simply clung to the possibility of feeling like part of the O'Malley clan, of being loved as one of their own, even if it required deception, even if only for a month.

None of which she could explain to Thomas, who, in spite of his now flawless necktie, was looking more and more like an angry bear in the wake of her silence.

When she made the observation aloud, he was unamused.

Chastened, she looked at the floor, studying the wide oak planks beneath her feet. "I couldn't bear it."

Thomas paused, but she didn't look up. "Couldn't bear what, Miss Whitley?"

"Hurting her. Adeline. It was foolish, embarking on this charade to begin with, and I know we're already hurting her by lying, but… she's very kind, Thomas. And gentle. I couldn't bear to see her hurt, if we just up and disappeared from the wedding."

"You wouldn't be there to see her." His voice was even, but not unkind.

"I know I wouldn't. But just the thought of it… and Aunt Bess. She gave me her ring, you know. Because she saw I wasn't wearing one." Harper lifted her hand to him, showing him the jewel that she had guiltily accepted. "And Claire and Claudia and Rhys and Uncle Hugh. They've fussed over me and called me dear and darling and… they've been so *kind* to me, Thomas. I couldn't bear to disappoint or hurt them. Not now."

She lifted her eyes to him, willing him to understand, willing him not to call her silly or foolish or ridiculous. She knew that she was—she just didn't want to hear him say it.

But he didn't say anything. Just regarded her steadily, his expression unreadable.

Harper felt guilty that she had forced him to maintain the charade as well; she knew he meant to write while on the island, and with the pre-wedding festivities that the O'Malleys had planned, his free time would be limited indeed.

In a desperate bid for his approval, she bit her lip. "You'll still have time to write while you're here. I'll make sure of it."

Her words seemed to startle him, and for a moment, his face went curiously blank.

"If that's what you're worried about," she clarified.

The longer he remained silent, looming over her the way that only the very tall can loom over the very small, the worse she felt. It had been wrong to give her word without discussing it with him first.

"That isn't what I'm worried about," he surprised her by saying.

"Oh. Then what…?"

His jaw clenched. "I'm not worried about the writing, Miss Whitley."

"Harper," she corrected, but he didn't seem to hear her.

"I'm worried about *you*."

Oh. Well, that was…. rather lovely, actually. It occurred to her then that there were perhaps other rather lovely things about his character, all hidden beneath that gruff grizzly bear reserve.

"That's very kind of you."

"I'm not kind," he said rigidly.

"But you need not worry."

"Miss Whitley, you do understand the potential ramifications of your behavior if our ruse is discovered?"

Harper bit her lip again. She understood all too well. Her father's crushing disappointment, her grandmother's inevitable wrath. The loss of her reputation, her prospects.

I'm glad you're here Viv.

As strange as it seemed, maintaining their charade seemed like the best way to avoid hurting Adeline and embarrassing the O'Malleys. Counterintuitive as it seemed, lying to them seemed kinder than telling the truth at this point. And she had understood the potential consequences of her actions from the moment she agreed to this scheme at Point Judith. Would prolonging the lie somehow make her actions worse?

She had no idea.

But she had already given Rose her word to continue.

"I do," she told him, sensing him begin to bristle anew. "I am sorry, though, Thomas."

She glanced up at him, wondering what she would see, not sure if she should prepare for a fresh wave of condemnation. Though *prickly* seemed to be his general temperament, she loathed the idea of him being genuinely angry with her. He was.... not exactly her friend. *Friend* didn't do justice to whatever he was to her. Her ally? Her partner in crime? He was her… Thomas.

Her grumpy, would-never-admit-that-he's-kind Thomas.

When she accepted his apology for assuming she was pregnant and told him that she forgave him, she had meant it. Because in that apology, his voice had been stripped of that ever-present sternness, and he had seemed so sincere, so genuinely… *grieved* that he had hurt her. The forgiveness had come surprisingly easily.

But before he could accept her apology, or bring a fresh onslaught of disapproval, they both noticed the clock and saw how late they already were for dinner.

And so down to dinner they went, silent but arm-in-arm, but as she walked beside Thomas, she had the strangest impression that she was his jailer, and he was a man condemned.

She could make no sense of the thought, and so she shrugged it away as they stepped into another evening with the O'Malleys.

Chapter 15

Harper woke early the following morning.

Though she was uneasy about continuing their charade and deceiving the family, she was also confident that it had been the right decision. Still, she felt as if she had forced Thomas to agree to the charade, and compelling him to do anything sat heavily with her. With that in mind, she went down to the breakfast room, hoping to find a moment alone with him.

Instead, she found nearly everyone *except* for Thomas sitting down to breakfast. At one end of the table were Hugh, Rhys, Max, and Lyle talking eagerly over a newspaper, and at the other end were Claire, Claudia, Isla, and Adeline. Harper stopped short at the threshold when she saw an unfamiliar figure striding toward her.

He was as tall as Rhys, and except for threads of gray in his hair and a hardness to his lined face, he looked almost identical to Adeline's brother. He must be the shipbuilding titan himself, Charles O'Malley. Because he had been absent from aperitifs on her first night on the island and had eaten dinner in his room while working the night before, Harper had never actually set eyes on the man. He was broad and imposing, radiating the sort of restless energy and impatience that one expected of a man who had built the world's largest shipbuilding empire. Though he was Hugh's brother, it was obvious that the men's temperaments were worlds apart.

He paused beside her in the doorway and gave her a perfunctory kiss on the cheek. "Vivi dear," he said curtly. "Glad you could make it."

"Oh, yes. I—I'm glad to be here, Uncle." If he noticed that she was flustered, he didn't comment on it. He simply nodded distractedly at her, then back to the room at large, before leaving the room.

In spite of the shipbuilder's brusque greeting, the rest of the family greeted her warmly and encouraged her to make a plate at the sideboard. Bess recommended the eggs and sausages, Adeline insisted she try the muffins, *"one of each kind,"* and Rhys gave her two of the biscuits from his own plate. When she finally sat down in one of the empty chairs near the middle of the table, her plate was overflowing. But Hugh—eyeing her plate and decrying the fact that she hadn't tried the oatmeal—proceeded to procure her the largest serving of oatmeal in the history of human oat consumption.

Apparently, they were breakfast food enthusiasts.

Their concern for her appetite was touching but baffling, and she felt a measure of relief when Wesley walked into the room to offer a distraction.

"Good morning all," he said easily, looking around the room until his eyes rested on Adeline. "Ah, there's the most beautiful woman in the world." Wesley strode towards his fiancée with easy confidence and grace, kissing her on the cheek. "Sleep well, darling?"

Adeline blushed at the attention but smiled up at him. "I did, thank you. And you?"

Wesley rested his hand against the back of her chair. "Indeed, though we had a bit of a late night finalizing some details of the Navy contract."

"You were working on the Navy contract last night?" Rhys's sharp question elicited only a slightly raised eyebrow from his future brother-in-law.

"Only some minutia, Rhys. Nothing that we needed to disturb you for," Wesley said easily.

Rhys's answering smile was tight. "I wouldn't have minded the disturbance. Would welcome it, actually. Is something amiss with the negotiation?"

In the pause before Wesley responded, Harper sensed the irritation simmering through the room. Hugh looked warily at his nephew, and Max's mouth was pinched.

"Not at all. You know how the bureaucracy can be in the Navy and government. Just a few misunderstandings we're ironing out."

"Misunderstandings," Rhys repeated, his voice speculative. "About the cost of the steel?"

Wesley smiled, but the edges of his mouth were strained. "Indeed."

Rhys nodded, not bothering to return the smile. "You'll let me know if the contract requires further negotiating." Though he was usually all that was charming, there was a hardness in his voice that Harper hadn't heard before.

Wesley straightened from where he had been resting his hand on the back of Adeline's chair, moving languidly to the sideboard so that his back was towards them. "I'm certain that won't be necessary. We managed to smooth out any hiccups last night."

"Just the same, you'll let me know," Rhys said to Wesley's back as the other man loaded his plate.

Adeline sent her brother a quelling look, which he pointedly ignored.

Wesley took his time perusing the sideboard, filling his plate high with meats and fruit.

Hugh looked back and forth between the men, his face inscrutable.

When Wesley turned, his expression was composed and friendly. "Of course. Now," he said, settling in across from Adeline, "what do we have planned for today, darling?"

Harper, relieved that the tense moment had passed, set to tackling her mountain of food as the others talked about the portraits planned for the afternoon. Rhys was something of an amateur photographer and wanted to take a few photographs of the family before the wedding day. Though his mother was apparently distrustful of photography in general—*"it isn't as if people haven't had perfectly lovely portraits painted for hundreds of years,"* she remarked acidly—when she heard that Consuela Vanderbilt had had a photographer at her wedding, the mother-of-the bride relented.

For her part, Harper had few plans other than finding Thomas.

Absurdly, she wished he was here with her now. She wasn't sure why—he was always glowering or disapproving or offending, yet somehow his presence reassured her. But at the moment, sitting in close proximity to Wesley, she felt a need for that assurance.

It wasn't that she was afraid of Adeline's fiancé, but something about him unsettled her. In spite of his claim that he slept well, there were faint purple smudges beneath his green reptilian eyes, and when he went to pour coffee from the urn, his hands were not quite steady. She thought back to his inquisitive stare when she said she had never been sailing before, then took a scalding sip of coffee to mask her unease.

Though the headlines surrounding the wedding of the century made the couple seem otherworldly and glamorous, it struck Harper then that the man and woman at the table with her were human, vulnerable even. They were, of course, exquisitely beautiful, far more than anyone she had ever seen. They radiated youth, vitality, and elegance. Their aesthetic qualities alone might have made them subject for newspaper fodder, even if Adeline hadn't been the shipbuilding titan's daughter and Wesley hadn't been the wunderkind.

Not in a hundred years would she ever have expected to be enjoying a casual breakfast with the wedding of the century's bride and groom.

As handsome as Wesley was, though, Harper preferred Thomas's more rugged appearance. His broad shoulders and stiff jaw, the improbable puppy-dog eyes set against such a saturnine face.

Not that she *preferred* him in any special way, of course. He was rude and grumpy and had a poor bedside manner.

But it seemed that the night before they had reached some sort of accord. He hadn't wanted to continue the charade any longer, nor had he wanted to give Rose his word.

But he had.

And Harper couldn't help but think it was because of her.

Then, as if conjuring him with her thoughts, Thomas Montgomery stepped through the doors of the breakfast room.

The breakfasters all greeted him with cheery *"good mornings,"* and he gave a curt nod to the room at large, scanning the table until his eyes rested on her. She gave a timid smile, and he inclined his head. His expression, always so shuttered, was difficult to read.

Was he still angry with her for agreeing to continue their charade? Or angry about sleeping on the floor again? Or angry because… well, because he didn't know how to be anything else?

As he made his way to the sideboard to fill a plate, Bess called out to him.

"Neville, be a dear and fetch your wife some fresh fruit while you're there."

"Oh Viv," said Adeline, genuinely dismayed. "Did you not get any fruit earlier? Rhys, you should have gotten her some fruit."

Rhys frowned at Harper's plate. "Well, Ada, I very well would have if I had noticed that she lacked fruit."

"Is there something special about the fruit?" Lyle asked.

When no one responded, the man moved to the sideboard himself, presumably to sample the fruit.

"Berries *and* oranges, please Neville," Bess clarified.

"Grab her another biscuit while you're at it," added Rhys. "I see you enjoyed the jam with them, Viv."

Harper stared at them, nonplussed. Her plate, other than the eggs, was very nearly full still. Was there some sort of general conspiracy to fatten her up?

"Do you need more oatmeal too, dear?" Hugh's voice was rife with solicitude and concern.

"Please, I'm actually quite full," Harper intervened, patting her stomach for emphasis.

Thomas glanced at her over his shoulder, his brows pulled together, but he did as he was bid and brought over both his own plate and another towering one for her.

Harper regarded the plate with faint alarm.

Thomas sat beside her, eyeing her two plates and the bowl of oatmeal with a similar expression. "Are you… hungry this morning?"

"Your wife is quite starved, my good man," Bess answered for her.

"Famished," Hugh added, his tone inexplicably laced with approval.

Strange, that.

As conversations resumed at the table and everyone tucked back into their plates, Harper leaned over to Thomas. "I meant to speak with you again last night."

"We did quite a bit of speaking last night, as I recall." His tone did not invite further conversation.

She spoke anyway.

"You're upset with me," she said, careful to keep her voice hushed.

He paused with his butter knife hovering over a biscuit, and after a quick glance at her, he resumed the motion. "I am not upset with you."

Well, that was… a relief. Although he didn't seem exactly *pleased* with her either. He seemed… remote. As if he needed to put some sort of imaginary distance between them.

Which was strangely… disappointing.

They hadn't actually spoken since their discussion the night before. He had been seated on the opposite side of the table during dinner, and he joined the other men for drinks on the veranda after dinner. When the other men returned, he had not. She must have been asleep already when he came into the room for the night, and he was already gone when she woke in the morning.

She couldn't actually verify that the man slept at all.

If he wasn't upset, perhaps he was… tired?

"I'll take the bathtub tonight."

His fork clattered onto his plate at the non-sequitur, but no one seemed to notice, and he regained his composure quickly.

"Excuse me?" To his credit, his voice was steady, as if she had not just offered to sleep in the bathtub.

"What I mean is, you can sleep in the bed tonight, and I can sleep in the bathtub. We can alternate so that we each get some proper rest."

"I'm quite well-rested."

She raised her eyebrows. "You cannot possibly be well-rested. You went to sleep later than I did and you were awake earlier. *And* you spent the night on a tile floor."

"The tiles are exquisite."

"Yes, they are. They are also a hard, nonporous substance that is meant for walking on, not sleeping."

"You'll not sleep in the bathtub, Mrs. Jones."

He still didn't look at her, and she felt her own temper irk. She angrily foisted several of her sausages onto his plate to show her displeasure.

"Yes, I will." Her words were muffled because she said them through a clenched-tooth smile, eager to ensure that the O'Malleys didn't notice their marital discord.

"No, you won't." He jabbed roughly at the sausages on her plate, slicing them with excessive force.

"Yes, I will." Two of her muffins made their way to his plate.

"Not." He bit into the muffin as if it had mortally offended him.

Stubborn man. She walloped a scoop of berries onto his plate. "Enjoy the bed tonight, Mr. Jones."

He managed to spear eight berries onto his fork at once, then stuffed them into his mouth, chewing quickly and angrily. "I will not, as *you* will be enjoying it, Mrs. Jones."

"If by *bed,* you mean *tub,* then yes, I shall enjoy it." She put her mammoth bowl of oatmeal in the exact spot where the berries had recently resided.

He eyed the bowl morosely. "For goodness sake, will you—"

"You'll join us, won't you Vivi?" Adeline's question yanked them from their escalating argument.

Harper, at a complete loss as to what Adeline was asking, smiled warily. From the corner of her eye, she saw the bride's mother glowering at her. She swallowed roughly. "Oh, well, I..."

"I'm sure Vivienne has other plans, this morning," Isla cut in, taking a delicate sip of coffee that belied her curt tone.

Bess glared at her sister-in-law, then softened as she looked at Harper. "Vivi dear, if you could spare the time, we would all love it if you joined us for Adeline's final wedding dress fitting this morning."

Adeline nodded encouragingly, and Claire and Claudia shot her hopeful smiles.

"I'm sure I could make time," she said, trying to ignore the resentment radiating from Adeline's mother.

When Thomas tensed beside her, she knew he noticed it as well.

"How lovely." Isla said the words as if the cook had just announced she was serving cod liver oil for dinner. "Shall we, then?"

Apparently, the dress fitting was to happen now, then. Harper looked to Thomas, unable to stifle a small snort when she saw how much food was still on his plate.

His eyebrow raised sardonically.

As she rose to leave, Thomas stood as well, surprising her as he leaned close.

"You'll be all right?" His voice was soft but gruff, as if he was out of practice with such a question.

She looked over at him, tilting her head. "It's only a dress fitting."

"It's not the dress I'm worried about." His eyes flitted to Isla, then back to Harper.

It was actually rather nice that he asked.

"I'll be just fine. Bess will keep me safe," she said with a crooked smile, and they both looked over at the woman in question, who was waiting for Harper in the doorway. "You'll… keep busy?"

"Indeed," he said, nodding stiffly.

"Right. Good. Well, until later, Mr. Jones."

"Until later, Mrs. Jones."

After a beat, she tore her eyes from his, eager to break whatever spell of irritation and enchantment that seemed to come over them whenever they interacted.

Harper hurried out the door, but not before she intercepted a penetrating look from Wesley.

"Wesley," she murmured, hurrying past him.

"Vivi," he said, inclining his head.

Eager to escape his regard, she hurried to meet her not-aunt at the door, and together they followed the other women upstairs.

Chapter 16

In spite of her assurances to Thomas, the dress fitting was an unmitigated disaster.

Though Adeline looked a dream in her dress—it was a Worth gown, fabulously expensive and beautifully crafted—Isla O'Malley had the bride in tears within moments. When Adeline emerged from behind the screen in the gown, her aunt, cousins, and maid had sent up a collective gasp, quite literally in awe.

Her mother was not similarly enamored.

She called Adeline unnaturally tall—an Amazon at best, an ogre at worst, and announced that it simply would not do to have a bride who towered over her guests. The gown itself was dismissed as a disappointment, doing too much to emphasize Adeline's excessive height and washing out her complexion, and she bemoaned the fact that there was no time to return to Paris for a new one.

The comments were as cruel as they were ridiculous—Adeline could have walked down the aisle in a moth-eaten sack and still been a vision—but judging by the crestfallen look on Adeline's face, she accepted her mother's words as truth.

While Rose and Bess looked like they were contemplating several different ways to smother the mother-of-the-bride, Harper had timidly commented that Adeline was statuesque, to be sure, but since Wesley was a tall man himself, they would suit perfectly.

Which only served to redirect Isla's anger toward Harper herself. On her first night on the island, Isla had cornered her during aperitifs, warning her not to ruin her own daughter's wedding as she had so scandalously destroyed her own prospects. *"You're treading on thin ice, girl—I will not let you taint Adeline's marriage as you did your own. If your parents weren't out of the country, you wouldn't be here at all."*

Harper had been shocked by the woman's venom for her niece, or at least the woman she *thought* was her niece, but after seeing the way Isla spoke to her own daughter, the woman's behavior made sense. Not *much* sense, to be sure, but Harper supposed the woman was bitter as a general rule, rather than because of Harper.

In the wake of Adeline's tear-streaked face, it was hardly comforting.

When Isla stormed from the room, apparently too disgusted with the dress and her daughter to remain, Bess had promptly rang for tea, and the remaining women worked together to bolster Adeline's confidence in the wake of her mother's criticism.

In the interest of doing just that, Rose declared Isla O'Malley to be a dunce, Claire and Claudia announced that she had feathers for brains, and Bess had called her an unparalleled ninny. With each insult, the women cheered and clanged their teacups together in a show of solidarity for Adeline. As the corners of Adeline's mouth had reluctantly begun to tip up in a smile, Harper added her two cents, calling her supposed aunt a nincompoop. At this, the women had let out elated whoops, raising their cups to Harper so enthusiastically that tea splashed down the front of her dress.

It seemed a small price to pay for seeing the smile return fully to Adeline's face, and she excused herself from casting cheerful aspersions on the mother-of-the-bride to go and change her dress.

Adeline's room, however, was on a separate floor from Harper's, and after one wrong turn trying to find the staircase, then another while retracing her steps, she found herself helplessly lost.

When she heard voices, she moved instinctively towards them, hoping to find a footman or another guest who could point her in the right direction. But the closer she got to the voices, the angrier they became, and she was about to turn in the opposite direction when she heard a crash and realized that the voices belonged to Wesley and his father.

They must have been in one of their rooms, but the door had been left ajar, wide enough that any passerby could clearly see in.

Without pausing to consider her actions, Harper padded silently towards the crack in the door, careful to remain concealed. She peered in, curious and concerned, but immediately wished she hadn't.

Because there was Wesley—handsome, confident, Wesley—pushed roughly against the back wall of the room. His father's hands, wrapped tightly around Wesley's crumpled collar, held him in place.

Wesley's green reptilian eyes had gone so huge that Harper was afraid he wasn't breathing. His father's hands were massive, and they were now pressing against Wesley's throat.

"You're an idiot, boy!" Marcus shouted, slamming his son against the wall.

Harper flinched as the hallway lights rattled.

"You're going to ruin our connections before you even marry the girl!"

"It's fine, father," Wesley rasped. "I have the matter well in hand."

His father loosened his hold on him, only to slap him across the face.

Harper's hand flew to her mouth to conceal her gasp, even as an angry red welt bloomed across Wesley's face. Though she distantly recognized the need to walk away, to leave the men to whatever it was they were discussing, she couldn't seem to move. Harper stood rooted on the spot, horrified but transfixed.

Wesley took a handkerchief from his pocket, touching it to his lip. It came away with blood. With infinite patience, he folded the cloth again, replacing it in his pocket. His movements were calm and measured, as if what had happened was perfectly natural, commonplace even.

The thought sent Harper's hand instinctively to her heart.

"I heard the brother talking at breakfast before your mother and I came in. He *knows*, boy."

Wesley smoothed his collar where his father's hands had crumpled it. "He doesn't know anything. He's jealous, that's all. He can't bear that his father trusts my judgment over his. The deal will go through." His voice still held a faint rasp.

"You said you were discreet in your… *arrangements*."

"I was. The deal with the Navy *will* go through. They need the oceanliners, and we're the only company that can produce them within the necessary timeframe. The negotiations are just a technicality at this point."

Wesley's father leveled him a look of such disdain that Harper marveled that he didn't crumble under it. "You'd better hope so, boy. You know what's riding on that deal. Think of Jacob."

For the first time, Wesley's face blanched, even as his jaw tightened.

Marcus seemed to take a perverse pleasure in his son's reaction, and he turned from him to walk across the room. On a small writing desk by the window sat a bottle of amber liquid. Moving with deliberate slowness, he filled the two glasses beside it, then brought them to his son.

Stopping directly in front of Wesley, he tilted his head back and finished the glass in a single swallow, hissing out a breath.

He extended the second glass to Wesley.

When he reached for it, his father hurled the tumbler across the room. The glass shattered against the wall, its liquid dripping down to puddle on the ground like blood.

Harper jumped back from the door at the clatter, but Wesley didn't even flinch.

"Now go see to your arrangements, boy."

Marcus turned his back, dismissing his son.

Hesitating for only a moment, Wesley turned for the door.

Turned towards *her*.

Harper scrambled down the corridor, but at the sound of the door creaking open she inadvertently turned towards it.

He was staring at her, and the dark look on his face told him that he knew exactly what she had just witnessed. His expression was a mix of anger and something else. Something very like shame.

She ached for Wesley even as she acknowledged to herself a very real fear of him right now. His eyes were blazing green and impenetrable.

"Wesley." Her voice was a trifle breathless. Her heart was still beating too quickly from what she had seen. "What a coincidence, seeing you here."

"Here?" His voice, by contrast, was deceptively calm. "As in, the River House Hotel? Where all the guests are staying?"

For a newly christened con-woman, she was a terrible liar. "Yes! Here, at the River House."

He nodded, his face hardening, though he indulged the obvious falsehood. "And what brings you to this particular corridor, at this particular time of day, cousin Vivi?"

His cheek was still red, and she forced her eyes away from the sight. She could still hear the sound from when his father slapped him.

"Oh, well I didn't mean to be here at all, actually." That much was true. "We were with Adeline for her dress fitting, and I spilled a spot of tea on my dress." She lifted the tea-stained sleeve as proof of her innocence. "I meant to head back to my own room to change, but I'm afraid I got a bit turned around."

"Did you? And you ended up here, just outside my father's room?"

He glanced back at the door behind them.

"I did," she said faintly, then looked longingly down the hall. "And now I'm off to change, so… good-bye, cousin Wesley."

His eyes glinted, and he stepped towards her. "Now now, Vivi dear. You don't mind if I call you that, do you? You're lost, are you not? Allow me to escort you."

"That won't be nece—"

"Walk with me, Viv. Tell me, is your room on the second floor?"

Seeing no way of avoiding his company, she nodded. "Yes. Yes, it is. And I'm sure that my *husband* will be looking for me." She was suddenly very glad to have a fake husband. She had no idea if he was looking for her or not, but the possibility seemed a sort of safety in itself.

"Then I'll just deliver you to him, and we can get to know one another along the way."

He offered his arm, and after eyeing it warily, she accepted.

"You know, Adeline has told me so much about you. She was beside herself when you and Neville accepted the invitation."

"Yes. We're so glad to be here," she said carefully, aware he was studying her.

"I'm sure you are. And Adeline's happiness is my happiness." In spite of the *happy* theme, his words held an unmistakable warning.

"You're a devoted fiancé, then."

"Yes, I am."

They walked in silence a bit, passing frame after frame of ocean and boat-themed paintings. They were all so similar in color that it was no wonder Harper had gotten lost.

"Your husband breeds horses, does he not? A family business?"

She had no idea what Neville Jones or his family did, so it seemed safest to agree. "Indeed."

"Excellent. I'm in the market for a bit of horseflesh myself."

"Oh. Well, I'm sure Neville would be happy to advise you." She would have to warn Thomas about a forthcoming interrogation.

"Indeed. Not an especially social man, your husband."

Harper bristled at his tone, feeling oddly protective. Never mind that she agreed with Wesley. "Crowds tend to make him uneasy."

"Of course," he said smoothly, but his tone was cold. "And I must admit, Vivi dear, *you* are not at all what I expected."

Harper paused, taking a bolstering breath. "No?" Her palms began to sweat, but she was pleased with how calm her voice was.

He went on as if he hadn't heard her. "Adeline had told me so much about you, you see. Scrapes you had gotten into as children and the like. The woman she described was fearless, a veritable firecracker."

Harper thought back to her one glimpse of the real Vivienne Jones, of how she had roared at her husband at a train platform and nearly pushed him off the docks into the water. Firecracker indeed.

"Well, as I'm sure you'll find after the wedding, marriage tends to change a person."

"I'm sure I will." He certainly looked sure of *something*, but she couldn't guess what.

"Since I already know so much about you from Adeline, allow me to tell you about myself."

Harper tensed, and she knew he felt it. "That would be lovely." Her voice was as stiff as her smile.

"I adore my fiancée, Vivi dear, and her family has become very dear to me as well. But at heart, I'm a businessman. I began as a welder on the shipyards, did you know that?"

She was genuinely surprised. "I did not."

He nodded. "I worked my way up to where I am in the company today. Mostly I negotiate deals and contracts for O'Malley. Millions of dollars worth of deals. Do you know how I accomplished all of that?" He paused expectantly.

"Hard work?" she ventured.

"Indeed. Hard work has served me well. I have one other skill, though, that has served me well and helped me to achieve all that I have today. Do you know what that might be?"

She shook her head, refusing to meet his eye.

"I am an excellent judge of character, *Vivi dear*. I am able to tell a great deal about a person by observing them. What motivates them, what frightens them, what delights them. I also know when someone is hiding something from me. When someone has been… *lying* to me."

Unease prickled up her spine, and she felt the fine hairs on the back of her neck rise in trepidation.

Their linked arms forced her to stop when he did. He turned to face her, and she took an instinctive step backward, which seemed to amuse him.

"Now now, Viv, no need to be afraid of me. We're almost family, aren't we?" Wesley smiled at her, and she could see clearly where his father's hand had split his lip. "And since we are, I'll tell you something important about me. I am not a man to be trifled with. And if someone were to say, *lie* to me, or try to *hide* something from me, especially during this month of wedding celebrations… well, I would be very, *very* put out."

His eyes bored into hers, and she knew a sudden, frantic wish for Thomas beside her. Thomas, who was so tall and broad and gruff, who could be so innately intimidating, but who had gently pulled her from a stampede and cradled her when she swooned. Who had gamely eaten the largest bowl of oats in Christendom.

When Harper spoke, she was proud that her voice was steady. "I understand completely." And she did. She understood that she was in irrevocably, desperately over her head.

"Good," he said smoothly, as if he hadn't just subtly threatened her, as if his own father hadn't just slammed him against a wall or raised his hand against him. "The stairs are that way."

He motioned to the left with his chin, and she saw that mercifully, he had led her to the stairs, was letting her leave now.

"Thank you, Wesley, for your… guidance."

"My pleasure."

She turned, barely resisting the urge to run down the stairs.

When she finally reached the haven of her own room, she hardly knew what to make of the exchange.

What she did know was that Wesley had the potential to be very, very dangerous.

Chapter 17

Thomas drummed his fingers against the front desk of the telegraph office, waiting for the clerk to return with the form. He was supposed to message Luther as soon as he got to the island but in the chaos of encountering the O'Malleys on the ferry and Harper fainting, telegraphing his editor had been the last thing on his mind.

Although if he were being honest, he could have made the time to telegraph Luther before today.

He just preferred avoiding the task.

He had reconciled himself to what he needed to do to publish his exposé, but he was far from happy about it, and meeting the O'Malleys had only compounded his guilt.

He had never had any reason for nor inclination towards subterfuge in the past, and the weight of deceiving Harper on one front and the O'Malleys on the other had him wondering if he was becoming some sort of pathological liar; the guilt of it weighed on him like a boulder. But he had spent years channeling his guilt into anger, so instead of dwelling on his guilt, he allowed himself to feel good and angry.

For starters, he was angry at Luther for asking him to cover this story in the first place, for making him choose between atoning for his father's sins and lying and deceiving his way into this ridiculous situation.

Initially, he had tried to justify himself—Charles O'Malley was no innocent, after all. He was wealthy and powerful and had become so by any and all means necessary, and Wesley was no different. Thomas took a moment to feel good and angry at them as well, then forced himself to admit with reluctance that Adeline *was* different. Harper seemed genuinely fond of her, and he had seen for himself that she was warm and kind where her father and fiancé were arrogant and calculating.

Her father and Wesley would have been more than eager to capitalize on the wedding, using Adeline's beauty and the public's fascination with her to enjoy a healthy dose of free publicity for the Gray Star Line. Which meant that the request for a private wedding must have come from Adeline herself.

Thomas drummed against the desk with greater impatience.

How long did it take the man to retrieve a simple form? How long had he been standing there? Five minutes? Ten minutes? Thomas glanced down at his watch.

Thirty seconds.

Well. The longest thirty seconds of his day.

Thomas took the next thirty seconds to feel angry at the clerk as well.

After that second eternal bout of thirty seconds, the clerk shuffled out of the backroom, form in hand, apologizing profusely for the wait. Since the wait had only been one minute, Thomas decided that there was an infinitesimal possibility that his anger was misplaced, and he withheld his harsh retort and took the proffered form.

He hastily scrawled out the message and direction for his editor, then handed the form to the clerk and walked out the front door, pausing briefly to feel angry at the bell above the door for tinkling in such a needlessly cheerful way.

He squinted at the sudden brightness outside, waiting a moment for his eyes to adjust. The day was already warm, and the sun shone brilliantly in the sky. The very cheerfulness of the weather seemed to mock his foul mood.

The scene he was met with back at the River House did nothing to improve it. The O'Malleys had gathered together on the veranda for portraits, and Rhys was setting up the tripod of a large camera while Hugh watched eagerly over his shoulder. He cast a cursory glance around the veranda and lawn but didn't see Harper. Rhys wasn't quite ready to begin yet, but it struck Thomas as odd that Harper should be missing. He was about to go into the hotel to look for her when Wesley intercepted him.

"Neville, so pleased you've made it back in time for portraits."

Thomas tried to conceal his irritation at the interruption. "Yes, of course. I wouldn't miss it."

"No, I'm sure you wouldn't," he said with an easy smile. "I

wondered where you went off to after breakfast."

The question felt strangely pointed, but he had no idea why it should be. No one from the wedding had seen him enter the telegraph office, and even if they had, they had no reason to suspect that he was sending a telegram to a newspaper editor. But Thomas knew better than to underestimate Wesley, and he met his gaze squarely. "Just exploring the island. Since my wife was otherwise detained with the dress fitting, it seemed like an appropriate time to take in some of the sights."

"Yes, the island is charming, isn't it? I had an interesting morning myself." Wesley's smile turned suddenly wolfish. "I spent some time getting to know Mrs. Jones."

Thomas was instantly tense. "Did you?"

"Mm. I think we've come to understand one another, your wife and I."

Thomas balled his fists, but before he could do or say anything unwise, Adeline called out to Wesley, and with a nod and a smirk he left Thomas to walk towards his fiancée.

"Hello," came a soft voice from behind him.

Harper.

Thomas turned, and though she had been smiling, she took one look at his face and her countenance fell.

"What's wrong?" she asked.

"Nothing," he ground out.

She raised an eyebrow. "Nothing?"

He sighed, running a hand through his hair. "I heard you and Wesley have been getting to know one another."

Her face blanched. "Who did you hear that from?"

"Wesley. What did he mean?"

"Oh, I.... Nothing. I got turned around trying to find our room after the dress fitting, and he helped me find my way."

"He helped you?"

She nodded, raising her chin defiantly, but he saw through the veneer.

She was rattled. What wasn't she telling him?

Before he could press the issue, Rhys announced that they were ready to begin, and for the next hour, he was forced to stand beside Harper, close enough to touch her but unable to speak with her. Eager to avoid leaving any evidence of their deception, he and Harper had done their best to tuck themselves behind the other O'Malleys during the pictures, which was much easier for diminutive Harper to accomplish than it was for him.

When Rhys was finally satisfied that he had taken enough photographs for the day, Thomas meant to resume his discussion with Harper, but Claire and Claudia had approached her, talking animatedly about the festivities planned for the coming weeks.

"Oh Viv, you'll just love the outdoor ball. The River House is setting up an entire ballroom floor on the front lawn. They have a giant tent to go over it all, and little torches to set all around to make it look like a fairy garden, just like we always imagined as girls!"

Claire continued to describe the outdoor ball, but the more she talked, the paler Harper looked.

It sounded like something any woman would adore. Women liked dancing, didn't they? And dresses and lights? Claudia moved on to describe the planned hot air balloon, fireworks, and wine tasting—O'Malley had spared no expense—and although Harper smiled at the girls' enthusiasm, he could see the strain at the edges.

Her whole demeanor was downright… *unHarper*.

Strange that he should know her well enough to identify such a thing.

Stranger still that he should notice. And *care*.

When the girls had exhausted their descriptions of the wedding festivities, they invited Harper to join them in their rooms for tea, but Thomas cut in before she could respond.

"I think Mrs. Jones and I will go and explore some of the trails instead."

Harper looked up at him in confusion but did not contradict him. When the sisters happily loped off to see if Adeline would join them, Thomas took her arm and led her towards the wooded trails around the back of the River House.

"*Now* would you care to enlighten me about what happened this morning with Wesley?"

She was still subdued, but she stiffened at the question. "I already told you."

"You began to tell me, and then we were interrupted. I'll have the whole account now."

She scoffed, then simply kept walking.

She.

Kept.

Walking.

No one kept walking when he asked a question.

When he caught up to her, he tried a different line of questioning.

"Why were you upset when Claire and Claudia mentioned the ball?"

Her cheeks flushed, and her stride increased. She took four steps to every one of his.

"Mrs. Jones," he warned, shocked that he was short of breath from their pace.

She ignored him. *Again.*

"Miss Whitley."

Five steps to every one of his.

"Harper!"

Either his volume or the use of her given name startled her enough to stop her.

"Is it so important to you?" Curls were falling loose from her bun, and her eyes were bright. In full sunlight, they were a striking verdant.

"Yes. It is."

"Why?" She sounded genuinely curious, and a trifle desperate.

"Because you were upset."

"Again, why should that be important to you?"

"Because…" he found himself at a loss for words.

Her question was valid. Why *should* it be so important to him? The information wasn't necessarily vital to maintaining their charade. Though to be fair, he didn't know *what* the information was.

When he didn't reply, she shook her head roughly, then raised her chin to look him in the eye. "Fine. You see, the girls mentioned the ball, and the thing is…. well I never learned to…" she looked down at the ground, crossed her arms over her chest—a gesture that was both defiant and protective—and then sighed. "I can't dance."

Chapter 18

Thomas met her eyes, his expression surprised. At least she *thought* it was just surprise. They had stopped in a clearing beside a pond, and it was difficult to tell.

The light rained down on them through the wide pointed sycamore leaves, casting strange shapes and shadows across the two of them. A diagonal line extended from his left temple down to the right side of his chin, dividing his face equally between shadow and light. She had not learned the lines and contours of his face well enough to decipher this expression.

She only knew that he was studying her, that handsome face only half illuminated.

She wished it wasn't so handsome. He was being pushy and insufferable again, and she felt that irritating men ought to be unattractive as a general rule.

Thomas Montgomery was…. decidedly not.

And it was downright embarrassing, a woman her age not knowing how to dance. Grandmother had been appalled when she realized, which only added to Harper's mortification. The reason she never learned to dance was more embarrassing still. It harked back to a time in her life that she would happily erase from memory.

A cloud passed over the sun, and the diagonal line across his face got smaller and smaller until it disappeared altogether.

With his whole face set in shadow, his eyes were a deeper shade of brown, his lids hooded. What did hooded lids mean?

On another day she might have been able to manufacture the bravado to feign indifference to his opinion, but after enduring Isla's ire at the dress fitting and then Wesley's interrogation, she didn't have it in her.

For some reason, she didn't want to tell Thomas about what happened with Wesley back at the River House. She had felt an unexpected compassion for Wesley during his encounter with his father, and she couldn't yet reconcile that compassion with his thinly-veiled threats. Even now she felt confused and unsettled and wasn't ready yet to relive what had happened with Thomas. She wasn't ready to be that vulnerable with him.

Although it occurred to her that in confessing her inability to do something as simple as dance, she had done just that.

Finally, mercifully, the cloud lifted, and he spoke.

"Then we'll just have to teach you."

The words, delivered surprisingly gently, stunned her.

Could Thomas Montgomery actually... *dance*? She couldn't imagine him in a ballroom at all, let alone *dancing*.

If she had to imagine Thomas in a ballroom, he would be frowning in a corner somewhere, silently disapproving of the general merriment.

But he had just offered to teach her, hadn't he?

Which implied two equally unexpected things: one, he *did* know how to dance, and two, he was willing to teach her.

His offer was... kind.

Needlessly so.

She thought again of their first night on the island, the night of her regrettable first venture into champagne.

You're going to be fine, he had told her. Gently, confidently.

She understood then that there was so much more to the man than what he showed to the world, to strangers. To perhaps anyone who hadn't agreed to act as his pretend wife.

Even to her, she suspected he had no idea that he had revealed anything of himself.

"You would teach me? To dance?"

His eyes, once more divided neatly between shadow and light by a passing cloud, were inscrutable. "If not knowing how to dance worries and upsets you, then it's going to worry and upset me as well. And it may very well be necessary to maintain our charade." He said the words gruffly, but they lacked rancor. "So yes, I would teach you."

"But... do you think I can? Learn, that is? Usually, women learn these things when they're young, and I am... well, not ancient, precisely, but..."

"No, certainly not ancient."

His voice was so serious still. Or maybe it wasn't so much serious as… steady. His voice, so like the man, was steady. After all that had happened in her life in the last month, that steadiness was a balm.

She wanted to lean into it, wrap up in it like a blanket and hide away for a time. The thought was as outrageous as it was compelling.

"It will be simple enough," he continued.

"Simple enough?"

"You don't need to learn all the dances," he clarified. "You need to be seen twirling and enjoying yourself for at least one, but the rest of the time can be spent chatting or drinking lemonade. Debutantes usually dance more, but as far as everyone knows you're a married woman."

He didn't sound overly concerned about it. In fact, it sounded like he had actually been to numerous balls before. Which made her wildly curious.

Did he stand and glower in the corners? Did he *dance*? Apparently, he knew how. What sort of women did he dance with? For some reason, this question seemed urgent.

She wouldn't ask.

"Do you think that will work?"

He considered her for a moment. "If it doesn't, we could always find you a large fern to hide behind."

Her jaw nearly dropped. Was he *teasing* her?

And was she… *enjoying* it?

"Well, as long as there are ferns."

Apparently, she was.

She had the sense that he was fighting a smile.

Suddenly, seeing him smile seemed urgent, too.

What would happen to those big puppy-dog eyes when he did?

"Now, if you're only going to learn one dance, it ought to be a waltz."

He took a step towards her, and she realized that he meant to teach her now, here in the clearing. Which made sense, of course. Their room at the River House was spacious but was hardly sufficient for waltzing, and they couldn't very well conduct a waltz lesson in the parlor.

"All right," she said, her voice unsure. "Why a waltz?" She smoothed several imaginary wrinkles from her skirts.

"Compared to a cotillion or a reel, it's quite simple. If you have a competent partner to follow and can count to three, you can waltz."

He took another step, so that he was only inches from her, and extended his hand. "May I?"

He was so tall that she had to look up, up, up at him. It was rather like tying the necktie again, with one critical difference: when she fixed his necktie, *she* had been in control. The task and rote movements had distracted her from his nearness, his largeness.

Now, their roles were reversed. He held the control. But the notion of surrendering control to him felt oddly safe.

She nodded, fitting her hand in his.

He clasped it gently. "Your other hand goes on my shoulder." She lifted her hand obediently. "And mine goes here."

His hand rested on her waist, and the heat and deliberate gentleness of his touch sent a sudden flurry of starbursts through her. At each of the points where their bodies were touching, the starbursts buzzed and thrummed as if they had been released straight into her bloodstream, as if luminosity itself had jolted through her.

The sensation was so sudden and strong that rational thought fled, and if he hadn't been holding onto her, she thought she just might float off the ground from the infusion of light and energy that had begun to spread in her.

They stood there for a moment, hedged in by the pond and the dense canopy of trees, saturated in colliding prisms of sunlight. A pair of ducks glided over the water's surface, and a chorus of cicadas and bullfrogs in the high grasses sang around them as the water lapped against the pond's shores.

"The waltz is set in three."

So close to his chest, his voice sounded even lower, more gravelly. She was feeling as well as hearing it.

"One two three, one two three. *Back side together, forward side together*."

Harper nodded, but she was having trouble focusing. His nearness was doing strange things to her brain. Knocking loose its judgment. Interrupting its frequencies. Jumbling thoughts and sensations.

"Follow my lead, all right?" Since her brain had recently lost control over coherent speech, she didn't reply. "We'll start slowly. Step back, left, then feet together. Three beats. Ready?"

No.

She nodded.

On his first count of three, she tripped on her own feet. They tried again, and she stepped on his toes. By the third round, she stumbled on a tree root, and they moved away from the tree line. Over and over, he kept counting to three, shaking his head when she apologized. She was a newborn calf, unsteady on her feet and liable to collapse at the slightest provocation.

One two three, one two three.

She huffed in frustration, but he just steadied her and started again.

For a man with such an irascible disposition, he was a surprisingly patient teacher.

On and on they went, dancing—or trying to dance—in and out of the sunlight, and she tripped but never fell because his hands maintained that same steady hold on her. Always, he steadied her.

She had the sense that if the earth began to tilt off its axis, he could simply lift his hands and steady it, putting the universe to rights with those warm, gentle hands.

And slowly, somewhere between the fifteenth and twentieth attempts, she stopped apologizing, not because he shook his head every time she did, but because she didn't need to anymore.

Because she was dancing.

Waltzing.

For the first time in her life.

In the woods, by a pond.

Gliding, floating, turning.

One two three, one two three.

She was at once weightless and grounded, lost in the copper glow of the sun as it slipped lower in the sky.

"How is it you never learned to dance?" he asked.

She lost her footing.

He pulled her in closer to steady her. "I didn't mean to startle you." She was so close to his chest now that his words were more sensation than sound.

"No, it's fine." She tightened her own grip on his shoulder, easing back into the smooth *one two three* of the dance.

"You don't have to tell me if you'd rather not."

She knew he meant it, and she was grateful to him. But he already knew about her mother, and explaining this wouldn't be any more difficult. If she just kept dancing, kept following the triple heartbeat of the movements, she could tell him.

She set her eyes on his chest, rather than on his face.

"We did have assemblies in Exeter, where I grew up. The local school taught most of the dances, but... I wasn't at the school long enough to learn them." She risked a look up at him and saw a shallow line appear between his brows. "After my mother died, I struggled in school. Not the work—I still passed all of the exams. But… the other students, well they…"

His hand tensed in hers, inadvertently drawing her closer. "Were they unkind to you?"

Both of their voices were soft, as if they were afraid to speak too loudly, afraid to push against whatever haven the cicadas and cattails and copper-glazed sun had built around them.

"No, not truly. Even if they had been, our teacher would have intervened."

How to explain it? He spun her around, and she was facing the pond. Lilypads dotted the surface, enough for a frog to hop from one to another straight across the pond. The ducks had drifted to the opposite end. Her hand felt small and guarded in his, and she wondered if she could absorb his steadiness through it.

She hoped so.

"I came to school one morning, and I was so proud. I had taught myself to braid, and that morning I had put my hair in two braids, tied the ends with ribbons…" In her mind's eye, she could see herself in the mirror, timid but pleased, eyeing her handiwork.

The moment that had loomed so large in her memory sounded trivial as she explained it now. So unremarkable in its retelling that she felt a flare of shame across her cheeks.

"You must have looked charming."

She couldn't look at him. He was being so *kind*, so different from the ogre who had demanded to know why she was sniffling at Point Judith. Some people were like that. Their kindness lived beneath callouses from the things that had hurt them.

What had hurt Thomas?

She held his hand more tightly, strangely upset by the notion that anything should be allowed to hurt him.

Harper cleared her throat.

"Yes, well, I thought so. Out in the schoolyard, though, one of the girls in my class laughed at me. Susie Baker. She said it looked like I had done them myself."

Her eyes met his again, and she was shocked by the fierceness in them.

"That was unkind." His voice was measured, but she sensed a sort of a leashed tension in it, as if the words and tone required great control.

Harper tried to shrug and missed a step. He steadied her instantly.

"She wasn't trying to be, and I *had* done them myself. But Susie's older sister Anna overheard us, and she scolded Susie. She told her *of course* I had done them myself." Harper shook her head, pushing back the visceral pain of the memory. *She doesn't have a mother, Susie. Who else would do them for her? Her father?* The boys on the schoolyard had laughed wildly at that.

Thomas seemed to hear all the words that she was too ashamed to speak out loud.

"Anna was trying to defend me, but it was a clear reminder that I was motherless. A lot of the families in our town thought my father should have sent me away to live with relatives after my mother died. They didn't approve of a gruff farmer raising a daughter by himself and had no compunction in sharing that opinion." Their comments to and about Harper had ranged from thinly-veiled disapproval to outright scorn. Even after so many years, their disdain for her and her father tore at her.

As if there were anywhere better or safer for a little girl to be than with the father who loved her.

The pain that he was now sending her away to live with her grandmother throbbed anew.

"Your grandmother, Mrs. Verbeek. Did she offer to raise you?"

Harper thought back to the fight that day and closed her eyes.

"Yes. But my grandmother had never approved of my parent's marriage—she didn't attend the wedding, and our visits with her were rare and uncomfortable. But my parents were happy together. My mother was happier living as a farmer's wife than she ever was as the wealthy Verbeek debutante, and I don't think my grandmother could ever understand or accept that. On the day of my mother's funeral, my grandmother announced to us that she would raise me herself. Told me to pack a bag and we would leave within the hour."

Thomas's eyes flared. "I imagine that your father had something to say to that."

"My father was breathing fire by the time he got through with all he had to say to that."

He spun her again. "So even now, you aren't close to your grandmother. Because he chose to raise you himself."

"To the complete scandalization of Exeter, he did. And if that wasn't enough to condemn him in their eyes, he educated me himself after what Susie Baker said to me." Thomas tilted his face in question.

"When I came home and told him what happened at school, I said I didn't want to go back, not ever, and he just said, *'of course you won't, Hopsy.'* Just like that.

"From then on, he taught me himself. I'd follow him around the farm, book in hand, reading Plato in the barn loft or on fence rails while he worked. He taught me math by showing me how to balance the ledgers. He pinned maps to the walls and made me memorize them. Any book in his study was mine to read. I spent my school years in strawberry patches and on hay bales, and as unconventional as it was, my childhood was actually rather wonderful.

"And then when he and my grandmother told me that I was to go to New York to live with her, I...."

Realizing what she was about to say, she clamped her mouth shut. There was no need to tell him all of *that,* to open that particular Pandora's box of emotions.

She blamed the waltzing. It truly had knocked something loose in her brain. Why else would she have told him about her childhood, things that she had never said aloud to another person before?

Thomas spun her again, and she was facing the tree line.

"So that's why you are the way you are," he whispered.

Harper looked up at him, embarrassed. "Yes, I suppose that's why I've become such an oddity."

He stopped dancing so abruptly that she would have fallen over if he hadn't kept his arms around her. "That isn't what I meant."

"Oh." She bit her lip, unsure of herself.

He was looking at her with an unfamiliar glint in his eye, with such intensity that she half expected to melt, or maybe burst into flames, like Icarus. When neither happened, she found her voice.

"What *did* you mean?" She realized she was holding her breath. Her father had always taught her not to worry about other people's opinions. *"They're like armpits,"* he'd say. *"Everyone has them, and most of them stink."* She would always laugh afterward, which had been his intent, even as she recognized the truth of it. People's opinions of her only had as much weight as she chose to give them.

Harper didn't know until that moment how much weight she gave Thomas's opinion. The weight of one of O'Malley's ocean liners. Or maybe a hundred of them. Far more than her fragile heart could bear to admit.

A breeze rushed at them, blowing his hair onto his forehead.

She knew a fleeting urge to brush it back for him.

"You're different. Unspoiled. From the world. From everything." His eyes were bright and intense, searching her face as if he'd never seen it before.

"Because I was so sheltered?"

"Because you were so loved."

Oh.

Oh.

"An extraordinary thing, to be so loved. Extraordinary."

The way he said extraordinary the second time was different. The sound and weight and tautness of it were uniquely charged.

It felt very much as if he was calling *her* extraordinary.

Her heart stuttered in her chest.

"I… well I… thank you."

"Don't change, when you go to New York, when you join your grandmother. Don't ever change." His words held the force of an oath and the essence of a benediction.

"I…"

Her eyes held his, as if his expression bound her there.

"I imagine I *will* need to change, once I'm there. My grandmother has a whole campaign of sorts planned for me. New dresses, lessons in manners and comportment and dancing… although at least I can tell her I know the waltz now." Her lips tipped up in a facsimile of a smile. "It's just that… I feel as if I'm a replacement for my mother, in my grandmother's eyes. She always felt that my mother married below her, and when she looks at me she doesn't see her grandchild, her own flesh and blood."

"What does she see?" he prompted gently.

A weary sigh escaped her. "She sees an untamed berry farmer's daughter. A woman with dirt under her nails instead of pristine kid gloves. A project to fix and reform instead of, of…"

"Someone to love."

"*Yes*. That's exactly it."

The admission both shamed and relieved her. She was so tired of buttoning up her emotions. She had done it for her father's sake before she left home, but it exhausted her, unhinged her so completely that she had run off the train and agreed to act as a stranger's wife so that she could hide away on Block Island.

"So that's what you meant by a day of freedom. One last day to be yourself."

She looked up at him. His face was caught between shadow and light. "You remembered that."

"I remember everything you say."

Her breath caught.

Who would have imagined that the cold, gruff man from the bench would be the one person in the world to see her, to understand her?

In that moment, it felt like there was a string pulling her toward him. The breeze that had mussed his hair changed direction and came from behind her now, pushing her gently, slowly, forward. They were already standing so close—neither had moved since they'd stopped dancing. Their hands were still clasped. At some point, her hand had slid from his shoulder to his chest. His hand had inched from her waist to her low back, and the starbursts were moving frenetically now, coming to some sort of brilliant, inevitable crescendo.

She was close enough to see that his brown puppy-dog eyes had flecks of gold in them, like something elusive and precious had only just now come to the surface. The breeze, soft at first, was more insistent now, and the string between them pulled tighter. He was so close that if she leaned just a breath closer, pressed up on her toes, she could—

"That's *enough*."

His voice was so loud and harsh that it startled the ducks from the pond. The bullfrogs and cicadas fell silent, too, as if the meadow itself was as shocked by the words as she was.

Harper drew back as if he had slapped her.

Something flashed across his face, and he set her away from him, gently but definitively.

The movement felt very much like an elegy.

He returned those warm starburst hands safely to his side as her own fell limply into the folds of her dress. She blinked rapidly to dispel the sudden moisture behind her eyes.

What had she been about to do? What had she been *thinking*? It was a *dancing* lesson. He was giving her a *lesson* so that she wouldn't embarrass them or jeopardize their charade at the ball.

Because it was all a *charade*, she reminded herself.

Their words, their motions—their whole relationship—was a charade.

Without the starbursts, without the warmth and steadiness of Thomas Montgomery holding her, she felt confused and embarrassed and small.

Well. Small*er*. Which was really saying something.

"I mean," he said, his voice still gravelly, but unmistakably firm, "that's enough dancing for today. You're quite proficient. More than enough to dance at the ball."

More than enough indeed.

She nodded at the ground, unable to look at him.

Their lesson thus concluded, they walked back to the River House in complete silence.

Only when he had deposited her at the front porch and announced a sudden interest in seeing the lobster cages at the docks did she allow the moisture in her eyes to return.

Chapter 19

Thomas dropped down roughly on the lobster crates beside the boats.

The lobstermen began their work before the sun, and they had long since finished, leaving their crates neatly stacked and their boats well secured for the next day's haul.

He dropped his head in his hands, scrubbing them roughly down his face.

Even now, his hands trembled.

It had been madness, teaching her to waltz. Madness to listen and care when she talked about her childhood, her father. Madness to call her extraordinary, to have thought for even the most infinitesimal fraction of time that he could ever be anything to her, or she to him. Madness to have succumbed that the subtle pull towards her, to have contemplated—

Thomas tugged at his hair, then raised his head to look out over the water.

He didn't even deserve the right to touch her, to be in charge of protecting her during their ridiculous charade.

Because the crux of the matter was that Thomas Montgomery was neither a good man nor an honorable one.

Even if he could ever forgive himself for his past—he knew he could not—the fact remained that even now he was deceiving Harper, allowing her to believe that he was simply a novelist, here to write and be inspired on an idyllic island. There had been ample time to correct the misconception, and he had chosen not to.

He had chosen not to let her see what a dishonorable man he truly was.

What he was doing to Adeline was even worse. Her nature was

sincere and gracious, and she showed no evidence of being the spoiled heiress he had expected. And thanks to Thomas's need for absolution and Luther's greed for selling newspapers, Thomas was writing a whole newspaper spread about her. *Exploiting* her.

It had never sat well with him, writing about the wedding to meet his own ends, but now that he knew her, knew her family—it made him want to retch.

And what would Harper think of him, if ever she found out the real reason he had needed to get on the ferry that day, the real reason he had taken those tickets from the ground at Point Judith?

He could imagine the way her eyes would change color to match her temper, that perfect heart-shaped lip jutting out in anger.

Stop. He couldn't think about her like that—the colors and shapes of her. He didn't have the right.

He meant what he said to her—she was unspoiled. Pure and untarnished and so very, very different from him.

Which is why he needed to keep his distance from her.

No more touching, no more dancing, no more hushed conversations.

Until the wedding was over and their charade was complete, there needed to be as little interaction with Harper Whitley as possible.

The thought tore at him.

He felt for the letter from his sister in his jacket pocket, tugging it out and smoothing it over his legs.

He would reread it as penance, to remind himself of exactly why someone like him needed to stay far away from someone as pure as Harper.

His sister's tidy, swooping penmanship lept out at him from the page, and that familiar clench of guilt and shame flared hot in his gut. The day Thomas had overheard the dockworkers and inadvertently discovered the location of the O'Malley wedding, his sister had been out to lunch with him while her husband was in town for business. The dockworker's carousing had amused her at first, until he told her what it all meant, the bargain he had made with Luther.

Thomas closed his eyes, remembering too well how her brown eyes, so similar to his own, had narrowed in disapproval.

That day was the closest they had come to a family argument. She had been adamant that there was another way to share his exposé with the world, that any respectable newspaper or magazine would publish him instantly. She had always thought so highly of him, believed he was better and braver than he had ever been.

Even after the accident.

But it had taken him years to work his way up as a journalist, and even now, he had little autonomy in choosing what he covered. *Yellow journalism*. That's what Luther had called his research on child labor in mills. *"Surely conditions aren't as bad as all that,"* he had scoffed. He hadn't even bothered looking at what Thomas had written. Only when the editor needed Thomas's knack for research to track down the O'Malley wedding had he considered publishing it.

Still, his sister's disapproval stung. In her letter, she apologized for her sharp words but begged him not to write about Adeline's wedding. Hers was the only opinion that actually mattered to him now. Kate, and by association, her husband Michael, were the only ones he allowed into the tightly welded chambers of his heart.

And he had disappointed her.

Because he was exploiting someone for his own sake.

Because in spite of the fact that he was doing all of this—the charade, the wedding article—to publish the exposé and atone for all that he and his father had done, he was still his father's son.

Selfish, reckless, dishonorable.

Ironic, that the means to his atonement for being Samuel Montgomery's son should make Thomas himself so like the very man he despised.

A man like that shouldn't be within fifty feet of Harper Whitley.

It would be difficult, but not impossible, to maintain the charade while keeping his distance from her. Couples in the upper echelon of society often eschewed public affection anyway, and there were enough wedding activities planned in the coming weeks that he could be seen participating in everything without ever actually being seen with Harper.

His mind resolute, Thomas folded his sister's letter against its well-worn creases, returning it gently to his pocket.

He knew what he had to do.

***

Thomas was avoiding her.

Since the day of their ignominious waltzing lesson, he hadn't spoken to her, hadn't even met her eye when they were in the room together. Other than the slight rearrangement of Neville's clothes in the wardrobe and the presence of his toothbrush and shaving kit in the bathroom, she never would have known the man shared a space with her.

Which was for the best, of course. Sharing the room was wildly inappropriate in the first place, and honestly, respectable women didn't run around waltzing with and leaning into and almost kissing their pretend husbands.

They simply didn't.

And because Charles O'Malley had spared no expense for his daughter's wedding celebrations, the days were filled to the brim: there were boat rides and treks to the lighthouse, excursions to Water Street and extravagant picnics on the lawn of the River House, and every day ended in a lavish formal dinner. With so many activities to choose from and people to company with, it was a fairly simple matter for him to avoid her.

He was proving impressively adept at it.

"But why should he be avoiding you?" Rose's voice was muffled, as it came from somewhere inside the wardrobe, where she was hunting through Vivienne's dresses for tonight's ensemble.

Harper had earned the maid's respect when she stood up to Adeline's mother during the wedding dress fitting, and since Rose was the only person other than Thomas who knew Harper's true identity, the maid had become both a friend and a confidant. Only Rose knew the true, unbearably convoluted nature of her relationship with Thomas.

Harper only groaned in response to Rose's question, falling backward onto the bed. She covered her face, the humiliation of the waltz lesson flooding her anew.

Rose's head peeked out from behind a ruffled scarlet skirt. "You're not still worried about the waltz kiss, are you?"

"We didn't kiss!" Harper's voice was muffled now too, filtering out from the cracks between her fingers.

"Which is likely the problem."

"Rose!"

"Don't you *Rose!* me. It's true. There's clearly something between the two of you, and denying it is giving both of you some sort of emotional constipation. You should just kiss already. It will clear the air." Rose's arm extended from the wardrobe to twirl in the air like some sort of fairy godmother.

"It will do the exact opposite of clear the air. And has anyone ever told you that you're awfully cheeky for a maid?"

"Thank you, dear. So lovely of you to say so." Rose peeked her head out long enough to give a saucy wink. "I mean it though, Harper. Just clear the air. Talk to him." Hangers creaked in the wardrobe as Rose continued her search.

Talk. As if she could ever just talk to him after the day by the pond. The day he had called her *unspoiled*, told her never to change. The day he had steadied her and pulled her close.

"Even if I were brave enough to clear the air, he won't give me the chance. He's become as slippery as an eel. Any time I come within ten feet of him he slinks away. The other night after dinner, I'm fairly certain he hid behind the fern to avoid me!"

Rose, who had since heard all about the giant fern incident, snorted. "You mean.... The *handsy* fern?"

Harper groaned and dropped her face into her hands.

Finally, Rose emerged from the depths of the wardrobe. "Then we'll just have to get his attention."

"I've tried, Rosie." Harper knew she sounded petulant, but she was too morose to care.

"I said *we* will get his attention. As in *I* will help you. And as any lady's maid worth her salt will tell you, the right dress can get any man's attention."

"Do you really think so?" She peeked at the maid from between her fingers.

"I *know* so. And I know the perfect dress for the job."

***

A few minutes later, Harper had shimmied into the alleged *dress for the job*, and one look in the mirror had her turning mutinously at her friend.

Rose, who was apparently immune to mutinous looks, gave a satisfied nod. "Just as I said. *Perfect*. A dress like this is bound to get his attention."

"Rose, a dress like this is going to get *everyone's* attention. The neckline plunges halfway to China!"

The dress in question did not plunge *quite* to China. It did, however, have a provocative V neckline, and used as little fabric as necessary to cover her chest.

Apparently very, *very* little fabric was necessary.

Rose began to pin up Harper's hair, unfazed by the outburst. "Don't you think you're being a tad dramatic? The dress looks lovely on you."

The dress itself was divine, more a work of art than an article of clothing. The fabric was a luscious oxblood silk, devoid of embroidery or embellishments but exquisitely tailored. The sleeves hung off her shoulders, dipping low in both the front and back and cinching at the waist. Delicate tiers of silk draped down to the floor, and it was by far the most gorgeous thing she had ever worn.

But again, there was the *small* matter of the appallingly *small* amount of fabric covering her chest.

"Dramatic?" Harper narrowed her eyes at Rose. "No, I don't think I am. Nor would it be a tad dramatic to say that a *blind man* could get a glimpse of my—"

"This dress is a bit lower than what you've been wearing, that's all," Rose interrupted in a frustratingly sage voice. "You'll get used to it after a bit. It will just feel… breezier." Rose waggled her fingers in the air and gave a mischievous grin.

Harper scowled. "Rose!"

Rose laughed outright, enjoying Harper's discomfiture. "Harper, necklines are lower this season. It's a perfectly respectable dress for a married woman."

"Exactly. A married woman. I am *not* a married woman."

"In the eyes of everyone on Block Island, you are," Rose sang happily.

Harper blew out a breath. "Yes, well, be that as it may, I think I ought to change into the gold gown." Harper turned determinedly towards the wardrobe.

"Absolutely not!" Rose scurried to bar the way. "You look like a dream wearing this."

"Rose, I *can't* wear this."

"You can and you will. Now stop moving your head so I can get your pins in."

Harper complied but frowned at Rose through the mirror.

"Don't you think we ought to leave a little to the imagination?" Harper asked hopefully.

"No." Rose jabbed a pin into Harper's hair with more force than necessary. "You're trying to get his attention, not inspire him to poetry."

"Can't I do both?"

Another pin was violently inserted. "No."

"But—"

"Harper, do you or do you not want to send Thomas hiding behind the handsy fern again?"

Harper eyed her balefully. "I wish I had never told you that story."

"I'm sure you do, dear. Now, are you ready to get his attention, or will I have to drag you down there myself?"

Harper eyed herself in the mirror. With her hair braided and pinned up, her décolletage was even more prominent.

Which had probably been Rose's intent.

"And you're sure I don't look like a..."

Rose folded her arms across her chest, then lifted an eyebrow. "A...?"

"Well... a... *ahem*... perhaps a lady of...."

When it was apparent that Harper was incapable of finishing her sentence, Rose rolled her eyes.

"You look like a woman who is going to have the attention of every man in the room tonight, Thomas Montgomery included. Now, go have fun, and make sure to share all the details with me later tonight."

While she spoke, Rose had been determinately propelling Harper towards to door. When Harper realized her intent, she tried to dig in her heels, but the flimsy red slippers under her dress only skidded and bumped along the rug.

"Rose, wait, I don't think I can—"

Harper was already halfway in the corridor when she had the presence of mind to swipe an enormous urn of flowers off the table by the door.

The door rattled on its hinges as Rose slammed it behind her.

Cheeky maid indeed.

Harper held the vase to her chest like a talisman.

The porcelain was *extremely* cold.

But when she heard the door lock behind her, Harper had no choice but to lift her chin and walk down to dinner.

Chapter 20

By the time the guests gathered for aperitifs before dinner, Thomas had already been dressed and ready for hours. In recent days, this had often been the case. He only entered their room when he knew Harper to be elsewhere or was sure that she was already asleep, and avoiding Harper in their own shared room in addition to everywhere else had become a juggling act.

But even as he avoided her—averting his eyes whenever she glanced his way, circumventing her whenever she got too close—he could *sense* her. It was as if her presence caused a sudden drop in barometric pressure, like an impending storm. The air would shift and tingle the closer she got, the atoms charging with energy and portent.

Which is why he knew she had entered the room for aperitifs, even as he carried on a conversation with Uncle Hugh. In recent days he had gravitated towards Hugh and his wife, along with their daughters; all four of them possessed the singular ability to hold an entire conversation with minimal involvement from other parties. Thomas could while away hours in their company without uttering more than an occasional *Ah*, *Oh?*, or *Really!*

Hugh was currently expounding on the return of his chronic gout—he was convinced his nascent intake of fresh seafood was causing it to flare—and his new set of ivory teeth. *"Excellent, excellent, my new set of chompers,"* he enthused, clamping his jaw for effect. Except for when he ate sweets, apparently. Sugar in his dentures made his gums ache, so he preferred to savor dessert *sans* his new ivory dentures, much to the chagrin of his wife (and anyone unfortunate enough to be beside him at the time).

"Watches me like a hawk, every time dessert is served! Wives,"

Hugh whispered conspiratorially to Thomas.

Thomas gave a sympathetic nod, even as he tracked Harper's movement from the corner of his eye. She was holding an enormous urn of flowers, making her way through the room with a tight smile. The vase alone probably weighed twenty pounds. Why on earth was she carrying it around?

He watched her as she took a seat in the corner of the room, then flushed as Lyle walked towards her and settled on the couch beside her. They were too far to hear anything, but Lyle was talking animatedly, leaning towards Harper as he did so. She kept her rigid smile in place, but held the urn in front of her like a shield, nodding and occasionally swatting an errant flower from her face.

A footman entered the room, announcing dinner, and he watched Harper's cheeks flush as Lyle stood and held out a hand towards her.

"Shall we, Neville? I'm told there's seared halibut on the menu tonight!" Hugh rubbed his hands eagerly.

Thomas nodded distractedly at him. "You go ahead. I'll be in in a moment."

Seeing the direction of his gaze, Hugh smiled at him. "Wives," he said happily, even as Thomas was already striding away from him.

He was halfway across the room when Harper reluctantly rose, setting the urn on the table beside her and turning to take Lyle's outstretched hand. When she did, Lyle's jaw dropped. Literally *dropped*.

His eyes dropped next.

To her chest.

And now Thomas was not striding, but barreling across the room. Why had he never noticed how infernally long this room was? Utterly impractical, having such a long room. He wanted to have sharp words with the architect who designed the River House. Right after he had sharp words with Lyle, whose jaw had snapped back into place but whose eyes were still wandering south of where they ought to be.

Which was on her face.

If he didn't move his eyes to her face, Thomas was going to pummel that chauvinistic, good-for-nothing—

"Good evening, Lyle. So good of you to keep my wife company for me." Thomas's tone was positively glacial.

Lyle had the good sense to recognize both the tone and the dismissal, and with a hasty *"of course"* he turned and offered his arm to Claudia instead, who took it with alacrity.

Thomas waited until Lyle and Claudia ambled out of the room with the rest of the guests before he looked down at Harper.

She looked back at him, her eyes surprised, but not displeased.

They were caramel, tonight, her eyes. Or maybe gold.

She was breathtaking.

"Good evening, Mr. Jones."

"Good evening, Mrs. Jones."

They stood there a moment in silence, as if they both needed to reacquaint themselves with the nearness, the erratic vacillations of atmospheric pressure.

It had been days since he had seen her up close, been near enough to smell strawberries and spring rain, and as he looked at her now it was like he could breathe again.

Suddenly he didn't want to escort her into dinner, didn't want her where everyone else would get to see how utterly stunning she was. He recognized the impulse as proprietary and tried to quash it.

She was *not* his wife.

He should *not* be near her.

But tonight, so help him, he was going to stay beside her and make sure that every other man on the island knew that *he* didn't belong near her either.

"May I escort you in to dinner?"

Caramel eyes met his, a smile in them now. "You may."

Which is how in spite of his best intentions, Thomas found himself seated beside Harper at dinner, eating the excess portions that she surreptitiously moved to his plate and searching for a polite way to smash his wine glass against the table and throw the shards into the eyes of every man who was foolish enough to ogle his pretend wife's torso.

Lyle and Wesley's father were especially conspicuous.

In lieu of throwing shrapnel at his fellow male diners (there was simply no socially acceptable method for it), he glared generally at anyone whose eyes lingered on his wife.

Thomas *excelled* at glaring.

He had been so busy glaring that the general conversation had been lost to him until Adeline's surprisingly sharp voice cut across the table to Harper.

"Oh Viv, don't eat the vegetables!"

Uncle Hugh, who had been hefting an enormous mound of vegetables onto Harper's plate, froze mid-scoop.

A floret of broccoli dropped unceremoniously onto her plate.

Everyone's attention swung to Adeline, whose voice was normally as gentle as a lullaby.

She flushed. "It had eggplant."

Harper's brow furrowed even as Bess shouted across the table. "Eggplant!" She was as outraged and horrified as if a loaded gun had been found in the bowl, rather than a purple vegetable. "Surely we've told the kitchen about your allergy, Vivi."

Hugh eyed the offending bowl of vegetables as if it had suddenly grown fangs, and a footman rushed to take it from him.

"Apologies, ma'am. I'll have a word with the kitchen right away." The footman, polite as he was, could not resist a peek south of Harper's face.

Thomas's knife and fork clattered against his plate as he cut into his halibut with blistering force. It had the desirable effect of redirecting the footman's gaze and rapidly sending him out the door.

"Thank heavens you noticed, Ada! Otherwise poor Vivi's lips would have swollen up like a pufferfish!"

"Have you ever seen her after she eats eggplant, Neville?" This from Rhys. "She truly does look like a pufferfish."

"Rhys!" Isla was scandalized, either by the attention given to her least favorite niece or her son's unseemly delight in the prospect. Possibly both.

"A very pretty pufferfish though, Viv." Rhys grinned unrepentantly.

"You would make a lovely pufferfish." Lyle smiled warmly at Harper, letting his gaze stray several inches below her face. When he intercepted Thomas's glare, he blanched, then hastily—and wisely—averted his eyes.

Harper, still pink from the unexpected attention, mustered a smile for him.

"Well, I'm certain our Dr. Grayson would have taken good care of you if you *had* eaten the eggplant and become a pufferfish," Bess said confidently.

The table at large turned admiring eyes on the good doctor, who inclined his head in acknowledgment.

"Pufferfish or not, I'm here for whatever you might need."

There was nothing particularly provocative about the statement. Grayson said it in the same soothing, gentle manner in which he said everything else.

No one would accuse *him* of having the bedside manner of a wet blanket.

Since he was already out of sorts from his proximity to Harper and inability to blind the resident males, Thomas could hardly be blamed for what came out of his mouth next.

"She doesn't *need* anything from you, Grayson. She didn't *eat* the EGGPLANT!" His sentence finished at a half decibel below a roar.

A hush fell over the table as several sets of wide eyes stared at him. More specifically, the fish being violently disembodied on his plate.

Under the table, Harper's foot collided with his shin.

"Indeed, dear." She smiled over at Thomas, but her eyes flashed a warning. "Thank you for your kind assurance, Dr. Grayson. But I suppose all's well that ends well."

Harper smiled sweetly to the table at large, and such was her innate charm that everyone smiled back, slowly returning to their dinners.

"I'm curious, Vivi dear." Wesley leaned across the table towards her. "Didn't you notice the eggplant in the vegetables? Surely you wouldn't have actually eaten them, as you're *allergic*?" Wesley sipped his wine, regarding her with interest.

His tone was conversational but oddly pointed. Thomas thought again of the morning when Wesley and Harper had gotten to know one another, and how reluctant Harper had been to tell him about it afterward.

He would have the full story by the end of the night.

"No, I'm certain I wouldn't have, though I'm grateful to Adeline for pointing it out to me." She lifted her glass to Adeline, who lifted her own with a smile.

"I didn't notice the eggplant either, Wesley," Uncle Hugh chimed in.

"Of course, of course. An honest mistake from the kitchen, then." Wesley flashed a smile.

"But you know, I'm certain I told them about Vivi's allergy." Adeline wrinkled her brow thoughtfully. "Wesley, didn't we discuss it with them when we looked through the menu plans at the beginning of the month?"

"I know that we did, darling. I'll need to have another word with them, it seems. I'm only glad that you noticed before Vivi ate any. We wouldn't want you swelling up like a pufferfish, Viv."

Adeline nodded gratefully, and Harper gave a tight smile.

Unfortunately, she was not to have a reprieve just yet.

"Viv," Rhys began, "do you remember when we were all at George's house, the one he built down in Asheville?"

Thomas felt Harper tense at his side.

Uncle Hugh chuckled. "Yes! Vanderbilt outdid himself on the Biltmore. A spectacular home he built."

"Impractical place for a home," Charles groused. It was one of the few dinners he had attended in person. "Who builds a mansion seven hundred miles from New York City?"

"Oh, but the casserole, Viv!" Claudia laughed around a bite.

"I had forgotten about the casserole!" said Claire, clapping her hands at the memory.

"I sense a story there," said Wesley. "Do tell us, Viv. What happened with the casserole?"

Harper flushed, and Thomas began to seriously consider smashing his wine glass against the table and hoping the shards made their way to Wesley's face. If he threw it at just the right angle, it would almost certainly hit him, possibly even maim him, if Thomas's aim was very precise.

Thomas could make it look like an accident.

His hands were on the stem of his glass when Aunt Bess spoke. "The corn and eggplant casserole! Oh, you poor dear. Your lips were swollen for days after that. Dear Georgie felt awful about it."

"They were diced so finely!" Caire added.

"It *was* delicious, though. Vanderbilt maintains an excellent cook!"

The rest of the O'Malleys continued to reminisce about their visit with the Vanderbilts, but Wesley's gaze remained fixed on Harper.

Thomas tried and failed to think of a way to change the conversation, to redirect it to something that did not involve memories that Harper knew nothing about. She was holding up admirably, but lying and obfuscation didn't come naturally to her. Their charade could only bear so much scrutiny.

"And then George's dog came bounding into the dining room that one night, do you remember?" Rhys shook his head ruefully.

"He was enormous, wasn't he?"

"He about ruined your dress, Viv, when he jumped up on you!" Adeline's comment, innocuous enough, sent Wesley's shrewd gaze back to Harper.

"Poor Vivi. It seems like you had a rough visit to the Biltmore, didn't you? Tell me, what kind of dog does Vanderbilt have?" Wesley smiled, but the effect was downright wolfish.

Harper's mouth froze on an *O*.

Why was Wesley working so hard to unsettle her? There was no doubt that he was suspicious of her, but Thomas couldn't think of a reason why he should be. They still had two weeks before the wedding, and it would be far more difficult to maintain their charade if Wesley continued to interrogate her.

Thomas felt the anger building in him.

What exactly had been going on in the days since he had been avoiding Harper? He had assumed that the greatest threat to Harper on Block Island was himself, but that was not necessarily true. How had he not realized the foolishness of the assumption?

From the moment he proposed the charade on Point Judith, he had assumed responsibility for her. She was *supposed* to be under his care. The decision to keep his distance from her had seemed wise that day after the waltz, but what had been happening in his time away from her?

What if she had needed him in the last few days, and he had continued to evade and ignore her?

The thought made him oddly desperate.

"Yes! Largest dog I've ever seen, old George had." Hugh sat forward, drumming his fingers on the table.

"A great dane, was it?" Charles ventured.

"No, must have been an Irish wolfhound," Rhys disagreed.

Harper's eyes flashed between the men, her panic barely disguised.

Wesley's eyes continued to bore into her.

"Hound? Couldn't be. The fur was all wrong."

"Not just a hound, Uncle, an *Irish* wolfhound."

"Nope. Nope." He drummed his fingers some more. "Bernese Mountain dog, that was it!"

"An English mastiff?"

"Maybe a Newfoundland?"

"Some sort of shepherd? Or an Alsatian?"

"It was a Saint Bernard!" Claire shouted triumphantly, followed by a chorus of agreement from the rest of the table.

Thomas could feel the breath that Harper exhaled.

He exhaled one of his own.

"I'm sure you were eager for that particular visit to end, weren't you Viv?" Wesley regarded Harper with what Thomas knew to be feigned sympathy.

After a pause, Harper met his gaze, lifting her chin. "On the contrary, Wesley. It takes far more than that to unsettle me."

He could feel her shaking with nerves, but her gaze was steady.

Thomas looked over at her, feeling oddly proud.

Brave girl.

But her bravery did nothing to curb his anger toward the man who had made it necessary for her to be brave.

Thankfully, the conversation moved to and remained on the fireworks planned for that night, and both he and Harper went mercifully unnoticed.

When the family rose to retire to the parlor, Thomas excused himself to walk out on the veranda, needing the space and cool air to settle his temper.

Unfortunately for his temper, he was not the only guest who had sought shelter on the veranda.

***

"Out for a smoke, Neville?" Wesley stepped out from the corner of the porch, a cigar in his hand.

Thomas tensed, not trusting himself to behave civilly towards Wesley just yet. "Just taking in the air. I don't smoke."

"No?"

Wesley blow out a ring of smoke, directing his gaze to the River House lawn. Blankets had been set out for the guests to sit on while they enjoyed the fireworks, and footmen were busy preparing the crates of explosives.

"I don't either, normally."

"Special occasion, then?" Thomas didn't bother to disguise the bite in his voice.

"Yes, I suppose so. A man only gets married once, doesn't he?"

Wesley turned toward Thomas, puffing out another breath. The cigar smelled expensive, and if Thomas wasn't mistaken, Wesley had been enjoying a fair amount of whiskey with his smoke. "Perhaps you could give me some advice, as an old married man yourself. I'm sure Vivi keeps you on your toes."

Thomas clenched his fists at his side. "You seem to have taken an uncommon interest in my wife."

Wesley met Thomas's gaze squarely. His smile was slow and wolfish. "Your wife is uncommonly interesting."

Thomas's jaw clenched so tightly that he was in real danger of cracking a tooth. "You know, the staff and kitchen at the River House have been excellent thus far. It beggars belief that they would make such a blatant mistake in serving eggplant at dinner this evening. Not when you *specifically* mentioned Vivienne's sensitivity to them. You wouldn't happen to know anything about that, would you?"

Wesley gave him an appraising look before lifting his lips in a smirk. "I'm sure I don't. But rest assured, I'm as relieved as anyone that your wife is well."

Both men recognized the lie, but neither acknowledged it. Instead, they stood in the shadows of the River House, studying one another, assessing for strengths and weaknesses.

After a moment, Thomas gave a decisive nod. He spoke with deliberate slowness. "Let me make something clear to you. I don't care that you're the groom of the wedding of the century. I don't care that you're the right-hand man to the wealthiest shipbuilder in the world. I don't care that we're almost family. If you ever bother my wife again, I will personally and very happily ensure that you live to regret it. Am I understood?"

In spite of Thomas's barely contained rage, Wesley regarded him cooly, almost disinterestedly. With another smirk, he raised the cigar to his mouth, blowing the smoke into the inches of space between Thomas's face and his own.

Neither man moved, though Wesley flicked his gaze back to the lawn.

"The fireworks will be starting soon, Jones. You'd better go and keep that pretty wife of yours company."

Thomas wanted to throttle him. He might be able to get away with it. But he knew better than to do it here and now. Guests were beginning to filter onto the lawn to claim their places for the fireworks, and if he was going to kill a man for disrespecting his fake wife, he would prefer fewer witnesses.

With a parting glare, Thomas walked off the veranda, intent on releasing his frustration on a long walk by the water.

But the blankets on the lawn were filling quickly, and Bess had already seen him.

"Neville! You hoo, dear! Vivi is just over there waiting for you." She gestured to her left, where he saw Harper curled up by herself on a blanket. When she heard Bess, she turned to him, her smile timid and her eyes luminous.

He couldn't refuse her.

Like a moth to the flame, he walked towards Harper, sitting a respectable distance from her on the blanket.

They were silent a moment, both a little awkward now that it was only the two of them. They were surrounded by people, but in the dark with just the two of them on the blanket, the setting felt surprisingly intimate. She picked idly at a loose thread on the blanket, not meeting his eye.

"Are you all right?" he asked carefully.

"Yes, yes I'm fine."

"Are you sure? Dinner was…" he ran his hands roughly through his hair.

"It certainly was." She gave the string a tug, tearing it from the blanket, then set to work on another one. "But I'm fine. Truly. Thank goodness I didn't eat the eggplant." She rolled her eyes, trying for a joke, but her voice was flat, and the smile she gave him didn't reach her eyes.

It made his chest ache, that smile.

"The day we took the photographs. Something had happened between you and Wesley, earlier in the morning. You never did tell me the story."

Thomas hadn't meant it as an accusation, but she stiffened at his tone.

He closed his eyes, gusting a breath. Gentleness did not come naturally to him. "That is… *would you* tell me what happened? Please?"

"It doesn't signify."

It was not an answer. What was she hiding?

The other guests were several feet away on their respective blankets, but he lowered his voice anyway. "Harper." She looked up at him in surprise. He shouldn't be calling her Harper, for the sake of propriety and the sake of the charade, but he knew it would disarm her, and for some reason that seemed important. It was important that she felt safe with him.

"Why don't you want to tell me what happened?"

Still, she didn't meet his eye. "I'd rather talk about something else."

He frowned. "Something—"

"Why have you been avoiding me?" The words rushed out of her like a waterfall, fast and uncontrolled.

His head jerked back in surprise. He hadn't expected her to call him out on his behavior. "I haven't been avoiding you." It was a blatant lie, and her expression told him she knew it. But he couldn't tell her the truth.

You've cracked something open in my chest—some errant fissure of tenderness. You remind me that I know how to feel. I care for you in spite of myself, and I cannot care about you because the things in my care get hurt.

"I'm very sorry, you know," she hurried on, her voice unsteady. "About the waltz that day. I didn't mean anything by it—I have no idea what came over me, and I just, I just..." she floundered for words, biting down hard on her lip.

He hated it. He hated seeing her uncomfortable, hearing her apologize.

Because she hadn't done anything wrong the day of the waltz. She had simply been herself. Beautiful. Enchanting. Unspoiled.

Far, far too good for someone like him.

He was not an honorable man, but he was also not a brute.

"Harper. Look at me." She did, and her eyes were colorless in the darkness of the lawn. "Please don't apologize. You didn't do anything wrong."

She shook her head roughly. "But you've been avoiding me since then."

"I haven't been avoiding you exactly. It's only that... I've been very busy."

He wracked his brain for a plausible excuse, but she supplied one before he could. "Busy with... researching for your novel?"

Her words landed like a blow. There it was, that lie of omission that he couldn't seem to correct. It was his deception within a deception—lying to her about his occupation while also lying to everyone on Block Island about his identity.

To use it as an excuse for avoiding her was both convenient and reprehensible.

He hated himself a little when he nodded. "Yes. I'm behind on my novel, so I've just been trying to carve out some extra time during the days to catch up. Forgive me if it came across as deliberate. I will endeavor to be more present for you in the future."

It was a dangerous promise. He *shouldn't* be more present. But if Wesley continued to bother her the way he had tonight, Thomas needed to be with her. The risk and weight of the charade were not hers to bear alone.

She tilted her head, studying him. He was terrified that she could see through him, that she could sense the lie. He actually held his breath.

Then she tucked her legs up in front of her, shaking out her dress and resting her chin on her knees. When she smiled at him, it was slow and warm, an invitation and a balm.

The air around them hummed with the energy and radiance of it.

"Thank you. I would like that."

He couldn't respond—he didn't trust himself to. He didn't deserve that smile. Instead, he looked up at the sky, frowning into the darkness.

"I've never seen fireworks before." Her voice was closer now. She must have shifted toward him on the blanket. "Have you?"

"I have not."

When he looked down at her, she was studying him, her lips pursed to one side.

To his surprise, she lifted her hand to his face and swiped her thumb between his brows, across his forehead.

He was so shocked that his face went blank, which, oddly, seemed to please her.

"There." She lowered her hand, satisfied.

"There?" His voice was embarrassingly hoarse.

"I've been wanting to smooth those out since the day we met. I smoothed out your frowny lines," she clarified. "They'll get stuck that way, you know." When he didn't respond, she continued. "It's just that you're always so... " she scrunched her face tightly, furrowing her brow to imitate his habitual expression, "and all those frown lines are bound to become permanent if you keep that up." She sat back and regarded him, grinning happily. "Now it matches your eyes."

He stared at her, stunned.

She was at once childlike and wise, playful and serious.

It was intoxicating.

She was intoxicating.

He was so awed by her that he didn't notice the footmen lighting the fireworks until the first boom blistered through the night sky, followed by a kaleidoscope of color and light. Suddenly the darkness was radiant, the night ethereal.

She let out a delighted laugh, then leaned into him."Have you ever seen something so completely wonderful?" Her voice was breathless, and her eyes reflected the sparkling hues of the night sky.

When he looked down at her, he answered in complete honesty.

"I have not."

Chapter 21

After debriefing her night with Rose and changing out of her evening gown, Harper laid down in bed, a contented sigh escaping her lips.

The evening had been perfect.

Well, almost perfect. Dinner had been a bit of a disaster—Wesley had clearly been trying to rattle her. But everything after that—clearing the air with Thomas, smoothing those furrows from his brow, the fireworks—that had been lovely.

Magical, even.

It was already late, but she wasn't tired yet. The night still felt aglow, thrumming with possibilities. The aftereffects of the fireworks, perhaps.

Or maybe just the aftereffects of Thomas Montgomery.

She still had another hour or two before he would return to the room for the night. She never did see him in the room between twilight and dawn, and since she couldn't sleep anyway, she slipped out of bed, drifting towards the wardrobe.

It was still ajar from when Rose had hung up her gown. The maid had been unapologetically smug about the success of the dress and her own sartorial prowess. Harper smiled; the dress *had* been effective at gaining Thomas's attention. She peeked into the wardrobe, running her hands over the smooth silk of the hanging gowns.

All of Neville's clothes hung in the wardrobe as well. The real Mr. and Mrs. Jones probably had no idea that their trunks that had arrived at the River House without them would get so much use. Harper grimaced at the thought.

As uncomfortable as Wesley had made her at dinner, his suspicions were completely justified. She *wasn't* Vivienne Jones. She wasn't allergic to eggplant and had never met George Vanderbilt's Saint Bernard. If his scrutiny and suspicions continued, there was bound to be trouble.

Perhaps she *should* have confided in Thomas about Wesley's subtle threats on the morning of the dress fitting, but if she had, she would also have felt compelled to tell him about what she had witnessed between Wesley and his father. She couldn't honestly say that she *liked* Wesley, but she had seen the hurt and shame in his eyes that morning. Somehow she couldn't bear to expose his shame to anyone else, even Thomas.

Harper shook her head, willing the thought away.

Her hands skimmed idly over Neville's neatly pressed suits, his array of crisp neckties.

She really ought to replace the one she had ruined with the Madeira.

She smiled ruefully at the memory of their first night on Block Island, then let her gaze drift to the bottom of the wardrobe. Thomas's satchel and his typewriter case, gleaming and black, were set in the corner. She knelt down beside it, curious. She had never actually seen a typewriter before—her father's ledgers were all kept by hand—and she succumbed to that tug of curiosity, pulling it slowly from its case.

Surely Thomas wouldn't mind if she just peeked at it.

The keys sat upright in a row, like soldiers in battle lines, with a curved fan-like apparatus framing the back. The contraption was foreign to her, but she itched to touch it. Maybe he would teach her to use it if there was time before the wedding. He *did* say he would endeavor to be more present. He was so difficult to read that she still wasn't sure how he felt about her, but at least it was *less* exasperated than it had been at the beginning of their charade.

She was glad she had smoothed away the frowny lines.

Tomorrow, at breakfast if she saw him, she would ask him to teach her.

Harper lifted the typewriter back into the case, but when she heard the unmistakable sound of crinkling paper, she quickly pulled it out again. She had accidentally set the typewriter on a notebook, the same one she had seen Thomas scribbling in during the ferry ride. It must have been tucked in the case earlier and she hadn't noticed. She cringed when she saw where the typewriter had bent back the cover and front pages. She picked it up out of the wardrobe, anxious to smooth the pages she had mangled.

Snooping was not her intent, so she was careful to avert her eyes when she opened the notebook. Her efforts were too slow, though. Before she looked away, something caught her eye. *Someone*, actually.

Adeline.

Harper felt a prickle at the back of her neck.

Why was Adeline's name on the paper? She was probably a character in his novel, that was all. A coincidence that they were here for Adeline's wedding.

Harper really did try not to look, but her eyes glossed over the page without her permission, and her attention was suddenly rapt.

Beneath Adeline's name was a physical description of her, followed by one of Wesley, and details about the River House.

The notes went on and on. About the O'Malleys and the scenery, about the clever decision to have the wedding on Block Island.

These were not notes for a work of fiction, nor were they written in the style of a personal journal. Their direct and concise nature was much more in the manner of a journalist.

Thomas *had* said he was a novelist, hadn't he?

But when she replayed their conversations about his occupation, that particular detail was opaque. She had assumed he was a novelist, but he had never actually confirmed it, had he?

The public intrigue and scarcity of details regarding Adeline's wedding would make any account of the wedding a veritable gold mine for any journalist. And if Thomas was a reporter, here to write about the wedding of the century… then she was his accomplice. By agreeing to impersonate Vivienne Jones, she had given him the perfect opportunity to insinuate himself with the family. To *spy* on them.

She shook her head roughly, willing away the thought. Surely there was another explanation. This was *Thomas*, for goodness sake. He might be grumpy and perpetually frowny, but he was not a liar or some intrepid reporter. He would never use her to advance his career. He cared about her too much to do such a thing.

Didn't he?

But now that the idea had been planted, her mind began to whirl, replaying their every interaction in a new light. And as much as she tried to find confirmation that he cared for her beyond what their charade necessitated, she couldn't.

Because their entire relationship was based on a charade.

When had she forgotten that this was all a charade?

How could she have forgotten?

Harper moved away from the wardrobe, clutching the notebook

against the ache in her chest, then began to pace the room. These last two weeks, while he had been writing in his notebook, planning to write about the wedding of the century, what had she been doing?

She had been confiding in him.

Dancing with him.

Literally, stupidly, falling for him.

She didn't know how long she stood there, holding the notebook and feeling lost and lonely and unbelievably foolish, until the door creaked open and Thomas appeared in the doorway. He was visibly shocked to find her still awake, but after a second's surprise, he seemed to take in the state of her. Whatever he saw had him before her in two strides.

"What's wrong? Has something happened?" His eyes were roving over her, looking for some physical indicator of her distress.

She could only stare at him, searching those warm brown eyes, trying to find a way to reconcile the Thomas she knew with the notebook she had found.

After a moment, his expression morphed from concerned to thunderous. "Harper." His adam's apple bobbed as he swallowed. "Has someone hurt you?"

The concern in his face nearly undid her, and she bit her lip, not trusting herself to speak. He stood so close to her that she could feel the heat of his body and smell the subtle scent of shaving soap on his skin. She couldn't think straight with him so close, and so she shook her head, walking backward until her back was pressed against the wardrobe.

The typewriter lay forgotten on the floor by her feet, and she stumbled over it. He came toward her, extending his hands to catch her. The sight of him there, strong hands ready to steady her, warm brown eyes fixed on her while he stood silhouetted in the soft glow of the lamp—it was unbearable.

Unsteadily she pulled the notebook away from her chest, holding it out to him. "Please." Her voice was weak, so desperate that she hardly recognized it. "Please tell me this isn't what it seems."

His brow creased, but as he looked between her and the notebook and saw the typewriter on the floor, realization dawned. He made no move to take it, but still, she held it there, questions and fears hanging heavy in the foot of space between them.

"Harper." His jaw ticked and he said nothing more, but he didn't need to. The stricken look on his face was answer enough.

She shook her head, feeling as if she understood far too much but not nearly enough. "You're not a novelist, are you?"

He didn't meet her eye but kept his gaze on the notebook that she still held between them. When her arm fell limply to the side, he was forced to look up at her.

"That's why you needed to get to Block Island that day, isn't it?"

When he nodded, her throat grew tight. "That's why you stayed with me at Point Judith, then? So that you could use me to get to the O'Malleys? I must have seemed the perfect Trojan horse, sitting there while Vivienne stormed by and left her ferry tickets. Even I can admire the poetry of it." She could feel herself unraveling, but she was powerless to stop.

"My goodness, you must think me so unpardonably stupid. Prattling on about finding enough time to write your novel, telling Rose how much I care about Adeline, would never do anything to hurt her. And this whole time—this *whole* time—that's exactly what I've been doing." She pushed the heels of her hands roughly against her eyes as if she could push the tears and the hurt that caused them back to where they came from.

Though Thomas had stood silent and unmoving, something about the action seemed to re-animate him.

"No. Harper, no," he said, his voice hoarse but steady. She felt rather than saw him step towards her. "Yes, I am a journalist. And yes, I was at Point Judith that day to get to the wedding. But it has never been my intention to *use* you."

She dropped her hands from her eyes. "Do you expect me to believe that it was only out of the goodness of your heart that you contrived this charade to get me to Block Island? That you did that for *my* sake?"

"I understand it's hard to believe, but yes. I had no notion that the woman whose ferry tickets we were taking was related to Adeline. I had no idea that Vivienne Jones was actually Vivienne *O'Malley* Jones. I never intended to do anything more than escort you to the island and make sure that you had a way to get back home at the end of the day. You cannot believe that I planned to run into Hugh and Bess, or that I wanted you to get sick when we arrived?"

That much, at least, she did believe. But there was more that he needed to answer for.

"What happened that first day, I understand. You could not have controlled that. And heaven knows that it was my own fault for what happened with the aperitifs and missing the ferry that night. But afterward... why didn't you tell me why you were really here? You must have thought me so stupid, not realizing the truth."

"No, I would never think such a thing of you. And you cannot think that I would ever use you."

"I don't know what to think! If I had been thinking clearly I would have realized the truth of the situation long before now. If I had been thinking I would have known that you're a newspaperman, that you..." her voice trailed off as she remembered what he had called her. *The long-lost Verbeek granddaughter.* "You knew who I was. Before we met, you had already heard of me, of my grandmother. Because you're a *journalist,* and they've written about me in the gossip sheets."

How had it never occurred to her that in assuming the mantle of official Verbeek debutante, she would also be exposing herself to public censure and gossip? No wonder her mother had felt well rid of New York Society. Like Adeline, her personal life would soon be fodder for newspapers.

For *newspapermen,* like Thomas.

He stood like a stone before her. He did not contradict her.

"So, when you're done writing about Adeline's wedding, will you write about me next? The wild Verbeek granddaughter who ran away to Block Island, who sullied her reputation and threw away her prospects for a day of freedom? Tell me, whose gossip reel will run first, Adeline's or mine?"

His adam's apple bobbed roughly. "Do you honestly believe that I would do such a thing?"

She turned away from him, feeling hurt and humiliated, and it was easier to lash out and accuse him than deal with her own battered heart. After a moment, she turned back to him. "You know, you continue to question what I can and cannot believe, but the very fact that we're having this conversation is proof that I can believe just about anything, isn't it, Mr. Montgomery? Bravo, sir. You've had me fooled from the moment we met."

If she had slapped him across the face, he could not have looked more stricken. He ran his hands through his hair so roughly that it stood on its ends.

"This has not *all* been an act for me. You're right. I willfully misled you about being a journalist. I should have told you from the beginning what I was, and it was unconscionable to mislead you for so long. For that, I can only say that I am sorry and beg forgiveness. I know you have little reason to hear me out, even less to trust me, but

I'll ask it of you all the same. I never meant for you to be my Trojan horse, to use or deceive you. I offered you those ferry tickets for your sake. I heard what you said, about your day of freedom. I would never *use* you."

Those wide puppy-dog eyes pled with her, a silent entreaty more potent than anything he could have said to her.

She *wanted* to trust him. More than anything, she wanted to believe him. But how could she? She didn't know him at all, not in the way she had let him know her. From that first day on the bench to the night she fixed his necktie and the afternoon when they waltzed, she had confided in him about her childhood and her family, yet she knew only the basic facts of his life.

Not even that. She hadn't even known he was a *journalist*.

"There's no need to pretend you ever cared about me or my day of freedom, Mr. Montgomery—this is the kind of story to launch your name in the newspaper industry, isn't it? You were the one reporter who found out where the wedding of the century would take place and actually got there in time. Well done, sir." She couldn't believe what she was saying—in her entire life, she had never spoken so unkindly to anyone.

Had she thought this night was magical? It was a nightmare.

At her words, his whole body turned rigid. "You think that I have done all of this for the sake of my own career?" His voice was as taut as his stance, but there was a sudden glint to his eyes, and if she had been more in her right mind she would have tried to understand it. As it was, it was all she could do not to break down and weep.

"What reason have you given me to believe otherwise?" she asked.

His eyes bored into hers, and she forced herself to hold his gaze. There was a riot of emotion in those brown orbs, but she had no idea what to make of it. The dim lighting and the late hour were disorienting her, and she had an unbidden desire to dive into the tangled world that lay beyond his eyes, to try and make sense of him. Because somewhere, in the deepest part of her, she *wanted* to understand him. She wanted to know what would make a man like Thomas Montgomery—a man who until tonight she had thought could keep the earth in its orbit with his steadiness alone—lie to her.

After a moment, he replied. "None. I haven't given you a single reason to believe otherwise." He didn't expound, didn't offer any further explanation. Perhaps there wasn't any.

But she desperately, desperately, wanted him to have a reason. "If not for the sake of your career, then why? Why is it so important to write about the wedding?"

Please have a reason. Please have a reason.

He scrubbed a hand down his face, looking tense and weary. "I cannot explain the whole of it to you. It's… complicated."

"Then simplify it." Her voice was just shy of begging.

His jaw ticked. "I can't."

She waited, hoping that there was more, but he only stood there, unmoving and immovable.

"Can't or won't?" she whispered.

The answering silence told her all she needed to know.

***

A tear had escaped from her filling caramel eyes, but she scrubbed it away fiercely. Even with puffy eyes, she was beautiful.

And she despised him.

Thomas had never intended to use Harper, but when he thought back to that day at Point Judith, isn't that exactly what he had done? But she had interpreted his actions in the worst possible way. To her, he was despicable and conniving, the worst sort of intrepid reporter. For that, he could only blame himself.

Yet to have her within arm's reach and not be able to touch her, to have her pleading for an explanation and not be able to give it, to see her looking lost and forlorn and not be able to comfort her—it gutted him. But what had he expected? That he would be able to keep her in the dark for an entire month? Or that she would forgive his betrayal without knowing the reasons behind it?

To tell her everything, though, the real reason why he had to write about the wedding for Luther, the things he had to atone for, the things he and his father had done—it was unthinkable. If he thought her censure stung now, how much worse would it feel if she knew all that he was guilty of?

"I wish I could," he said stiffly.

"Then do! It's just us, Thomas. There's no one else here to hear it, and in spite of my rampant naïveté, you can trust my discretion in keeping quiet about whatever reasons you have to justify your actions."

The casual derision she directed at herself tore at him.

"Don't do that. You aren't naive—the fault, all the fault, lies with me. And it's better that you don't know the reason why I need to write about Adeline's wedding."

"You know, I've heard quite a bit of that in the last month. My father and grandmother agreed that it's *better* for me to give up my home and who I am to have a coming-out as a New York debutante. You tell me it's *better* for me that I don't know why you've used me to insinuate yourself into the O'Malleys to profit off of Adeline's wedding day. Thank goodness everyone knows so much *better* than I do."

Her tears began to fall in earnest, and something in his chest roared and lurched. Because seeing her fall apart in front of him was like taking a mallet to his own heart.

And *he* was the reason. Because in her eyes, he was a consummate liar. Selfish, reckless.

Beyond redemption.

Not that he hadn't known it before.

But *she* hadn't.

The tears kept falling. It was excruciating.

He didn't try to justify himself. Thomas had never considered himself an affectionate man, but at that moment, the urge to comfort and hold her was almost overwhelming.

But he resisted. He didn't pull her into his chest and stroke her hair. He didn't kiss the top of her head and tell her everything would be fine.

He had been wrong earlier; he *was* a brute.

She shook her head, angrily swatting the tears from her face. "I can't do this anymore, Thomas. I can't be here on Block Island, here with you, and pretend that we're, that's everything is… I can't."

Of course she couldn't. He was anathema to her, now that she knew who he really was.

"Do you wish to tell the O'Malleys the truth?" he asked tightly.

"Even if I did, we can't." She wilted at the words, miserable. "I gave Rose my word that we would finish the charade, and I can't imagine what the confession would do to Adeline, the pallor it would cast on her wedding. We have to make it through the wedding, but I cannot stomach the deceit. I need to…." She trailed off, biting her lip.

"What do you need?" His voice was cold, inflectionless. It had to be so; how else could he keep himself from folding her into his arms?

But he felt strangely disembodied from his own voice. As if he was watching the scene play out from above, rather than living through it. As if it wasn't his own heart that was breaking.

"I need to tell someone. That we're not the real Vivienne and Neville Jones."

He nodded once, careful to keep his face expressionless.

"Maybe Aunt Bess? She wouldn't tell Adeline, not if I asked her not to, and at least she would know the truth. With her, at least, I want to be honest. She has been so unfailingly kind to me, so much kinder than I deserve." Absently she fumbled with the ring on her hand. The one he hadn't given her. He could *never* give her a ring. "You… you would let me?"

Let her? Did she think he was such a monster that he would try to stop her?

"You don't need my permission to tell anyone anything. But if the deception of the charade has become too much for you, and if it's important to you, then you should tell her."

She let out a shuddering breath, wrapping her arms around herself. "And… you'll agree not to write the article? About Adeline's wedding?"

At his hesitation, her face crumbled.

"But you can't. Not now that you've met them! Adeline just wants to get married in peace. What bride would want her wedding day to become a public spectacle, open to critics and gossips?"

"My situation with my editor at the newspaper is… complicated."

"*Complicated*. There's that word again. Do you think so little of my intelligence that you think I cannot understand?"

"That isn't what I meant, and for pity's sake, will you stop belittling yourself?"

"Belittling *myself*? Has it occurred to you that if I am feeling belittled in this conversation, perhaps *I* am not the cause?"

"I'm not trying to belittle you."

"Then stop telling me that things are too complicated for me to understand! I just want the truth, Thomas. Why does this article matter so much to you? If it's not about your career, what is it about?"

He wanted to tell her. He ached to unburden himself to her. About his father and the accident, the exposé he wrote about the children working in mills, Luther's ultimatum about covering the wedding. But the shame of it all was a fortress around him, erected high to keep others at bay, built strong to ensure no one ever saw the hideous truth about his past.

If there was anyone in the world he would spare the knowledge of his past, it was Harper.

"It isn't important."

"Isn't important?" Her eyes flitted between pain and disbelief, and for a moment, she stared at him. "If you truly believe it isn't important, then I think this conversation is finished." She took a shuddering breath. "We'll make it through the wedding as planned, with as little contact between us as possible. We will converse when other people are around and it's expected of us, but otherwise, I would appreciate it if you kept your distance. I think it would be easier—*better*—for the both of us."

Each word landed like an anvil.

He clenched his jaw, absorbing her anger, accepting it as his due. "If that's what you want."

Her lower lip trembled. "It is."

It took all the strength he had not to let her see the effect her words had on him. "Very well. Let me assure you, though, that should you need anything for the remainder of our charade, anything at all, you may still depend on me."

She turned her face from him, not acknowledging his words.

"I'll leave you, then. Good night." He made to leave, but as his hand gripped the doorknob her voice stopped him.

"Where are you going?"

He glanced at her over his shoulder. "I agreed to as little contact as possible, Miss Whitley. Our living arrangements have been suspect from the beginning of this charade. I'm sure I can find accommodation elsewhere."

She looked less sure of herself. "Well, yes, but I hadn't meant to evict you from our room—it's yours as much as it is mine. I..."

Thomas allowed himself one last look at her—he took in her slight frame, the hair cascading down her shoulder, her hazel eyes reflecting the lamplight—then set his face to the door. "No, you were quite right. It would be better for the both of us to keep our distance. Good night, Miss Whitley."

And then he left her.

Chapter 22

Harper hesitated in the hallway, her knuckles hovering over the door to Bess's room.

She could do this.

She *could* do this.

She *had* to do this.

After her fight with Thomas, she had spent the remainder of the night tossing in bed, alternately weeping and punching her pillow until the first slivers of lavender dawn crept through the window.

During their argument, she had the incongruous urge to pound his chest in rage or wrap her arms around his neck and beg to be held. After a night of reflecting on all that had happened, she could make no more sense of Thomas and his motives. When she finally crawled out of bed that morning, she felt as unrested and miserable as she had the night before.

She also looked an absolute fright, but she was beyond vanity now. Rather than waiting for Rose to check on her or ringing the bell to the servants' quarters, Harper had put on her own simple traveling dress from the day she arrived, tucking her hair in a half-hearted chignon. The less she resembled Vivienne during this conversation, the easier it would be. Not that anything could truly make it easier.

With a deep breath, she rallied her courage, shut her eyes, and knocked on Bess's door.

Bess's voice floated back to her from the other side. "Come in!"

Arranging her face into a facsimile of a smile, Harper obeyed and stepped into the room. "Good morning," she said, walking to the bed and kissing Bess's proffered cheek.

The bedroom was larger than the one she and Thomas shared—*used to share,* she amended—and had wide bay windows set against two of the four walls. Sprawling vines curved across the wallpaper, matching the pastel green bedspread that adorned the wide canopied bed. Bess was propped up in the middle of it, a tray set beside her with a porcelain cup of coffee and a variety of pastries, most of them missing at least one bite.

"Come have a coze with me, love. I'm spent from the fireworks last evening—a glamorous affair, wasn't it? So pleased Adeline thought of it—and when your uncle was up and about at seven to get his breakfast, I told him in no uncertain terms that I couldn't be roused from my bed for another hour, at least. Do you need coffee, darling? I can ring for a fresh pot."

"I'm fine, thank you," Harper demurred, settling down where Bess patted the bed beside her. In truth, she was desperate for a cup of coffee, but the sooner she unburdened herself, the better.

"Mm, I completely understand, dear. Coffee doesn't always agree with one in the mornings, does it? But come, have a pastry. These pinwheels have the most delectable strawberry jam in the middle. And the morning bun is simply divine." Harper lifted her hands to decline the tray, but Bess was undaunted. "A muffin, at least, dear. There's blueberry and lemon poppyseed. And a croissant! This one has ham and cheese, but the others are just plain. If those don't suit, I'll just ring down to the kitchen and get you a fresh batch of confections, yes?"

She was already reaching for the bell when Harper found her voice.

"Truly, I'm not hungry. Please don't trouble anyone on my account." Bess gave her a searching look, but after a moment it turned to sympathy.

"You've no appetite this early, I suppose. Poor darling. Have you been suffering terribly?"

Heavens, did she look as bad as all that? A cursory glance in the mirror beside the bed told her that *yes, yes she did*, but she didn't want Bess's sympathy, nor did she deserve it.

"No, nothing so terrible. Just a sleepless night."

Bess clicked her tongue. "You poor dear. I've heard that can happen as well."

Harper shook her head, eager to have her confession over and done with. "Really, I'm quite fine. It's only that, there's something I need to tell you." She paused, looking down at the bed and running her hands across the soft linen.

Bess, observing her closely, reached out to rest her hand on Harper's arm. "It's all right, child. Just tell me, hm?"

Harper nodded, but when she opened her mouth to confess, her words lodged in her throat, caught on the sudden lump. She shook her head roughly to shake away the well of tears gathering behind her eyes.

Exhaustion had rendered her weepy, but it wasn't just that. The fight with Thomas and the guilt of her own deceit made her feel hollow with shame and misery, and before she could master her emotions, the floodgates opened behind her eyes and Bess was gathering her in her arms, smoothing her hair back from her face and shushing her as if she was a small child.

Harper knew that when she made her confession Bess would likely be throwing her out of the room, not stroking her back and consoling her, and the realization made her cry even harder.

Before she came to Block Island, she had considered herself too old to be held or coddled or consoled in such a way, and it wasn't until this exact moment that she understood that no matter how old a woman is, she will always need someone to hold her while she cries. Every woman of every age needs someone to *mother* her.

It had been so very, very long since anyone had mothered her.

When she could finally speak again, she pulled back from Bess, prepared to tell her all.

But when she saw the unrestrained affection on Bess's face, she stopped short.

It proved to be a crucial mistake.

"Dearest, does whatever you need to tell me have something to do with your sleepless night?"

Harper swiped under her eyes and nodded. "But before I say more, please know how sorry I am to have kept you in the dark until now. I never meant to hurt you."

"Of course you didn't, darling," she soothed. "And you needn't look so worried, dear. I suspect I know what you're about to say."

Harper's puffy wet eyes snapped to Bess. "You do?" She couldn't know, could she? Harper and Thomas had been so careful. She had assumed Wesley was the only one who was suspicious of their charade. And Rose, of course, but she never would have told.

"Well, I understand that you and your beau wanted the matter to remain private, but your uncle and cousins will confirm that I suspected from the day we ran into one another at the ferry. I knew from the moment I set eyes on you that something was different."

"From the first day!" Surely Bess hadn't known she was an imposter from the first day, had she? And if she had, why continue the ruse? Why continue treating her like her own niece? Then the rest of her statement sank in. "Hugh and the cousins know too!?"

Bess laughed. Laughed! As if the situation was all a grand lark. *I'm a charlatan—hah! And a con-woman—how droll! I've become a compulsive liar—how uproariously amusing!*

"Oh yes. Most of us do, actually."

"Most of us?" Harper squeaked. She gripped the blankets to steady herself.

"Adeline, Rhys, Hugh, Claire and Claudia, Dr. Grayson, of course."

"The doctor!"

"Why, yes. He was the first to realize it. After myself, naturally."

Harper struggled to make sense of Bess's words. They had *all* known that she and Thomas were imposters? And played along? For goodness sake, why? Perhaps the O'Malleys wanted to conceal the scandal from their soon-to-be in-laws? Seen in that light, it made sense. But still…

"But… but aren't you angry with us?"

"Angry? Why would we be? Surely the pair of you are entitled to your privacy."

Harper frowned, shaking her head. The confession was not progressing at all as she expected. "Be that as it may, our prevarication affected all of you. I expected you would be ready to turn us out on our ears."

"Oh child, such a vivid imagination! We'll do nothing of the sort. And I wouldn't call it prevarication."

"You wouldn't?"

Bess was certainly taking the news better than Harper expected. All things considered, her nonchalance was rather shocking, actually. But the woman heaved a contented sigh, then took Harper's hand and met her gaze squarely. "My darling, believe me when I say that none of us are upset." Harper's face was incredulous, and Bess laughed back at her. "You and Neville chose not to tell us about the pregnancy right away, and there's nothing wrong with that, my love. Keeping a matter private is not at all the same as prevaricating, you know. And we're all just thrilled to bits about the baby!"

The baby?!

Harper gaped at her. During this whole conversation, Bess had assumed that Harper was about to tell her she was *pregnant*?

But as she thought back on their exchange, this time from Bess's perspective, her assumption made a strange sort of sense. All things considered, it was somewhat horrifying, but not at all outside the realm of reason. It also explained the family's near-fanatical commitment to feeding her. She touched her stomach absently.

"Baby." Harper repeated the word in dull amazement.

But Aunt Bess neither heard nor noticed Harper's reaction, as her own loudly expressed raptures about the baby quite drowned her out. For a time Harper just sat on the bed, stupefied, allowing Bess to ply her with pastries and wax poetic about the delicate embroidery she had planned for the baby blanket she was making.

Harper dropped her croissant mid-bite. Which was probably a good thing, as it was already her fourth in as many minutes. Or possibly her fifth? Time was revolving around her in erratic arcs, and sleep deprivation and emotional exhaustion had her head feeling feather-light.

"You've already begun making a blanket? For the baby?"

"Yes, dear. As I was just saying, the rose border will take me eons, and if I'm to make a christening gown to match, I need to press my nose to the grindstone. Tell me again, when did you say the baby is due?"

"I didn't," she said faintly.

"You know, being away from home for an entire month is rather risky at this stage, isn't it? Will you reconsider having Dr. Grayson examine you?"

Examine her? To check on the baby who was definitely not growing in her womb? Harper thought back to her first night on the island, on Bess's insistence that she meet the good doctor.

Sweet heavens. She had made a grave misstep in this confession.

Enough. Her lies had gone on for long enough. She needed to tell Bess who she was, and she was going to do it right now.

Which would have been a more feasible plan if Bess took more than half a shallow breath between thoughts.

"Oh, my child, I'm just so ecstatic to be adding to the family!"

And then, to Harper's horror, Bess began weeping tears of joy over her, and in their unexpected reversal of roles, Harper found herself rubbing the woman's back in comfort.

Which was unacceptable. She came here to confess the truth. But as her shoulder and collarbone were steadily soaked in Bess's tears, there was no way she could own up to her perfidy.

Because when Bess looked at her and told her she was happy about adding to the family, it felt like she was talking about *her*. Not Vivienne's baby, but *Harper*.

And while she had never wanted for love as a child, since meeting the O'Malleys and being grafted into their clan, she found something she never realized she was missing. The affection and chaos of a large family who loved and teased with abandon.

And if the truth would only affect her, Harper might have found the strength to tell her everything. But she understood then how it would crush Bess. How could she crush this lovely, affectionate, tender-hearted woman who was already making a baby blanket for her unborn (and non-existent) baby?

The icing on the cake came with another knock on the door. Adeline peeked her head in the door and, taking in the tableau before her, shouted with delight, *"you've told her about the baby!"* A heartbeat later Adeline was calling down the hall. *"Girls! She's announced the baby!"* And with great whoops and shrieks Claire and Claudia bounded into the room, proclaiming their unparalleled euphoria at becoming aunts.

For the next hour, Harper endured the singular experience of having four sets of hands touch her stomach in hopes of feeling a kick or flutter from the baby in her (empty) womb.

And so instead of clearing her conscience that morning, Harper compounded her guilt, not only by deepening the charade but by spreading a rumor about the real Vivienne Jones, whose current state of motherhood (or lack thereof) Harper knew nothing about.

Only when she was on her way back to her own room did it occur to her that she would have to tell Thomas about the unexpected development in their charade.

The thought of talking to him at all, even being *near* him, made her dizzy with anxiety.

But their first meeting after the fight was bound to be awkward no matter what; she might as well find him quickly and get it over with.

After she had gone back to her room to change and had finally tracked Thomas down, he could not have been in a less ideal location.

The picnic blankets from the fireworks had been cleared from the River House lawn, and in their place were improvised tennis courts. The men were spread out on the courts with rackets in hand, and lawn chairs had been set out for the women along the edges.

Unfortunately, it looked like every single wedding guest and staff member was already present. Which meant that Harper had to tell

Thomas about their baby before someone else mentioned it to him.

She needed to get Thomas somewhere private. *Quickly.*

She saw Aunt Bess on a lawn chair on the grass, beckoning her husband towards her and speaking animatedly. Harper couldn't hear their conversation, but based on the level of enthusiasm their exchange was reaching, she could hazard a guess.

She was already at the bottom steps of the River House, but nearly broke into a run when she saw Uncle Hugh making a beeline towards Thomas. His stride was at once determined and jovial—the kind of stride a man has when he's about to congratulate another man on his impending fatherhood.

No, no, no, no.

Harper moved as quickly as her corset would allow, but her legs were tangling in her petticoats, and an errant breeze sent her straw bonnet careening across her face.

She swiped it back with a careless tug, then kicked her legs free of the cumbersome petticoats.

Thomas saw her from the corner of his eye. His face was pure granite, hard and impenetrable.

Harper was going to strangle whoever invented the corset. Was it the French? Might be a bit much to strangle an entire nation. She was not usually so unilaterally violent. But honestly. To take the sharp bones of whales and fashion them into a tiny prison for ribs and waists and childbearing hips?

The French had it coming.

Hugh reached Thomas, then clapped him on the back affectionately.

"Congratulations," his lips said. Harper could see the words forming, but didn't hear them. The blood roaring in her ears was too loud to admit sound.

Rhys approached next. *"Couldn't be happier for you."*

Who knew Harper had such a knack for lip-reading? The revelation would have been more welcome if she wasn't watching all of her best intentions implode in spectacular fashion.

She could only see Thomas's profile—the set jaw, the tousled brown hair blowing over his temple—but she knew when he tensed, could feel it as if it were her own body stiffening, tightening, drawing into itself.

It was the doctor who finally delivered the news. *"You'll be a wonderful father,"* his lips said.

Thomas's eyes connected with hers so quickly that it was as if he knew exactly where she was on the grass, as if they were the only two people in the universe and his eyes could always, only, inevitably connect with hers. The thought left her breathless.

Or that might have been the corset.

The French could be so galling.

With so many people on the lawn with them, the abrupt meeting of their gazes shouldn't have felt intimate. But something happened in that moment—the connection was a bolt of lightning slamming straight against her chest, a shocking jolt of energy and animation and sheer life matter that had the power to re-animate the lifeless lump hidden behind her ribs.

Did he know, the effect the contact was having on her? Did he feel it too?

She suspected so, because just as she came abreast of him, she watched the stone mask slip right off his face and shatter.

Chapter 23

Thomas stood stock still, resisting the urge to adjust his collar or run his hands through his hair. Everyone was congratulating him, talking to him, slapping him on the back. There were too many faces, too many voices.

Right now, there was only one face he wanted to see and one voice he wanted to hear.

He wanted to clap his hands and stop time, make everyone else freeze in motion while he turned to Harper and asked her to explain how he had gone from persona non grata to the father of her child in less than twelve hours.

He had no doubt that she knew what was going on—he recognized the guilt and chagrin on her face as she crossed the lawn to come beside him, felt her standing beside him with the same tension and stillness that was ruling his own limbs.

Had she spoken to Bess already? And if she had, how in the world had Bess come away from the conversation with the understanding that there was a *baby*? That would be the first question he asked Harper when they disentangled themselves from the growing crowd of misinformed well-wishers.

The crowd dispersed of its own accord when Dr. Grayson gently but firmly reminded them of the need to begin the lawn tennis tournament before the day grew too warm. Thomas nodded his thanks to the doctor, and Grayson inclined his head with an understanding smile. The doctor was a good sort, Thomas decided. But so help him, if the man made one more offer to *examine* Harper at Bess's behest, he was going to launch the tennis ball straight at his cranium.

Apparently, Thomas was still on edge from the fight last night.

He had roamed the River House until the wee hours of the morning, then collapsed in a spare bed in the servants' quarters. When an alarmed butler woke him up at the crack of dawn, he fumbled out an excuse that he had inadvertently been locked out of his room but was unwilling to wake anyone at such a late hour. The shocked butler accepted his story, being too well-mannered to ask further questions.

And, on edge or not, Thomas would not have the opportunity to launch a ball at Grayson's cranium, since the two were paired together for the doubles tennis tournament. Their first match was against Wesley and Lyle, which provided a much more appropriate, not to mention satisfying, outlet for his mounting frustration.

He hit the ball with such force and frequency that after a particularly grueling volley, Lyle cried out in indignation that it was a doubles tournament, after all, and to let the good doctor hit the ball once in a while. Wesley eyed him speculatively but made no comment.

Thomas, only slightly abashed and feeling the weight of Harper's gaze on him from the sidelines, reluctantly returned half of their side to Grayson but continued to hit with enough force to bloody noses and bring down a grown man, which is how that particular match ended.

"Ee oke mine nome!" Lyle cried, kneeling on the ground and cradling his nose as blood dripped down onto the immaculate green lawn.

Dr. Grayson knelt down beside him, prying Lyle's hands away and inserting his own handkerchief into the crimson fount.

"I'm not sure it's broken, but we'll have to stop the bleeding before I'm able to verify."

Thomas, though not at all contrite, sacrificed his own handkerchief to the cause, mumbling a soft apology to Lyle. He had been [mostly] joking about hitting anyone in the cranium and was genuinely dismayed to have spilled so much blood.

Their lawn *was*, after all, immaculate.

After Dr. Grayson escorted a still moaning Lyle off the lawn, Uncle Hugh tactfully suggested that perhaps Thomas needed a break after such a *rousing* match. Thomas, having already lost his tennis partner and quite possibly his mind, readily agreed. As he walked off the lawn, he caught Harper's eye. Since the exertion of the match had taken the bite off of his frustration, he decided it was time to have a frank conversation with her about her *confession* with Aunt Bess.

She was sitting still and tense in a lawn chair between Claire and Claudia, no doubt alarmed by his *rousing* tennis match.

"I believe I've had enough tennis for today. Will you walk with me?" His voice was measured, but she must have heard the steel in it, quickly falling into step with him after an apologetic smile at the cousins.

They walked side by side, inches apart but not touching. He didn't offer his arm, and she didn't move to take it. He could feel her trepidation but did nothing to assuage it. If she was uneasy, it was her own fault.

Last night, he had let her rage at him, acknowledging the truth in every accusation and accepting her need to confess to Bess and her desire to be away from him. Her reasons were good and her sense of betrayal was justified. So then why, for goodness sake *why*, had she told everyone that she was pregnant?

It felt like a grotesque recapitulation of the *first* time he had assumed she was pregnant and their ensuing argument.

It was torture enough, having to pretend that this beautiful, funny, gentle woman was his wife, knowing that she despised him, but to have to pretend to be the father of her child? To stand there and feign happiness while people congratulated him on becoming a father, on starting a family?

It was nothing short of agony.

With rapid, clipped steps he led them to the River House and up the stairs. When he continued ascending the stairs beyond their floor, Harper eyed him nervously.

"You've missed our room."

"It isn't *our* room." His voice was tight, sharp. The tip of a needle.

Harper clutched her skirts in her fists. "Right. Yes." When he neither slowed his steps nor explained himself, she spoke again. "Where are we going?"

"You'll see." He knew he was being brusque, but he couldn't bring himself to sympathize with her obvious distress.

He had held his temper in check the night before, kept his composure even when it hung by the thinnest thread, but he could feel himself unraveling now. She had tugged on the thread and it had torn him down the middle, ripping stitch after stitch until whatever shape his composure had once taken was unrecognizable, leaving only the barest hints of fabric and color and string.

By the time they reached the top of the steps, she was out of breath. He opened the door at the end of the dim staircase and sunlight flooded over them. Her caramel eyes flashed vibrant jade in the light, and he forced himself to look forward, holding the door open and extending his arm. "After you."

The doorway led out to a short ladder, and after a moment's hesitation, she climbed it. He waited until he heard her gasp before following her and stepping out onto the cupola at the top of the River House.

The highest point of the River House had one of the most spectacular views on the island—it was a panorama of sapphire ocean, the New Harbor and its cacophony of ships and schooners, the rise and fall of green fertile hills on one side and imposing gray cliffs on the other.

Harper stepped out towards the railing, shielding her eyes from the sun and turning in a circle. Her unease momentarily forgotten, she leaned towards the view. "It's beautiful up here," she breathed.

"I'm glad it suits you," he grunted, startling her out of her reverie.

She flushed scarlet from her cheeks to where her throat met the scalloped collar of her dress. An unexpected flame of remorse shot through him—he didn't need to be a brute. And the view *was* beautiful—he had inadvertently wandered out here the first week of their stay, and it had quickly become his haven.

If things had been different, if he was just an ordinary man spending time with an ordinary woman, he would have brought her here just to watch her reaction, to marvel at the wonder and quiet awe in her hazel eyes. Instead, he had brought her here because they could not afford any witnesses to this discussion, and the cupola was the most secluded place he could bring her without breaking all bounds of propriety.

Not that they had many bounds left to break.

With difficulty, he steadied his breathing.

"I gather you've had an… eventful morning." There, that was nice, wasn't it? Far nicer than *why did you tell me to leave you alone and then tell the entire population of the River House that we're having a baby!?*

See? Nice.

"Yes, I have. Much more eventful than I was expecting." She was still wringing her skirts, hard enough that her knuckles were white.

A heron flew overhead, squawking.

"Would you care to elaborate?"

He heard her mutter *"not really,"* but then she lifted her chin to face him. "When I went to confess to Aunt Bess this morning, there was a bit of a misunderstanding."

"A misunderstanding," he drawled.

She bit her lip, and a fresh flood of remorse shot through his veins. "Why don't you start from the beginning?"

She did, and by the time she finished her explanation he had to make a conscious effort not to let his jaw drop down from his face. It was just outrageous enough to be believable. And it certainly explained her abundant portions at mealtime.

But still.

"So you just left the room? With all of them believing that your big confession was a *pregnancy*?"

She squared her shoulders. "Yes, Mr. Montgomery, I did. I know it was foolish and cowardly and I did it anyway. There. Are you pleased that I've admitted it? My only defense for my actions was that I wanted to spare people who I have come to care about the pain of the truth. Can you understand that?"

His head reared back, stunned. "Can I *understand* that? Can *I*? Miss Whitley, after last night you ought to know that I understand better than anyone the difficulty and misunderstanding inherent in withholding the truth from someone when you know that truth will cause them pain."

His barb hit the mark. "Is that what you were doing last night? Withholding the truth because it would cause me *pain*? This is not the same situation, Thomas."

"Isn't it? How is you intentionally keeping the truth from Bess any different from me keeping something from you? I'm not telling you why I have to write the article on Adeline's wedding because you don't truly need to know, and if you did know it would cause you pain. Please, enlighten me. The situations are nearly identical!" He felt his voice and temper rising but felt powerless to rein in either.

"They're different." Her eyes flashed, and he could feel her temper rising to match his.

"How? How could they possibly be different?"

"It's different because I never lied to *you*!"

The silence stretched between them.

Taut, tense. Fairly writhing.

She broke it with a whisper.

"I never lied to *you*. You don't think I'm ashamed, lying to everyone here, lying to my own father and grandmother? What would my father think of me, if he could see me now? He'd be so ashamed." She wrapped her arms around her waist, shaking her head. "I entered into this charade with my eyes wide open, from the day we sat on that bench in Point Judith. I cannot condemn you for deceit when I am just as guilty.

"The difference is that you always had all of me, the whole truth of why I wanted to come to Block Island, my family and my history. But…" She blew out a breath, frustrated. "Sometimes people lie for good reasons, and I understand that. You might have a good reason for lying to everyone here, to the O'Malleys and everyone else we've interacted with. Fine. Lie to the whole world if you must, Thomas—" her arms stretched wide—"but not to me. *Never* to me."

You've always had all of me.

The words both elated and crushed him.

He had had all of her. And lost all of her.

A cloud brushed past the sun, dimming the brilliant jade of her eyes.

"I never meant to lie to you," he said stiffly.

"Then why are you? And please, don't tell me it's complicated. Just tell me the reason." Her eyes were begging him, and he knew what that vulnerability must have cost her after their fight the night before.

But he could not give her what she wanted. He shook his head, turning back towards the water and resting his elbows on the railing.

She nearly crumpled beside him, and he felt the space in his chest do the same.

The frustration he had felt with her a moment ago vanished, yielding to an instinctive and nearly overpowering desire to comfort her, to hold her.

His arms stayed rooted on the railing.

"He wouldn't be ashamed of you." He felt her eyes on his back. "Your father," he clarified.

"What makes you say that? You've never met him."

"No, but I've met you. There's not a father in the world who would be ashamed of raising a daughter like you. And based on everything you've told me about him, that man loves you down to his bones. I'm not sure that he could be anything but proud of you, no matter what you do."

She moved and rested her arms on the railing beside his. *Strawberries and spring rain,* he noted absently.

"Thank you for saying that," she said softly. "I'm not sure it's true, but it's kind all the same."

Silence fell again, but this time it felt different. Like a tentative peace offering.

"I truly am sorry that I didn't correct Bess this morning. Everyone was right though. You'll make a good father someday." She looked out at the water, unaware of the effect her words had on him.

Thomas was *very* aware of it—the familiar spasm of fury and shame. His words snapped out before he could stop them. "I don't plan on being a father."

From the corner of his eye, he saw her turn to look at him. "You don't? Not… not ever?"

"No."

"Oh." She was quiet for a moment, but he could feel her working up to a question. "You don't like children, then?"

"I don't mind children," he said carefully.

"But surely someday, when you're married, you'll decide you want —"

"I don't plan on marrying, either."

"I see." Her tone indicated that she did not. "Have you always felt this way?" Her voice was tentative, curious. A bit embarrassed.

His jaw clenched, and he glanced at her briefly. "Not always, no."

"Then what made you—"

"My life decisions are not up for discussion right now, Miss Whitley."

The *Miss Whitley* might as well have been a curse word, the way her eyes widened in hurt, then anger.

The sound of their peace offering shattering was nearly audible.

"Yes, of course, Mr. Montgomery." Her voice was clipped. "Well, again, I apologize for my errors in judgment this morning and any further difficulty they may cause you." She stepped back from the railing. "If you'll excuse me, there's a lawn tennis tournament that I'm eager to return to, so the sooner we can work out how to move forward with the charade in light of this little hiccup, the better."

"Little hiccup? You consider the pregnancy a *little* hiccup?" The pregnancy would change everything in their charade—nothing *little* about it. But his own anxiety about maintaining their ruse made his words sharper than he intended, and he regretted them instantly.

He was generally gruff and insensitive, but he was never carelessly cruel.

It was like kicking a puppy. Except the puppy was the most beautiful woman he had ever seen and quite possibly the woman he had fallen in love with.

Her cheeks flamed. "I believe I've already apologized for my mistake, Mr. Montgomery. There's no need to be mean."

There really wasn't. Hadn't he just told himself the same thing moments ago? And hadn't he just told her that any man would be proud to have a daughter like her? What was the matter with him? Why were the thoughts in his head and the words in his mouth and every one of his actions so completely dissonant?

That shift in barometric pressure that he always felt around her was jarring him, setting him off balance. For the first time in a long time, he felt raw, vulnerable.

When he didn't respond, she took another step back from him, clenching her hands against her skirts.

"I beg your pardon, sir. I did not realize that having to pose as the father of my child would be so repulsive to you."

Repulsive? Is that what she was taking away from their conversation? He wanted to bash his head against the railing. There was nothing *repulsive* about pretending to be Harper Whitley's husband, about pretending to love and care for and protect her. There was nothing *repulsive* about pretending that they were bringing a child into the world together.

Repulsive? Never.

The thought was wonder itself.

Pretending to have a life with Harper was the first firefly of summer.

It was orange and purple sunrises and blushing crimson sunsets. The smell of honeysuckle and the sound of rain. Ripe strawberries and climbing purple wisteria. All the grandeur of the mountains and the vastness of the sea. Yellow daffodils in spring and scarlet leaves in autumn.

Repulsive? It was every yearning joy and every promised happiness, but without any of its fulfillment.

Harper would never be his, no matter what this charade was doing to the cavern in his chest.

There would never be a little girl with pigtails running into his arms shouting *daddy.* There would never be a chubby hazel-eyed boy riding on his shoulders. There would never be Harper's hand in his with a ring—a ring that *he* gave her—on her finger. And until that exact moment, he hadn't realized how much he wanted all of it.

Did she not understand that?

The mingled hurt and confusion in her face told him that she didn't. He ran his hands through his hair, feeling so untethered and broken that he couldn't think straight.

Was she *trying* to bring him to his knees?

He hadn't meant to say those last words out loud.

With a flood of self-loathing, he watched her face crumble and her eyes fill.

"Miss Whitley, I apologize, that was uncalled for." He straightened and faced her, reaching for her.

She ignored him, already adjusting her skirts to climb down from the cupola.

"Please, I only meant—"

"I understood perfectly what you meant, Mr. Montgomery." No, she truly didn't. "As much as possible, I will remain in my room from now on and feign illness. No one would question that. Pregnant women feel unwell all the time."

"You don't need to do that." He was climbing down the ladder now, skipping the last rung to catch up with her.

"The only one who might give me trouble is Dr. Grayson." She was flying down the stairs at an alarming pace, and he struggled to keep up with her.

"Dr. Grayson will not be touching you with a ten-foot pole. Slow down, will you? You'll fall down the stairs."

"I'm fine." Her foot slipped on her skirts, but she righted herself and hiked them up with a violent tug.

"You're not fine, you're upset. Let me explain myself. Would you *please* slow down?"

She rounded the staircase, deliberately ignoring him.

"Harper." Even with his long legs and her short ones, she was difficult to catch.

"Don't call me—"

Her words broke off as her feet slipped out from under her, her body tilting back in a terrifying arc towards the stairs. For one unbearable second, he saw her fall backward, could imagine what the sound would be when the back of her head cracked against the wooden steps.

He leaped down half a dozen steps to get to her, catching her in his arms an inch before his worst imaginings were realized.

She laid still in his arms, wide eyes locked with his, their chests heaving in synchronized, rapid breaths.

Suddenly he wondered if he actually *had* clapped his hands and frozen time. The whole world was still, and he saw only her. Nothing existed outside of the two of them—the world would begin and end at this precise interval in time. Hazel eyes, brown curls. The feeling of silk under one hand and the velvet texture of her hair under the other.

Wonder itself.

They may have stayed like that for one minute or ten, for one heartbeat or a thousand. His hold on her was like the dip of a waltz. They were dancing without motion, lost in the soft tug of their locked gazes and the steady beats of their hearts. He was going to stay here forever, hold her forever.

There was no wedding and no article and no charade.

Only here and now and her.

But when he blinked, the world crashed and ricocheted into motion. He felt the blast of the impact straight against his ribs.

The world outside *did* exist—they were in a dim stairwell—and she was shoving against his chest, grappling to get free.

Instantly he righted and released her, and she stepped as far back from him as the staircase would allow.

"Are you all right?" His voice was like gravel.

"I'm grand. Never better." Her words were livid and caustic. She pushed back errant curls with rough, quick movements. "If you'll excuse me, I think I'll retire to my room for the day."

"You're not returning to the tournament?"

"I am not. I trust you're capable of making my excuses for me. No need for anything elaborate. I would hate to *bring you to your knees*."

He dragged his hand down his face. She was already walking down the stairs again.

"Please, you misunderstood me. I only meant that—"

"Good day. " She didn't even turn her head.

"Just one moment—"

"I'll be in my room, *dear*."

The acerbic *dear* hit him straight in the solar plexus.

What had he done?

He studied her retreating form with aching remorse.

"I'll see you soon, then." His voice carried enough in the stairwell that she heard him even from a flight away.

He knew that because he heard hers float back up to him.

"I should hope not."

Chapter 24

Harper wasn't sure she was going to survive the next seven days.

Rose knew that she and Thomas had fought, but Harper hadn't shared the details with her. She was convinced Rose might inflict bodily harm on him if she knew he was a journalist. When Harper told her that she planned to keep to her room as much as possible, feigning fatigue from pregnancy, and that Thomas was no longer using the room, Rose had been both curious and concerned. But once Harper had assured her that the charade would remain intact, the maid had accepted the explanation without further questions.

Rose's unquestioning acceptance of the new status quo was the only spot of relief Harper had known.

The last week had been miserable—whenever her "pregnancy symptoms" abated enough for her to join the other wedding guests, Thomas had treated her with steady solicitude; she was confident that only *she* could see the cool detachment with which he performed his husbandly attentions. In return, she had smiled at him with unyielding benevolence, and she was equally confident that only *he* could see how much the act strained her.

She hated that even when she was angry with him, she was still so in tune with him. Any time they were in the room, she could sense where he was standing, could pick his voice out of a crowd, could feel his eyes on her even when her back was turned. She had assumed that with all of the tension between them, with all the weight of unspoken disappointment and hurt, she would have been able to sever the connection between them, the one responsible for drawing her towards those warm brown eyes even when she was livid with him.

But she couldn't.

Instead of breaking the thread that pulled them together, the strain in their relationship somehow made it heavier, stronger. Since the curtain had come up on their newest act of lovestruck parents-to-be, that tight thread had become an iron band between them.

Every time their eyes met she felt a lurch in the left side of her chest. Every time she looped her arm through his without ever actually touching him, her traitorous heart would turn hummingbird, threatening to burst out of her and lift her from the ground. Every forced smile and held gaze between them for the sake of the O'Malley clan held something deeper, something unexpected—it was a simmering pot that had been turned up too high, and the boiling contents were beginning to spill out over the top.

It was unbearable, the weight of whatever it was between them, but there was no resolving it. Even if they had both wanted to, there wasn't time.

There was only one week before the wedding, and for the first time since their charade began, Harper let her mind wander to life after the wedding. She would turn up on her grandmother's doorstep, a full month late, and though she had sent a weekly letter to her father assuring him that she was well and to her grandmother assuring her that her delay to New York was only temporary, she would have quite a bit of prevaricating to do regarding her unexpected delay. After that the whirlwind would begin—her grandmother had explained the need for a new wardrobe befitting a Verbeek, then there would be the introductions and events and balls, the gradual cleansing of everything she had been until this point in her life.

All traces of the Rhode Island berry farmer's daughter would be erased, replaced with the prototype of a prim Knickerbocker debutante. She would be molded into the exact thing that her own mother had repudiated when she chose to marry her father. Harper Whitley would cease to exist—by the time her Grandmother was done with her, she would be known only as the long-lost Verbeek granddaughter.

And when she reminded herself that after this week, she would never see Thomas Montgomery again, the hummingbird in her chest turned to stone.

Because angry or not, leaving Thomas after their month together on Block Island would be like turning her back on the sunrise. It would feel like willfully walking away from the blush-dusted promises of a perfect dawn and newborn hope. She wanted to hate him. She thought she might despise him. But even in the midst of that, she felt like she had given something of herself to him, and she didn't know how to get it back.

She was terrified that it was her heart.

He sat beside her now, rigid and straight-backed in his chair. There were only inches between their legs, but they both avoided the space as if it contained the plague. Always close, but never touching. Always smiling, but never happy. Since their fight and the misunderstanding with Bess, this was their new normal, and every moment of it was like chewing glass.

A ripple of applause washed through the room as Claire and Claudia stood up from behind the piano. Tonight's entertainment was an impromptu soirée after dinner, and footmen had lined up chairs in front of the piano in the music room. The sisters were the first to volunteer to play, but already the evening seemed interminable.

Time with Thomas was like that now.

So when Uncle Hugh remarked that he hadn't heard Adeline sing in ages and Bess pointed out that Adeline and Wesley had stepped out on the veranda, Harper happily volunteered to fetch her cousin.

She and Thomas were sitting in the middle of the row, so she carefully made her apologies as she shimmied in front of the other guests and out of the room.

She slipped out the French doors onto the veranda, letting the polite smile slide off her face. The music room was stuffy with all the bodies huddled together, and the cooler night air was a balm to her fractured nerves and flushed cheeks.

Once she was around the corner and out of view from the River House's windows, she let herself fall back against the hotel's tidy white siding. She meant to take advantage of the reprieve, to rest there a moment with her eyes closed, until her breathing was steady and she found the energy to continue playing the part of Vivienne Jones, adoring wife and mother-to-be.

But a soft cry interrupted her just as she closed her eyes. A cry that sounded suspiciously like *"don't."*

Harper jerked herself upright.

"No, *please,* don't." This time the cry came more like a whimper, definitely a woman's.

The porch of the River House wrapped all the way around, with potted plants scattered throughout the east side. The moon hung timidly behind a veneer of clouds, and as she crept towards the voices she could just make out two shapes huddled behind one of the potted plants in the corner, and she realized with a small trickle of panic that the shapes were Adeline and Wesley's, and the soft pleas were coming from her.

"Come now, darling, we're as good as married already, aren't we?" Wesley's voice was looser than usual, not quite slurred, but not quite sober, either.

"Wesley, please, no. Let's wait, all right? It's only another week." Adeline's voice was muffled now, and a shift in the dark shapes in front of her gave Harper a fair idea of just what was muffling her.

Wesley let out a small growl. "I have been more than patient."

Harper's mortification on stumbling upon such a scene was matched only by the fury welling up in her. The only reason that Harper wasn't already jumping on Wesley's back and wrapping her arms around his neck was that she knew Adeline's mortification would exceed even her own if they were discovered in such a position.

Taking a few steps back, Harper called out in a soft, sing-song voice. "Adeline. Oh Adeline, dearest. Are you out here? We're all dying to have you sing for us."

Wesley let out another growl, and in the silver-laced moonlight, she saw his hulking figure step away from his fiancée. It was just light enough for her to see how disheveled Adeline was—her hair had fallen loose in several places, her dress was stretched and pulled to one side, and her elegant evening gloves had slipped down to her wrists. When Harper saw the way Adeline's hands shook as they smoothed down her elegant sapphire gown, she wished she had gone ahead and throttled the groom.

Harper bit down her umbrage, trying for Adeline's sake to feign ignorance, and stepped in front of the couple.

"Oh! There you are, darling."

"Here I am!" Adeline's voice was too bright, too sharp. Harper tried not to notice.

"Claire and Claudia have just finished a lovely duet, and we were all wondering if you might come back and sing for us?"

"Of course. I'd be happy to sing."

"Lovely. You go on in, Ada," Harper said. "I'll be in in just a moment. This cool air feels wonderful."

"Yes, it's… lovely. The air is lovely." Adeline's voice was breathless, detached.

It made Harper want to cry.

Or simply pummel the man next to her. Unfortunately, she would have needed a step stool to do the act justice, and she hadn't the foresight to have brought one to the veranda.

It was a bitter disappointment.

"I'll be just behind you, darling." Wesley gave Adeline a tight smile, but she didn't see it. Her eyes were on the ground.

"I'll see you in there, then." Adeline swept past them and made for the beckoning light of the music room.

Though Wesley had kept silent so far, Harper could feel the tension radiating off of him.

Good, she thought. She had enough tension radiating through her to match his. She might have been more than a foot shorter and about a hundred pounds less, but outrage was a powerful motivator.

When she could no longer hear Adeline's footsteps, she stepped toward him.

"How dare you. *How dare you* treat her like that. You ought to be ashamed of yourself."

He raised a mocking brow at her. "How dare I, Vivi?" He leaned towards her, his breath awash with liquor. "I don't have anything to be ashamed of."

For a moment, the audacity of his words and her own outrage robbed her of speech.

"Because you didn't see anything," he said cooly. "Just your cousin and her fiancé having a private moment."

"A private moment? You were forcing yourself on her! She told you *no*." She fisted her hands in her dress.

"And I told *you*," he said, grabbing her wrists, "you didn't see *anything*."

Harper realized then what a foolish thing it had been to confront a large, not-quite-sober man in such a dark and secluded place. She tried to reclaim her arms, but his grip was a vise.

"Get your hands off of me—I am a married woman!"

"Then you should understand that certain matters ought to be kept private between a man and a woman." He raised that mocking brow again, and if her arms weren't trapped she would have slapped him.

"What exactly is that supposed to mean?" She forced herself not to struggle in his grip, or to show him how afraid she was. His questions had unnerved her in the past, and she had certainly been afraid of being exposed as a fraud, but she hadn't been afraid that he would actually *hurt* her.

The scene between Wesley and his father flashed again in her mind's eye. His father's rough hold on him. The tumbler of amber liquid.

There were men with tempers, and then there were *drunk* men with tempers. Harper sensed it was the first time she was encountering Wesley as the latter.

She had no idea what this version of Wesley was capable of.

"It means that I know that you and your husband are hiding something. Perhaps you've fooled everyone else, *Vivi dear*, but I am no fool. I know that things are not as they seem between the *happy couple*. And I will not permit you or anyone else to interfere in my marriage."

Harper raised her chin, feigning a confidence she didn't feel. "You're not married yet."

"Funny. I just had a similar conversation with Adeline."

It was *not* funny. It was despicable, vile, unacceptable in every possible way.

His grip had tightened on her wrists, and she had no doubt that if he had a mind to, he could snap them like twigs.

Physically, she was no match for him. Amidst her mounting panic, she recognized the need for another type of defense.

"Tell me about Jacob."

The words tumbled out of her before she could think better of it. It was a gamble, of course, mentioning the name she had overheard between Wesley and his father, but it was the only time she had seen him look vulnerable. She had been curious about the name since that morning, but she also sensed that Jacob, whoever he was, was a weakness for him. Perhaps his only one.

In this moment, it seemed wildly important that Wesley have some weakness.

Something flared in his eyes, and his grip momentarily loosened, but not enough for her to reclaim her wrists.

"I'm surprised Adeline hasn't mentioned him to you before. Since you two are so… *close*." He uttered the last word in undisguised scorn.

Harper was undeterred. "It's been a busy month. You'll remember that I haven't seen my cousin since my marriage. We've had many other things to discuss these last weeks."

Wesley studied her, gauging whether her question warranted an honest response.

Finally, he spoke.

"Jacob is my brother. He's ten."

Brother. He had a brother. She couldn't imagine him with a child. But instinct told her that the current intensity of his gaze, the flash of vulnerability in his confrontation with his father, concealed a genuine concern for his brother, affection even.

The possibility was almost enough to soften her towards him.

"He's away at school right now. Jacob is extremely bright, and he's involved in a mathematics program in Boston for the summer. We thought it best not to interrupt his schooling for the wedding."

Harper thought back to the morning of Adeline's dress fitting. Wesley had been a welder before he worked his way up in O'Malley's company. A common welder did not come from affluence; the finery that his parents wore must have come from Wesley. She suspected the tuition for Jacob's schooling did as well.

His engagement to Adeline had come only after Wesley had won the Navy contract for the oceanliners, and it was widely understood that winning the contract had essentially also won him the hand of the shipbuilder's daughter. It likely also signaled an enormous pay raise, one that would elevate a welder's family into the luxury of the upper class.

Wesley had a great deal to lose if the Navy contract was not finalized, and based on what she had overheard, it was not nearly as secure as Wesley hoped.

It certainly explained the constant presence of a tumbler in his hands in the past weeks. His current agitation as well. When she met his eyes again they were a reptilian green and glinting, and for a heartbeat, she thought he would break her wrists after all.

She looked down at their hands, and for the first time since he had seized hers, he looked down as well. He frowned darkly at their interlocked hands as if he couldn't remember how they had gotten there. In a flash he released her, stepping back hurriedly and scowling at the ground.

He took a breath that was almost steady, and after a moment he smoothed down the elegant folds of his evening jacket and straightened his cuffs. When he met her eyes again, his face was composed. If she didn't know better, she would think he had just spent an uneventful ten minutes enjoying the cool air on the veranda. The quicksilver change was terrifying.

"If you'll excuse me," he said, "Adeline is about to sing, and I wouldn't miss it for the world." And with a derisive bow, he was gone, walking towards the light of the River House.

She collapsed the second he was out of sight.

There were no tears, no sobs, but she was trembling all over, from fear or shock or anger she couldn't say. But she couldn't indulge her feelings now—Adeline and Wesley were both back in the music room, and even if no one else noticed her absence, Thomas would. The last thing she wanted was to be discovered here, curled up with her arms around her legs and chin on her knees, like a child lost in the woods.

So she set her jaw and tugged up her silk evening gloves, just as she had seen Adeline do moments before. She stood and shook out her skirts, and by the time she was back in the music room, no one would have remarked on her appearance anyway. Everyone's attention was on Adeline, standing beside the piano and singing something beautiful and haunting in Gaelic, her flawless face and voice betraying nothing of the scene Harper had just witnessed.

Wesley was in the front row, smiling beatifically at her, the portrait of an adoring fiancé, and she wondered with a sickening lurch how often this had happened. How many times had Wesley said or done something, and Adeline had just shrugged it off, had just schooled her beautiful features to hide all of the discomfort she must be feeling right now?

Thomas must have felt that string that was still between them tug because he turned and looked directly at her. When he saw her face, he froze. The longer he held her gaze, the more thunderous his own became.

He knew.

He knew something was wrong. But because he was in the middle of the row, he couldn't leave his seat now without disrupting the performance. She read the question in his furrowed brow, and she only shook her head, her eyes flashing a warning.

She wouldn't tell him what happened.

She wouldn't let him see her raw and vulnerable and afraid.

Not again.

His brow creased even further, but he turned around, returning his attention to Adeline.

She breathed a sigh of relief, letting herself sink against the wall in the back of the room.

She breathed too soon.

When she had come back into the music room, she had been distracted looking at Wesley and Adeline, and then Thomas, and hadn't even noticed Dr. Grayson standing by the back windows. Apparently, not everyone's eyes had been on Adeline because he approached her with a worried frown.

"Mrs. Jones," he said in a hushed voice, inclining his head.

She could feel her palms sweating through her gloves, but gave a polite smile. "Dr. Grayson. Such a lovely performance, isn't it?"

"Indeed. Are you quite all right?" Though his voice was hushed and considerate, it also held an uncharacteristic hint of impatience.

"Of course. I was just outside enjoying the cool evening." She was still jumpy from her encounter with Wesley, and she felt her face heat from a mix of nerves and the overcrowded room. "It's terribly warm in here, don't you think?"

He didn't agree with her, although he did look more flushed than usual.

"I noticed Miss O'Malley seemed distraught when she came in."

He had? He must have been looking closely because Adeline was doing a fair job of convincing everyone else that she was perfectly fine.

"Oh, well… I believe she was just a bit nervous to sing for everyone."

Grayson looked over at Adeline thoughtfully. "Yes. Miss O'Malley has always been modest."

Harper followed the line of his gaze, then looked again to the doctor.

After a moment he shook his head, as if to clear it. "And you're feeling all right? No more light-headedness?"

Harper grimaced, regretting her comment about the warm room. "Never better."

He considered her, and she felt a knee-jerk fear that he would use the *e* word again. The last thing this night needed was an *examination* of her empty womb.

"Mrs. Jones."

Oh no.

His tone was not at all light or indulgent. It was clinical and direct and meant that she needed immediate evidence of her robust health, along with that of her unborn child.

"I have only been the physician for the O'Malleys for a few years, but believe me when I say that I care for each of its members. Not just their physical needs, but mental and emotional as well. I am here for the well-being of this family, in every possible sense."

Her gaze strayed to Thomas, remembering his words from that day. *Dr. Grayson will not be touching you with a ten-foot pole.* She knew instinctively that he meant it.

"If Adeline is in distress, physically or otherwise, then I ought to be made aware of it."

Though her mind had been wandering, Harper yanked her eyes back to the doctor, stunned by his words. His present concern was not for Harper at all.

The man was usually so reserved, essentially unflappable. But when he said *I ought to be made aware of it,* he didn't look self-contained or reserved or clinical. His gray eyes were intense but inscrutable. At that moment, he looked... flappable.

Adeline was finishing her song now, and both of their eyes moved to her.

"Thank you, Dr. Grayson. I will keep that in mind."

And she meant it. But before she talked to anyone else about what happened on the veranda, she needed to speak to Adeline.

He acknowledged her words with a nod, then silently returned to his seat in the back row.

Adeline's clear voice rang out on a final note, and the room filled with applause.

At the front of the room, Isla O'Malley stepped forward, letting the guests know that they would take a short break from the music for drinks and desserts in the other parlor.

The ensuing shuffle created the perfect distraction for her to slip away to her room. She had lingered long enough for the evening and could hopefully keep to her room for a few more days before making another appearance.

Sensing Thomas's eyes on her, she turned, hoping to escape through the crowd before he reached her. But there were too many people moving towards the door, and in the time it took her to navigate three steps forward, Thomas was already beside her.

"What's wrong?" He bent his head to whisper in her ear, and she could feel the warmth and solidity of him, the sheer steadiness of his presence. She shook her head, scanning the room for an alternative exit, and she would have made for the door to the veranda if he hadn't cupped her elbow in his hand.

Still rattled from her encounter with Wesley, she flinched at his touch, pulling her arms towards her and crossing them across her stomach.

The concern in his face hardened, then, and though he returned his arms to his side, he leaned towards her to speak. "Something happened while you were on the veranda."

It was a statement, not a question. How could he do that, see through her so fully without her ever uttering a word? But this was not the place to talk about what had happened, and Thomas was not the person that she would confide in.

"Nothing you need to concern yourself with."

"If it involves you, then it *is* my concern."

"I'm telling you that it isn't." The stress of the last half-hour made her voice jagged and sharp.

"But Dr. Grayson, it was his concern?"

Her head jerked back in surprise. "Dr. Grayson? What does he have to do with anything?"

"That's exactly what I would like to know. You didn't seem to have any problem sharing your concerns with *him*."

"What are you talking about? Were you *watching* me?"

"I didn't need to watch you. Your voices carried well enough across the room while Adeline was singing. It was badly done."

Was he in earnest? Was he lecturing her on *manners*? Her fear from the confrontation with Wesley abated in the face of growing anger, born of defensiveness and embarrassment.

"Badly done of *me*? And you don't think it's at all badly done to weasel your way into a wedding party to violate someone's privacy and write a *news story* about their wedding?"

His eyes flashed even as the rest of his body stiffened. "Don't. You don't understand what you're talking about."

"No, I don't, which I believe is why we agreed to interact as little as possible while we finish out this charade." She moved to the left, but he blocked her path.

"We did agree to that, but if something has happened, then you can be certain that we are going to have an interaction about *that*." His eyes told her that he already knew something had happened, that all he needed was a handful of details and he would be shouting for pistols at dawn and naming his second.

She wouldn't have thought it would be painful, to have someone care for her in this way, to feel protective of her, but with him, it was. Because she couldn't trust him, and because his withholding the truth meant that he didn't trust her either.

So where she should have felt gratified and warm, she felt only bereft and cold.

The last few guests walked out the door, and it was only the two of them.

She took a deep breath, narrowing her eyes. "Let me be clear. You are neither my father nor my brother, neither my betrothed nor my husband. You have no right or responsibility to be my protector on this island, and if you have some sort of misguided idea that you should be, I will disabuse you of that notion right now. The only thing I need from you is to carry on this farce for another week, and then we'll both get on that steamship back to the mainland, and that will be the end of our association. You need not worry about me after that, and you need not worry about me now."

Other than a tick in his jaw, Thomas made no response.

"Now, if you'll excuse me."

She lowered her arms from her stomach to brush past him, but when his eyes followed the motion, the look on his face stopped her short.

She had seen him irritated and frustrated before, but she had never seen him like this.

He looked like a Viking warrior of old, ready to raze villages to the ground.

When she followed the direction of his gaze, she understood why.

Her gloves had slipped down again, and wrapped around her forearm was a group of angry red welts—five of them, arranged four in a row with one on the opposite side. Their origin was unmistakable.

Thomas's eyes were riveted on her arm, and for a moment, he looked so thunderous that he could have passed for Thor himself.

"Who? Who did this to you?"

Harper froze, arrested by the naked fury in his eyes. His eyes didn't look warm or brown anymore—they were obsidian and fire, wild and seething. He didn't frighten her—it was nothing like the way Wesley had looked at her earlier—but his expression caused something to flare to life in her chest.

Stupid, treacherous hope.

Hope for what she couldn't say—there could be no future between them. She was a farmer's daughter who was being thrust into the limelight of New York Society, and he was a journalist with a hidden agenda, a locked-vault heart that couldn't be cracked.

"I—"

"It was Wesley, wasn't it?" The force of his gaze was like gravity, pulling her in towards him. Insistent, powerful, impossible to resist.

For a fleeting moment, she wanted to tell him everything.

She wanted to tell him about the morning with Wesley and his father, about what happened just now on the veranda. His broad shoulders would enfold her easily, and she could bury her head in his chest and pour out all of the anxiety of the last week. The prospect of telling him everything, laying her burdens on his steady shoulders, was so alluring that she very nearly succumbed.

Instead, she jerked her gloves back up to her elbows. As if hiding the welts could solve the problem of the man who put them there. The man who, if she wasn't careful, might just unravel their charade. The man who almost certainly did not belong with someone as inherently gentle and lovely as Adeline O'Malley.

Through clenched teeth, she met his gaze squarely. "It's been a trying evening, and I'm tired. I believe I will return to my room now. Good night, Mr. Jones."

With that, she turned her back on the stricken look on Thomas's face, walking steadily until she reached the landing of the stairs.

Only then did her steps and composure falter.

Chapter 25

The River House lawn had been transformed into a midsummer night's dream.

A pathway framed by twinkling bell-shaped lanterns led down to the grass where an elegant parquet floor had been constructed for dancing. Though gray clouds had hung heavy and swollen throughout the day, the lanterns bathed everything in soft vanilla light. Enormous urns of lilies were set along the perimeter of the makeshift ballroom floor, their scent sweet and refreshing against the rush of salty sea air coming off the coast.

Tables flanked the east and west sides, piled high with graceful, edible towers of macaroons and tarts, eclairs and cakes, as ushers flowed unobtrusively through the guests with an endless supply of champagne. A small orchestra sat between the dance floor and the path to the ocean, quietly tuning their instruments.

Tonight was the last of the pre-wedding festivities. The wedding rehearsal and a formal dinner were the only events planned for tomorrow. The wedding would take place late Saturday morning, and then the ferries would resume their schedules shuffling tourists back and forth from the mainland.

After tonight, Thomas would only need to endure two more days, and the charade would be finished. On Sunday, he would accompany Harper back to Point Judith on the ferry, then see her safely on a train to Grand Central Station. That would be the end of their charade, of them.

The thought brought him intense relief alongside a searing pain right in that cavern on the left side of his chest.

Though recently, any thought of Harper had that effect on him.

He hadn't seen her since the night of the musical when he had seen the marks on her arms. Not once. But the image of her slender arms, red and swollen where rough hands had touched her—had *hurt* her—was branded into his memory.

It had taken a three-hour walk around the island to cool his temper, and even then, only the firm conviction that murder is wrong had kept him from ripping Wesley from his bed and throttling him.

Because he was certain it was Wesley who had done it. He had yet to parse together what had happened between them, and it made Thomas wild with frustration. He didn't know if Harper was protecting Wesley or afraid of him, or maybe both, but the mere sight of the groom provoked some primal violence in him.

At one point he was so unhinged that he had actually come to Harper's room, prepared to break down the door and demand an explanation. Instead, a stony-eyed Rose had barricaded the doorway and made clear that any interaction he had with Harper going forward would be done through her. He admired the maid's protectiveness even as he had contemplated moving her bodily from the doorway. When he heard what sounded like a sniffle from the other side of the doorway, he very nearly did.

His only consolation was that since Harper hadn't left her room and Rose had admitted no visitors, she had been safe from Wesley. Everyone had been concerned but understanding regarding Harper's *pregnancy sickness,* though she would need to make an appearance at the ball tonight. To miss such an extravagant event would only arouse suspicion, and the O'Malleys would insist that Dr. Grayson become involved in Harper's care.

So with Rose acting as their go-between, Thomas and Harper had arranged to meet outside the River House to walk down to the ball on the lawn together. He saw Harper step out onto the porch, and since he was tucked behind several tall hydrangeas, he could study her openly.

She was wearing a diaphanous bronze gown, and though fitted at the top, it billowed out into a full train in the back, trailing behind her elegantly. When she walked down to the trees and into the vanilla light of the lanterns, she had the appearance of a glowing woodland fairy. Her hair was swept high on her head, with curls falling artfully down her shoulders, her back.

Wonder itself.

He shook his head to ward off the thought.

She was achingly beautiful, but as she got closer, he saw that beneath her eyes—they looked gold tonight—was the faintest hint of purple smudges. Her face looked thinner, her cheeks slightly more hollow than when he had seen her last.

Thomas swallowed roughly.

"Good evening, Mrs. Jones."

She inclined her head, keeping her distance from him. "Mr. Jones."

With that, it seemed they had exhausted their store of things to say to one another and stood in awkward silence for a moment.

"Well, I suppose we ought to…" Harper looked to the lawn behind her.

The orchestra was playing the opening strains of a cotillion, and they watched as Adeline and Wesley moved to the middle of the dance floor. Thomas restrained his murderous instincts.

But only just.

"Yes. In just a moment. We need to speak before we go down there." His words came out rougher than he intended, but he didn't apologize. She already thought he was a brute.

"I don't think that's necessary." She turned to walk away from him, but he stepped around her, careful to keep his hands away from her, though he had effectively blocked her path. She raised her eyebrows.

"It will only take a moment."

Her lips pursed, but she relented. "Fine. You have one minute."

He nodded briskly. "We need to discuss the protocol for tonight."

Harper stiffened. "Protocol?"

He nodded, fisting his hands at his sides to keep from reaching for her. "I won't ask you again about what happened on the veranda the other night, but I'm going to ensure that nothing like it happens again. So tonight, you won't be leaving my side."

Her eyes flared in mutiny. "I beg your pardon?"

"For the duration of the evening, you're not to leave my sight." Even to his own ears, he sounded brusque and domineering, but he didn't care. He may not have a *sunshiney disposition,* as she had put it, but he knew he was right in the matter, and he wouldn't compromise. "It's for your own good. I'm not trying to be controlling, and I'm not trying to tell you what to do."

"I believe you just did both. *Twice*."

She was livid with him, but that was fine. He could take her anger. What he *couldn't* take was seeing another mark on her body from a man who couldn't control his temper.

"Harper."

"It's Miss Whitley to you."

"Actually, it ought to be *Mrs. Jones.*"

She narrowed her eyes but seemed to deflate a bit. "Touché."

"Mrs. Jones. Whether you have *asked* for it or not, whether you *want* it or not, whether you will *accept* it or not, you will have my protection for as long as you and I are on Block Island together. I gave you my word of that when we began this charade, and I intend to keep it. To do that tonight, I need you with me, regardless of how distasteful the prospect is to you. We'll mingle and eat and dance, but we'll do it *together.*"

She looked down at the ground, but he saw the debate taking place in her—anger and indignation warring with the need to maintain a peaceful front for the sake of their farce. Perhaps even a reluctant acknowledgment of the truth of his words.

"Fine." Her gaze snapped to his. "But I want to add to the protocol."

Thomas regarded her warily. "Very well."

"No dancing."

Their gazes met and held, a silent battle.

"It *is* a ball," he said dryly.

"I'm aware. But you yourself said that a married woman could get away with mostly chatting on the fringes of the ballroom. And allow me to clarify. I will not be dancing with *you.*"

Thomas clenched his jaw. "Right. No dancing together."

Harper nodded. "Agreed."

"Agreed."

In the taut silence that followed, he could hear the echoes of their first negotiation, standing together at Point Judith. He remembered that first errant fissure of tenderness for her. He had had no idea then that it would eventually tear him open and shred everything within.

With the solemnity of a funeral march, they walked down to the twinkling vanilla light of the River House lawn.

***

Harper held herself rigidly beside Thomas, watching Adeline and Wesley dance alone in the center of the dance floor.

"Promise you won't tell anyone."

The morning after the veranda incident, Adeline had visited Harper in her room. She had directed her words towards the floor. *"Promise you won't tell anyone."*

The bride's face, normally almost angelic in its radiance, had been pale and wan, her body tense rather than graceful.

For a moment, Harper had been speechless. When Adeline said nothing further, Harper's brain had slowly begun to formulate responses. *You cannot marry him. Call off the wedding. Tell your father, your brother. Tell someone. Tell anyone.*

But she didn't say any of those things. Instead, she asked, "Has he done it before?"

"No, never," Adeline answered hastily, her cheeks flaming. "He's never acted like that with me. He's always been a perfect gentleman. It's only that…"

Harper felt a sliver of trepidation. "Only what, Ada?"

For the first time, Adeline looked directly at her. "Please Vivi, you have to understand the pressure he's under. He and daddy have been working day and night to finish negotiating the Navy contract. It's been terribly stressful for him. Sometimes he drinks, just to relax, and he overdoes it a bit."

"He didn't seem to be overdoing it a bit. He seemed out of control."

Adeline blanched. "I know you two haven't gotten along as well as I had hoped, and he hasn't been himself the last few weeks, but Wesley isn't a bad man, truly." Harper must have looked incredulous because Adeline hurried on. "Once the wedding is over and the contract is finalized, he'll be back to himself. He only drinks when he's anxious. And he was so miserable about it when he apologized this morning. Please, Vivi. Promise you won't tell anyone."

While Adeline spoke, Harper's own anger had been building to a fever pitch. But then Adeline's violet eyes filled with tears, and Harper knew she had to choose her words carefully. It would be wrong for someone as sweet and gentle as Adeline to marry a man like Wesley. But it also felt wrong to go directly against Adeline's own wishes and share with anyone what she had seen, even Rose. Especially because the night before, Harper had gone out of her way to conceal from Rose the bruises that Wesley had left on her own arms.

And the fact of the matter was that Harper was not Adeline's beloved cousin at all but the worst sort of imposter.

She also didn't relish the prospect of single-handedly breaking up the wedding of the century.

The only person on the island she felt comfortable talking to about such a thing was Thomas, but she couldn't, not now that she knew he was a journalist. And if she had read his mood correctly the night before, he would have gladly removed Wesley's head from his shoulders even before knowing the way he treated his own fiancée.

Which, she reflected, would have solved the problem of Adeline marrying Wesley but created quite a few more.

So Harper begrudgingly gave her word to Adeline and gave her the only other thing she could think to give: a succinct lesson about the diverse uses for a parasol and an overview of the vulnerable points of the male anatomy. Harper had no idea if Adeline would ever use the defense maneuver but now shared her father's conviction that every young woman ought to know how to defend herself.

Tonight, Adeline was radiant in ivory silk, and Wesley was the perfect foil to her, dressed in black, crisply cut evening attire. They gave no outward sign of what had happened earlier in the week. Everything about the couple and the backdrop was aesthetically perfect.

The dissonance between the tableau before her and the true state of the couple made her want to weep.

And the tension she felt in Thomas's presence only compounded her uneasiness. His high-handed manner regarding the *protocol* for the evening rankled, and the only reason she had agreed to his demands was that the slowly yellowing bruises on her arm were a poignant reminder of her vulnerability.

But when the orchestra switched to a faster dance and other couples flocked to the dance floor, Harper's anxiety over her own impending debut in New York, her fear for Adeline, and her agitation in Thomas's presence made her restless. She would only be on the island for another two days, and after that, she would never see Thomas or the O'Malleys again.

The thought should have been a relief, but it made her feel frantic and desperate instead.

As the night progressed, the influence of the vanilla light and the ethereal aura of the outdoor ball made her feel reckless as well.

And so she threw herself headlong into mingling and smiling, acting like the vivacious, carefree Vivienne Jones that the O'Malleys all expected. Everyone was happy enough believing that her pregnancy nausea had abated and that she was feeling more like herself.

Everyone except Thomas. The longer the ball lasted, the darker his scowl became. Since he had begun the evening with a fierce scowl, the progression was truly formidable.

But true to her word, she had stayed by his side throughout the evening. She had also flirted shamelessly with Lyle and laughed boisterously at Wesley's father's more colorful comments.

True to *his* word, Thomas didn't ask her to dance. He did, however, glare draggers at any man who seemed likely to ask her, and himself only narrowly avoided having to ask Claire or Claudia to dance by spouting some outrageous nonsense about being unable to leave his beautiful wife, even for a moment.

Incandescent, he had called her.

What rot.

She hadn't expected him to hear her when she mumbled the words under her breath, but when Claire and Claudia moped away to find another dance partner, he scrubbed a hand down his face before frowning down at her.

"Is that really necessary?" he asked.

"What?" She widened her eyes, a portrait of innocence.

"I understand that you hate me, but if you could at least contain your condescension while we're in company, I'd be much obliged."

Her pride smarted at that. She *had* been rude. But so had he! He was a liar, wasn't he? He was still exploiting Adeline by writing about her wedding, wasn't he?

"I don't hate you," she ground out, hiding her own frown behind her fan.

"You could have fooled me."

"Don't do that." She snapped her fan closed, then faced him with a hand on her hip.

"Do what?"

"Say things like that. Sarcastic things."

"Right. I can't imagine what it might be like for someone to use such sarcasm when you're trying to have a civilized conversation."

She narrowed her eyes. "Oh, is that what we've been having lately, civilized conversations? Perhaps you don't know this, but in civilized conversations, gentlemen don't normally point out how abhorrent it is to be mistaken for a father."

"Is that what this is about? How I reacted to your confession with Bess?"

Harper could have kicked herself. Why had she brought that up? It only served to remind her of her own cowardice in not telling Bess the truth and the mortification she'd felt at Thomas's reaction.

"No, it's not about that."

"Then what is it about, *dear*?" The sarcasm was so heavy on the last word that she was shocked it didn't become corporeal and land on the ground between them.

"It's *Mrs. Jones.*"

Thomas gave a brittle laugh. "Enough with the names. If I called you the Queen of England, could you manage one straight answer?"

"I'm sorry, *I'm* the one who can't give a straight answer?" Harper was suddenly furious. It was oddly satisfying, though, saying what she thought, *fighting* with him. Such an utter relief from the polite tension that had begun to define them.

"There you are, Vivi dear!" Bess's ringing voice jolted them both.

She and Uncle Hugh were walking towards them, wreathed in smiles that were completely at odds with the outright battle about to break out between Harper and Thomas.

But her greeting served to remind them of the impropriety of their argument at the ball. In an instant, both of their faces had smoothed into casual smiles and she stepped closer to his side, careful not to actually touch him.

"Darling, I've just spoken with Charles, and the orchestra is setting up for the last waltz of the night. I haven't seen the pair of you dance together at all this evening. Neville, I insist you take her out there at once." Bess said it playfully, but there was nothing playful about the awareness that was suddenly humming between Harper and Thomas.

With almost anyone else, they could have talked their way out of the dance. But Harper had already been acting too brashly tonight to feign illness, and Vivienne's aunt was looking at them like she had just caught Father Christmas about to sneak up the chimney without leaving any presents—eager anticipation happily bordering on blatant accusation.

"I'm not much of a dancer," Thomas said tightly. "I would hate to inflict my two left feet on anyone."

Bess accepted his excuse like it was a clever joke. "Two left feet! Nonsense! Those thighs are like tree trunks, and you walk with such natural grace. My Hugh here, now he has two left feet. His thighs are all twigs and his gait is unavoidably marred by the gout in his knee."

Her husband took umbrage with the comparison. "Now I say, Bess, a man can't help his own gout."

She ignored her husband, turning back to Thomas. "Now Neville, it's been an age since I've seen my niece on the dance floor, and she's simply too beautiful to spend the evening on the side like a wallflower. You used to have a partner for every dance, my darling."

Harper bit her lip, realizing the futility of arguing with her pseudo aunt.

Before she or Thomas could produce another excuse, Bess swatted Thomas on the back with her fan, effectively launching him towards the dance floor. "Off you go then, my dears."

And like a puppet on a string, Harper let Thomas take her arm and lead her toward the other dancers.

She might have felt sorry for how hard Bess had thumped him if she was not on the verge of a very public breakdown.

She was walking onto the dance floor.

To waltz with Thomas.

In warm vanilla light in a fairy tale dress.

His hand claimed hers. Harper watched her own hand move to his shoulder and felt his on her waist. He felt her tense, and his brow furrowed.

"I apologize." His voice was tight as a string and rough as gravel. "I didn't know how to avoid the dance without calling attention to us. If you'll bear with me half a minute, I'll move us to the far side of the floor and we can edge behind the lilies there."

Inscrutable brown eyes looked down on her, and her hand tightened on his shoulder inadvertently.

She had told him she wouldn't dance with him because she was angry and embarrassed, but as she looked up at him now, those wide, puppy-dog eyes so incongruous with the furrows in his brow, she could admit the truth to herself.

She didn't want to avoid waltzing with him, not truly. Since the minute he stepped away from her by the pond, all she had wanted was to be wrapped in his steady arms again, safe and hidden. In a way, Block Island was already a world away, and under the guise of Vivienne O'Malley Jones, the real Harper was anonymous, set aside somewhere between the real world and this charade. What did it matter if she waltzed with him, just once more? She suspected her heart was already broken. One more dance would hardly make a difference.

The musicians teased out the first notes of the waltz, and she looked up at him. "It's all right."

He inclined his head, already eyeing the space across the dance floor where they could disappear.

He had misunderstood.

"No. I mean… it's all right if we dance."

He tilted his head, a question in his eyes. Even with the heels that went with her dress, he still towered over her. But he came to some sort of conclusion.

Without a word, he began to move them in the *one two three, one two three* that he had taught her what felt like a lifetime ago.

Out of her peripheral vision, she saw Adeline and Wesley twirl by, then Charles and Isla, and even Bess and Hugh, who actually *was* an awful dancer. But she wouldn't have known it from their faces—Bess was laughing at Hugh, her eyes bright, and he was leaning down, whispering in her ear. The look they shared was easy and intimate, a sort of wonder known only to them.

It was the way that her father had always looked at her mother.

Longing swept over her so strong and fast that her knees buckled, and if not for Thomas's strong hands keeping her upright she would have fallen to the ground.

She wanted *that*. She wanted what her mother and father had, what Bess and Hugh had. And the painful truth was that she wanted it with Thomas. The gruff, frowny-faced, angry bear who could steady her world with the touch of his hands. But she could never have it—even if he had been honest with her about why he was writing the article, he said he didn't want to marry, didn't want children.

He didn't want *her*.

Suddenly the lanterns and the music and the flowers didn't feel lovely or ethereal. They felt daunting and nightmarish. Before he could ask her what was wrong, she had slipped free of his arms and backed away towards the edge of the dance floor.

"I'm sorry, I can't do this." She bit her lip. "I'll see you at the wedding on Saturday."

She turned away from him, lifting the hem of her dress and running away from the light and laughter and music as quickly as her heels would allow.

When he said her name, she was already halfway to the River House.

***

Without waiting for Rose, Harper slipped out of her dress, wrangling the corset off and tossing it to the floor. Her breath was coming too fast. The room was silent, but the roaring in her ears wouldn't stop. What was she doing right now? Why in the world had she ever gotten onto that boat with Thomas Montgomery?

Her limbs were restless, and after pacing her room failed to expend her manic energy, she threw open the closet door and fished out Vivienne's swim costume. It was late for a swim, already past midnight, but she felt trapped in the room. Trapped in her thoughts, her fears.

All the time alone in her room during the last week had wreaked havoc on her nerves; in the quiet of the room, she had been increasingly panicked about life with her grandmother in a world that she had never belonged to. She was homesick and missed her quiet life with her father. And as absurd as it seemed, she missed Thomas too, or rather, what she *thought* she had with him.

How had this room ever felt luxurious to her? It was a prison, the walls shrinking. She needed to get away. Surely she could slip down the back stairs easily enough and take the dirt path down to Crescent Beach.

The ball was over now, and the guests were leaving the dance floor, making their way back to their rooms. The staff would all be occupied breaking down the wonderland they had created on the lawn.

No one would notice her slipping out through the servants' stairs.

A swim would calm her. Hadn't the ocean always felt like freedom? Hadn't the allure of endless waters and freedom been what enticed her from the train at Point Judith in the first place? She could swim off her energy and then slip back to the hotel with no one the wiser.

She threw a dressing gown over her swim costume, choosing to go barefoot so that one no would hear her in the hallway.

Not that it mattered anyway—she didn't see a soul on her way out.

The moment she stepped onto the beach, she heaved a sigh of relief.

An ocean's worth of freedom swelled before her, and in the space of a minute, she had folded the dressing gown on the rocks away from the encroaching tide and run to the water's edge. The moon still hid behind the silver puffed clouds, but the dark didn't bother her. The idea of a hideaway suited her just fine.

At the first shock of cold water, she felt alive, invincible. She swam out further, her strokes steady. Her body was weightless, the saltwater washing off the anxiety that had clung to her. It was perfect. Back and forth she swam, never too far from shore, never out of sight of the River House.

Except at some point, her body had stopped moving in the right direction. She was moving too fast, too far away from shore. When she tried to turn, tried to adjust her stroke, she couldn't. The strength of the water was too strong against her.

Rip current.

The words rang through her mind like an alarm bell. Her father had taught her about rip currents when they were here together, hadn't he? Just breathe. She could swim out of it, couldn't she?

She was strong.

She was invincible.

Parallel to shore. She needed to swim parallel to shore. But she hadn't realized how cold her limbs had gotten in the water. Summer had only just begun, and the ocean was still bracing and cold.

She was a rag doll now, pliant and weak and propelled helplessly by the current. How long had she been swimming? The rip current felt endless, inescapable.

Her mind, like her body, was growing too slow, too tired. Sight and sound and sense faded until there was only cold and black and wet.

Like the rip current was all there ever was, all there ever would be.

Her life—the plan to go to New York, the charade she had so foolishly begun—it was all a rip current. Silly girl, thinking she had ever had control, that she could have ever done anything but float passively along, calm and accepting in the face of plans and people stronger than she could ever be.

Everything on her was tired now. Her arms were filled with lead, too heavy to lift above the water. She tried, she did, but she couldn't raise them. Her body was limp with fatigue and cold, and as the water rose up to her chin, she realized how very easy it was to mistake freedom for emptiness, escape for self-destruction.

She wished then that she had just told Thomas everything that had happened, had asked for his help.

In the last seconds before her head slipped under the water, she could almost hear his voice again, that familiar warm timbre calling her name.

It sounded like home.

And then it was no more.

Chapter 26

Cold black water collided with his chest.

A heartbeat later it was over his head, cloaking him in the same darkness that had just engulfed Harper.

Thomas had been wandering the coastline since she left him at the ball. He had slipped into the shadows away from the dance floor before anyone took notice of the obvious rift between Mr. and Mrs. Jones.

He could have followed her, could have easily outrun her, but to what end? There could be no consoling her when he was the one who had caused her pain.

The absence of any celestial light had made it easy to slip away from the ball, easy to roam the water's edge unnoticed and unperturbed.

It was *not* so dark, however, that he failed to notice Harper's furtive escape from the hotel down the path to the beach. It was reckless, swimming in the ocean alone, even if it had been daylight. He knew she hadn't told anyone what she was doing because the only person she would have confided in would have been Rose, and there was no way that Rose had sanctioned a lone swim well after midnight.

He watched from afar as she folded her robe and ran into the sea, her movements swift and determined, as if the same buzzing energy that kept him walking up and down the coast had infected her too. Her stroke looked strong, but still, what was she thinking, sneaking out of the hotel to swim alone in the middle of the night?

Unnoticed, he moved closer to the rocks where she had left her robe, determined to keep a silent vigil until she returned to the River House. He hadn't planned to approach her, hadn't planned to let her know he was there at all.

Except the night was so dark that his eyes strained to see her slight form bobbing up and down through the waves, and with a slow-growing terror he realized that her strokes were no longer strong or measured or in rhythm with the crashing waves.

That barely visible head was getting further and further from shore, and in a heartbeat, he registered that her arms weren't making strokes at all—she was flailing, drifting, sinking.

Drowning.

His jacket was off and in the sand in less than a second, the pounding of his feet against sand accelerating in perfect rhythm with the pulse roaring in his ears. Three strides into the tide and he threw himself into the sea, managing just one word before he was under.

Harper.

When he had called her *incandescent* at the ball earlier, he had meant it. Not just in the light of the lanterns, but everywhere, always. She was earnest and open and kind and warm. *Wonder itself,* he thought again.

Seeing her disappear in the water was like watching the sun fall out of the sky. If it had been the sun instead of Harper that had sunk down into the water, he would have been less afraid.

He hadn't been in the water for years, but his body remembered the motions well. Even if it hadn't, the adrenaline pumped through his veins with such violence that he could have swum all the way to the mainland if he had to, if that's where Harper was.

The problem was that he didn't *know* where Harper was—he swam towards where he had seen her go under, careful to avoid whatever current she had been caught in, but he couldn't find her. Tangles of seaweed wrapped around his ankles, and he kicked them off impatiently, trying not to think about the creatures likely swimming around him.

It was so dark that his eyes were useless underwater, scarcely better above it. He could do little more than reach blindly and pray.

Please, please, please. The words drifted through his mind like an aching, broken prayer.

They were enough.

His hand clasped around her arm, and in one motion his free arm was around her torso. His legs pumped wildly as he struggled to keep both their heads above water. Harper was completely limp in his arms, her head lolling from side to side. He doubted she was conscious at all, but he talked to her the whole time he paddled to shore.

"Just hold on. A moment longer. Please. Just hold on."

He collapsed with her on the shore, forcing himself to be calm, to think. Adrenaline had given him the strength to reach Harper, but it clouded his brain now. He wanted to pound against the sand, to shout to *wake up* until she opened her eyes. He had seen her like this once before, the day she lost consciousness in the heat on the docks, but that was different.

She had been *breathing* then.

Harper lay completely still, her skin an unnatural white, her lips tinged blue.

He put his ear up to her mouth, listening for even the slightest rasp of air passing through.

He heard and felt nothing.

Breathe, breathe, breathe.

Think. He had to think. He had read a newspaper article about this before, hadn't he? A German scientist who had revived a patient by breathing air back into him, by simulating heartbeats with chest compressions.

He crouched over her and pinched her nose, matching his lips to hers and blowing air through.

Her lips against his were cold and lifeless.

He interlocked his hands and aligned them over her heart, mimicking heartbeats with steely resolve.

She didn't move.

Another breath. More compressions.

Motionless. She was utterly motionless.

He wasn't going to lose her like this. He wasn't going to lose her while she was far from home, cold and pale, lungs drenched in saltwater.

Losing her was inevitable—he understood that. But not tonight. He would watch her walk away from him, see her step off the ferry and onto a train, say goodbye to her so that she could live a full, beautiful life and have a family full of ruddy-cheeked, hazel-eyed children, all while he spent his life atoning for being his father's son. For being a *murderer*.

More breaths. More compressions.

Again and again and again.

Had he thought watching her walk away from him before was painful? That was nothing compared to this. Leaning over her lifeless form, *this* was pain. Jagged, searing, excruciating. This pain? He would never move on from this.

The tide was still coming in, and though it had been feet away when he carried Harper out of the water, it lapped at his heels now, each wave closer than the last, a tangible reminder that he was running out of time.

Once more he aligned his lips with hers and breathed, found that spot over her heart and pushed, beat after beat after beat.

Nothing happened.

What had he done?

The exact same thing his father did. By his own carelessness, his own reckless impatience to get what he wanted, he had put Harper in harm's way. He was the reason she was lying here on the beach, cold and lifeless. He was no better than his father—in his mad quest to distance himself from the man, to publish the exposé, he had hurt her.

He had *killed* her.

Thomas's fingers went slack. He moved them to rest on either side of her, his eyes roving over her face, lovely even without animation.

Even without life.

The continuous rumble of the waves faded to nothing in his ears. He didn't smell the subtle bite of fish and salt in the air, didn't feel cold or wet even as the water engulfed his ankles.

He felt nothing at all. Body and mind felt curiously vacant.

Then finally, after he didn't know how long, Thomas let that beast in his chest come roaring free, and a single sob tore out of him. Followed by another, and then another, until his forehead dropped against her and he crumbled, cradling her as he fell apart. His limbs shook uncontrollably with every new sob, tears mixing freely with the saltwater dripping from his hair, his clothes.

Since the day he found out what he and his father had done, he hadn't shed a single tear.

He made up for it now.

You always had all of me.

That was what she had told him the night after she learned he was a journalist. Only now did he feel the full weight of the gift she had given him in her trust and the full pang of guilt at how he had squandered that trust, broken it with complacent lies and his own shame.

All at once, he felt everything and nothing, like his heart had grown too big for his chest but too broken to function.

A cloud skittered through the sky, and for a fraction of a second, the moonlight punctured the darkness, a fleeting flash of silver light brushing over their huddled forms.

It was the exact moment that Harper's eyes opened.

By the time the moonlight was spent she had rolled to her side, coughing and sputtering, her small frame seizing with the effort of expelling the water from her lungs. Thomas rocked back on his heels, the sound of her struggle jolting him back to the present.

He set his hand on her back and raised her up as she struggled for breath, then used the other hand to stroke her hair out of her eyes, down her neck, over the whorls of her ears. He knew a frantic need to touch her, as if his hands had the power to tether her to the land of the living.

He hadn't even realized he was speaking until she caught her breath and replied.

"You don't have anything to be sorry for."

"I'm sorry." He had been whispering it to her, over and over.

Her voice was hardly more than a scrap of sound, but it was enough to stir him to action.

"Warm. Harper, we have to get you warm." Her breaths came steadily now, but she was shaking, as much from trauma as from the cold.

With preternatural calm, he slipped an arm under her knees and the other behind her back and lifted her, his hold unwavering as he gathered her robe and his coat.

The walk back to the River House was a blur of motion.

He didn't remember laying Harper in her bed or ringing the bell for Rose. Later, he couldn't recall the look on Rose's face when she walked through the door and took in the sight of them, wet and bedraggled.

What he did remember was Rose shoving him into the bathroom, throwing a pair of Neville's clothes at him and demanding he change and wait in there until she called him out.

When she did, Harper was changed and tucked beneath the blankets. Rose eyed him and pointed at the hearth, a silent command to light the fire. His hands shook with jittery relief, and it took him three times as long as it should have to strike the match.

When the fire was burning steadily in the grate, he turned to see Rose watching him, tilting her head in thought. Harper's eyes were closed, but her breathing looked too sporadic for her to be sleeping yet.

But she was breathing, and that was enough.

"A word, Mr. Montgomery?" Rose's mouth was turned down in a frown.

He followed her to the far corner of the room, scrubbing his hands down his face. "How is she?"

"Steady, as far as I can tell, and slowly warming up. Based on what she told me, she inhaled quite a bit of water. Obviously, she isn't sure how long she went without breathing." Rose looked down, her usual indomitable nature subdued now. "You saved her life. She was lucky she had you looking out for her."

Thomas gave a bitter laugh. "It would have been better if I hadn't tried looking out for her in the first place. None of this would have happened."

Rose hesitated, then looked back up at him. "Don't say that. She's all right now, and for all the nonsense you two have put me through, I'll admit that having you here has been good for Adeline. Heaven knows how you've been able to fool everyone, but cousin or not, it's meant the world to Adeline, having you two here."

Knowing how she felt about her mistress, Thomas recognized the understated praise for what it was.

"Now, what happens after the wedding is up to you and Harper, but I'll say this. What you two have together, whatever it is… it doesn't go falling off of trees and knocking just anyone in the head." Rose regarded him as if she would very much like to knock *him* in the head. "That woman over there is a treasure, and for some reason, she seems to think you're one as well." She quirked a brow, her tone only half teasing.

"Rose, I…"

She held out her hands. "No no, don't tell me anything. I don't want to hear it. Tell *her.* I've been your go-between for long enough. If I had known this tiff between you would end up with this sort of late-night escapade and a three-in-the-morning bell call, I would have sat you both in the corner from the beginning and given you a proper scolding." Her voice was gentle, but he didn't doubt that she meant every word.

Thomas looked down at his feet, unsure of how to respond. She took his silence in good grace, moving on to practical matters.

"We ought to wake Dr. Grayson to check on her."

"I agree."

"But she's refusing. Insists she's just fine."

Thomas clenched his jaw. "She's not just fine. She almost drowned."

"Yes, she did. But in spite of my misgivings, she's in no state to be bullied right now. She seems to be breathing easily and remembers her name and where she is. It's only a few hours until dawn. Let her rest now, and we'll reassess in the morning."

He opened his mouth to protest, but she cut him off with a look. "It's what she wants, Mr. Montgomery." Her face softened, and she went on. "She had a bad scare, and she's embarrassed."

"She doesn't need to be—"

"Eh eh eh—not me who needs to hear it." She looked like she wanted to knock him in the head again. "For now, she just needs rest. And I think one of us should stay beside the bed, keep an eye on her."

He spoke without hesitation. "I'll do it."

Rose gave him an appraising look. "I thought so." She nodded curtly, then puffed up like a mother hen. "And I trust you'll behave like a gentleman?"

"You have my word."

Satisfied, she nodded. "Good. I'll be back to check on you both first thing in the morning. Keep her warm, yes?"

"Of course."

Rose gave him a look, then walked to the door. "I'll see you in a few hours, then. And Mr. Montgomery?"

He was already walking towards the bed but looked back at her. "Where on earth have you been sleeping?"

A rueful smile tugged at his lips. "In a spare bed in the servants' quarters. I told the footmen that pregnancy has made my wife restless in the evenings and that she prefers the space to herself."

Rose shook her head, a weak smile on her lips. "If nothing else, this charade has kept things interesting. Good night, Thomas."

"Good night, Rose."

The door shut with a soft click, and Thomas eased himself into the chair beside the bed. Harper was still pale, but no longer shaking. Her damp curls made a haphazard frame around her face, tumbling across the pillow and flowing down her shoulders.

She opened her eyes and gave him a wan smile.

"Hello."

"Hello."

For a moment they said nothing else. Thomas looked down at his cuticles, and Harper bunched the blankets in her hands.

"Thank you," she said abruptly. Her voice was weak, but he was close enough to make out her words.

He didn't need to ask her what she meant. "You don't need to say that."

She scrunched her brow. "Of course I need to say that." Her pale cheeks flushed. "You saved my life."

"I *endangered* your life. If I had never asked you to pose as Vivienne in the first place—"

"Then I would have missed out on the time of my life." He shook his head, running a hand down his face, but she persisted. "You gave me a month of freedom before going to my grandmother's, gave me the chance to see the ocean every day and meet the most wonderful people and—"

"I *abducted* you on your way to your grandmother's, *stranded* you on an island, and forced you to *lie* to a perfectly decent group of people."

She frowned. "That's not how I see it."

Thomas locked his jaw, not meeting her eye.

"Will you ask me? How I see it?"

He sighed. "How do you see it, Miss Whitley?"

"Harper," she corrected, and something fluttered in his chest. He ignored it, trying to focus on her next words. "Every decision we made since Point Judith we made together. And throughout this outrageous charade, even when I irritated you and yelled at you and made your life difficult, you were always…" She shut her eyes tightly, pursing her lips.

A log popping in the hearth was the only sound in the room. With her head bowed, he could see the streaks of red and gold in her hair. He was close enough that if he dared, he could have brushed back the curl that had tumbled down over her eye.

He moved closer but kept his hands to himself. "I was always what, Harper?"

She took a shuddering breath, her hand reaching up to her throat. "Steady. You've always been so steady, Thomas. The day I left the train that day, I felt like I was slowly falling apart. I didn't know what I wanted, or what I planned on doing, exactly. I just knew I wasn't ready for New York, for my life to change so drastically. And there you were. Gruff and grumpy and so utterly, wonderfully, steady."

She met his eyes then. They were moss green in the glowing firelight.

He tried to form words, but they wouldn't come. He didn't feel steady, not at all. Since the moment he met her, his life had been like a train derailed, an object careening off course. But it had been wonderful. Everything she touched was wonderful.

He felt himself leaning towards her on the bed, his elbows resting on her blankets even as he forced himself not to reach for her.

"And after the wedding, I don't want you to go. I mean, *I* don't want to go." She bit her lip. "What I mean to say is, I don't want everything to be over on Sunday. I don't want to say goodbye. I want..."

Her voice caught, and he felt another fissure in his chest. But it wasn't a break or a fracture this time. This time, it was a release, letting something wild and dangerous out into the world.

Something very much like hope.

He leaned forward, so close he could see his own reflection in her eyes. "What do you want, Harper?"

Hope was shooting out of him fast and fierce now, like brilliant fireflies flitting across the room. They were swirling through the tangles in her hair, beneath his fingertips. A whole host of them, illuminating every nook and cranny of the room, their luminescence so bright it about put the sun to shame.

Her eyes met his, unflinching. "You. I want *you*, Thomas."

In one fluid movement, Thomas closed the space between them, cupping the back of her head and joining his lips to hers. Desperately gentle, insistent and urgent, the kiss was apology and promise and hope. All the words they couldn't say, all the parts of them that were bruised and battered, the kiss bridged and bound them, hedging them in to keep the world at bay.

Her hands were trembling, but she fisted his shirt, pulling him closer, holding him steady. As if she was afraid he might leave.

As if the world even existed outside of her.

It didn't.

Wonder itself.

Everything about this woman—her eyes and her laugh and her honesty and her kiss—sheer wonder.

When they pulled apart her cheeks were flushed, her hair even more tousled, but he kept his hand around the back of her head, unwilling to break contact, unwilling to trust that this moment was real. When he spoke, his voice was thick.

"Harper, I'm so sorry."

She shook her head, her eyes glossy. "Shh, don't."

"No, I am." He forced himself to pull back from her now, to look at her properly, to show her his sincerity. "I'll tell you why I have to write the article, why I came here. I'll tell you everything."

"Thomas, you don't have to—"

"I want to." His voice was firm, and for a moment she held his gaze, studying him.

She lifted her hand to his cheek, her thumb brushing against the rough stubble that had formed there.

The easiness, the *rightness*, of the gesture hit him straight in the solar plexus.

"All right. I want to tell you everything, too."

She swallowed, glancing down at her wrist, the crescents across them fading but still evident. The sight still made him want to tear walls down, but he set aside his rage in favor of considering the woman before him, understanding that her trust was not given lightly. Her trust was a gift he hadn't earned and didn't deserve, but he would be a fool not to take it with outstretched arms.

"All right." He took a breath, wondering where to begin or if he should hear her out first. But when he looked at her, her face was lined with fatigue, her complexion still too pale even with the pink tinge in her cheeks that their kiss had kindled. He took her hand. "Not tonight, though. Tonight you rest, and we'll talk tomorrow. Is that all right?"

She nodded and smiled at him, such a simple, lovely, trusting smile, one he never thought to see directed at him. But after a moment her smile dropped, and she bit her lip. "But you'll stay here with me, won't you?"

Wild horses couldn't drag him away.

"I'll be here." He wrapped her small fingers in his and squeezed lightly.

"Until the morning?" she asked.

Until forever.

"Until the morning."

She gave him another wan smile, and her lids seemed to close of their own accord. In less than a minute she was asleep, her breath a lullaby in the quiet of the room. In the steady song of her breathing, he allowed himself to think that maybe, just maybe, he could actually be more than just his father's son.

For Harper, he could.

Chapter 27

Harper opened her eyes in a haze of dizzying happiness.

She woke with her fingers still entwined with Thomas's, and when he lifted his head from the edge of her bed with a gravelly *good morning*, her heart fluttered to life in her chest.

His face was rough with stubble, purple half-moons hung beneath his eyes, and half his hair stood on end. He looked every inch like a bear just woken from hibernation.

And when he looked over and their eyes met, the corners of his mouth tipped up into a smile—and *oh*, his smile. She had never seen him smile properly before, not once, and it was like watching his entire face light up, the sun rising on his features. Those usually serious lines were suddenly as warm and inviting as his big puppy-dog eyes, and her heart lurched inside her chest.

It was the most beautiful smile she'd ever seen, and she wanted to spend the rest of her life waking up to it.

But when Rose bustled into the room with breakfast and a list of questions about Harper's well-being, there had been no time to talk. The maid was equal parts lioness and mother hen, and she shooed Thomas to the bathroom to clean himself up while she checked on Harper.

Harper was still against sending for Dr. Grayson, in spite of both Rose and Thomas's protests. He would insist on checking the baby's health as well, and there could be no positive outcome to that particular scenario. She only convinced Thomas and Rose not to bring in the good doctor by agreeing to rest in bed for the day, which turned out to be surprisingly easy. When Harper woke again, it was already time to dress for the wedding rehearsal.

Since she had slept the day away, there had been no time for a private moment with Thomas, but every time their eyes met during the rehearsal, she saw the heat and promise in them. The look was enough to banish all of her fears about the charade and her debut.

It was not, however, enough to banish her fears about Adeline marrying Wesley.

Throughout the rehearsal, both bride and groom were distracted and on edge, missing most of their cues. Father Jessup had to repeat instructions several times before either of them noticed or complied.

Isla had been livid, and while her criticism of her daughter was not quite as severe as it had been the day of the dress fitting, it was enough that Bess and Rhys forcibly removed her from the sanctuary under the pretense of checking the floral arrangements in the back room.

The father-of-the-bride did not even deign to attend the rehearsal. He had received a telegram just before the rehearsal and left for his room with only a hurried word to Wesley.

Wesley's own father had the foresight to bring a flask, much to everyone's chagrin. Throughout the rehearsal, he offered both unsolicited advice and lingering touches to the female members of the bridal party. Since Harper, Claire, and Claudia were all standing up with Adeline, they shared equally in the discomfort. When Thomas, Rhys, Hugh, and Wesley began to quietly steam at the ears, Lyle had the unexpected wisdom and tact to hurriedly invite the father-of-the-groom for a walk around the grounds.

After the disaster of the rehearsal, dinner was hardly better.

Harper urgently needed to tell Thomas about what happened with Wesley that night on the veranda, and she was seriously reconsidering her decision not to break up the wedding of the century. But she had yet to find a moment alone with him. They had shared a carriage to and from the rehearsal with Hugh and Bess, and they were seated at opposite ends of the table during dinner.

By then, Wesley's father had finished his flask and made his way through several glasses of wine while his wife tried earnestly to melt into the floor. Wesley hadn't touched his wine, but his tanned face looked pale and taut, and in spite of the cool evening there was sweat beading at his temples. Isla's face was brittle enough to crack in half, and Charles O'Malley had returned in such a foul mood that even perennially good-natured Hugh was tense.

When the wedding guests retired to the parlor after dinner, everyone seemed grateful for the opportunity to put the length of a room rather than just a table between one another.

Thomas found his way to Harper on the settee, and she took her first deep breath of the evening. When his hand found hers, it was like the universe was set to rights.

Everything would be fine. If Thomas was beside her, everything would be fine.

But when Charles stood from his chair and rested his elbow on the hearth beside them, Harper felt a fresh flicker of unease. Thomas sensed the tension in her and shifted her closer to his side.

Fine. Everything would be fine.

"I had an interesting message from the office in New York today, Wesley." Though Charles's voice and stance were casual, there was an edge to his words.

Harper felt the fine hairs on the back of her neck rise.

Wesley, who had been talking quietly with Adeline across the room, turned to look at his soon-to-be father-in-law. His gaze was carefully neutral. "Is that so?"

Charles nodded, and though he smiled, it didn't reach his eyes. "I've told you the story of how I started the Gray Star Line, haven't I Wesley?"

Though the man had spent decades in the United States, his voice still held the melodic lilt of a native Irishman. Harper felt herself leaning towards him in spite of her trepidation.

"I worked the ferry to Long Island as a boy. Not the mammoth steamers we have now, but the simple boats. Just a man and an oar and a heap of wood. Not a lot of glory in it." He held up his bare hands, the gesture of a showman. "I still have scars from the winter when my chilblains burst and turned septic." Even in the dim gaslight of the room, the scars and calluses across his hands were prominent. They would have been excruciating at the time.

"It wasn't glamorous work, but there was enough of it that I saved my money. The first time I rented a place on the docks to build a ship, they laughed. Most storefronts advertising for help at the time still had a sign in the front window: no Irish need apply. And I didn't. Not once did I apply to someone else for what I could earn with my own hands."

Peripheral conversations had quieted now. The whole room was riveted on Charles O'Malley. No doubt everyone had heard the story before, but the rise and fall of the Irishman's voice was compelling.

"They laughed for years as I brought the scrap metal to the docks, welded myself and brought in engineers and laborers. I could barely afford to pay them hourly wages. I could barely afford to feed my family." Charles cast a cursory glance at his wife and children, but the look was cold and unfeeling; he might have looked the same way at his first pile of scrap metal. "But when that first boat was finished, when they heard what I'd sold that first steam engine for, they didn't laugh. *No one* laughed after that."

Wesley had held O'Malley's gaze, but Harper could see the tremor that shot through him. Only one, and he recovered quickly. When Thomas tensed at her side, she knew he saw it too.

"I walk back there sometimes, to that first dock. Did you know that?" Wesley shook his head, his face taut. "To remember. To remind myself that no one laughs at me now. Who would dare laugh at the shipbuilding titan?" He straightened from the hearth and smiled, but it was sardonic.

His eyes skirted the room, combative, challenging. Inviting anyone to question his success.

No one moved. No one spoke. His voice held them all tightly in his web. Even if they wanted to, it was unlikely they could have.

His eyes narrowed on Wesley. "So I have only one question, Wesley. *Wesley, Wesley.*" The words were not affectionate. They were a warning. "My wunderkind. My *son*. Tell me, Wesley, why did *you* see fit to laugh at me?"

Wesley's face blanched. "Charles, I would never—"

O'Malley lifted his hand in the air, his face like granite. "Would you like to know what my telegram this evening was about, Wesley?"

Isla, whose face had been growing more and more pinched, glanced sharply between the two men. "My dear, I'm certain now is not the time to talk business."

No one acknowledged her words.

Adeline, who had been hovering behind her fiancé during the exchange, moved to stand beside him.

Wesley didn't seem to notice.

"We had a communication from a representative of Carnegie Steel. Do you remember the low price you negotiated for the latest shipment of steel? The one we ordered to begin the ocean liners for the Navy?"

A muscle ticked in Wesley's jaw. "Yes."

Tension blanketed the parlor, and Harper felt the room at large holding its breath.

"He made an interesting accusation." *Interesting*. He had said it twice now, and it sounded very much like a threat. "I must say, Wesley. I've not made my fortune by playing nicely in the schoolyard. But I always did know to stop short of outright *blackmail*."

Charles's words landed in the room like an elephant. Heavy, unexpected, and very, very dangerous.

Rhys stepped towards his father, his own face rigid. "Father, why don't we take this—"

"And the only reason I can think of to explain why you would do something so idiotic as to blackmail a member of the country's largest steel company is to make my name a joke." His voice, rising steadily, had ended at a roar.

"Charles, I can ex—"

With quick strides O'Malley crossed the room to Wesley. The men were nearly nose to nose. "I'm a shrewd businessman, Wesley. You know that as well as anyone. But I never broke a law to make my fortune. And if I had, I would have been smart enough not to leave *evidence*."

Wesley stood unmoving, holding Charles's gaze. Neither man spoke.

Slowly, Adeline moved to stand between the two men, her violet eyes inscrutable. She lifted a hand to her father's sleeve. The gesture was almost childlike. She said only one word. "Papa."

But he didn't look at her. Didn't acknowledge the hand on his arm.

"Wesley James, you are through with this company."

Wesley's father, who had been sitting silently in an oxblood armchair throughout the exchange, rose suddenly. His immense alcohol intake made the movement erratic, and when he reached Charles's side, the shipbuilder looked at him in undisguised disdain.

"You can't fire him. You don't have the right—"

"It's my company. I have *every* right."

For the first time, Wesley tore his gaze from his erstwhile employer. "Father, don't—"

"Shut up, boy." Marcus's words snapped like a whip.

Adeline flinched, but Wesley barely batted an eye. The only sign of his discomposure was the tremble in his hands. Instead of addressing his father again, he looked to Charles. "And the wedding?"

At this, the mother-of-the-bride stood and moved towards the epicenter of the tension. "That's *enough*. We will move this discussion to the library. *Now*."

In the middle of the room now stood a semicircle of wary,

combustible tempers. Wesley and his father on one side, Rhys, Adeline, and Isla on the other.

Charles O'Malley stood at the center of it all. "That remains to be seen."

Harper was shocked that Isla O'Malley's head did not spontaneously combust.

"I suppose that means he doesn't know what happened on the veranda." Harper whispered the words under her breath, and she had only meant to say them to herself. But in the deafening quiet following O'Malley's statement, she might as well have screamed them.

Several sets of eyes diverted from the center of the room to her.

Thomas's, wide and chocolatey brown, were bright with emotion.

"What was that?" Thomas and Dr. Grayson, who had been standing behind them, said the words in unison.

It might have been funny if Harper was not suddenly mute with horror.

Adeline's eyes cut to Harper's immediately, the plea in them earnest and panicked. Wesley's eyes closed on a stuttering breath.

As if in slow motion, Charles turned to face Harper. The lines in his face were implacable, but when he spoke it was very, very soft. He echoed Thomas and Dr. Grayson. "What was that?"

The force of his gaze was like fire. Bright and brilliant, easily lethal.

Presently, none of the men in the room looked controlled. If they had been a pack of wolves rather than men, the fur on their backs would be raised, and fangs would have been bared. Though she was surrounded by the latter rather than the former, bloodshed still felt imminent.

"No-nothing. Nothing at all."

Thomas increased the pressure on her hand and shifted on the settee to place himself between Harper and the shipbuilding titan.

"Vivi dear?" Bess's voice seemed to float to her from far away.

Charles stepped towards her, his voice deceptively light. "No, dear. Enlighten me. What happened on the veranda?"

Harper froze. It must have been a catching condition because everyone in the room did the same. When motion returned to the room, it came from an unlikely quarter.

Dr. Grayson, that gray-eyed, soothing presence, joined the semi-circle. Though he was no taller than any of the other men, they all took a step back at the unexpected flint in his face. Isla and Adeline, startled by the intensity of the usually mild-mannered doctor, stepped back to the divan.

"I imagine you can tell us, Wesley." Gone was the calming bedside presence. At the moment, Grayson was standing more like a prizefighter than a healer.

For a beat, Wesley didn't move.

Harper had been squeezing Thomas's hand so tightly that she was leaving white imprints on his knuckles. The poor man was probably losing circulation.

Wesley's jaw worked for a moment, and when his eyes cut to hers, she was taken aback by the menace in them. He stepped out of the semicircle and directly towards her.

"You foolish, meddling—"

Thomas was on his feet in half a second. In the half-second that followed, his fist had knocked out whatever words Wesley was about to say.

Later, no one could say for certain where the next punch came from.

Hugh claimed it was Rhys. He was certain because he remembered advising him to follow through with his hips when he threw a punch.

Bess thought it was Marcus, and had screamed *"cease the fisticuffs!"* at the angry, inebriated man. Unfortunately, her husband's own commentary somewhat undermined the sentiment.

Claire and Claudia would always maintain that it was their Uncle Charles, because *"hell hath no fury like an angry Irishman."*

Harper privately thought it was Dr. Grayson, but even she could hardly countenance the kind, sensible doctor doing such a thing.

Whoever actually threw the next punch was debated for years after the fact, but it was universally agreed that what happened thereafter was nothing short of a violent, tavern-style brawl.

Rhys, Grayson, and Thomas aimed for Wesley, in retribution for whatever had happened on the veranda—the details seemed moot by that point. Marcus aimed for Charles O'Malley because *he* was the only one allowed to publicly shame his son. The shipbuilder himself was angry enough to swing at anyone nearby and did so with efficacy and tenacity. Hugh and Lyle entered the fray, presumably to pry the men apart, but a dodged tackle sent the large mass of bloodthirsty men into the handsy fern, straight through the French doors, and out onto the now ignominious veranda.

By then the footmen became involved, but they were no more successful in breaking up the fray than Hugh and Lyle. Hanging pots of petunias and begonias were dislodged and crashed to the ground in the mayhem, sending sprays of dirt and crazed petals spiraling through the air. Grayson was shoved hard enough to shatter the banister and tumble to the grass and was followed shortly by Wesley and two burly but ineffectual footmen.

The women's shouts went either unheard or ignored amidst the pandemonium.

Everyone was so caught up in the chaos that no one noticed the entrance of three newcomers into the parlor.

A large middle-aged man walked through the door beside a diminutive but formidable-looking white-haired woman. They were accompanied by an ancient sea captain.

Even in the cacophony surrounding her, Harper heard her name from across the room, instantly recognizing the voice.

"Harper Jane Whitley." The words were like a rumble of thunder, so deep and dangerous that they managed to cut through the sound of knuckles against jaws and splintering furniture.

Harper felt the blood drain from her face, turning towards the direction of the voice. Her own words were softer than a whisper. "Daddy."

Thomas had since been pushed back to the veranda, but he was only a few feet from her still, and close enough to hear her. When she turned to face him, he saw her own horror mirrored in his face.

"Daddy?" he repeated, his face aghast.

Motion and violence slowed and stopped as everyone noticed the newcomers.

"Daddy?" Aunt Bess's head bounced between Harper and her father. "Vivi dear, who is this man?"

Adeline, who had found her way to Harper's side in the erstwhile brawl, looked down at her in confusion. "Vivi? Do you know him?"

"Oh… well, you see…" Harper floundered, looking desperately to Thomas.

But he didn't speak either. His face looked shell-shocked.

"Harper? See now, that's Mrs. Jones," the ancient mariner explained in a matter-of-fact tone. "Mrs. Vivienne Jones. Have you been practicing your knots, my girl?" he asked expectantly.

Only then did Harper notice who was standing with her father and grandmother.

"Silas?" Her mind stuttered, struggling to make sense of the distorted reality before her. Her father, grandmother, and the Block Island mail-by-sea captain stood together in the parlor, and she couldn't for the life of her fathom how that could be.

It was like a grotesque manifestation of every lie she had told for the last month.

Silas, ever the gentleman, tipped his hat, completely heedless of the friction surrounding him. "At your service, my dear."

"But… what are you doing here?" She must be dreaming. Surely she was dreaming. Because there was no way her father and grandmother could be here, in the River House parlor.

It was impossible.

"Well, this fine couple here needed a ride to the island. Said it was an emergency. Now, normally I don't do personal shuttles, and especially not with the travel ban in place right now on account of the wedding." Silas's eyes found Adeline, and he tipped his hat again. "Congratulations, by the way, Miss O'Malley." Harper could practically hear Isla's eye roll.

Adeline didn't respond, apparently in some sort of stupor.

Harper could relate.

"Anyhow, these fine folks here told me their girl was missing, and they thought she might have ended up here on the island. Now I heard that and I knew, I just *knew*, I had to help. The missus always says I'm too tender-hearted." He touched his hand to his chest, apparently taking a moment to savor the words of his missus. He beamed at the room, completely unfazed by the rapidly swelling purple eyes and bloody body parts of the immaculately-dressed guests.

"I don't understand," Aunt Bess cut in. "Surely you must be mistaken. There's no *Harper* here."

"Actually…." Harper's voice was threadbare.

Harper's father stood stock still, his large figure imposing even in a room full of other large men. "Harper Jane," he said again, looking directly at her.

Oh, she was in trouble. *Deep* trouble. Underground, pit-of-the-earth trouble.

"Sir, you must be mistaken. This is our Vivienne." Apparently, Aunt Bess was determined to dig Harper's hole deeper. "And this is her husband, Neville."

For the first time, Harper's father noticed Thomas, who had moved to stand at her side.

John Whitley's brow, already furrowed, became a thundercloud.

"Husband?" His voice was a rumble, low and deep enough that it seemed to vibrate through the floorboards. His eyes were bright and livid, a live coal seconds away from bursting into flames. Harper hadn't seen him so angry since the day of her mother's funeral when her Grandmother announced that she was taking Harper.

Actually, his present state made his temper that day seem tame in comparison.

Which was nothing short of terrifying.

"Daddy," Harper began, holding up her hands in a placating gesture.

"Husband," he repeated, taking a step towards Thomas.

Even the O'Malley-James collective seemed cowed by the unexpectedly furious newcomer.

"Daddy, I can explain. He isn't my husband. He's—"

"Not your husband?!" Claudia's mouth dropped open in shock.

Harper ignored her, directing her words toward her father. "No, he's —"

"But what about the baby!?" Claire cried.

Oh no.

OH no.

NONONONONO.

"Baby?" John Whitley rose up impossibly taller, advancing on Thomas like a wildfire. Although Harper was bitty, it wasn't for lack of genetic potential. Her father was a mammoth of a man, and the way he was hulking towards Thomas would have frightened even a fairy tale giant.

Harper learned then that looks could not, in fact, kill. If they could, Thomas would have expired on the spot.

Thomas straightened, putting his hands up in front of him. "Sir," he began, addressing Harper's father.

But Harper's father ignored him, continuing his death march towards Thomas.

He was going to kill him.

Her father was going to kill Thomas with his bare hands, and then he was going to spend the rest of his life in jail. Harper was going to die an old heartbroken spinster, and at her funeral when the pastor was addressing the sparse attendees, he would turn the eulogy into a graveside cautionary tale. *"This, my children, is why you should never lie and never get into boats with strangers."*

It was like watching lightning strike the ground in slow motion. All power and heat and impossible, inevitable danger.

"Sir, there's been a bit of a misunderstanding," Thomas tried again.

As Harper stepped in front of Thomas, prepared to act as a human shield, another unfamiliar voice cut through the room, this one shockingly bright.

"Surprise! What have we missed!"

All eyes now flew from the soon-to-be executioner to the door, where a young couple stood arm in arm, looking expectantly at the room.

Oh, sweet mercy.

Just when she thought the carnage could not get any more gruesome, Harper laid eyes on her doppelgänger, the indomitable Vivienne Jones herself.

She really, *really*, wished she could swoon on demand.

"Vivienne?" Bess's voice was clouded in confusion.

"Yes," replied Harper and Vivienne in unison.

Harper cringed.

From across the room, she saw her grandmother blanch.

The shock of seeing a woman who bore an impossible, uncanny resemblance to his own daughter stalled her father, and his steps faltered. Silas looked between Harper and Vivienne with undisguised interest.

There were enough jaws hanging open that Harper could count hundreds of teeth if she had a mind to.

Which was oddly appealing, in light of the alternative.

The alternative being, of course, dealing with the fallout of a month's worth of lies, deception, and prevarication.

The real Vivienne, undeterred by her lackluster reception and the disarray of both the River House parlor and the majority of its guests, looked eagerly around the room. "I see we're having a bit of our usual family drama," she added cheerfully.

Vivienne looked as elegant as Harper remembered from the day at the ferry, although instead of trying to shove her husband into a large body of water, she was tucked against his side, while his arm rested comfortably around her waist.

Apparently, they had since resolved their differences.

"Well, never mind that now." Her voice was airy and light, as if she didn't find it at all odd that the guests and bridal party of the wedding of the century had been engaging in an angry and impromptu bout of fisticuffs. "Everyone, this is Neville." The real Vivienne smiled brightly at her husband, who nodded congenially around the room.

Uncle Hugh scoffed. "Now, that's not Neville."

The real Neville frowned. "I beg your pardon?"

"I *said*, you're not Neville." Hugh pointed across the room at Thomas, whose lip had been steadily dripping blood onto his white shirt. "*That's* Neville."

"Uncle," Vivienne cut in with a trill of laughter. "I think I'd know my own husband."

"So would I," he replied, nonplussed. Then, as if only now realizing the inherent problems with his assertion, he looked back and forth between Harper and Vivienne.

"Wait—" Hugh began, just as Vivienne met Harper's eye and said "Who is—"

Harper was blushingly so furiously she was certain her face was about to incinerate. This whole situation was a figment of her worst imaginings.

Silas eyed the real Joneses thoughtfully. "I say, how did you two get here?"

"We bribed a fisherman," said the real Neville easily. "He wasn't cheap either, but well worth it to make it to the wedding and finally meet my wife's relations." He smiled genially, though his expression wavered a bit as he seemed to finally notice the dishabille of his new family.

"I knew it." Wesley's voice shot through the room. "She's a fraud."

Adeline let go of Harper's arm, studying her. "I don't… but I…"

"Is that my waistcoat?" Neville asked, his eyes resting on Thomas.

"I daresay it is, darling." Vivienne's face was bemused, rather than perturbed. She looked again at Harper, and though she tilted her head, she showed no other signs of being appalled or shocked or disconcerted by the appearance of a woman who could be her twin. "Well, I'm sorry we're late to the party. It seems it's been eventful." She rolled her shoulders, and her lips curled in an amused smile. "Care to fill me in?"

While Isla stared daggers at her niece, her husband stood to his full height on the veranda. His face was smeared liberally with dirt and blood, and a limp begonia clung to his shoulder.

The deceased perennial on his person did not make him any less formidable.

Charles O'Malley looked directly at Wesley when he spoke. "The wedding is off."

Apparently, *that* little pronouncement was enough to finally shock Vivienne O'Malley Jones. Her mouth fell open in shock.

The words reverberated through the room, their implications

dawning on the faces of the guests, both invited and uninvited.

Slowly, Wesley rose battered and muddy from the ground beyond the veranda. When he raised his hand to point at Harper, his fingers were shaking. "You. This is *your* fault. You filthy, conniving little—"

Like the last time he had wound up for a dramatic accusation, Wesley's words were cut short by a large fist. Naturally, this one also belonged to Thomas. He had leaped an impressive distance—not to mention over the corpse of the handsy fern and out the shattered French doors—to accomplish the feat.

The action had the effect of releasing the dam that had temporarily held tempers in check, and suddenly the pandemonium resumed with newfound zeal.

Harper stood in the center of it all, horrified and shaken and completely untethered.

The idiocy of this scheme hit her fully, then. How could she have done this? How could she have ever thought to hide her deception?

"It's time to go, child." She hadn't noticed her grandmother move to stand beside her, and when the woman's hands clasped Harper's arms, they felt like ice. Harper looked over at her, at the hazel eyes so like her own.

Harper opened her mouth to explain, to say something, to say *anything*, but her Grandmother only shook her head. The lines of her face were severe and unyielding. "Get your things. We're leaving." She glanced at the mayhem before them, her eyes filled with disdain.

Harper looked to the door. Her father's eyes moved between his daughter and the melee. He was torn between dragging his daughter from the room and wading into the fray to dismember the man who he believed had eloped with his daughter, and who may or may not be the father of his unborn grandchild.

For fear that his impulse to kill Thomas would win out, Harper allowed her grandmother to lead her out of the room, away from the chaos that she had so unwittingly released.

But she couldn't leave—not now. She had to talk to Thomas. They needed a plan, a way to be together. They were going to be together—they *had* to be.

Her grandmother's arm continued to propel her across the room.

Then, as if sensing her regard, Thomas turned to face her, their gazes tangling and holding from across the room. For a moment the noise and chaos of the room faded away, and there was only him. Even half-beaten and bloodied, he was the most handsome man she had ever seen.

She didn't need to hear him to know what he was saying to her.

Harper.

She nodded, her heart in her throat.

The word was a promise and a plea, and she knew it was all he could offer her in that moment.

As she walked out of the room, she slipped Bess's emerald off her finger, setting the ring gently on a side table before leaving.

It felt oddly like a metaphor.

And then, tucked between her father and grandmother, with a befuddled Silas trailing behind them, she went to pack up her life on Block Island.

Chapter 28

The boat ride to the mainland passed in portentous silence, but the moment her father closed the door on their waiting carriage at Point Judith, the invectives from her grandmother began. Heidi Verbeek waxed poetically and surprisingly creatively about Harper's utter lack of sense, decency, familial loyalty, and feminine decorum.

Not that the lecture was undeserved. Harper had well and truly earned the censure.

But the colossal loneliness she felt at leaving Thomas on Block Island prevented her from feeling the sting of her grandmother's words. Away from Thomas and the O'Malleys and the tucked-away charm of the island, her surroundings had taken on an otherworldly quality.

Though she had left the charade to return to the real world, it felt just the opposite. As if she had walked away from where she belonged and entered a strange dreamworld without Thomas.

She felt oddly numb.

After two minutes of uninterrupted vitriol, her father cut off his mother-in-law with one sharp word.

"Enough."

Though not generally a man of many words, when John Whitley spoke, he did so with an understated sort of power. He hadn't said a word since they left the River House and had been emanating a sort of leashed energy that Harper found more unnerving than her grandmother's diatribe.

Harper's grandmother narrowed her eyes but mercifully complied.

For all of ten seconds.

"I suppose your mother never told you I have a twin."

Though Harper had closed her eyes and was resting her head against the plush interior of the carriage wall, the non-sequitur jolted her upright.

"You do?"

Her grandmother scoffed. "Well. That's just like your mother, trying to erase our family from—"

A dangerous rumble from her father's side of the carriage stopped the flow of what promised to be a fresh diatribe.

Mrs. Verbeek pointedly cleared her throat, but wisely chose not to finish her sentence.

"Yes, well. My sister Moira and I both married during our first season, but her husband's family was from Chicago, and they moved there after the wedding. Visits were sparse, but we kept in touch through letters. Both of us gave birth to baby girls within a year of one another. Your mother and Lydia, Moira's daughter, were never close, but they did have something in common." She paused ominously. "Your mother threw her life away on a man beneath her station, and —"

Harper's father sent her grandmother a quelling look that would have felled a lesser woman. Her grandmother simply gave him a Cheshire smile.

"And Moira's granddaughter did the same. Apparently, Lydia and her husband had an appropriate marriage arranged for their daughter, but instead of doing her duty, the girl eloped. With some common horse breeder." Her lip curled in derision.

As Harper parsed through her grandmother's words, she felt her eyes go wide.

Mrs. Verbeek met Harper's gaze squarely, giving an infinitesimal nod. "My sister's granddaughter is named Vivienne."

Of course.

Of course.

Why hadn't Harper understood before? The uncanny resemblance between herself and Vivienne could not possibly have been a coincidence. They were cousins, of a sort. Her brain was too tired to name their exact connection, and she was still reeling from the disastrous end to her time on Block Island, but it made sense, such perfect sense that she didn't know why she hadn't realized it herself.

The physical likeness between her grandmother, mother, and herself had always been pronounced, and it was the same case with Moira's branch of the family.

Two generations later, she and Vivienne were as good as another set of twins.

She had been so occupied with her own reaction that she hadn't noticed her father rising up in his seat.

"Did you know?" His voice was low and dangerous. "Before we arrived at the River House, did you know that Harper had been impersonating Vivienne?"

Her grandmother scoffed, which Harper privately thought was either reckless or stupid, in light of her father's rising temper.

Although this was the way *most* of her father and grandmother's interactions unfolded, so the powerful Knickerbocker was probably confident that her father would not actually throttle her.

Harper was less sure.

"Of course I didn't, John." Her words were crisp and cutting. "I never expected the girls to meet at all. Moira and her husband live in Chicago, and although her daughter married into that nouveau riche boatman's family, one could hardly expect them to find their way to rural Rhode Island." Only her Grandmother would refer to Charles O'Malley, the world's wealthiest shipbuilder, as a *nouveau riche boatman.*

Harper had so many questions for her grandmother that her brain stuttered trying to sort through them all.

Finally, she managed one.

"But... if you didn't know that I had taken Vivienne's place, how *did* you know that I was on Block Island?"

Her father sighed, his face looking so lined and weary that she felt a fresh pang of guilt. "I missed you and took the train to New York, to see for myself how you were getting on in your debut. Imagine my surprise when I arrived at Fifth Avenue only to be told that your arrival had been delayed indefinitely."

Harper had never truly understood what people meant when they said the floor dropped out from under them.

In that moment, she understood.

When she managed to meet her father's eye, she was shocked to find the ghost of a smile, rather than the fire and brimstone she was anticipating. His next words were similarly unexpected.

"Your mother loved the ocean. Do you remember that?" Harper felt her eyes prick with tears, nodding mutely. "She used to say it made her feel free. If she ever needed to escape, she need only run to the water's edge. And you, Hopsy, are nothing if not your mother's daughter." His voice was a mix of exasperation and delight. "I remembered that the train stopped at Point Judith. I couldn't be sure, but… hopping a train for a jaunt on Block Island seemed like just the sort of thing your mother might have done."

Harper bit her lip, and when she could speak, her words were very, very soft. "I'm sorry, Daddy."

Never a demonstrative man, he rested his warm, calloused farmer's hand on hers, and in a tight voice he whispered, "I know."

And just like that, she knew he had already forgiven her for her foolishness, knew he would always forgive her, no matter what she did.

But suddenly the question that had nagged her for the last two months finally made its way to the surface.

"If you missed me… why did you send me away?"

Her grandmother, who had sat in tight-lipped silence during their exchange, looked sharply between her son-in-law and granddaughter. "You didn't tell her, John?"

A trickle of cold foreboding shot through Harper as she turned to her father. The rueful smile had been replaced with a tight-lipped frown.

"Tell me what?"

So much time passed that she thought he wouldn't answer. When he did, her stomach clenched in dread.

"You remember my accident in the hayloft last fall?"

Remember? How could she forget? A crash in the barn had sent her running inside, only to find her father sprawled and unconscious, face down on the floor. For a terrifying minute, she had thought him dead.

"I remember."

He sighed. "I didn't fall off the ladder. On the faulty rung, I mean. I had a… the doctor explained that it was…" he cleared his throat. "An issue with my heart."

Harper's own heart, already beating too quickly, gave a sickening lurch.

His heart? Something was wrong with his heart, and she was only now learning of it?

"I… but why didn't you tell me?"

"There was no reason to worry you, Harper."

Her mind whirled, trying to assimilate the revelation with the last several months. "That's why you've finally hired help on the farm."

He inclined his head. "Dr. Morgan also believed it prudent to ensure that you were settled, that I make accommodations for you, should anything happen to me."

She shook her head roughly, as if it could erase his words, erase the defect in her father's heart that had nearly taken him from her. "Nothing is going to happen to you. You're fine. You're strong and healthy, and we need a second opinion. I've always thought that Dr. Morgan was on the shady side of senile."

Her father quirked a brow. "Dr. Morgan is the one who delivered you into the world."

"Yes, well, back in his prime! He's practically in his dotage now."

"He's my age."

Harper opened her mouth to protest, but it was her grandmother who forestalled her. "Your father wrote to me, Harper. This winter. He asked if my offer to take you in and give you a proper dowry and debut was still standing. Obviously, you know my response."

Though her grandmother's mouth was perennially tipped down in disapproval, her voice and eyes held an unprecedented gentleness. If she had to name her current expression, Harper would have called it... *broken*. Her grandmother, tyrant of the Knickerbockers, formidable society matron, one-woman force of nature, looked broken.

A historic moment.

Harper understood, in an objective sense, that her grandmother must have been heartbroken by the death of her only daughter, but Harper had never seen so much as a crack in her iron facade, nothing to indicate grief or sorrow. It had been nothing but anger that day at the funeral, at least the part that Harper could recall. And then, when her grandmother had shown up unannounced on their doorstep, years later, she showed nothing but the haughty grandeur befitting a wealthy New York matron.

For the first time, Harper wondered if offering to raise Harper on the day of her mother's funeral had less to do with control and spiting her father and more about grieving her only child. Harper sat forward, rapt and not unmoved by this new and unexpected version of her mother's mother.

"As difficult as you might find it to believe, I do want what's best for you," said her grandmother.

Harper looked down at her lap, humbled and more than a little ashamed of herself.

Her grandmother straightened, the momentarily softness replaced with a martial light in her eyes. "And now that you've had your questions answered, Harper Jane, I believe you have some explaining of your own to do." Her grandmother's eyebrows rose, and she felt her father turn to look at her.

Yes. She supposed she did.

What followed was an account of what had happened from the day she left the train at Point Judith to that very night, with emphasis on the happy fact that she was neither married nor pregnant and careful omission of champagne and neckties and waltzing and kissing. Even in its redacted form, however, her behavior had been foolhardy at best and reckless at worst.

After absorbing her unlikely and scattered account, her father and grandmother sat in stony silence and then spoke at once.

"That brute ruined your reputation!" her grandmother cried. "You'll have to marry him now!"

"I'm going to kill him," vowed her father.

In a shocking turn of events, Harper found herself agreeing with her grandmother.

Harper already felt hollow and miserable after leaving Thomas, and more than a little guilty about abandoning him to deal with the aftermath of the brawl and the unraveling of their charade, but a fierce protectiveness for Thomas rose in her, energizing her.

He was gruff and insensitive, but he was not a brute, and he certainly hadn't done anything to justify murder. Obviously, her father disagreed.

"No, you don't understand, he's—"

"A dead man walking," supplied her father.

"A conniving little snit of a journalist who abducted you from Point Judith to compromise you for the sake of your dowry," concluded her grandmother.

Harper squared her shoulders. "No, he isn't." Her father was glowering again, so she spoke quickly. "I know what you must think. But he isn't conniving, and he never did anything to compromise me."

She studiously avoided thinking about the kiss and the fact that they shared a room for a time. Hardly the sort of thing to endear her relations to the man.

"He's not perfect, I know he's not. He's made mistakes, but I did too. I share as much blame for our farce as he does, perhaps more. And he was always a gentleman to me, Daddy—he was my protector, there, my friend. If you only knew him, the *real* him, not just what he's done, you'd know that deep down he's as caring and gentle as he is prickly.

He can be maddening and downright infuriating, but I… I love him."

The truth of the words washed over her like a wave. She loved him. And suddenly they were her favorite words in the English language.

I love him, I love him, I love him.

Her father studied her carefully, then seemed to weigh his words before he spoke them. "And does he love you?"

Harper swallowed. "I believe so, yes."

He hadn't said it outright, but she could see it in his eyes, in the way his hand wrapped around hers.

Her father's adam's apple bobbed, and he nodded once. "Well. The plan remains for you to return to New York with your grandmother," he said grimly. "You will do as your grandmother says and have your debut. But if this man seeks you out… then I will give him a chance to prove to me that he's worthy of you."

Little pinpricks of joy flowed through her, and she could only nod, too happy to speak.

"But I won't make it easy for him," he warned.

"Nor will I," her grandmother added.

Harper didn't doubt it.

But as the carriage continued to roll towards New York City, deep into the night, Harper felt content for the first time since she had left Thomas on Block Island.

He would come for her. She knew he would.

Chapter 29

Thomas's ferry left for the mainland at two o'clock.

Shortly after Harper left the night before, the burly footman of the River House finally managed to break up the assorted brawlers, but not before they had torn apart half the veranda, the entirety of the parlor, and destroyed several hundred dollars worth of haute couture.

Dr. Grayson, bloodied and bruised, had returned to himself, methodically cleaning wounds and stitching gashes before sternly sending each man off to his room.

Thomas himself was exhausted and battered, with a fresh row of stitches running down his jaw. He had been up all night and wanted nothing more than to put the whole nightmarish affair behind him, but before he left Block Island, he had one final task.

When Thomas knocked on Adeline's door that morning, he had every expectation of being hit, spat upon, or some combination of the two.

Though Rose had looked inclined to do just that before slamming the door in Thomas's face, Adeline's soft voice had floated through the doors, asking Rose to admit him.

When Thomas walked past a fuming Rose and entered the room, he found not only Adeline, but Bess, Claire, Claudia, and Vivienne all huddled on the bed, their eyes as red and swollen as the bride's. Or rather, the *former* bride's. His eyes lingered briefly on Vivienne, and her impossible resemblance to Harper struck him anew.

Watching Harper walk away was like watching someone tear open his chest and empty its contents, and it hurt too much to consider. Right now, he owed it to Harper and to all of the O'Malleys to tell them the truth.

Without preamble he told them the whole of their charade, accepting all of the blame and making they sure knew about Harper's scruples in deceiving them and her sincere affection for everyone in the family. He did not try to justify or condone his actions. The apology he offered was sincere, though he had little expectation of receiving their forgiveness.

The unusually subdued O'Malley women had accepted his story and apology with only hushed words, though Vivienne had stared curiously at him throughout his explanation.

The pall of the broken engagement on the eve of the wedding and the ensuing full-family brawl had cast enough of a shadow on them without his presence adding to their unhappiness, so Thomas had quietly left the River House. After a quick stop at the telegraph office to message his sister, he had boarded the ferry and watched Block Island shrink and disappear into the distance.

After catching the train back to New York, his first stop was at the newspaper office. He had tendered his resignation in a contentious meeting with Luther, further enraging him by refusing to disclose even a single detail about the wedding. That done, he had packed up his desk and made the three-mile trek home on foot.

By the time he finally arrived back at his rented rooms, he was ready to collapse into his bed for the better part of a month.

It was not to be.

Because there, sitting patiently on his front stoop, was his sister Kate, alongside her husband Michael.

Thomas swiped at his eyes to see if they were deceiving him but regretted the action immediately. His left eye was enormous and a riotous shade of purple, and the rest of him looked even worse.

With wide eyes, Kate took in his disheveled state. "Thomas Montgomery, what ever is wrong with your face?"

Thomas sighed. "Lovely to see you too, Kate." He walked past her to the door, every step feeling heavy as lead. "Care to come in?"

Thomas hefted his typewriter to his hip and fished out his key from his satchel, unlocking the door and holding out a hand to his sister and her husband. "After you," he said drily.

Kate walked primly through the door and her husband followed, giving him a commiserating smile and a bracing pat on the back. "Hope you gave as good as you got."

In spite of his misery, Thomas had to smile. He *had* given as good as he got.

Michael settled himself at the small table in the kitchen, unfolding a newspaper without delay, while Thomas followed his sister into the living area, dropping his bags at the threshold and collapsing onto the threadbare couch.

The moment he leaned back and closed his eyes, Kate's impatient voice shot through the room. "Let's have it, then."

Thomas groaned. "Have what, Kate?" His knuckles, cheeks, and jaw still thrummed with pain, and his chest throbbed at the memory of his goodbye—or lack thereof—with Harper. He was in no mood for an interrogation.

Kate, either unaware of or indifferent to his state—unlikely on both counts, based on her earlier question about his face—was undaunted by his tone.

"Have what? Thomas! You send me a cryptic telegram saying you won't be covering the wedding *and* make an unprecedented offer to visit me?" Her jaw took on a mulish set. "Now, I'm going to say it again. Let's. Have. It."

Thanks to his sister's unexpected appearance and excessive volume, Thomas could now add a blistering headache to his list of maladies. He leaned forward, dropping his head into his hands.

"I apologize, Kate. The telegram was impulsive and unnecessary. There was no need for you to show up on my doorstep."

Kate raised an eyebrow. "Then perhaps you ought to have sent a letter instead. You know, the non-urgent mode of communication that allows for multiple sentences and actual explanations? But never mind that now." She swept her hand carelessly through the air. "I sensed that you needed me, and so I'm here."

"I didn't mean to worry you." He checked his watch with a frown. "You must have taken the first train out to get here at this hour."

She balled her first in her lap. "Thomas Morgan Montgomery, if you don't give me a straightforward explanation of what's happened *right now*, then I'm going to kick you in the shins."

He believed her.

"You're my only brother, and in spite of your supremely dissatisfying telegram, I think the world of you and can count on one hand the times in my life that you've needed my help. Did you think I wouldn't come?"

He ran his hands through his hair, wondering how to explain the events of the last month to his sister.

Even the last forty-eight hours had been a whirlwind.

Watching Harper walk away from him, flanked by her grandmother and father, had about undone him.

The punch Wesley landed only hurried his inevitable descent to his knees.

"What happened is all rather… complicated."

Complicated was a comically mild way of putting it. Thomas cursed himself as the worst kind of fool for ever hoping that he could have a future with Harper. The elation he felt when she opened her eyes on the beach, her whispered confession by the light of the fire, the way she yielded and responded to his lips on hers—all of it had blinded him to the reality of their situation. He had allowed himself to be swept away in a dream, a reverie that existed only in the confines of their charade—he was not only a fool, but a cad.

He was the son of a murderer, a journalist who until very recently had been willing to exploit an innocent woman's privacy for his own gain, his own undeserved atonement.

A disgrace in his own right.

The recrimination in her father's eyes that night had brought all of those unsavory and indisputable truths back to him. How could he ever be worthy of a woman like Harper? How could he ever even consider making her his own, ever soil her with his name? Honor now demanded that he marry her to save her reputation (which he doubted her father would ever sanction), or never darken her doorstep again.

The latter and only acceptable course of action sent a surge of pain through his chest.

Had he thought the situation only complicated? It was outright impossible. There was no scenario in which he could do what was best for Harper and still be with her.

Too drained to try and filter them, he gave his sister a full recounting of events, only glossing over their kiss.

Kate, in spite of her rampant curiosity, listened without interruption, but when Thomas ended his recounting of events, she nearly jumped out of her chair at him.

"And?"

He frowned. "And?"

She rolled her eyes. "What are you going to do about it?"

He sighed, feeling as if he had aged a decade overnight. He would check for gray hairs later. "Before I came home, I stopped at the newspaper office and gave Luther my notice. Which means I am now unemployed and no closer to publishing the exposé on the mills than before I went to Block Island." He straightened, feeling the tension and strain pulsing up and down his spine. "But I'll find another way."

He *had* to find another way.

Except that for years his main purpose in life had been to atone for his past, but now that he had met Harper, now that he had reawakened that beast in his chest, reminded himself that it could, in fact, beat and feel and love in spite of all the previous evidence to the contrary, he didn't know what he would do with himself once the mill articles were published.

What his life might be after the articles had run had never occurred to him. He would carry on as a journalist, he supposed, but the prospect of continuing to follow stories, to write, only to end up at home alone, night after night… how had he never considered before what a lonely path he had chosen for his life?

The truth was, he had never *felt* lonely until he met Harper.

But now?

Now that he knew what it was to love her, to guard and protect and cherish her, to do and say ridiculous things just to see her smile… the thought of never doing that again was like a physical blow.

"I always knew you could, Thomas." Kate's voice was laced with pride and confidence. "However, that is not what I was referring to."

Thomas wrinkled his forehead, then winced in pain. He would really need to learn to control his facial expressions until his wounds had time to heal. "Kate, please. In the last forty-eight hours I have slept a combined total of about three hours. I've been pummeled and knocked down and stitched back together, and as you so kindly pointed out, I look as wretched as I feel. Do me a favor and be specific about what it is you want to know."

Now she did leap out of her chair, eyes blazing. "Thomas, you enormous twattering oaf! What are you going to do about *Harper*?"

A fresh jolt of pain slammed between his ribs, but he kept his face impassive. "I'm not going to do anything. She's going to live with her grandmother and will move on with her life. She'll marry someone wealthy and respectable and have a dozen fat babies."

The thought made him want to bloody his knuckles all over again.

Kate remained standing while he was seated, so she towered over him. "Yes, a dozen fat babies with *you*, you impossible buffoon!"

"Language, darling," came her husband's mild voice from the kitchen.

Kate scowled in his direction, then turned back to Thomas, wrath undiminished. "Thomas, you're in love with this woman!"

This time, he did flinch. "Which is why I need to leave her be."

"Which is why you need to clean up your sorry face and go track her down!"

He sighed. "I've already tracked her down." He pointed to a sheet of paper sticking out of his satchel, where he had written her address. A half hour's worth of research in the archives room before he left the newspaper office had given him the address of both her father's farm and her grandmother's Fifth Avenue residence.

It was an exercise in futility, though; he knew he couldn't use the information, could never seek her out. She deserved far, far better than him. Kate looked behind her at the hastily scrawled address, then back at him, her eyes wide.

Thomas exhaled raggedly. "Please, don't make this harder than it already is."

Her face was incredulous, and for a moment he had a real fear that she would make good on her threat against his shins. With forced calm, his sister lowered herself back to her chair and regarded him steadily. "Thomas. You're not still holding onto that ridiculous notion that you'll never marry?"

"It is not a ridiculous notion. And yes, I am."

"But why!?"

"You know better than anyone why!" He struggled to lower his voice, to keep his heart from falling out of his chest onto the floor. "I could never risk becoming *him*. Becoming to some woman what he was to our mother. Becoming to a child, to multiple children, what he was to *us*." He turned his face away from her, unwilling for her to see his unshed tears.

He hadn't expected her to kneel down in front of him.

Her face was inches from his own, but he averted his eyes, unwilling for his younger sister to see his brokenness.

The unnamed specter of their father hovered around them like a tomb. They had never talked about all that had happened, only acknowledged it from a distance, bearing with the day-to-day fallout without words. Thomas and Kate had always understood one another implicitly, the result of a harrowing childhood, and had supported one another in their own way.

After the death of their parents, he had told Kate about his resolution never to marry and have his own family. She had accepted it with aplomb, but perhaps never understood the seriousness of his resolve.

She seemed to understand now.

When she spoke, her voice was impossibly gentle. It was the voice she had used on the wounded animals she rescued as a child.

"Thomas, please. I know better than anyone all that you've suffered. But he's taken so much from us already.... so much joy lost irrevocably. Don't let him take this, too. Don't let him take *her*." Kate's own eyes began to overflow. "You're not him. Never in a million years could you ever be like him. I know you don't believe in yourself, but believe *me*, Thomas." She increased the pressure on his hand. "Thomas, you *love* this woman."

His jaw clenched. "Which is why I need to let her go. I don't deserve her."

She shook her head roughly. "Thomas, no. *No*. No one can earn love. Mothers don't love their children because they've somehow *earned* it. You don't love me because I *deserve* it. Love is not a merit-based system. It's grace. Pure grace. It's offering yourself fully to someone for *their* sake, not because some invisible scale has found them worthy. To love is to give yourself away. Would you be willing to give yourself away for Harper? To sacrifice your own comfort and dreams and success for her?"

Thomas paused, swallowing around the lump in his throat. "I would move heaven and earth for her. I would *die* for her."

Kate regarded him steadily. "I know that you would. What I want to know is why you are unwilling to give her the chance to do the same for you?"

Thomas looked down at their clasped hands, unable to speak. She would never understand what he felt, the shame and guilt that clung to him like a disease.

"Go to her, Thomas. Give her the chance to love you."

Gently, he removed his hand from hers, straightening in his seat. She looked up at him, moving to sit beside him. "It was kind of you to make the trip here, Kate. If you don't mind, I believe I'll go and lie down. Perhaps clean myself up a bit." He tried for a self-effacing smile but knew that between his stitches and swollen eye and the fierce ache in his chest, he did little more than grimace.

"Yes, yes of course. We should be going anyway. Michael has some business in the city." She stood, looking towards her husband in the kitchen. "But Thomas... once you've rested and recovered, you'll go to her? You'll tell her how you feel?"

When he trusted himself to reply, he spoke to the space above her shoulder. "Thank you for coming today, Kate. It means more than you know."

Chapter 30

Two weeks. Harper had been with her grandmother for two weeks, and not a word from Thomas.

She knew he could find her—he had been the only journalist on the eastern seaboard able to track down the time and location of the O'Malley wedding. Surely the Verbeek family mansion would be simple by comparison.

After seeing her settled at her grandmother's, her father had taken the next train home, leaving Harper at the mercy of the army of seamstresses and dance masters that her grandmother had recruited to make her presentable for high society.

It had been exhausting, and the only thing that made it bearable was the thought that any day, at any hour, Thomas would appear. He would come for her.

Which is why she had nearly flown down the stairs when a footman came to her room to announce the arrival of a guest come to see her.

When she walked into the elegant morning room downstairs, she had stopped short at the sight of wide eyes her very favorite shade of chocolate brown.

"Hello, Miss Whitley."

Harper opened her mouth but could emit no sound; the shock of the moment had rendered her mute.

Because those chocolate brown eyes were set in a face that she had never seen before. It was admittedly a very pretty face—sun-kissed peach cheeks and a pert little nose set above a wide smiling mouth—but unknown to her nevertheless.

Soon enough a lifetime's worth of manners gained the upper hand,

and Harper returned the smile and gestured to the wingback chair.

"Hello," she managed in an almost normal voice. "Please, won't you have a seat?"

Her guest obliged, and Harper sat down only to rise up immediately after. "May I offer you some tea? Or coffee? Or perhaps you would like something to eat? I believe our cook has made some lemon tarts." She felt skittish and uncomfortable and nearly sagged with relief when her guest took control of the conversation.

"You're too kind, Miss Whitley, but I'm just fine. Please forgive me for calling on you unannounced—I realize how forward this must seem to you. Allow me to introduce myself." She extended a gloved hand. "My name is Kate Anderson, though you're more likely to place me from my maiden name."

"Montgomery," Harper said faintly, taking the woman's hand and sitting before her legs gave way beneath her.

"Yes." Kate beamed back at her.

What did it mean that Thomas's sister was here to see her, but not Thomas? She tried to smooth the emotions from her face but knew her success to be dubious at best.

"I cannot tell you how pleased I am to finally meet you, Miss Whitley."

"Please, call me Harper."

Kate flashed her another smile, and when the afternoon sunlight caught her brown eyes, she looked so much like her brother that a stab of longing shot through her heart, pumping out into veins and extremities with such force that her whole body felt limp with it.

"Again, I recognize the unorthodox nature of the visit, but I hoped you would hear me out."

Hear her out? Harper wanted to shake the woman by the shoulders and demand to hear anything and everything she knew about Thomas, past and present. Her manners, however, still retaining the upper hand, kept her hands tucked firmly in her lap and guided her reply. "Of course. Any relation of Thomas's is more than welcome. Is your brother… is he well?"

The longing began to morph into dread.

"He is, yes. Well," she paused, and Harper nearly doubled over in anxiety, "when I saw him last he looked rather the worse for wear after a bit of a scuffle, although I assume you knew that already." Harper confirmed with a grimace. "He's quite well, only…" Kate's gaze wandered around the room, from the ornate velvet curtains and plush

Aubusson rug to the imposing family portraits hanging on the walls, then returned to Harper with startling directness. "May I speak plainly with you, Harper? It's only that I feel as if I know you already, with all that Thomas has told me about you, and I think it might save us both time if I skipped the delicacy."

Harper nodded fervently. She hated delicacy. Delicacy was abominable. "Please do."

With a relieved sigh, Kate straightened in her chair, leaning towards Harper. "You see, Thomas doesn't know that I'm here today. He would be livid with me for meddling, but he'll thank me for it later. Honestly, if that man doesn't get a swift kick in the right direction, he'll end up a crotchety old monk."

Kate rolled her eyes, and Harper tried to pass off a laugh, but inside the dread was solidifying, pumping lead into her veins instead of blood and hope and longing. Why wasn't Thomas here himself, and why would his sister see fit to insert herself into his affairs?

Unless... unless he wasn't coming for her?

With that terrifying prospect, the dread seeped out of her veins and filled the nooks and hollows of her anatomy until she wondered how her now metallic lungs could still manage to move air and carbon dioxide into and out of her body.

"I imagine Thomas didn't tell you much about our parents, did he?"

The change of subject was jarring, but Harper kept her posture ramrod straight. "No, not much. Only that they've since passed away."

"They did, yes, though I suppose I had better start from the beginning. You see, our father was a mill owner, a self-made man. He was hard-working and proud, and ever since Thomas was a young boy our father had impressed upon him that he would one day take over the mills. Which sounds like a natural enough thing, I suppose, to want to pass your business down to your son.

"But my father was... a hard man. Less criticism was the closest he ever gave to praise, and he demanded perfection. When either of us inevitably fell short, his temper would..." she looked down at her hands, then gave a shrug that was likely meant to be indifferent, but told Harper worlds about Thomas and Kate's childhood.

"Failure in anyone was unacceptable to him, but Thomas always bore the brunt of our father's temper. As long as his anger wasn't directed at her, my mother saw fit to absent herself, to the effect that she was almost a nonentity in our childhood. And so Thomas bore the burden not only of our father's expectations but of being my protector and friend and parent. He is only one year my senior."

Kate was looking out the window now, and Harper had to swallow back tears. She remembered the waltz by the pond when she had told Thomas about her own father. *An extraordinary thing, to be so loved*, he had told her. She tried to imagine Thomas as a child, the little boy who learned to frown and scowl at the world to conceal the pain inflicted by a cruel father. The ache it caused her was almost unbearable.

"When Thomas finished school, he went to work for our father. Now for years, the mills had been dependent on child labor, which is often the case. Small hands and slim bodies can maneuver the intricate machinery where adults cannot. And of course, children are paid far less. Once Thomas was officially part of the company, however, he proposed a change. He wanted to replace the child workers with adults and acquire and reconfigure existing mills to offset the cost. My father was nearly apoplectic at the prospect, but somehow Thomas convinced him."

Harper looked down at her lap. "He can be very persistent."

"Yes, he can. It was decided that while our father ran the existing mills, Thomas would travel to acquire several more in the area, which meant that he was away for weeks at a time. On the day of the fire, he had only just returned home."

The fire. At those words, Harper had such a premonition of grief and loss that she hardly dared to breathe. "Fire?"

Kate didn't seem to hear her. "No one was allowed to smoke in the mills; it was a well-known rule, but one day a foreman was careless, and he discarded a cigarette outside the mill. An errant wind blew it into the door, and within moments the dry cotton was up in flames."

Kate's eyes cut to Harper's, and Harper both felt and saw her premonition take shape in those steady brown eyes.

"The problem was that the mill was still being worked exclusively by children. My father had yet to follow through with Thomas's plan to phase out child labor, and because Thomas had been away so frequently, he didn't realize. When the fire caught, the children on the lower level were able to get out in time, but those on the second floor…" Kate took a shuddering breath, and suddenly the lovely woman before her was Atlas, bent and weary, laboring under the weight of the world.

Harper, struck by the impossible horror of Kate's story, felt her own breath release in unsteady fits.

"The wind sent the fire up the stairwell. Someone had run to the house and alerted Thomas to the fire, but by the time he arrived, the whole building was an inferno. Thomas ran into the blaze anyway, and he managed to reach the children on the second floor. Ten children. One-by-one, he carried all ten children out of the fire." Kate's breath shuddered, and she met Harper's eye. "Only nine of them survived."

Suddenly, Harper felt sick, dizzy with the horror of the loss, of children who never should have been in harm's way. The loss would have eviscerated Thomas. In her mind's eye, she could almost see him crumbling to his knees in shock and sorrow and impotent rage.

"A jury convicted the foreman of criminal negligence, but my father was never charged, never apologized to Thomas or anyone else. Not that it mattered in the end. Shortly after the fire, our town had an outbreak of influenza, and both of our parents contracted it, succumbing within a week of one another. When they did, Thomas sold the mills, every one of them, and gave the money to the family who had lost their daughter. He moved to New York and started a new life as a journalist. For the last several years, he's been working on an exposé about child labor, specifically that in the mills."

Kate's voice became imploring. "The articles are brilliant and poignant and heartbreaking—every newspaper ought to print them across the front pages. But Thomas's editor, Luther, wouldn't print them outright. You see, Thomas presented them to Luther right after the O'Malley wedding was announced, and Luther made an agreement with him: he would only run the articles if Thomas found out where the wedding was held and covered the story. The agreement never sat well with Thomas, but he felt compelled.

"He blames himself for what happened the day of the fire. The guilt and shame haunt him, and to watch him suffer as he does…" Kate's brown eyes shone with tears, and Harper knew her eyes did the same. "It's not his fault. What happened was not his fault."

The fierce desire to protect and defend Thomas was a shot of adrenaline through her. "Of course it wasn't."

And didn't everything that had happened on Block Island make such perfect sense now? He had never wanted to cover the wedding in the first place—he had been in an impossible situation. Hot anger for the editor who had put Thomas in such a position made her ball her fists, but as quickly as that anger came, it fled.

Because hadn't Harper made terrible accusations against him for writing the article? Hadn't she called him a liar? Accused him of trying to advance his career? And with what reason? Because he had been unwilling to share with her the weight of his shame and guilt, misplaced as it was?

Remorse and mortification washed over her like waves. How could she have ever doubted him, ever been angry with him?

Why had it never occurred to her that the man who was so steady, steady enough to root her in place when she felt like the whole world was falling apart, would need someone to be steady for him as well? Why hadn't she just trusted him, let him lean on her?

Kate gave her a small smile, but it didn't reach her eyes. "You and I both agree that Thomas was not to blame, but my brother does not. This drive to atone for what our father did, it's consumed him. It's the reason he won't—" Kate stopped short, and with a sinking heart Harper understood what Kate did not say.

The mill fire was the reason Thomas never planned to marry or have children. As penance or punishment, or perhaps both, he would deny himself a family. And the implications of that decision for Harper…

Kate gave her a gentle smile. "I know it isn't my place to say, but he loves you, Harper. I believe he'll come around, I do. But in the meantime, I thought you should know the reason he's wary—that it has nothing at all to do with you."

Kate's words were meant to reassure her, but for the first time since her kiss with Thomas, a kernel of doubt spread through her.

"You also ought to know that he's quit his job at the newspaper. Which is a good thing for him, I believe. But he's having a difficult time just now. For so long he's believed himself to be beyond forgiveness, beyond love. And until he can come to terms with what happened, not just by publishing the mill exposé, but by letting someone love him…"

Kate's words trailed off, the unfinished sentence conjuring far more doubt and fear in Harper than anything she could have said aloud. Harper loved him, as surely as the sun rises in the east and sets in the west, but if he didn't believe himself worthy of love, if he never came for her…

All at once, she felt excruciating pain and a chilling numbness.

She hardly even noticed when Kate took her leave.

When her grandmother came into the room hours later to ask why Harper wasn't already upstairs getting dressed for their evening out, the feeling had yet to subside.

***

* * *

Thomas stepped out of the narrow brick building where he had had his interview and into the lank heat of the bustling street, feeling exhausted and heavy. And accomplished, he thought belatedly. He ought to feel accomplished.

He had a job offer, after all, and at a prestigious magazine at that. After an hour's meeting and a brief look at Thomas's exposé on child labor in New England mills, the editor of *Collier's Weekly* had offered him a job on the spot. Though Luther had dismissed Thomas's interest in child labor reform as yellow journalism and had all but blackballed him in New York newspaper circles, *Collier's Weekly* was an illustrated magazine that didn't shy from covering the appalling conditions of underage, vulnerable workers and immigrants. The publisher had just enough power and influence to actually instigate change, in both laws and public perception.

The pay was better than the newspaper, and the magazine was widely lauded as a forerunner in investigative journalism and social reform. He should have felt elated—the job was everything he could have hoped for. Kate had been right when she said that any editor with integrity would run the story. He had expected to feel light and free, or at the very least unburdened, knowing that he was finally in a position to atone for what he and his father had done all those years ago.

He felt nothing.

His chest was hollow. If he felt anything at all, he would call it misery.

Life away from Harper was absolute misery.

The weather certainly didn't help. The gray clouds and steady wind promised a thunderstorm before the afternoon was finished. He could easily hail a hansom cab to take him home, but he preferred walking.

Since his decision to let Harper go, he was both exhausted and almost maniacally restless.

No doubt seeing her face printed in the gossip pages of the newspapers didn't help. She had made her debut in Manhattan society with the dazzling splendor expected of Mrs. Verbeek's only granddaughter, and people were already speculating on who would win the hand of the stunning long-lost debutante. Society loved nothing better than beautiful novelty and fabulous wealth, and Harper had both in spades.

Thomas passed a cart selling newspapers, and Harper's face jumped out at him once again. She was surrounded by suitors and wearing an elaborate, puffed ballgown. Her features, so achingly familiar, were lovely as always, but she wasn't smiling. In all the pictures, she never smiled.

As if on cue, the sky ripped open with a slash of thunder, and rain came hammering down, soaking him within seconds. The man at the newspaper cart hurriedly pulled a cover over the papers, and Thomas picked up his pace. The swarming mass of people up and down the street did the same, and from the corner of his eye, he saw a slim man crossing the street, stopping halfway to right the umbrella that had been turned inside out by the wind.

Thomas also saw what the man didn't: a hansom cab barreling down the street towards him. The thunder must have spooked the horse because the creature was running helter-skelter on both sides of the road, creating waves of mud and startled yelps in every direction.

A heartbeat later, Thomas was running into the road. With a shout and the full force of his body, he knocked the man out of the way a split second before the horse and its cab came charging through the road.

Thomas, the man, and the umbrella tumbled onto the sidewalk in a muddy heap. He landed on his back and the breath whooshed from his lungs. His head made contact with the ground with a sickening crack.

Although his eyes remained open, his vision was dark, as if night had already fallen. He was only vaguely aware of tepid rain still falling against his face, of panicked voices shouting and calling over him.

The pain was everywhere—back, head, shoulders, legs—and though he blinked several times, he couldn't seem to clear his vision.

He wondered idly if he was dying.

He had read stories before of men and women who had near-death experiences and seen their lives flash before their eyes, a bright light beckoning in the distance.

Thomas saw neither of those things.

Instead of a bright light or his own life playing back to him, he saw only hazel eyes, brilliant and clear, smiling at him. The hazel eyes belonged to a woman, small and warm and breathtakingly beautiful.

Harper, his rattled brain told him.

He loved her. Oh, how he loved her.

The voices were growing louder now, more insistent, but he ignored them. Instead, he focused all of his energy on remembering her voice.

You, Thomas. I want you.

He had meant to tell her everything, the day after that confession.

About his father and the fire, about his agreement with Luther. He had meant to tell her he loved her.

But the real world had bowled him over with the appearance of her father and grandmother, of Vivienne and Neville Jones. And he had remembered all the reasons why he didn't deserve her, why she would be better off with almost anyone but him.

None of us deserve to be loved, Kate had told him. *It's grace, all grace.*

He didn't deserve her. But if Kate was right, maybe that didn't matter. Maybe he didn't need to deserve her to love her. And if that was true....

If there was even the smallest, most infinitesimal possibility that he could love her, have a life with her, even if he didn't deserve her, then there was no way he was going to lay down and die now.

A face came into focus then, a young man, wide-eyed and muddy. It was the man with the umbrella, the one he had pushed out of the way of the carriage. He was talking to him, asking him questions. *"Sir, can you hear me? Are you all right, sir?"*

The words tugged at a memory, of another time when he had been injured after pulling someone to safety. A memory of Harper. Pulling her out of the crowd at Point Judith, that lacy parasol knocking him to the ground. Her hazel eyes surprised and concerned, hovering above him. The smell of strawberries and spring rain.

It didn't smell like her now. The rain and heat had made the streets reek of sweating bodies and horse. The contrast made him ache for her.

Thomas blinked, gingerly lifting his hand to wipe the rain from his eyes. A futile effort, since the rain continued to crash down on him. But the movement meant he was alive.

No, he wouldn't die. He would go to her. She might refuse him, might have found a man who could give her all the things he couldn't. She might feel angry or betrayed, having given him up as a lost cause.

He had nearly given himself up as a lost cause.

With a strength he didn't know he possessed, he forced his eyes to focus, leaning up out of the mud and mire beneath him.

A crowd of spectators and samaritans had formed around him, and several hands reached out to steady him.

Weak as he was, he let them, breathing deeply.

The breath hurt his ribs, but it didn't matter.

Pain and rain and what he deserved didn't matter now. Only *she* mattered.

And then, to the cumulative shock and dismay of those around him, he rose to his feet.

He had to.

He was going to get Harper.

Chapter 31

The Right Honorable Matthias Robert Kennett Junior had turnip greens wrapped around the left canine—his left, not Harper's.

As the otherwise pleasant-faced young judge danced the cotillion with her at Mrs. Greenfield's ball, the rogue leaf monopolized Harper's attention. Unfortunately, the Honorable Matthias Robert Kennett Junior was in a happy mood and saw fit to flash those otherwise inoffensive teeth quite liberally, and when his good humor overflowed he even laughed, affording her a vinegar-scented reminder of what had taken residence in his tooth. Even without the unfortunate left canine, Harper could only have mustered a bland and entirely platonic liking for the man.

He had the distinct disadvantage of not being Thomas Montgomery.

But she had no choice but to go through the motions of having her debut, of dancing and smiling and doing her extremely illustrious Dutch forebears proud when all she really wanted to do was cry.

Because he hadn't come for her.

He.

Hadn't.

Come.

She knew that he lived under the guilt of what had happened, but that didn't matter to her, and if he would have come for her, she would have told him that. She would have told him that she loved him completely and irrevocably and that there was nothing he could ever do to change that.

But he hadn't given her the chance.

So she tried to smile as his Honor danced her around the room, but the effort was exhausting. Her misery only intensified as she heard the unmistakable whispers throughout the ballroom about Wesley and Adeline's broken engagement. The newspapers had finally broken the story last week, and the speculation regarding the reasons for their break-up ranged from the absurd to the salacious to the cruel.

She wanted to rage at all of the petty men and women whispering about Adeline like she had done something wrong—as if she was unworthy or tainted or otherwise deficient. Women always bore the brunt of broken engagements, and hearing strangers malign someone as lovely and sweet as Adeline was maddening.

But she couldn't say a word. Her grandmother had gone to great pains to conceal any hint of Harper's escapades on Block Island—apparently, she had told everyone that Harper had succumbed to a sudden and unseasonable bout of the flu—and so her defense of Adeline was left unspoken.

The music for the cotillion was fading, and her partner slowed and beamed down at her. "Miss Whitley, you are an exquisite dance partner. May I escort you back to your grandmother?" Turnip greens shimmied before her in a solicitous flash, and Harper tore her eyes from them long enough to reply.

"Thank you, sir. The honor was all mine."

When they reached her grandmother, however, she was busy gossiping with the other influential matrons about the season's changing hemlines, and once his Honor was out of sight she slipped away to the punch table, eager for a moment without her grandmother's intense scrutiny.

She was reaching for the punch bowl when she heard them.

"There she is, girls!"

"Where?"

"Oh, I see her!"

"Hello, Harper!"

Slowly, she turned.

Impossible.

It was not possible that Bess, Hugh, Claire, and Claudia—and oh heavens, Vivienne and Neville Jones—were standing behind her. And, what was even more improbable, *smiling* at her.

"Aunt Bess! I mean—Mrs. O'Malley. Hello. I..."

Her pseudo aunt waved her hand impatiently. "Nonsense. You must still call me Aunt Bess. I still am, in essence."

Harper must have looked as baffled as she felt because Vivienne touched her on the arm.

"Your grandmother reached out to mine, telling her about how you had taken my place on Block Island. My grandmother, in turn, sent me a scathing letter about my behavior at Point Judith that day. I haven't had the pleasure of scandalizing her so thoroughly since Neville and I eloped." She smiled winsomely. "I only wished we had known one another sooner. Imagine, all this time we could have grown up like twins!" She sounded genuinely delighted, and Harper could not reconcile all of their cheerful countenances with the chaos of the last time she had seen them. And it was still startling to encounter someone whose face was almost exactly like her own.

Harper bit her lip. "I never did get a chance to apologize properly to any of you. I'm so, so sor—"

"Pfft! None of that now!" Bess said airily. "Thomas explained everything to us, dear. No one is angry."

"But you should be," Harper insisted earnestly. "I lied to you and deceived you and accepted your hospitality—"

"You did what you believed was right in an impossible situation. You were a wonderful stand-in cousin to Adeline when she needed you."

"And I must say, dear, we've all grown fond of you in your own right," added Hugh. His eyes twinkled down at her with laughter and affection.

"What an adventure you had, Harper!" Vivienne added. "And honestly, it was partly my fault for losing my temper with Neville that day." She smiled up at her husband as he snaked his arm around her waist. "You see, I'm with child, and I find my moods to be just a bit…"

"Tempestuous?" Claire offered.

"Mercurial?" Claudia supplied.

"Frightening?" her husband suggested.

Vivienne laughed. "*Unpredictable*. I only wish I could have been a fly on the wall throughout the ruse! I'm dying to hear about it from your perspective." Her eyes twinkled merrily at Harper.

"I…" Harper's mind whirled, trying to accommodate so much new information at once. They weren't angry with her. And the real Vivienne actually *was* pregnant. "Congratulations. That's wonderful news." Feeling flustered, she tried to smile, but the mention of Thomas had brought on a fresh onslaught of longing. He had spoken to the O'Malleys after the fight. How could they be so kind and forgiving—laughing and joking, even—in light of all that she had done?

But before she asked any of those questions, she thought of one that was far more urgent. "How is Adeline?"

Their faces lost some of their mirth. "Bearing up. She's stronger than anyone gives her credit for, but people can be so needlessly cruel," Bess said. "She's going to stay on Block Island for a time, let the gossip die down a bit before returning to New York. Rhys and Rose are with her. She has a difficult road ahead of her, but she'll be all right. We O'Malleys are a hardy breed," she added fervently.

"And we have our marching order to socialize and gallivant throughout the city, letting everyone know that Adeline was not at fault and telling anyone who will listen that she's as well as ever, having a grand time off in Europe." Claire smiled sheepishly. "We thought it best to keep her true location a secret for now."

"Of course." Harper nodded, feeling a rush of compassion and affection for the erstwhile bride. But she sensed that what Bess said was true: Adeline was strong. She would be all right, and however painful the breaking of the engagement was, she was better off not married to a man with the quicksilver temper of Wesley James.

The group seemed to sense her mood because with quick kisses on her cheeks from the women and Hugh and a friendly handshake from Neville, they excused themselves, off to spread word of Adeline's glamorous jaunt through Europe and promising to call on Harper at her grandmother's mansion soon.

Once they were out of sight, Harper sighed in relief. As wonderful as it was to see the O'Malleys again and know that they held no ill-will, she felt suddenly drained. With a surreptitious look over her shoulder to ensure that her grandmother was still occupied, she slipped away from the punch table and the clamor of the dance floor. It wasn't a drink she needed, but somewhere quiet to collect her thoughts.

With nearly four hundred bodies packed into the ballroom on a balmy summer night and the acrid smells of sweat and perfume that accompanied them, the heat was nearly unbearable. Everything felt overstimulating—the noise of the musicians and the dancers and the blinding array of rubies and sapphires and diamonds refracting the splendor of the ornate gaslit chandeliers.

She slipped away from all of it, finding a dim, empty alcove at the periphery of the room.

As she rested her head against the cool pillar of the alcove, the orchestra began the opening notes of a waltz.

With a new wave of sadness, she shut her eyes.

Because even with all the dancing and socializing she had done to please her grandmother, she had steadfastly refused to waltz. It would be wrong, somehow.

The waltz would always belong to Thomas.

But the now-familiar *one two three, one two three* of the dance conjured such strong memories that she could almost imagine Thomas's handsome face across the ballroom, stern and frowning. But when he looked in her direction, the face transformed, those deeply trenched frown lines disappearing in the wake of a smile, slow and beautiful as a flower opening to the sun.

That smile.

Rare and elusive and so achingly precious.

Likely a troubling sign, that she missed him so badly that she was hallucinating. Her grandmother would have an aneurysm if she knew Harper was still thinking about him, especially if she was doing it often enough to imagine his face in a crowd.

When it had become clear that Thomas would not come for her, her grandmother had declared Harper well rid of *that scheming opportunist.*

As if her beaten, scarred remnant of a heart needed any reminding that he wasn't coming for her.

Except that at that moment, her hallucinogenic Thomas Montgomery was scything through the crowd towards her.

She shrunk further into the relative shadow of the alcove, now genuinely alarmed that the figment of her imagination appeared so remarkably real and corporeal and broad and handsome, now only ten feet from her.

The distance shrunk to seven, then to four—the phantom Thomas Montgomery had *enormous* strides—and then he was before her, a foot away, close enough to touch.

So that's exactly what her trembling hand did.

Fully expecting the mirage to vanish with a puff and to find herself swooning or vomiting or whatever women generally did when they were unwell enough to hallucinate, her mouth dropped open when her gloved hand came in contact with actual flesh and bone cheek, warm and smooth enough that it must have been freshly shaved.

The cheek tugged up again in the smile that she had been so hungry for. She was famished, and that smile was her feast in the wilderness.

"Hello, darling."

That voice.

So deep that she felt it rumble in her chest. That rough timber of a voice could not possibly be in her head, which could only mean that the freshly-shaved face and achingly-familiar voice belonged to the man himself.

Her knees buckled beneath her, and in a fluid motion, his arm was around her waist, steadying her, like he did the first time she ever saw him.

Her hand fell from his cheek to his chest. His heartbeat was a wildfire beneath her palm, a tattoo against her hand.

Vaguely aware that they were only scantily hidden in an alcove in a very crowded ballroom filled with various important and dignified members of New York Society, she knew she ought to put a respectable distance between them. But since even a respectable distance from him would be too far, she settled for pulling her face back enough to meet his eye.

"You're here."

"I am," he confirmed.

"How are you here?" Her eyes searched his face, reacquainting themselves with the lines fanning out from his eyes, the straight angle of his jaw, the slope of his nose. A small pink scar ran down the length of his jaw, and she smoothed her hand over it.

She couldn't move away from him, couldn't stop touching him. He was the gravity of her world now. She would always move irresistibly towards him.

"Why didn't you come for me?" she whispered. She hadn't meant to ask—there were a thousand other things she could have said. *How are you? I met your sister. I missed you. I love you.*

But seeing him again—touching him and smelling him and hearing him—was disorienting, like breathing pure oxygen after subsisting off of a cheap imitation.

"I'm sorry, so very sorry, darling. But I... No, please don't cry." She hadn't realized she was crying, but he took her face in his hands, his thumbs swiping gently beneath her eyes. "Please, I can't bear to see you unhappy."

A sob escaped her before she could stop it. "But I *was* unhappy. You didn't come for me. I waited and I hoped and.... you were just gone." She sniffled, frustrated with herself for crying when he was finally here. "How can I be anything but unhappy without you?"

He cradled her face tenderly in his hands, his warm brown eyes looking as if they might cry too. "There were... things I needed to do, to come to terms with before I could come for you." He looked away from her, his beautiful face looking so sad that she felt it deep in her chest. Until the day she died, she was certain she would feel his sadness as an ache in her own chest.

"Do you mean about the fire?" she asked gently, afraid to pry at a wound so deep.

He met her eye. "How do you know about the fire?"

"Your sister came to see me." His head reared back in surprise, but she tugged him forward again, unwilling to surrender even an inch of space between them. "Please don't be upset with Kate. She told me about your father, about what happened at the mill. She also told me that you quit the newspaper, about your editor and why you were going to write about the O'Malley wedding." She took a shuddering breath. "I'm so sorry for the things I said to you Thomas, so terribly sorry.

"And you must know what happened the day of the fire wasn't your fault. The foreman was careless and your father dishonest, but you ran into that building and risked your own life to rescue those children. That doesn't change the fact that one precious child died, nothing could ever change that, but it wasn't your fault. And nothing could ever change the way I feel about you. Past, present, or future."

Her face was still in his hands, those warm, gentle hands, and the motion of his thumbs told her that she was still crying. For a long while, he didn't respond. He simply looked at her. His gaze was so intense and warm that she remembered what Claire and Claudia had said all those weeks ago, that he looked at Harper as if she was the only pearl in the ocean. As if he meant to keep her.

Finally, he tilted his head, a rough exhale escaping him. "Truly, Harper? Can you truly be with a man with that sort of blood on his hands?"

She turned her cheek against his palm, savoring the feel of him, then slowly pulled his hand from her face and pressed a kiss in his palm. "I don't see any blood here." She held his hand in hers, tracing the lines of his palm, wanting to memorize every groove of him.

"No?" His voice was gravel. The pulse in his wrist galloped beneath her thumb. "What do you see?"

After a moment, she pulled her eyes from his hand and met his gaze squarely, willing him to listen and understand and believe. "I see hands that were willingly scorched and burned to carry ten children out of a burning building. I see hands that pulled me from a tourist stampede and caught me when I fell. I see hands that have worked to write an exposé that is going to change the very fabric of our society. I see hands that taught me to dance and held me when I cried." She looked at his hand again, so large and powerful in her own smaller one. "Blood, Thomas? No. They've been scarred and battered, but these are hands that give life, not take it."

"Harper." His voice was ragged, and for a second she was terrified that he would contradict her. "I don't deserve you. I probably never will. But a wise woman once told me that love isn't about getting what we deserve."

Love. The word was a firework. Brilliant color and light.

"I have a question for you, Harper." His voice was steady now, serious and intent. "A proposal, actually."

It was an echo of that day they first met at Point Judith, and she felt fresh fireworks begin to explode in her chest. She willed them to quiet. "All right."

"But I must warn you. It may involve… canoodling."

A laugh bubbled out of her, watery and bright, and he rewarded her with a smile. "Does it?"

He nodded solemnly. "I'm afraid so. There is also a possibility—no, a strong probability—of liberties."

Playful. He was being playful with her. The most serious, stoic, gruff man she had ever known was being *silly*—she knew instinctively that he was never silly, would never *be* silly with anyone but her—and she fell that much more in love with him.

"Liberties?"

He nodded again, his eyes never leaving hers. "That's right, Miss Whitley. Canoodling *and* liberties. My honor also compels me to warn you of a real danger of tomfoolery, perhaps even—" he brought his head even closer to her, so close that if she only tipped up onto her toes their lips could brush—"monkey business."

Sunlight. Riots of sunlight inside her chest.

"Well," she said, amazed that she could speak around the cascade of radiance and light in her chest. "I think you had better say your piece, Mr. Montgomery, before I get the wrong idea."

"I daresay I better." He let go of her and pulled back, only to drop to one knee. He reached for his pocket, looking up at her now. In his hand, he held a velvet-lined box. Inside it was a perfectly smooth, glossy pearl set in a thin, gold band. His mock severity was gone now, replaced with only a shining sort of wonder.

"Harper Jane Whitley, during our short acquaintance, I have done a number of idiotic things. But I've also done the smartest thing that I ever have in my life."

"Oh?" Her voice was little more than a breath.

"Yes. I fell in love with you. And I know I've mishandled almost everything about our relationship—I've been dishonest and thoughtless and I've hurt you, and for that, I have no excuse. I confess I'm not a wealthy man, nor am I an especially smart man, based on how badly I've bungled things. It's possible that I am the worst possible choice of husband for you, especially in the crowd here tonight. But Harper, if you'll have me, I give you my word that I will work every day to be a *good* man."

"Thomas." Her voice was so thick, the rest of the words lodged in her throat, and she could only nod.

The warmth in his eyes grew. "Yes?"

She nodded again, then swallowed back her tears. "Yes. Of course. For you, it will always be yes."

Before she knew what was happening she was in his arms, her feet hovering above the floor and skirts whirling around them as he spun her. When he set her down he slipped the ring on her finger with aching tenderness, but her eyes weren't on the ring, exquisite as it was.

Her eyes never left his face.

The heat in his eyes threatened to make her knees go weak all over again, but he wouldn't let her fall. This man was steady as a rock. And she would be steady for him. Never again would he be left by himself to let guilt and shame break him. She loved him too much to ever let that happen again.

Slowly she became aware that the dancers around her were slowing, that the music of the waltz was fading, and a thought managed to break through her haze of happiness.

"My father—Thomas, we'll have to speak to my father."

"Already done."

"What?" She frowned in confusion, and his thumb smoothed the lines from her forehead. The gesture would have charmed her, had she not been so baffled.

"I've already spoken to him," he said reasonably.

"You spoke to my father? When?"

"When I saw him at the farm yesterday. He's waiting outside in the carriage, by the way."

Her mouth dropped. "My father is *here*?" The night had been one shock after another—all good ones, but disorienting nevertheless.

"And you came for him before you came for me!?"

His lips tipped up in a half-smile. "I didn't exactly come for him. But I did owe him an explanation for what happened on Block Island."

Remembering the look on her father's face the last time the two men had met, Harper felt a grim fascination with how the visit has passed. "What did you say to him?"

"I started by telling him what a colossal idiot I've been. He seemed to like that, so I continued in the same vein. I must have said something right because he eventually gave me his blessing."

She felt a wondering smile bloom on her face, only to have another thought break through her happiness.

"But my grandmother! She'll be livid. She's invested so much in my debut." She began to worry her bottom lip, but his thumb brushed across it to stop her, leaving a thousand fresh starbursts in its wake.

"My love, even *she* will not object to our engagement."

"How can you be so sure?"

"Do you really want to know?"

She nodded eagerly.

"Have you noticed the waltz is ending?"

"Yes." She tilted her head in question.

"Now that it has, the alcove is about to be far less conspicuous." Harper looked behind her, and just as he said, the couples were beginning to slow and separate. She looked back at him, her eyebrows raised in question. "So here is what I'm going to do. I'm going to put my hand behind your head." His hand slid gently into her hair, releasing several curls. "Then I'm going to lean scandalously close to you." He did, so close that she could feel his breath on her lips when he spoke. Her eyes clung to his, rapt, her lips tingling in anticipation. "Do you know what I'm going to do next, Harper?"

She was humming with such wild hope that she couldn't move or speak to reply. That seemed to please him, and he smiled down at her. She would never tire of that smile.

"Next, I'm going to kiss you in full view of four hundred of Manhatten's most elite citizens, your esteemed grandmother included. And this kiss, my darling," he shook his head reprovingly, "it will not be a peck. I'm going to take my time, as long as I'd like." He teased her, moving his lips scant millimeters from hers. "And I would like a very, *very*, long time," he whispered. Her knees nearly buckled, and he tightened his hold on her waist. "This kiss is going to be so indecently long that the scandalized members of this ballroom will all agree that the only way to salvage your reputation will be for me to marry you."

And when she closed her eyes and finally—*finally*—felt the warm relief of his lips on hers, that is *exactly* what happened.

The End.

Acknowledgments

Writing a book has always been a quiet dream of mine, but I never expected it to become a reality.

But one day in January 2021, in the midst of pandemic loneliness and winter blues and cabin fever, I decided to write a story of warmer days and happy endings.

That story became *The Block Island Charade*, but without the love and encouragement of several people, it never would have existed outside of my head.

Eli, thank you for being excited for me and proud of me every step of the way, and for getting takeout ten thousand times because I was writing and forgot to cook dinner. You're my best friend and my very happiest of endings.

Theo, Mary, and Emma, thank you for always asking what's happening in my story and for playing outside in the afternoons so that I could write. You're the most outrageous, most wonderful little people in the world, and I love you oodles of poodles of noodles.

Mommy, thank you for always laughing at my jokes and believing that I could do this!

Ramona, you've been my faithful friend and my hawk-eyed editor, and I cannot imagine what sort of grammatically incoherent sloop I would have produced without you. For your diligence and patience, I am so grateful!

Bronwyn, you brought my story to life in the most beautiful, perfect way possible. Thank you for dreaming and imagining with me!

And to *you*, dear reader, thank you for taking this journey with me! I hope you enjoyed reading this story as much as I enjoyed writing it.

Author's Notes

Readers and friends,

In spite of being a romcom, *The Block Island Charade* touches on the weightier issues of guilt, shame, and how our past defines us. If, like Thomas, you've ever felt a guilt that cripples or a shame that robs you of joy, I hope you have people in your life like Kate and Harper, who love you relentlessly, through every deep valley and every dark night.

But I would be remiss if I did not also say that the only real answer to guilt and shame is Jesus. In dying on the cross, Jesus took on himself the unbearable burden of our guilt and shame, and in rising from the grave, he obliterated it entirely. In the love of Jesus—that vast, unmeasured, boundless love—there is no room for guilt or shame. The wild extravagance of his love for us eclipses any and every weight that would pull us down.

And if this sounds strange to you, or unbelievable even, level with me. Take the next ten seconds and ask Jesus to make Himself real to you, to take the weight of your guilt and shame. At worst, you'll have wasted ten seconds. At most, it will change your life.

You've trusted me enough to read this far, haven't you?

Warmest hugs to you, friend,
Bekah

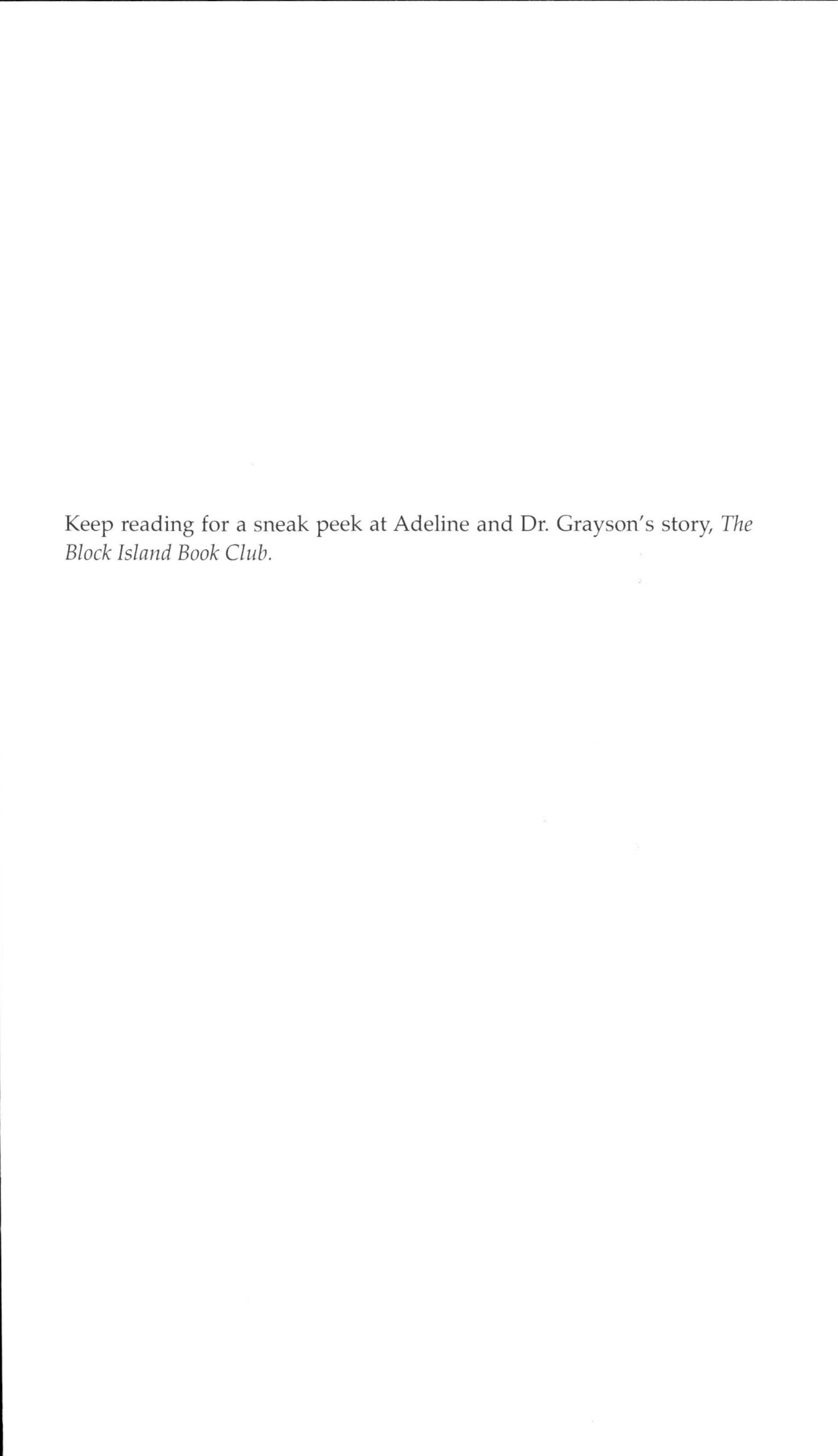

Keep reading for a sneak peek at Adeline and Dr. Grayson's story, *The Block Island Book Club.*

The Block Island Book Club

Adeline O'Malley, daughter of the world's wealthiest shipbuilder, former fiancée of Wesley James, and all-around woman on the edge, took the scissors to her hair like a novice lumberjack: with tremendous enthusiasm and very little skill.

Though the process itself was gratifying—she sawed off nearly two feet of hair, and her head felt light and free as a bird—the end result was somewhat unexpected. She hadn't accounted for the natural curl of her hair or the effect of so much weight suddenly lifted, and rather than the demure shoulder-length style she was expecting, her hair fell just below her chin.

Such a short bob was not at all the style—society would label her a bluestocking at best, a loose woman at worst. Her own mother would be downright scandalized.

Adeline decided that hacking off her hair had been the best decision of her life.

The issue was, her mother was generally scandalized *regardless* of what Adeline did, and New York Society was *already* gossiping about her.

All it took was one month for her to go from a modern Helen of Troy to persona non-grata.

It all began when Wesley James, her father's handsome, brilliant, right-hand man, had proposed to her at midnight on January 1, 1900. The press had deemed their upcoming nuptials the wedding of the century, and the public was elated, enraptured, obsessed with the very *idea* of them. Apparently, the thought of two rich, beautiful people marrying and producing more rich, beautiful people was the stuff gossip columnists' dreams were made of.

Such attention from the press had always made Adeline uncomfortable—she hadn't done anything more remarkable than being born an uncommonly pretty girl to an uncommonly wealthy man, and even in that, she had not actually *done* anything—but when the newspapers began harassing her every time she left the house, she had made the unprecedented decision to put her foot down. Instead of the spectacular society wedding everyone expected, she insisted on a quiet, private ceremony, with only their families and closest friends in attendance.

With careful planning, the wedding came together: Adeline and Wesley would marry on Block Island, an idyllic locale off the coast of Rhode Island, and would be Mr. and Mrs. James before the newspapers had any idea where or when the wedding was planned.

Except that was *not* what had happened.

Not at all.

They had made it to Block Island, of course, but that was about the only part of the plan that succeeded. When the stress and pressure of a shipbuilding contract led Wesley to drink to excess, he had changed from charming and thoughtful to unpredictable and volatile.

But *no,* thought Adeline, perhaps he *hadn't* changed. Perhaps Adeline had never actually known Wesley at all. Perhaps she had no more known the true Wesley than he had known the true Adeline.

To be fair, very few did.

And when her father and Wesley finally had a confrontation about the shipbuilding contract, and that confrontation led to a whole family brawl that destroyed the parlor of one of Block Island's finest hotels and ended their engagement, all of that careful planning went up in flames.

Metaphorically, of course.

In the fisticuffs that ensued after her broken engagement, there had been no real fire. Only a great deal of blood and quite a bit of splintered furniture.

So that was something.

But as with any broken engagement of any high-profile couple, the gossip was swift and cruel, and public opinion was decidedly against her. The unspoken rule in such matters was that the woman was at fault, and Adeline's case was no different.

Some said she was simply a spoiled heiress, demanding and mercurial, and Wesley was well rid of her. Others speculated that she was secretly an intellectual and a radical, promoting such heinous vices as bloomers and women's suffrage—there were few things that society distrusted more than women in pants and women in power. The most bitter rumors claimed that she was loose and faithless, a strumpet and a temptress, and wasn't it a fine thing that Wesley found out *before* the wedding?

The fact that her father had also fired Wesley when he ended the engagement did Adeline no favors; Wesley was cast as the victim, losing his livelihood in addition to his future when Adeline did whatever it was everyone supposed she did. Whether it was because she was spoiled or a radical or a loose woman made no difference. The fact of the matter was, she was a danger to respectability everywhere, and therefore welcome nowhere.

All of which Adeline found a bit ironic: she was a natural introvert, and during the years when she had been in high demand at parties, balls, and soirees, she had wanted nothing more than to go home and read in bed.

In lieu of her current social status, she was free to do that to her heart's delight.

Except she didn't feel even the least bit delighted.

She *did* feel more than a little bit unhinged.

Her first reaction to the family brawl and broken engagement had been shock mingled with horror. She had been concerned about Wesley's drinking and worried about his working relationship with her father, but in spite of those reservations, she had been prepared to marry him. She had been determined to be a good wife, regardless of Wesley's many flaws.

But without even consulting her, without even *looking* at her, the two men, only one of whom was an active participant in their upcoming marriage, had ended her engagement and thrown her future into chaos.

And once the initial shock and horror had worn off, something very remarkable had happened.

Adeline had been… angry. *Furious*, in fact.

The emotion was almost totally foreign to her—she was familiar enough with irritation and annoyance and frustration, but anger… well. That was as unprecedented for her as putting her foot down.

All her life, Adeline had been eager to please. To please her parents, and then her governess, and then the world at large, when she came of age. And all that time—all twenty-two years of her life—it had never occurred to her that being *too* eager to please could actually be a very dangerous thing.

It was certainly occurring to her now.

But at the time, she had stood by silently while her father and Wesley decided her future, because heaven forbid she interrupt or inconvenience anyone by having an opinion about the rest of her life. Heaven forbid she be treated like a sentient, valuable, human being, rather than a prized object. Heaven forbid she have a voice worth listening to simply because she existed.

In retrospect, *furious* actually seemed a rather tepid word to describe how she felt.

And so after a full night of weeping into the arms of her aunt and cousins—her mother would never deign to be present for something as distasteful as her only daughter's breakdown—Adeline made a decision.

No more would she be eager to please. She would be eager to do good, eager to be kind, but never again would she indiscriminately aim to please.

Whether the impromptu haircut was some sort of celebration of this decision or a sign of her precarious grip on sanity, she couldn't say. What she could say was she *liked* it. She would feel the breeze on the back of her neck and brush her hair in ten minutes flat. She would look different than every other woman her age and she wouldn't even care.

She was a woman on the edge, after all.

So with her head held high and her hair cropped dangerously short, she walked out the door of her room to find her parents and demand a say in her own future.

Unfortunately, her dramatic exit was interrupted when she entered the hallway and crashed directly into the arms of Dr. Daniel Grayson.

***

"Oof!" Adeline's forehead collided with his chin with a forceful thwack, and the momentum and shock of it were enough to set Daniel off balance.

The two of them stumbled back against the wall of the corridor, almost displacing an expensive gilt-framed painting in the process. Out of sheer instinct, he lifted his hands to steady her, but she had been flailing her own to regain her balance, to the effect that she slapped him across the face.

He let out an "*oof*" of his own.

His back was braced against the wall, keeping them both upright, but she had tripped after slapping him and was now sprawled against his chest.

Daniel's first thought was that he should set her safely upright, but his second, and ultimately more compelling thought was, *I'm holding Adeline O'Malley*.

At long last, he was holding Adeline O'Malley.

He half expected a beam of light shine to down on them from the heavens.

But when she abruptly pushed back from him, righting herself and putting a respectable amount of space between them, the moment was lost. With a rough shake of his head, he returned to reality.

What had he been *doing*?

What had he been *thinking*?

A man did not simply stand in the hallway in broad daylight and *hold* Adeline O'Malley.

Except that for about five seconds, he *had*.

And it had been the best five seconds of his life.

With a steadiness that belied his discomposure, he righted himself as well, determined to act like the grown man and respectable doctor that he was. But when he looked over at her again, that inexplicable phenomenon occurred, the same one that always took place when he saw her: the sight of Adeline O'Malley took his breath away.

Dr. Daniel Grayson had been in love with her since the first moment he saw her.

Daniel was a man of logic and science, and he didn't believe in love at first sight as a general possibility, so even *he* could not explain the way he felt.

It was four years ago, though he had the strangest feeling that he had always loved her. The day he first saw her, Daniel had come to the shipbuilding yard to interview with Charles O'Malley for a position as a physician at the Gray Star Line. The dangerous nature of welding and construction meant accidents were likely, if not inevitable, and O'Malley was hiring a team of in-house physicians.

To get to O'Malley's office, Daniel had taken a shortcut through one of the rougher sections of the dockyards. Although poverty and crime were proportionally high around the docks, Daniel had never much feared for his own safety. His work had brought him into contact with all sorts of people and places much worse than that one, and though he could defend himself well enough, he had always thought that if God wanted him to get somewhere, He would see him there safely.

It was in the darkest, filthiest section of the dockyard that he first laid eyes on her. She had been dressed in a simple white eyelet dress, looking for all the world like a springtime daisy against the gray squalor of her surroundings. More remarkable than the simple fact of her presence there was what she was doing: perched on an old crate, with at least a dozen malnourished, grubby children at her feet, she was reading aloud, just as naturally as if she was in a lavish parlor on Fifth Avenue.

When one of the children climbed onto her lap, likely exposing her to all manner of lice and disease, she had simply wrapped an arm around him, rested her chin against his head, and continued reading.

And as Daniel had stood there watching her, disbelieving and bemused, he had thought to himself, *someday, I'm going to marry her.*

The thought had not been emotional in nature—he had always been rational rather than sentimental. Instead, it had been as firm and definitive as a law of physics. *Every action has an equal but opposite reaction. An object at rest tends to stay at rest. Daniel Grayson is going to marry the daisy woman.*

But that had been a long time ago, before he realized she was his employer's daughter and before she had ever been engaged to Wesley James.

And before his mind had a chance to reminisce about *that* recent disaster, she looked up at him in concern. "Dr. Grayson, I'm so terribly sorry! Are you all right? I was in a bit of a hurry, I'm afraid, and wasn't watching where I was going, and I—"

"You cut your hair."

He recognized the rudeness of interrupting her—he was normally the height of manners, and widely known for having a soothing, unflappable bedside manner—but she had always been the exception. The exception to many things, in fact.

He *never* emoted. Except around her.

He was *always* polite. Except when she was distraught.

He was *unfailingly* calm and controlled. Except when she had been mistreated.

In that case, he was liable to punch hard enough to crack teeth and tackle soundly enough to shatter a floor-to-ceiling French door.

He had suspected that something was amiss between Adeline and her fiancé, but when it became clear to him that Wesley had hurt her in some way… the ensuing brawl with Wesley and the whole O'Malley clan was *not* his finest moment.

"I did," said Adeline, looking surprised and shy. But then, seemingly with effort, she raised her chin. "I cut it myself."

The style was unfashionably short, but on her, it was stunning. Her violet eyes looked wider and brighter, her cheekbones more prominent, and her curls appeared downright riotous. In the honeyed afternoon light, she resembled a woodland nymph, wild and radiant, and he had an almost irresistible urge to tug one of her curls, simply for the pleasure of watching it spring back into place.

Which he would *not* do. He had resolved to behave respectably and normally around her. Never again would he lose his head over this woman.

The words resonated with more far optimism than belief.

"It looks lovely," he said, careful to keep his voice neutral.

"Do you think so?" she beamed at him, and he had to dig his fingernails into his palms to keep from reaching for a curl.

"I do."

"Well, thank you. It's not at all the style, I know. But I just felt like I needed... like I had to..." she puffed her cheeks and blew out a breath, something she never would have done in public. The fact that she did it with him was untenably endearing. "It just feels like *me*. The haircut, I mean. But also... *I* feel like me. Like myself. Although I suppose that doesn't make much sense."

Daniel wasn't sure that it did, but he understood her all the same. In the years since he had first seen Adeline, Charles O'Malley had been so impressed with him that he asked him to switch his services from chief physician of the Gray Star Line to private physician of the O'Malley clan, and the transition had often brought him into close contact with her. Without ever meaning to, he had learned all about her, seen the kindness and spark of life that was concealed beneath the beautiful socialite that the rest of the world saw.

Which was problematic for all sorts of reasons, not least of which was that he was her *family physician*. He had a duty to her father and her family, and Dr. Daniel Grayson was nothing if not dutiful.

But whenever he was in close proximity with Adeline, whenever she looked up at him with wide violet eyes like she was now, he quite simply forgot.

He resisted the urge to clear his throat. "On the contrary, Miss O'Malley. I know just what you mean." There. That was dutiful *and* appropriate. "And I agree. The haircut suits you." And that was *polite*.

Not at all meant to be complimentary or forward.

She crinkled his nose at him, another gesture the public Adeline would never make. "You don't need to *Miss O'Malley* me, you know. How long have we known one another?" Her face bloomed into a smile. "Please, just call me Adeline."

"I'm sure that wouldn't be proper." It was bad enough that he regularly referred to her by her given name in his head.

At that she turned pensive, tilting her head to the side and studying him, as if he had given her a riddle to solve. "You know, I'm not sure that being proper is all it's cracked up to be. Propriety doesn't win wars or solve societal woes. Being proper doesn't make people any more compassionate, or even more likable. In my experience, it generally does the opposite. It's simply another socially acceptable opportunity to judge one another and decide who we're better than."

Daniel looked down at her, stunned speechless. He didn't disagree with her, of course—the observation was startlingly accurate—he had just never heard Adeline say such a thing before. Though her father was above all else a businessman, more concerned with making money than cultivating public approval, her mother was the opposite: few things mattered more to Isla O'Malley than propriety and what others thought of her, and by extension, her family. What Adeline had just said amounted to heresy in her mother's eyes, which Adeline would know better than anyone.

Whatever change had come over Adeline that had been the catalyst for her haircut, Daniel couldn't say, but he had a sense that the Adeline who had walked through that door and crashed into him was a much freer, much wilder version of the Adeline the rest of the world knew.

And beyond all sense of duty or self-preservation, he *desperately* wanted to know everything about this version of her.

So with as neutral a smile as he was capable of, he simply said, "You know, Miss O'Malley, I believe you're right."

To read more, watch for *The Block Island Book Club*, coming soon…

Made in the USA
Monee, IL
18 June 2022